THANKFUL BLOSSOM

Mr. Harte in 1890

The Writings of Bret Harte

THANKFUL BLOSSOM

AND OTHER EASTERN TALES AND SKETCHES

BY

BRET HARTE

Short Story Index Reprint Series

BOOKS FOR LIBRARIES PRESS
FREEPORT, NEW YORK

First Published 1896
Reprinted 1972

INTERNATIONAL STANDARD BOOK NUMBER:
0-8369-4105-5

LIBRARY OF CONGRESS CATALOG CARD NUMBER:
72-37546

PRINTED IN THE UNITED STATES OF AMERICA
BY
NEW WORLD BOOK MANUFACTURING CO., INC.
HALLANDALE, FLORIDA 33009

CONTENTS

[redacted] [redacted]

LIST OF ILLUSTRATIONS

THANKFUL BLOSSOM

AND

OTHER EASTERN TALES AND SKETCHES

THANKFUL BLOSSOM

A ROMANCE OF THE JERSEYS

(1779)

PART I

The time was the year of grace 1779; the locality, Morristown, New Jersey.

It was bitterly cold. A northeasterly wind had been stiffening the mud of the morning's thaw into a rigid record of that day's wayfaring on the Baskingridge road. The hoof-prints of cavalry, the deep ruts left by baggage wagons, and the deeper channels worn by artillery lay stark and cold in the waning light of an April day. There were icicles on the fences, a rime of silver on the windward bark of maples, and occasional bare spots on the rocky protuberances of the road, as if Nature had worn herself out at the knees and elbows through long waiting for the tardy spring. A few leaves, disinterred by the thaw, became crisp again, and rustled in the wind, making the summer a thing so remote that all human hope and conjecture fled before them.

Here and there the wayside fences and walls were broken down or dismantled, and beyond them fields of snow, down-trodden and discolored and strewn with fragments of leather, camp equipage, harness, and cast-off clothing, showed traces of the recent encampment and congregation of men. On some there were still standing the ruins of rudely constructed cabins, or the semblance of fortifications equally rude and incomplete. A fox stealing along a half-filled ditch, a wolf slinking behind an earthwork, typified the human abandonment and desolation.

One by one the faint sunset tints faded from the sky, the far-off crests of the Orange Hills grew darker, the nearer files of pines on the Whatnong Mountain became a mere black background, and with the coming on of night came, too, an icy silence that seemed to stiffen and arrest the very wind itself; the crisp leaves no longer rustled, the waving whips of alder and willow snapped no longer, the icicles no longer dropped a cold fruitage from barren branch and spray, and the roadside trees relapsed into stony quiet. So that the sound of horse's hoofs breaking through the thin, dull, lustreless films of ice that patched the furrowed road might have been heard by the nearest Continental picket a mile away.

Either a knowledge of this or the difficulties of the road evidently irritated the viewless horseman. Long before he became visible his voice was heard in half-suppressed objurgation of the road, of his beast, of the country folk, and the country generally. "Steady, you jade!" "Jump, you devil, jump!" "Curse the road and the beggarly farmers that durst not mend it." And then the moving bulk of horse and rider suddenly arose above the hill, floundered and splashed, and then as suddenly disappeared, and the rattling hoofbeats ceased.

The stranger had turned into a deserted lane, still cushioned with untrodden snow. A stone wall on one hand

— in better keeping and condition than the boundary monuments of the outlying fields — bespoke protection and exclusiveness. Half-way up the lane the rider checked his speed, and, dismounting, tied his horse to a wayside sapling. This done he went cautiously forward toward the end of the lane and a farmhouse from whose gable window a light twinkled through the deepening night. Suddenly he stopped, hesitated, and uttered an impatient ejaculation. The light had disappeared. He turned sharply on his heel, and retraced his steps until opposite a farm-shed that stood a few paces from the wall. Hard by a large elm cast the gaunt shadow of its leafless limbs on the wall and surrounding snow. The stranger stepped into this shadow, and at once seemed to become a part of its trembling intricacies.

At the present moment it was certainly a bleak place for a tryst. There was snow yet clinging to the trunk of the tree, and a film of ice on its bark; the adjacent wall was slippery with frost and fringed with icicles. Yet in all there was a ludicrous suggestion of some sentiment past and unseasonable — several dislodged stones of the wall were so disposed as to form a bench and seats, and under the elm-tree's film of ice could still be seen carved on its bark the effigy of a heart, divers initials, and the legend, "Thine forever."

The stranger, however, kept his eyes fixed only on the farm-shed, and the open field beside it. Five minutes passed in fruitless expectancy. Ten minutes! And then the rising moon slowly lifted herself over the black range of the Orange Hills, and looked at him, blushing a little, as if the appointment were her own.

The face and figure thus illuminated was that of a strongly built, handsome man of thirty, so soldierly in bearing that it needed not the buff epaulets and facings to show his captain's rank in the Continental army. Yet there was something in his facial expression that contradicted the manliness of his presence, — an irritation and querulousness that were inconsistent with his size and strength. This fretfulness increased as the moments went by without sign or motion in the faintly lit field beyond, until, in peevish exasperation, he began to kick the nearer stones against the wall.

"Moo-oo-w!"

The soldier started. Not that he was frightened, nor that he had failed to recognize in these prolonged syllables the deep-chested, half-drowsy low of a cow, but that it was so near him— evidently just beside the wall. If an object so bulky could have approached him so near without his knowledge, might not she —

"Moo-oo!"

He drew near the wall cautiously. "So, Cushy! Mooly!" "Come up, Bossy!" he said persuasively. "Moo" — but here the low unexpectedly broke down, and ended in a very human and rather musical little laugh.

"Thankful!" exclaimed the soldier, echoing the laugh a trifle uneasily and affectedly as a hooded little head arose above the wall.

"Well," replied the figure, supporting a prettily-rounded chin on her hands, as she laid her elbows complacently on the wall, "Well, what did you expect? Did you want me to stand here all night while you skulked moonstruck under a tree? or did you look for me to call you by name; did you expect me to shout out Captain Allan Brewster?"

"Thankful, hush!"

"Captain Allan Brewster of the Connecticut Contingent," continued the girl with an affected raising of a low pathetic voice that was, however, inaudible beyond the tree. "Captain Brewster, behold me — your obleeged and humble servant, and sweetheart to command."

Captain Brewster succeeded, after a slight skirmish at

the wall, in possessing himself of the girl's hand. At which, although still struggling, she relented slightly.

"It is n't every lad that I 'd low for," she said, with an affected pout, "and there may be others that would not take it amiss. Though there be fine ladies enough at the Assembly balls at Morristown as might think it hoydenish."

"Nonsense, love," said the captain, who had by this time mounted the wall and encircled the girl's waist with his arm. "Nonsense! you startled me only. But," he added, suddenly taking her round chin in his hand and turning her face toward the moon, with an uneasy half suspicion, "why did you take that light from the window? What has happened?"

"We had unexpected guests, sweetheart," said Thankful; "the count just arrived."

"That infernal Hessian!" He stopped and gazed questioningly into her face. The moon looked upon her at the same time — the face was as sweet, as placid, as truthful as her own. Possibly these two inconstants understood each other.

"Nay, Allan, he is not a Hessian; but an exiled gentleman from abroad. A nobleman" —

"There are no noblemen, now," sniffed the trooper contemptuously. "Congress has so decreed it. All men are born free and equal."

"But they are not, Allan," said Thankful, with a pretty trouble in her brows. "Even cows are not born equal. Is yon calf that was dropped last night by Brindle the equal of my red heifer whose mother came by herself in a ship from Surrey? Do they look equal?"

"Titles are but breath," said Captain Brewster doggedly. There was an ominous pause.

"Nay, there is one nobleman left," said Thankful, "and he is my own — my nature's nobleman."

Captain Brewster did not reply. From certain arched gestures and wreathed smiles with which this forward young woman accompanied her statement, it would seem to be implied that the gentleman who stood before her was the nobleman alluded to. At least he so accepted it, and embraced her closely, her arms and part of her mantle clinging around his neck. In this attitude they remained quiet for some moments, slightly rocking from side to side, like a metronome, — a movement, I fancy, peculiarly bucolic, pastoral, and idyllic, and as such, I wot, observed by Theocritus and Virgil.

At these supreme moments weak woman usually keeps her wits about her much better than your superior reasoning masculine animal, and while the gallant captain was losing himself upon her perfect lips, Miss Thankful distinctly heard the farm gate click, and otherwise noticed the moon was getting high and obtrusive. She half released herself from the captain's arms, thoughtfully and tenderly, but firmly. "Tell me all about yourself, Allan dear," she said quietly, making room for him on the wall, "all, everything."

She turned upon him her beautiful eyes; eyes habitually earnest and even grave in expression, yet holding in their brave brown depths a sweet, child-like reliance and dependency; eyes with a certain tender deprecating droop in the brown fringed lid, and yet eyes that seemed to say to every man that looked upon them, "I am truthful, be frank with me." Indeed, I am convinced there is not one of my impressible sex who, looking in those pleading eyes, would not have perjured himself on the spot rather than have disappointed their fair owner.

Captain Brewster's mouth resumed its old expression of discontent.

"Everything is growing worse, Thankful, and the cause is lost. Congress does nothing, and Washington is not the man for the crisis. Instead of marching to Philadelphia and forcing that wretched rabble of Hancock and Adams at the point of the bayonet, he writes letters."

"A dignified, formal old fool," interrupted Mistress Thankful indignantly; "and look at his wife! Did n't Mistress Ford and Mistress Baily — ay, and the best blood of Morris County — go down to his Excellency's in their finest bibs and tuckers; and did n't they find my lady in a pinafore doing chores? Vastly polite treatment, indeed. As if the whole world did n't know that the General was taken by surprise when my Lady came riding up from Virginia with all those fine cavaliers, just to see what his Excellency was doing at these Assembly balls. And fine doings, I dare say."

"This is but idle gossip, Thankful," said Captain Brewster, with the faintest appearance of self-consciousness; "the Assembly balls are conceived by the General to strengthen the confidence of the townsfolk, and mitigate the rigors of the winter encampment. I go there myself rarely. I have but little taste for junketing and gavotting, with my country in such need. No, Thankful! what we want is a leader! And the men of Connecticut feel it keenly. If I have been spoken of in that regard," added the captain, with a slight inflation of his manly breast, "it is because they know of my sacrifices, — because as New England yeomen they know my devotion to the cause. They know of my suffering" —

The bright face that looked into his was suddenly afire with womanly sympathy, the pretty brow was knit, the sweet eyes overflowed with tenderness. "Forgive me, Allan, I forgot — perhaps, love — perhaps, dearest, you are hungry now."

"No, not now," replied Captain Brewster, with gloomy stoicism; "yet," he added, "it is nearly a week since I have tasted meat."

"I — I — brought a few things with me," continued the girl, with a certain hesitating timidity. She reached down and produced a basket from the shadow of the wall. "These chickens," — she held up a pair of pullets — "the Commander-in-Chief himself could not buy. I kept them for *my* Commander! And this pot of marmalade, which I know my Allan loves, is the same I put up last summer. I thought (very tenderly) you might like a piece of that bacon you liked so once, dear. Ah, sweetheart, shall we ever sit down to our little board? Shall we ever see the end of this awful war? Don't you think, dear (very pleadingly), it would be best to give it up? King George is not such a very bad man, is he? I 've thought, sweetheart (very confidently), that mayhap you and he might make it all up without the aid of those Washingtons, who do nothing but starve one to death. And if the King only knew you, Allan — should see you as I do, sweetheart — he 'd do just as you say."

During this speech she handed him the several articles alluded to, and he received them, storing them away in such receptacles of his clothing as were convenient. With this notable difference; that with *her* the act was graceful and picturesque; with him there was a ludicrousness of suggestion that his broad shoulders and uniform only heightened.

"I think not of myself, lass," he said, putting the eggs in his pocket, and buttoning the chickens within his martial breast. "I think not of myself, and perhaps I often spare that counsel which is but little heeded. But I have a duty to my men, — to Connecticut. (He here tied the marmalade up in his handkerchief.) I confess I have sometimes thought I might, under provocation, be driven to extreme measures for the good of the cause. I make no pretense to leadership, but" —

"With you at the head of the army," broke in Thankful enthusiastically, "peace would be declared within a fortnight!"

There is no flattery, however outrageous, that a man will not accept from the woman who he believes loves him. He will, perhaps, doubt its influence in the colder judgment of mankind, but he will consider that this poor creature, at least, understands him, and in some vague way represents the eternal but unrecognized verities. And when this is voiced by lips that are young, and warm, and red, it is somehow quite as convincing as the bloodless, remoter utterance of posterity.

Wherefore the trooper complacently buttoned the compliment over his chest with the pullets.

"I think you must go now, Allan," she said, looking at him with that pseudo-maternal air which the youngest of women sometimes assume to their lovers, as if the doll had suddenly changed sex and grown to man's estate. "You must go now, dear, for it may so chance that father is considering my absence overmuch. You will come again a' Wednesday, sweetheart, and you will not go to the assemblies, nor visit Mistress Judith, nor take any girl pick-a-back again on your black horse, and you will let me know when you are hungry?"

She turned her brown eyes lovingly, yet with a certain pretty trouble in the brow, and such a searching, pleading inquiry in her glance that the captain kissed her at once. Then came the final embrace, performed by the captain in a half-perfunctory, quiet manner, with a due regard for the friable nature of part of his provisions. Satisfying himself of the integrity of the eggs by feeling for them in his pocket, he waved a military salute with the other hand to Miss Thankful, and was gone. A few minutes later the sound of his horse's hoofs rang sharply from the icy hillside.

But as he reached the summit, two horsemen wheeled

suddenly from the shadow of the roadside, and bade him halt.

"Captain Brewster — if this moon does not deceive me?" queried the foremost stranger with grave civility.

"The same. Major Van Zandt, I calculate?" returned Brewster querulously.

"Your calculation is quite right. I regret, Captain Brewster, that it is my duty to inform you that you are under arrest."

"By whose orders?"

"The Commander-in-Chief's."

"For what?"

"Mutinous conduct, and disrespect of your superior officers."

The sword that Captain Brewster had drawn at the sudden appearance of the strangers quivered for a moment in his strong hand. Then, sharply striking it across the pommel of his saddle, he snapped it in twain, and cast the pieces at the feet of the speaker.

"Go on," he said doggedly.

"Captain Brewster," said Major Van Zandt, with infinite gravity, "it is not for me to point out the danger to you of this outspoken emotion, except, practically, in its effect upon the rations you have in your pocket. If I mistake not, they have suffered equally with your steel. Forward, march!"

Captain Brewster looked down and then dropped to the rear, as the discased yolks of Mistress Thankful's most precious gift slid slowly and pensively over his horse's flanks to the ground.

PART II

Mistress Thankful remained at the wall until her lover had disappeared. Then she turned, a mere lissom shadow in that uncertain light, and glided under the eaves of the shed, and thence from tree to tree of the orchard, lingering a moment under each as a trout lingers in the shadow of the bank in passing a shallow, and so reached the farmhouse and the kitchen door, where she entered. Thence by a back staircase she slipped to her own bower, from whose window half an hour before she had taken the signalling light. This she lit again and placed upon a chest of drawers, and taking off her hood and a shapeless, sleeveless mantle she had worn, went to the mirror and proceeded to readjust a high horn comb that had been somewhat displaced by the captain's arm, and otherwise, after the fashion of her sex, to remove all traces of a previous lover. It may be here observed that a man is very apt to come from the smallest encounter with his Dulcinea, *distrait*, bored, or shamefaced — to forget that his cravat is awry, or that a long blond hair is adhering to his button. But as to *mademoiselle* — well, looking at Miss Pussy's sleek paws and spotless face, would you ever know that she had been at the cream jug?

Thankful was, I think, satisfied with her appearance. Small doubt but she had reason for it. And yet her gown was a mere slip of flowered chintz, gathered at the neck, and falling at an angle of fifteen degrees to within an inch of a short petticoat of gray flannel. But so surely is the complete mould of symmetry indicated in the poise or line of any single member, that, looking at the erect carriage of her graceful brown head, or below to the curves that were lost in her shapely ankles, or the little feet that hid themselves in the broad-buckled shoes, you knew that the rest was as genuine and beautiful.

Mistress Thankful, after a pause, opened the door and listened. Then she softly slipped down the back staircase to the front hall. It was dark, but the door of the "company room" or parlor was faintly indicated by the light that streamed beneath it. She stood still for a moment, hesitatingly, when suddenly a hand grasped her own, and half led, half dragged her into the sitting-room opposite. It was dark. There was a momentary fumbling for the tinder-box and flint, a muttered oath over one or two impeding articles of furniture, and Thankful laughed. And then the light was lit, and her father, a gray, wrinkled man of sixty, still holding her hand, stood before her.

"You have been out, mistress?"

"I have," said Thankful.

"And not alone," growled the old man angrily.

"No," said Mistress Thankful, with a smile that began in the corners of her brown eyes, ran down into the dimpled curves of her mouth, and finally ended in the sudden revelation of her white teeth; "no, not alone."

"With whom?" asked the old man, gradually weakening under her strong, saucy presence.

"Well, father," said Thankful, taking a seat on a table, and swinging her little feet somewhat ostentatiously toward him, "I was with Captain Allan Brewster of the Connecticut Contingent."

"That man?"

"That man!"

"I forbid you seeing him again."

Thankful gripped the table with a hand on each side of her, to emphasize the statement, and swinging her feet, replied, —

"I shall see him as often as I like, father!"

"Thankful Blossom!"

"Abner Blossom!"

"I see you know not," said Mr. Blossom, abandoning the

severely paternal mandatory air for one of confidential disclosure, "I see you know not his reputation. He is accused of inciting his regiment to revolt — of being a traitor to the cause."

"And since when, Abner Blossom, have *you* felt such concern for the cause? Since you refused to sell supplies to the Continental commissary, except at double profits? Since you told me you were glad I had not politics like Mistress Ford" —

"Hush!" said the father, motioning to the parlor.

"Hush!" echoed Thankful indignantly; "I won't be hushed! Everybody says 'hush' to me. The count says 'hush!' Allan says 'hush!' You say 'hush!' I'm aweary of this hushing. Ah, if there was a man who did n't say it to me!" and Mistress Thankful lifted her fine eyes to the ceiling.

"You are unwise, Thankful; foolish, indiscreet. That is why you require much monition."

Thankful swung her feet in silence for a few moments, then suddenly leaped from the table, and seizing the old man by the lappels of his coat, fixed her eyes upon him, and said, suspiciously, —

"Why did you keep me from going into the company room? Why did you bring me in here?"

Blossom senior was staggered for a moment. "Because, you know, the count" —

"And you were afraid the count should know I had a sweetheart? Well — I'll go in and tell him now," she said, marching toward the door.

"Then why did you not tell him when you slipped out an hour ago? Eh, lass?" queried the old man, grasping her hand. "But 't is all one, Thankful — 't was not for him I stopped you. There is a young spark with him — ay, came even as you left, lass — a likely young gallant, and he and the count are jabbering away in their own lingo — a kind of Italian, belike — eh, Thankful?"

"I know not," she said thoughtfully. "Which way came the other?" In fact, a fear that this young stranger might have witnessed the captain's embrace began to creep over her.

"From town, my lass."

Thankful turned to her father as if she had been waiting a reply to a long-asked question. "Well?"

"Were it not well to put on a few furbelows and a tucker?" queried the old man. "'T is a gallant young spark; none of your country folk."

"No," said Thankful, with the promptness of a woman who was looking her best, and knew it. And the old man, looking at her, accepted her judgment, and without another word led her to the parlor door, and opening it, said briefly, "My daughter, Mistress Thankful Blossom."

With the opening of the door came the sound of earnest voices that instantly ceased upon the appearance of Mistress Thankful. Two gentlemen lolling before the fire arose instantly, and one came forward with an air of familiar yet respectful recognition.

"Nay, this is far too great happiness, Mistress Thankful," he said, with a strongly marked foreign accent and a still more strongly marked foreign manner. "I have been in despair, and my friend here, the Baron Pomposo, likewise."

The slightest trace of a smile and the swiftest of reproachful glances lit up the dark face of the baron as he bowed low in the introduction. Thankful dropped the curtsy of the period — *i. e.*, a duck, with semi-circular sweep of the right foot forward. But the right foot was so pretty and the grace of the little figure so perfect, that the baron raised his eyes from the foot to the face in serious admiration. In the one rapid feminine glance she had given him she had seen that he was handsome; in the second, which she could not help from his protracted silence, she saw that his beauty centred in his girlish, half fawn-like, dark eyes.

"The baron," explained Mr. Blossom, rubbing his hands together, as if, through mere friction, he was trying to impart a warmth to the reception which his hard face discountenanced, "the baron visits us under discouragement. He comes from far countries. It is the custom of gentlefolk of — of — foreign extraction to wander through strange lands, commenting upon the habits and doings of the peoples. He will find in Jersey," continued Mr. Blossom, appealing to Thankful, yet really evading her contemptuous glance, "a hard-working yeomanry, ever ready to welcome the stranger, and account to him penny for penny for all his necessary expenditure. For which purpose, in these troublous times, he will provide for himself gold or other moneys not affected by these local disturbances."

"He will find, good friend Blossom," said the baron, in a rapid, voluble way, utterly at variance with the soft, quiet gravity of his eyes, "Beauty, Grace, Accom — plishment, and — eh — Santa Maria! what shall I say?" He turned appealingly to the count.

"Virtue," nodded the count.

"Truly, Birtoo! all in the fair lady of thees countries. Ah, believe me, honest friend Blossom, there is mooch more in thees than in thoss!"

So much of this speech was addressed to Mistress Thankful that she had to show at least one dimple in reply, albeit her brows were slightly knit, and she had turned upon the speaker her honest questioning eyes.

"And then the General Washington has been kind enough to offer his protection," added the count.

"Any fool — any one," supplemented Thankful hastily, with a slight blush, "may have the General's pass — ay, and his good word. But what of Mistress Prudence Bookstaver? She that has a sweetheart in Knyphausen's brigade — ay, I warrant a Hessian, but of gentle blood, as Mistress Prudence has often told me; and look you, all her letters stopped by the General — ay, I warrant read by my Lady Washington, too — as if 't were *her* fault that her lad was in arms against Congress. Riddle me that, now?"

"'T is but prudence, lass," said Blossom, frowning on the girl. "'T is that she might disclose some movement of the army tending to defeat the enemy."

"And why should she not try to save her lad from capture or ambuscade, such as befell the Hessian commissary with the provisions that you" —

Mr. Blossom, in an ostensible fatherly embrace, managed to pinch Mistress Thankful sharply. "Hush, lass," he said, with simulated playfulness; "your tongue clacks like the Whippany mill. My daughter has small concern — 't is the manner of women folk — in politics," he explained to his guests. "These dangersome days have given her sore affliction, by way of parting comrades of her childhood and others whom she has much affected. It has in some sort soured her."

Mr. Blossom would have recalled this speech as soon as it escaped him, lest it should lead to a revelation from the truthful Mistress Thankful of her relations with the Continental captain. But to his astonishment, and, I may add, to my own, she showed nothing of that disposition she had exhibited a few moments before. On the contrary, she blushed slightly, and said nothing.

And then the conversation changed — upon the weather, the hard winter, the prospects of the cause, a criticism upon the Commander-in-Chief's management of affairs, the attitude of Congress, etc., etc., between Mr. Blossom and the count, characterized, I hardly need say, by that positiveness of opinion that distinguishes the unprofessional. In another part of the room it so chanced that Mistress Thankful and the baron were talking about themselves, the Assembly balls, who was the prettiest woman in Morristown, and whether General Washington's attentions to Mistress Pyne were only perfunctory gallantry or what, and if Lady Washington's hair was really gray, and if that young aid-de-camp Major Van Zandt were really in love with Lady W., or whether his attentions were only the zeal of a subaltern. In the midst of which a sudden gust of wind shook the house, and Mr. Blossom, going to the front door, came back with the announcement that it was snowing heavily.

And indeed, within that past hour, to their astonished eyes the whole face of nature had changed. The moon was gone, the sky hidden in a blinding, whirling swarm of stinging flakes. The wind, bitter and strong, had already fashioned white, feathery drifts upon the threshold, over the painted benches on the porch, and against the door-posts.

Mistress Thankful and the baron had walked to the rear door — the baron with a slight, tropical shudder — to view this meteorological change. As Mistress Thankful looked over the snowy landscape, it seemed to her that all record of her past experience had been effaced — her very foot-prints of an hour before were lost — the gray wall on which she leaned was white and spotless now; even the familiar farm-shed looked dim and strange and ghostly. Had she been there — had she seen the captain — was it all a fancy? She scarcely knew.

A sudden gust of wind closed the door behind them with a crash, and sent Mistress Thankful, with a slight feminine scream, forward into the outer darkness. But the baron caught her by the waist, and saved her from Heaven knows what imaginable disaster, and the scene ended in a half hysterical laugh. But the wind then set upon them both with a malevolent fury, and the baron was, I presume, obliged to draw her closer to his side.

They were alone — save for the presence of those mischievous confederates, Nature and Opportunity. In the half obscurity of the storm she could not help turning her mischievous eyes on his; but she was perhaps surprised to find them luminous, soft, and, as it seemed to her at that moment, grave beyond the occasion. An embarrassment utterly new and singular seized upon her, and when, as she half feared yet half expected, he bent down and pressed his lips to hers, she was for a moment powerless; but in the next instant she boxed his ears sharply and vanished in the darkness. When Mr. Blossom opened the door to the baron he was surprised to find that gentleman alone, and still more surprised to find, when they reëntered the house, to see Mistress Thankful enter at the same moment, demurely, from the front door.

When Mr. Blossom knocked at his daughter's door the next morning it opened upon her completely dressed, but withal somewhat pale, and, if the truth must be told, a little surly.

"And you were stirring so early, Thankful," he said; " 't would have been but decent to have bidden Godspeed to the guests, — especially the baron, who seemed much concerned at your absence."

Miss Thankful blushed slightly, but answered with savage celerity, "And since when is it necessary that I should dance attendance upon every foreign jack-in-the-box that may lie at the house?"

"He has shown great courtesy to you, mistress, and is a gentleman."

"Courtesy, indeed!" said Mistress Thankful.

"He has not presumed?" said Mr. Blossom suddenly, bringing his cold, gray eyes to bear upon his daughter's.

"No, no," said Thankful hurriedly, flaming a bright scarlet; "but — nothing. But what have you there — a letter?"

"Ay — from the captain, I warrant," said Mr. Blossom, handing her a three-cornered bit of paper; "'t was left here by a camp-follower. Thankful," he continued, with a meaning glance, "you will heed my counsel in season. The captain is not meet for such as you."

Thankful suddenly grew pale and contemptuous again as she snatched the letter from his hand. When his retiring footsteps were lost on the stairs, she regained her color and opened the letter. It was slovenly written, grievously misspelled, and read as follows: —

SWEETHEART, — A tyranous Act, begotten in Envy and Jealousie, keeps me here a prisoner. Last night I was Basely arrested by Servile Hands for that Freedom of Thought and Expression for which I have already Sacrifized so much — aye all that Man hath but Love and Honour. But the End is Near. When for the Maintenance of Power, the Liberties of the Peoples are subdued by Martial Supremacy and the Dictates of Ambition the State is Lost. I lie in vile Bondage here in Morristown under charge of Disrespeck — me that a twelvemonth past left a home and Respectable Connexions to serve my Country. Believe me still your own Love, albeit in the Power of Tyrants and condemned it may be to the scaffold.

The Messenger is Trustworthy and will speed safely to me such as you may deliver unto him. The Provender sanktified by your Hands and made precious by yr. Love was wrested from me by Servil Hands and the Eggs, Sweetheart, were somewhat Addled. The Bacon is, methinks, by this time on the Table of the Com^r-in-chief. Such is Tyranny and Ambition. Sweetheart, farewell for the present. ALLAN.

Mistress Thankful read this composition once, twice, and then tore it up. Then, reflecting that it was the first letter of her lover's that she had not kept, she tried to put together again the torn fragments, but vainly — and then in a pet, new to her, cast them from the window. During the rest of the day she was considerably *distraite*, and even manifested more temper than she was wont to do, and later, when her father rode away on his daily visit to Morristown, she felt strangely relieved. By noon the snow ceased, or rather turned into a driving sleet that again in turn gave way to rain. By this time she became absorbed in her household duties — in which she was usually skillful — and in her own thoughts, that to-day had a novelty in their meaning. In the midst of this, at about dark, her room being in rear of the house, she was perhaps unmindful of the trampling of horse without, or the sound of voices in the hall below. Neither were uncommon at that time. Although protected by the Continental army from forage or the rudeness of soldiery, the Blossom farm had always been a halting place for passing troopers, commissary teamsters, and reconnoitring officers. General Sullivan and Colonel Hamilton had watered their horses at its broad substantial wayside trough, and sat in the shade of its porch. Mistress Thankful was only awakened from her daydream by the entrance of the negro farm hand, Cæsar.

"Fo' God, Missy Thankful, them sogers is g'wine into camp in the road, I reckon, for they 's jest makin' theyseves free afo' the house, and they 's an officer in the company room with his spurs cocked on the table, readin' a book."

A quick flame leaped into Thankful's cheek, and her pretty brows knit themselves over darkening eyes. She arose from her work — no longer the moody girl, but an indignant goddess, and pushing the servant aside, swept down the stairs and threw open the door.

An officer, sitting by the fire in an easy, lounging attitude that justified the servant's criticism, arose instantly, with an air of evident embarrassment and surprise that was, however, as quickly dominated and controlled by a gentleman's breeding.

"I beg your pardon," he said, with a deep inclination of his handsome head, "but I had no idea that there was any member of this household at home — at least a lady." He hesitated a moment, catching in the raising of her brown-fringed lids a sudden revelation of her beauty, and partly losing his composure. "I am Major Van Zandt; I have the honor of addressing" —

"Thankful Blossom," said Thankful, a little proudly, divining with a woman's swift instinct the cause of the Major's hesitation. But her triumph was checked by a new embarrassment, visible in the face of the officer at the mention of her name.

"Thankful Blossom," repeated the officer quickly. "You are then the daughter of Abner Blossom?"

"Certainly," said Thankful, turning her inquiring eyes upon him; "he will be here betimes. He has gone only to Morristown." In a new fear that had taken possession of her, her questioning eyes asked, "Has he not?"

The officer, answering her eyes rather than her lips, came toward her gravely. "He will not return to-day, Mistress Thankful, nor perhaps even to-morrow. He is — a prisoner."

Thankful opened her brown eyes aggressively on the Major. "A prisoner — for what?"

"For aiding and giving comfort to the enemy, and for harboring spies," replied the Major, with military curtness.

Mistress Thankful's cheek flushed slightly at the last sentence; a recollection of the scene on the porch and the baron's stolen kiss flashed across her, and for a moment she looked as guilty as if the man before her had been a witness to the deed. He saw it, and misinterpreted her confusion.

"Belike, then," said Mistress Thankful, slightly raising her voice, and standing squarely before the Major, "Belike, then, *I* should be a prisoner, too, for the guests of this house, if they be spies, were *my* guests, and as my father's daughter, I was their hostess. Ay, man, and right glad to be the hostess of such gallant gentlemen. Gentlemen, I warrant, too fine to insult a defenseless girl, — gentlemen spies that did not cock their boots on the table or turn an honest farmer's house into a tap-room."

An expression of half pain, half amusement covered the face of the major, but he made no other reply than by a profound and graceful bow. Courteous and deprecatory as it was, it apparently exasperated Mistress Thankful only the more.

"And pray who are these spies, and who is the informer?" said Mistress Thankful, facing the soldier, with one hand truculently placed on her flexible hip, and the other slipped behind her. "Methinks 't is only honest we should know when and how we have entertained both."

"Your father, Mistress Thankful," said Major Van Zandt gravely, "has long been suspected of favoring the enemy; but it has been the policy of the Commander-in-Chief to overlook the political preferences of non-combatants, and to strive to win their allegiance to the good cause by liberal privileges. But when it was lately discovered that two strangers, although bearing a pass from him, have been frequenters of this house under fictitious names" —

"You mean Count Ferdinand and the Baron Pomposo," said Thankful quickly; "two honest gentlefolk, and if they choose to pay their devoirs to a lass — although, perhaps, not a quality lady, yet an honest girl" —

"Dear Mistress Thankful," said the Major, with a profound bow and smile that, spite of its courtesy, drove Thankful to the verge of wrathful hysterics, "if you establish that fact — and from this slight acquaintance with your charms, I doubt not you will — your father is safe from further inquiry or detention. The Commander-in-Chief is a gentleman who has never underrated the influence of your sex, nor held himself averse to its fascinations."

"What is the name of this informer?" broke in Mistress Thankful angrily. "Who is it that has dared" —

"It is but King's evidence, mayhap, Mistress Thankful, for the informer is himself under arrest. It is on the information of Captain Allan Brewster, of the Connecticut Contingent."

Mistress Thankful whitened, then flushed, and then whitened again. Then she stood up to the Major.

"It 's a lie — a cowardly lie!"

Major Van Zandt bowed. Mistress Thankful flew upstairs, and in another moment swept back again into the room in riding hat and habit.

"I suppose I can go and see — my father," she said, without lifting her eyes to the officer.

"You are free as air, Mistress Thankful. My orders and instructions, far from implicating you in your father's offenses, do not even suggest your existence. Let me help you to your horse."

The girl did not reply. During that brief interval, however, Cæsar had saddled her white mare and brought it to the door. Mistress Thankful, disdaining the offered hand of the Major, sprang to the saddle.

The Major still held the reins. "One moment, Mistress Thankful."

"Let me go," she said, with suppressed passion.

"One moment, I beg."

His hand still held the bridle-rein. The mare reared, nearly upsetting her. Crimson with rage and mortification, she raised her riding-whip and laid it smartly over the face of the man before her.

He dropped the rein instantly. Then he raised to her a face calm and colorless but for a red line extending from his eyebrow to his chin, and said quietly —

"I had no desire to detain you. I only wished to say that when you see General Washington I know you will be just enough to tell him that Major Van Zandt knew nothing of your wrongs, or even your presence here, until you presented them, and that since then he has treated you as became an officer and gentleman."

Yet even as he spoke she was gone. At the moment that her fluttering skirt swept in a furious gallop down the hillside, the Major turned and reëntered the house. The few lounging troopers who were witnesses of the scene prudently turned their eyes from the white face and blazing eyes of their officer as he strode by them. Nevertheless, when the door closed behind him, contemporary criticism broke out —

"'T is a Tory jade, vexed that she cannot befool the Major as she has the Captain," muttered Sergeant Tibbitts.

"And going to try her tricks on the General," added Private Hicks.

Howbeit, both these critics may have been wrong. For as Mistress Thankful thundered down the Morristown road she thought of many things. She thought of her sweetheart, Allan, a prisoner, and pining for *her* help and *her* solicitude, and yet — how dared he — if he *had* really betrayed or misjudged her! And then she thought bitterly of the count and the baron — and burned to face the latter, and in some vague way charge the stolen kiss upon him as the cause of all her shame and mortification. And, lastly, she thought of her father, and began to hate everybody. But, above all, and through all, in her vague fears for her father, in her passionate indignation against the baron, in her fretful impatience of Allan, one thing was ever dominant and obtrusive — one thing she tried to put away, but could not, — the handsome, colorless face of Major Van Zandt with the red welt of her riding-whip overlying its cold outlines.

PART III

The rising wind, which had ridden much faster than Mistress Thankful, had increased to a gale by the time it reached Morristown. It swept through the leafless maples, and rattled the dry bones of the elms. It whistled through the quiet Presbyterian churchyard, as if trying to arouse the sleepers it had known in days gone by. It shook the blank, lustreless windows of the Assembly Rooms over the Freemasons' Tavern, and wrought in their gusty curtains moving shadows of those amply-petticoated dames and tightly-hosed cavaliers who had swung in "Sir Roger," or jigged in "Money Musk" the night before.

But, I fancy, it was around the isolated "Ford Mansion," better known as the "Headquarters," that the wind wreaked its grotesque rage. It howled under its scant eaves, it sang under its bleak porch, it tweaked the peak of its front gable, it whistled through every chink and cranny of its square, solid, unpicturesque structure. Situated on a hillside that descended rapidly to the Whippany River, every summer zephyr that whispered through the porches of the Morristown farmhouses charged as a stiff breeze upon the swinging half-doors and windows of the "Ford Mansion," every wintry wind became a gale that threatened its security. The sentry who paced before its front porch knew from experience when to linger under its lee and adjust his threadbare outer coat to the bitter north wind.

Within the house something of this cheerlessness prevailed. It had an ascetic gloom, which the scant firelight of the reception-room, and the dying embers on the dining-room hearth failed to dissipate. The central hall was broad, and furnished plainly with a few rush-bottomed chairs, on one of which half dozed a black body servant of the Commander-in-Chief. Two officers in the dining-room, drawn close by the chimney corner, chatted in undertones, as if mindful that the door of the drawing-room was open, and their voices might break in upon its sacred privacy. The swinging light in the hall partly illuminated, or rather glanced gloomily from the black, polished furniture, the lustreless chairs, the quaint cabinet, the silent spinnet, the skeleton-legged centre table, and finally, upon the motionless figure of a man seated by the fire.

It was a figure since so well known to the civilized world, since so celebrated in print and painting as to need no description here. Its rare combination of gentle dignity with profound force — of a set resoluteness of purpose with a philosophical patience have been so frequently delivered to a people not particularly remarkable for these qualities, that I fear it has too often provoked a spirit of playful aggression, in which the deeper underlying meaning was forgotten. So let me add that in manner, physical equipoise, and even in the mere details of dress, this figure indicated a certain aristocratic exclusiveness. It was the presentment of a King — a King who by the irony of circumstances was just then waging war against all kingship; a ruler of men who just then was fighting for the right of these men to govern themselves, but whom, by his own inherent right, he dominated. From the crown of his powdered head to the silver buckle of his shoe, he was so royal that it was not strange that his brother, George of England and Hanover, — ruling by accident, otherwise impiously known as the "Grace of God," — could find no better way of resisting his power than by calling him "Mr. Washington."

The sound of horses' hoofs, the formal challenge of sentry, the grave questioning of the officer of the guard, followed by footsteps upon the porch, did not apparently disturb his meditation. Nor did the opening of the outer door and a charge of cold air into the hall that invaded even the privacy of the reception-room and brightened the dying embers on the hearth, stir his calm preoccupation. But an instant later there was the distinct rustle of a feminine skirt in the hall, a hurried whispering of men's voices, and then the sudden apparition of a smooth, fresh-faced young officer over the shoulder of the unconscious figure.

"I beg your pardon, General," said the officer doubtingly, "but" —

"You are not intruding, Colonel Hamilton," said the General quietly.

"There is a young lady without who wishes an audience of your Excellency; 't is Mistress Thankful Blossom, the daughter of Abner Blossom — charged with treasonous practice and favoring the enemy — now in the guard-house at Morristown."

"Thankful Blossom?" repeated the General interrogatively.

"Your Excellency doubtless remembers a little provincial beauty and a famous toast of the country side — the Cressida of our Morristown epic, who led our gallant Connecticut captain astray" —

"You have the advantages, besides the better memory of a younger man, Colonel," said Washington, with a playful smile that slightly reddened the cheek of his aid-de-camp. "Yet I think I *have* heard of this phenomenon. By all means admit her — and her escort."

"She is alone, General," responded the subordinate.

"Then the more reason why we should be polite," returned Washington, for the first time altering his easy posture, rising to his feet, and lightly clasping his ruffled hands before him. "We must not keep her waiting. Give her access, my dear Colonel, at once. And — even as she came — *alone.*"

The aid-de-camp bowed and withdrew. In another moment the half-opened door swung wide to Mistress Thankful Blossom.

She was so beautiful in her simple riding dress, so quaint and original in that very beauty, and, above all, so teeming with a certain vital earnestness of purpose, just positive and audacious enough to set off that beauty, that the grave gentleman before her did not content himself with the usual formal inclination of courtesy, but actually advanced, and taking her cold little hand in his, graciously led her to the chair he had just vacated.

"Even if your name were not known to me, Mistress Thankful," said the Commander-in-Chief, looking down upon her with grave politeness, "nature has, methinks, spared you the necessity of any introduction to the courtesy of a gentleman. But how can I especially serve you?"

Alack! the blaze of Mistress Thankful's brown eyes had become somewhat dimmed in the grave half-lights of the room, in the graver, deeper dignity of the erect, soldier-like figure before her. The bright color, born of the tempest within and without, had somehow faded from her cheek; the sauciness begotten from bullying her horse in the last half-hour's rapid ride was so subdued by the actual presence of the man she had come to bully, that I fear she had to use all her self-control to keep down her inclination to whimper and to keep back the tears that, oddly enough, rose to her sweet eyes as she lifted them to the quietly-critical yet placid glance of her interlocutor.

"I can readily conceive the motive of this visit, Miss Thankful," continued Washington, with a certain dignified kindliness that was more reassuring than the formal gallantry of the period, "and it is, I protest, to your credit.

A father's welfare — however erring and weak that father may be — is most seemly in a maiden."

Thankful's eyes flashed again as she rose to her feet. Her upper lip, that had a moment before trembled in a pretty infantine distress, now stiffened and curled as she confronted the dignified figure before her. "It is not of my father I would speak," she said saucily. "I did not ride here alone to-night, in the weather, to talk of *him;* I warrant *he* can speak for himself. I came here to speak of myself — of lies — ay, *lies,* told of me, a poor girl — ay, of cowardly gossip about me and my sweetheart, Captain Brewster, now confined in prison, because he hath loved me, a lass without politics or adherence to the cause — as if 't were necessary every lad should ask the confidence or permission of yourself, or belike my Lady Washington, in his preferences."

She paused a moment, out of breath. With a woman's quickness of intuition she saw the change in Washington's face, — saw a certain cold severity overshadowing it. With a woman's fateful persistency — a persistency which I humbly suggest might on occasion be honorably copied by our more politic sex — she went on to say what was in her, even if she were obliged, with a woman's honorable inconsistency, to unsay it an hour or two later — an inconsistency which I also humbly protest might be as honorably imitated by us — on occasion.

"It has been said," said Thankful Blossom quickly, "that my father has given entertainment knowingly to two spies — two spies that, begging your Excellency's pardon, and the pardon of Congress, I know only as two honorable gentlemen, who have as honorably tendered me their affections. It is said, and basely and most falsely too, that my sweetheart, Captain Allan Brewster, has lodged this information. I have ridden here to deny it. I have ridden here to demand of you that an honest woman's reputation shall not be sacrificed to the interests of politics. That a prying mob of ragamuffins shall not be sent to an honest farmer's house to spy and spy — and turn a poor girl out of doors that they might do it. 'T is shameful — so it is — there! 'T is most scandalous — so it is — there now. Spies indeed — what are *they*, pray?"

In the indignation which the recollection of her wrongs had slowly gathered in her, from the beginning of this speech, she had advanced her face, rosy with courage, and beautiful in its impertinence, within a few inches of the dignified features and quiet gray eyes of the great commander. To her utter stupefaction, he bent his head and kissed her, with a grave benignity, full on the centre of her audacious forehead.

"Be seated, I beg, Mistress Blossom," he said, taking her cold hand in his, and quietly replacing her in the unoccupied chair. "Be seated, I beg, and give me, if you can, your attention for a moment. The officer intrusted with the ungracious task of occupying your father's house is a member of my military family and a gentleman. If he has so far forgotten himself — if he has so far disgraced himself and me as" —

"No! no!" uttered Thankful, with feverish alacrity, "the gentleman was most considerate! On the contrary — mayhap — I" — she hesitated, and then came to a full stop, with a heightened color, as a vivid recollection of that gentleman's face, with the mark of her riding-whip lying across it, rose before her.

"I was about to say that Major Van Zandt, as a gentleman, has known how to fully excuse the natural impulses of a daughter," continued Washington, with a look of perfect understanding, "but let me now satisfy you on another point, where, it would seem, we greatly differ."

He walked to the door and summoned his servant, to whom he gave an order. In another moment the fresh-faced young officer, who had at first admitted her, reappeared with a file of official papers. He glanced slyly at Thankful Blossom's face with an amused look, as if he had already heard the colloquy between her and his superior officer, and had appreciated that which neither of the earnest actors in the scene had themselves felt, — a certain sense of humor in the situation.

Howbeit, standing before them, Colonel Hamilton gravely turned over the file of papers. Thankful bit her lips in embarrassment. A slight feeling of awe and a presentiment of some fast-coming shame; a new and strange consciousness of herself, her surroundings, of the dignity of the two men before her, an uneasy feeling of the presence of two ladies who had in some mysterious way entered the room from another door, and who seemed to be intently regarding her from afar with a curiosity as if she were some strange animal, and a wild premonition that her whole future life and happiness depended upon the events of the next few moments, so took possession of her that the brave girl trembled for a moment in her isolation and loneliness. In another instant, Colonel Hamilton, speaking to his superior, but looking obviously at one of the ladies who had entered, handed a paper to Washington, and said, "Here are the charges."

"Read them," said the General coldly.

Colonel Hamilton, with a manifest consciousness of another hearer than Mistress Blossom and his General, read the paper. It was couched in phrases of military and legal precision, and related briefly that upon the certain and personal knowledge of the writer, Abner Blossom of the "Blossom Farm" was in the habit of entertaining two gentlemen, namely, the "Count Ferdinand" and the "Baron Pomposo," suspected enemies of the cause, and possible traitors to the Continental Army. It was signed by Allan Brewster, late captain in the Connecticut Contingent. As Colonel Hamilton exhibited the signature, Thankful Blossom had no difficulty in recognizing the familiar bad hand, and equally familiar misspelling of her lover.

She rose to her feet. With eyes that showed her present trouble and perplexity as frankly as they had a moment before blazed with her indignation, she met, one by one, the glances of the group who now seemed to be closing round her. Yet with a woman's instinct she felt, I am constrained to say, more unfriendliness in the silent presence of the two women than in the possible outspoken criticism of our much abused sex.

"Of course," said a voice which Thankful at once by a woman's unerring instinct recognized as the elder of the two ladies, and the legitimate keeper of the conscience of some one of the men who were present, "of course Mistress Thankful will be able to elect which of her lovers among her country's enemies she will be able to cling to for support in her present emergency. She does not seem to have been so special in her favors as to have positively excluded any one."

"At least, dear Lady Washington, she will not give it to the man who has proven a traitor to *her*," said the younger woman impulsively. "That is — I beg your ladyship's pardon" — she hesitated, observing in the dead silence that ensued that the two superior male beings present looked at each other in lofty astonishment.

"He that is trait'rous to his country," said Lady Washington coldly, "is apt to be trait'rous elsewhere."

"'T were as honest to say that he that was trait'rous to his King was trait'rous to his country," said Mistress Thankful, with sudden audacity, bending her knit brows on Lady Washington. But that lady turned dignifiedly away, and Mistress Thankful again faced the General.

"I ask your pardon," she said proudly, "for troubling

you with my wrongs. But it seems to me that even if another and a greater wrong were done me by my sweetheart, through jealousy, it would not justify this accusation against me, even though," she added, darting a wicked glance at the placid brocaded back of Lady Washington, "even though that accusation came from one who knows that jealousy may belong to the wife of a patriot as well as a traitor." She was herself again, after this speech, although her face was white with the blow she had taken and returned.

Colonel Hamilton passed his hand across his mouth and coughed slightly. General Washington, standing by the fire with an impassive face, turned to Thankful gravely —

"You are forgetting, Mistress Thankful, that you have not told me how I can serve you. It cannot be that you are still concerned in Captain Brewster, who has given evidence against your other — *friends*, and tacitly against *you*. Nor can it be on their account, for I regret to say they are still free and unknown. If you come with any information exculpating them, and showing they are not spies or hostile to the cause, your father's release shall be certain and speedy. Let me ask you a single question. Why do you believe them honest?"

"Because," said Mistress Thankful, "they were — were — gentlemen."

"Many spies have been of excellent family, good address, and fair talents," said Washington gravely; "but you have, mayhap, some other reason."

"Because they talked only to ME," said Mistress Thankful, blushing mightily; "because they preferred my company to father's — because" — she hesitated a moment — "because they spoke not of politics, but — of — that which lads mainly talk of — and — and," — here she broke down a little; "and the baron I only saw once, but he" — here she broke down utterly — "I know they were n't spies — there now!"

"I must ask you something more," said Washington, with grave kindness; "whether you give me the information or not, you will consider that if what you believe is true, it cannot in any way injure the gentlemen you speak of, while, on the other hand, it may relieve your father of suspicion. Will you give to Colonel Hamilton, my secretary, a full description of them? That fuller description which Captain Brewster, for reasons best known to yourself, was unable to give."

Mistress Thankful hesitated for a moment, and then, with one of her truthful glances at the Commander-in-Chief, began a detailed account of the outward semblance of the count. Why she began with him I am unable to say, but possibly it was because it was easier, for when she came to describe the baron, she was, I regret to say, somewhat vague and figurative. Not so vague, however, but that Colonel Hamilton suddenly started up with a look at his chief, who instantly checked it with a gesture of his ruffled hand.

"I thank you, Mistress Thankful," he said, quite impassively, "but did this other gentleman, this baron" —

"Pomposo," said Thankful proudly. A titter originated in the group of ladies by the window, and became visible on the fresh face of Colonel Hamilton, but the dignified color of Washington's countenance was unmoved.

"May I ask if the baron made an honorable tender of his affections to you," he continued, with respectful gravity — "if his attentions were known to your father, and were such as honest Mistress Blossom could receive?"

"Father introduced him to me, and wanted me to be kind to him. He — he kissed me, and I slapped his face," said Thankful quickly, with cheeks as red, I warrant, as the baron's might have been.

The moment the words had escaped her truthful lips she would have given her life to recall them. To her astonishment, however, Colonel Hamilton laughed outright, and the ladies turned and approached her, but were checked by a slight gesture from the otherwise impassive figure of the General.

"It is possible, Mistress Thankful," he resumed, with undisturbed composure, "that one, at least, of these gentlemen may be known to us, and that your instincts may be correct. At least rest assured that we shall fully inquire into it, and that your father shall have the benefit of that inquiry."

"I thank your Excellency," said Thankful, still reddening under the contemplation of her own late frankness and retreating towards the door, "I — think — I — must — go — now. It is late, and I have far to ride."

To her surprise, however, Washington stepped forward, and again taking her hands in his, said with a grave smile, "For that very reason, if for none other, you must be our guest to-night, Mistress Thankful Blossom. We still retain our Virginian ideas of hospitality, and are tyrannous enough to make strangers conform to them, even though we have but perchance the poorest of entertainment to offer them. Lady Washington will not permit Mistress Thankful Blossom to leave her roof to-night until she has partaken of her courtesy as well as her counsel."

"Mistress Thankful Blossom will make us believe that she has, at least, in so far trusted our desire to serve her justly by accepting our poor hospitality for a single night," said Lady Washington, with a stately courtesy.

Thankful Blossom still stood irresolutely at the door. But the next moment a pair of youthful arms encircled her, and the younger gentlewoman, looking into her brown eyes with an honest frankness equal to her own, said caressingly, "Dear Mistress Thankful, though I am but a guest in her ladyship's house, let me, I pray you, add my voice to hers. I am Mistress Schuyler of Albany, at your service, Mistress Thankful, as Colonel Hamilton here will bear me witness, did I need any interpreter to your honest heart. Believe me, dear Mistress Thankful, I sympathize with you, and only beg you to give me an opportunity to-night to serve you. You will stay, I know, and you will stay with me, and we shall talk over the faithlessness of that over-jealous Yankee captain who has proved himself, I doubt not, as unworthy of *you* as he is of his country."

Hateful to Thankful as was the idea of being commiserated, she nevertheless could not resist the gentle courtesy and gracious sympathy of Miss Schuyler. Besides, it must be confessed that for the first time in her life she felt a doubt of the power of her own independence, and a strange fascination for this young gentlewoman whose arms were around her, who could so thoroughly sympathize with her, and yet allow herself to be snubbed by Lady Washington!

"You have a mother, I doubt not?" said Thankful, raising her questioning eyes to Miss Schuyler.

Irrelevant as this question seemed to the two young gentlemen, Miss Schuyler answered it with feminine intuition. "And you, dear Mistress Thankful" —

"Have none," said Thankful; and here, I regret to say, she whimpered slightly, at which Miss Schuyler, with tears in her own fine eyes, bent her head suddenly to Thankful's ear, put her arm about the waist of the pretty stranger, and then, to the astonishment of Colonel Hamilton, quietly swept her out of the august presence.

When the door had closed upon them, Colonel Hamilton turned half-smilingly, half-inquiringly to his chief. Washington returned his glance kindly, but gravely, and then said quietly —

"If your suspicions jump with mine, Colonel, I need not remind you that it is a matter so delicate that it would be as well if you locked it in your own breast for the present. At least that you should not intimate to the gentleman whom you may have suspected aught that has passed this evening."

"As you will, General," said the subaltern respectfully; "but may I ask," he hesitated, "if you believe that anything more than a passing fancy for a pretty girl" —

"When I asked your silence, Colonel," interrupted Washington kindly, laying his hand upon the shoulders of the younger man, "it was because I thought the matter sufficiently momentous to claim my own private and especial attention."

"I ask your Excellency's pardon," said the young man, reddening through his fresh complexion like a girl; "I only meant" —

"That you would ask to be relieved to-night," interrupted Washington, with a benign smile, "forasmuch as you wished the more to show entertainment to our dear friend, Miss Schuyler, and her guest. A wayward girl, Colonel, but, methinks, an honest one. Treat her of your own quality, Colonel, but discreetly, and not too kindly, lest we have Mistress Schuyler, another injured damsel, on our hands," and with a half playful gesture, peculiar to the man, and yet not inconsistent with his dignity, he half led, half pushed his youthful secretary from the room.

When the door had closed upon the colonel, Lady Washington rustled toward her husband, who stood still, quiet, and passive on the hearthstone.

"You surely see in this escapade nothing of political intrigue — no treachery?" she said hastily.

"No," said Washington quietly.

"Nothing more than idle, wanton intrigue with a foolish, vain country girl?"

"Pardon me, my lady," said Washington gravely. "I doubt not we may misjudge her. 'T is no common rustic lass that can thus stir the country side. 'T were an insult to your sex to believe it. It is not yet sure that she has not captured even so high game as she has named. If she has, it would add another interest to a treaty of comity and alliance."

"That creature!" said Lady Washington — "that light o' love with her Connecticut captain lover? Pardon me, but this is preposterous," and with a stiff courtesy she swept from the room, leaving the central figure of history — as such central figures usually are apt to be left — alone.

Later in the evening, Mistress Schuyler so far subdued the tears and emotions of Thankful that she was enabled to dry her eyes and rearrange her brown hair in the quaint little mirror in Mistress Schuyler's chamber, Mistress Schuyler herself lending a touch and suggestion here and there after the secret freemasonry of her sex. "You are well rid of this forsworn captain, dear Mistress Thankful, and methinks that with hair as beautiful as yours, the new style of wearing it — though a modish frivolity — is most becoming. I assure you, 't is much affected in New York and Philadelphia — drawn straight back from the forehead, after this manner, as you see."

The result was that an hour later Mistress Schuyler and Mistress Blossom presented themselves to Colonel Hamilton in the reception-room with a certain freshness and elaboration of toilet that not only quite shamed the young officer's *affairé* negligence, but caused him to open his eyes in astonishment. "Perhaps she would rather be alone, that she might indulge her grief," he said doubtingly, in an aside to Miss Schuyler, "rather than appear in company."

"Nonsense," quoth Mistress Schuyler. "Is a young woman to mope and sigh because her lover proves false?"

"But her father is a prisoner," said Hamilton in amazement.

"Can you look me in the face," said Mistress Schuyler mischievously, "and tell me that you don't know that in twenty-four hours her father will be cleared of these charges? Nonsense! Do you think I have no eyes in my head? Do you think I misread the General's face and your own?"

"But, my dear girl," said the officer in alarm.

"Oh, I told her so — but not *why*," responded Miss Schuyler, with a wicked look in her dark eyes, "though I had warrant enough to do so to serve you for keeping a secret from *me!*"

And with this Parthian shot she returned to Mistress Thankful, who, with her face pressed against the window, was looking out on the moonlit slope beside the Whippany River.

For by one of those freaks peculiar to the American springtide the weather had again marvelously changed. The rain had ceased, and the ground was covered with an icing of sleet and snow, that now glittered under a clear sky and a brilliant moon. The northeast wind that shook the loose sashes of the windows had transformed each dripping tree and shrub to icy stalactites that silvered under the moon's cold touch.

"'Tis a beautiful sight, ladies," said a bluff, hearty, middle-aged man, joining the group by the window; "but God send the spring to us quickly, and spare us any more such cruel changes. My lady moon looks fine enough, glittering in yonder treetops, but I doubt not she looks down upon many a poor fellow shivering under his tattered blankets in the camp beyond. Had ye seen the Connecticut tatterdemalions file by last night, with arms reversed, showing their teeth at his Excellency and yet not daring to bite — had ye watched these faint hearts, these doubting Thomases, ripe for rebellion against his Excellency, against the cause, but chiefly against the weather, ye would pray for a thaw that would melt the hearts of these men as it would these stubborn fields around us. Two weeks more of such weather would raise up not one Allan Brewster, but a dozen such malcontent puppies ripe for a drumhead court-martial."

"Yet 't is a fine night, General Sullivan," said Colonel Hamilton, sharply nudging the ribs of his superior officer with his elbow; "there would be little trouble on such a night, I fancy, to track our ghostly visitant." Both of the ladies becoming interested, and Colonel Hamilton having thus adroitly turned the flank of his superior officer, he went on: "You should know that the camp, and indeed the whole locality here, is said to be haunted by the apparition of a gray-coated figure, whose face is muffled and hidden in his collar, but who has the password pat to his lips, and whose identity hath baffled the sentries. This figure, it is said, forasmuch as it has been seen just before an assault, an attack, or some tribulation of the army, is believed by many to be the genius or guardian spirit of the cause, and, as such, has incited sentries and guards to greater vigilance, and has to some seemed a premonition of disaster. Before the last outbreak of the Connecticut Militia, Master Graycoat haunted the outskirts of the weather-beaten and bedraggled camp, and, I doubt not, saw much of that preparation that sent that regiment of faint-hearted onion-gatherers to flaunt their woes and their wrongs in the face of the General himself." Here Colonel Hamilton, in turn, received a slight nudge from Mistress Schuyler, and ended his speech somewhat abruptly.

Mistress Thankful was not unmindful of both these allusions to her faithless lover, but only a consciousness of mortification and wounded pride was awakened by them. In fact, during the first tempest of her indignation at his arrest, still later at the arrest of her father, and finally at the discovery of his perfidy to her, she had forgotten that he was her lover; she had forgotten her previous tenderness towards him; and now that her fire and indignation were spent, only a sense of numbness and vacancy remained. All that had gone before seemed not something to be regretted as her own act, but rather as the act of another Thankful Blossom, who had been lost that night in the snowstorm; she felt she had become within the last twenty-four hours not perhaps *another* woman, but for the first time a *woman*.

Yet it was singular that she felt more confused when, a few moments later, the conversation turned upon Major Van Zandt; it was still more singular that she even felt considerably frightened at that confusion. Finally she found herself listening with alternate irritability, shame, and curiosity to praises of that gentleman, of his courage, his devotion, and his personal graces. For one wild moment Thankful felt like throwing herself on the breast of Mistress Schuyler and confessing her rudeness to the major; but a conviction that Mistress Schuyler would share that secret with Colonel Hamilton, that Major Van Zandt might not like that revelation, and, oddly enough associated with this, a feeling of unconquerable irritability toward that handsome and gentle young officer, kept her mouth closed. "Besides," she said to herself, "he ought to know, if he is such a fine gentleman as they say, just how I was feeling, and that I did n't mean any rudeness to him;" and with this unanswerable feminine logic, poor Thankful, to some extent, stilled her own honest little heart.

But not, I fear, entirely; the night was a restless one to her; like all impulsive natures the season of reflection and perhaps distrust came to her upon acts that were already committed, and when reason seemed to light the way only to despair. She saw the folly of her intrusion at the headquarters, as she thought, only when it was too late to remedy it; she saw the gracelessness and discourtesy of her conduct to Major Van Zandt only when distance and time rendered an apology weak and ineffectual. I think she cried a little to herself, lying in the strange gloomy chamber of the healthfully sleeping Mistress Schuyler, the sweet security of whose manifest goodness and kindness she alternately hated and envied, and at last, unable to stand it longer, slipped noiselessly from her bed and stood very wretched and disconsolate before the window that looked out upon the slope towards the Whippany River. The moon on the new-fallen, frigid, and untrodden snow shone brightly. Far to the left it glittered on the bayonet of a sentry pacing beside the river bank, and gave a sense of security to the girl that perhaps strengthened another idea that had grown up in her mind. Since she could not sleep, why should she not ramble about until she could? She had been accustomed to roam about the farm in all weathers and at all times and seasons. She recalled to herself the night — a tempestuous one — when she had risen in serious concern as to the lying-in of her favorite Alderney heifer, and how she had saved the life of the calf, a weakling, dropped apparently from the clouds in the tempest, as it lay beside the barn. With this in her mind she donned her dress again, and with Mistress Schuyler's mantle over her shoulders noiselessly crept down the narrow staircase, passed the sleeping servant on the settee, and, opening the rear door, in another moment was inhaling the crisp air and tripping down the crisp snow of the hillside.

But Mistress Thankful had overlooked one difference between her own farm and a military encampment. She had not proceeded a dozen yards before a figure apparently started out of the ground beneath her, and leveling a bayoneted musket across her path called, "Halt!"

The hot blood mounted to the girl's cheek at the first imperative command she had ever received in her life; nevertheless she halted unconsciously, and without a word confronted the challenger with her old audacity.

"Who goes there?" reiterated the sentry, still keeping his bayonet level with her breast.

"Thankful Blossom," she responded promptly.

The sentry brought his musket to a "present." "Pass, Thankful Blossom, and God send it soon, and the spring with it, and good-night," he said, with a strong Milesian accent. And before the still amazed girl could comprehend the meaning of his abrupt challenge, or his equally abrupt departure, he had resumed his monotonous pace in the moonlight. Indeed, as she stood looking after him, the whole episode, the odd unreality of the moonlit landscape, the novelty of her position, the morbid play of her thoughts, seemed to make it part of a dream which the morning light might dissipate but could never fully explain.

With something of this feeling still upon her, she kept her way to the river. Its banks were still fringed with ice, through which its dark current flowed noiselessly. She knew it flowed through the camp where lay her faithless lover, and for an instant indulged the thought of following it and facing him with the proof of his guilt; but even at the thought she recoiled with a new and sudden doubt in herself, and stood dreamily watching the shimmer of the moon on the icy banks, until another and it seemed to her equally unreal vision suddenly stayed her feet, and drove the blood from her feverish cheeks.

A figure was slowly approaching from the direction of the sleeping encampment. Tall, erect, and habited in a gray surtout with a hood partially concealing its face, it was the counterfeit presentment of the ghostly visitant she had heard described. Thankful scarcely breathed. The brave little heart that had not quailed before the sentry's leveled musket a moment before, now faltered and stood still as the phantom, with a slow and majestic tread, moved toward her. She had only time to gain the shelter of a tree before the figure, majestically unconscious of her presence, passed slowly by. Through all her terror Thankful was still true to a certain rustic habit of practical perception to observe that the tread of the phantom was quite audible over the crust of snow, and was visible and palpable as the imprint of a military boot!

The blood came back to Thankful's cheek, and with it her old audacity. In another instant she was out from the tree, and tracking with a light feline tread the apparition that now loomed up the hill before her. Slipping from tree to tree, she followed until it paused before the door of a low hut or farm-shed that stood midway up the hill. Here it entered, and the door closed behind it. With every sense feverishly alert, Thankful, from the secure advantage of a large maple, watched the door of the hut. In a few moments it re-opened to the same figure free of its gray enwrappings. Forgetful of everything now but detecting the face of the impostor, the fearless girl left the tree and placed herself directly in the path of the figure. At the same moment it turned toward her inquiringly, and the moonlight fell full upon the calm, composed features of General Washington.

In her consternation Thankful could only drop an embarrassed curtsy and hang out two lovely signals of distress on her cheeks. The face of the pseudo ghost alone remained unmoved.

"You are wandering late, Mistress Thankful," he said, at last, with a paternal gravity, "and I fear that the formal restraint of a military household has already given you some embarrassment. Yonder sentry, for instance, might have stopped you."

"Oh, he did!" said Thankful quickly; "but it 's all right, please your Excellency. He asked me 'who went there,' and I told him, and he was vastly polite, I assure you."

The grave features of the Commander-in-Chief relaxed

You are wandering late, Mistress Thankful

in a smile. "You are more happy than most of your sex in turning a verbal compliment to practical account. For know then, dear young lady, that in honor of your visit to the headquarters, the password to-night through this encampment was none other than your own pretty patronymic, —'Thankful Blossom.'"

The tears glittered in the girl's eyes, and her lip trembled. But with all her readiness of speech, she could only say, "Oh, your Excellency."

"Then you *did* pass the sentry?" continued Washington, looking at her intently with a certain grave watchfulness in his gray eyes. "And doubtless you wandered at the river bank. Although I myself, tempted by the night, sometimes extend my walk as far as yonder shed, it were a hazardous act for a young lady to pass beyond the protection of the line."

"Oh, I met no one, your Excellency," said the usually truthful Thankful hastily, rushing to her first lie with grateful impetuosity.

"And saw no one?" asked Washington quietly.

"No one," said Thankful, raising her brown eyes to the General's.

They both looked at each other—the naturally most veracious young woman in the colonies and the subsequent allegorical impersonation of Truth in America—and knew each other lied, and, I imagine, respected each other for it.

"I am glad to hear you say so, Mistress Thankful," said Washington quietly, "for 't would have been natural for you to have sought an interview with your recreant lover in yonder camp, though the attempt would have been unwise and impossible."

"I had no such thought, your Excellency," said Thankful, who had really quite forgotten her late intention; "yet if with your permission I could hold a few moments' converse with Captain Brewster, it would greatly ease my mind."

"'T would not be well for the present," said Washington thoughtfully. "But in a day or two Captain Brewster will be tried by court-martial at Morristown. It shall be so ordered that when he is conveyed thither his guard shall halt at the Blossom Farm. I will see that the officer in command gives you an opportunity to see him. And I think I can promise also, Mistress Thankful, that your father shall also be present under his own roof, — a free man."

They had reached the entrance to the mansion and entered the hall. Thankful turned impulsively and kissed the extended hand of the Commander. "You are so good. I have been so foolish — so very, very wrong," she said, with a slight trembling of her lip. "And your Excellency believes my story, and those gentlemen were not spies, but even as they gave themselves to be."

"I said not that much," replied Washington, with a kindly smile, "but no matter. Tell me rather, Mistress Thankful, how far your acquaintance with these gentlemen has gone, or did it end with the box on the ear that you gave the baron?"

"He had asked me to ride with him to the Baskingridge, and I — had said — yes," faltered Mistress Thankful.

"Unless I misjudge you, Mistress Thankful, you can, without much sacrifice, promise me that you will not see him until I give you my permission," said Washington, with grave playfulness.

The swinging light shone full in Thankful's truthful eyes as she lifted them to his.

"I do," she said quietly.

"Good-night," said the Commander, with a formal bow.

"Good-night, your Excellency."

PART IV

The sun was high over the Short Hills when Mistress Thankful, the next day, drew up her sweating mare beside the Blossom Farm gate. She had never looked prettier, she had never felt more embarrassed as she entered her own house. During her rapid ride she had already framed a speech of apology to Major Van Zandt, which, however, utterly fled from her lips as that officer showed himself respectfully on the threshold. Yet she permitted him to usurp the functions of the grinning Cæsar, and help her from her horse, albeit she was conscious of exhibiting the awkward timidity of a bashful rustic, until at last, with a stammering "Thank ye," she actually ran upstairs to hide her glowing face and far too conscious eyelids.

During the rest of that day Major Van Zandt quietly kept out of her way, without obtrusively seeming to avoid her. Yet when they met casually in the performance of her household duties, the innocent Mistress Thankful noticed, under her downcast, penitential eyelids, that the eyes of the officer followed her intently. And thereat she fell unconsciously to imitating him, and so they eyed each other furtively like cats, and rubbed themselves along the walls of rooms and passages when they met, lest they should seem designedly to come near each other, and enacted the gravest and most formal of genuflections, curtsies, and bows, when they accidentally *did* meet. And just at the close of the second day, as the elegant Major Van Zandt was feeling himself fast becoming a driveling idiot and an awkward country booby, the arrival of a courier from headquarters saved that gentleman his self-respect forever.

Mistress Thankful was in her sitting-room when he knocked at the door. She opened it in sudden, conscious trepidation.

"I ask pardon for intruding, Mistress Thankful Blossom," he said gravely, "but I have here" — he held out a pretentious document — "a letter for you from headquarters. May I hope that it contains good news — the release, of your father, — and that it relieves you from my presence, and an espionage which I assure you cannot be more unpleasant to you than it has been to myself."

As he entered the room, Thankful had risen to her feet with the full intention of delivering to him her little set apology, but as he ended his speech she looked at him blandly — and burst out crying.

Of course he was in an instant at her side and holding her cold little hand. Then she managed to say, between her tears, that she had been wanting to make an apology to him; that she had wanted to say ever since she arrived that she had been rude, very rude, and that she knew he never could forgive her; that she had been trying to say that she never could forget his gentle forbearance, "only," she added, suddenly raising her tear-fringed brown lids to the astonished man, "*you would n't ever let me!*"

"Dear Mistress Thankful," said the major, in conscience-stricken horror, "if I have made myself distant to you, believe me it was only because I feared to intrude upon your sorrow. I really — dear Mistress Thankful — I"—

"When you took all the pains to go round the hall instead of through the dining-room lest I should ask you to forgive me," sobbed Mistress Thankful, "I thought — you — must — hate me, and preferred to" —

"Perhaps this letter may mitigate your sorrow, Mistress Thankful," said the officer, pointing to the letter she still held unconsciously in her hand.

With a blush at her preoccupation, Thankful opened the letter. It was a half-official document, and ran as follows: —

The Commander-in-Chief is glad to inform Mistress Thankful Blossom that the charges preferred against her father have, upon fair examination, been found groundless and trivial. The Commander-in-Chief further begs to inform Mistress Blossom that the gentleman known to her under the name of the "Baron Pomposo," was his Excellency Don Juan Morales, Ambassador and Envoy Extraordinary of the Court of Spain, and that the gentleman known to her as the "Count Ferdinand" was Señor Godoy, Secretary to the Embassy. The Commander-in-Chief wishes to add that Mistress Thankful Blossom is relieved of any further obligation of hospitality toward these honorable gentlemen, as the Commander-in-Chief regrets to record the sudden and deeply-to-be-deplored death of his Excellency this morning by typhoid fever, and the possible speedy return of the Embassy.

In conclusion, the Commander-in-Chief wishes to bear testimony to the Truthfulness, Intuition, and Discretion of Mistress Thankful Blossom.

By order of his Excellency,

General GEORGE WASHINGTON.

ALEX. HAMILTON, Secretary.

To Mistress THANKFUL BLOSSOM, of Blossom Farm.

Thankful Blossom was silent for a few moments, and then raised her abashed eyes to Major Van Zandt. A single glance satisfied her that he knew nothing of the imposture that had been practiced upon her — knew nothing of the trap into which her vanity and self-will had led her.

"Dear Mistress Thankful," said the major, seeing the distress in her face, "I trust the news is not ill. Surely I gathered from the Sergeant that" —

"What?" said Thankful, looking at him intently.

"That in twenty-four hours at furthest your father would be free, and that I should be relieved" —

"I know that you are aweary of your task, Major," said Thankful bitterly; "rejoice, then, to know your information is correct, and that my father is exonerated — unless — unless this is a forgery, and General Washington should turn out to be somebody else, and *you* should turn out to be somebody else" — and she stopped short and hid her wet eyes in the window curtains.

"Poor girl!" said Major Van Zandt to himself, "this trouble has undoubtedly frenzied her. Fool that I was, to lay up the insult of one that sorrow and excitement had bereft of reason and responsibility. 'T were better I should retire at once and leave her to herself," and the young man slowly retreated toward the door.

But at this moment there were alarming symptoms of distress in the window curtain, and the major paused as a voice from its dimity depths said plaintively, "And *you* are going without forgiving me!"

"Forgive *you*, Mistress Thankful," said the major, striding to the curtain, and seizing a little hand that was obtruded from its folds, "forgive you. Rather can you forgive me — for the folly — the cruelty of mistaking — of — of" — and here the major, hitherto famous for facile compliments, utterly broke down. But the hand he held was no longer cold, but warm and intelligent, and in default of coherent speech he held fast by that as the thread of his discourse, until Mistress Thankful quietly withdrew it, thanked him for his forgiveness, and retired deeper behind the curtain.

When he had gone, she threw herself in a chair and again gave way to a passionate flood of tears. In the last twenty-four hours her pride had been utterly humbled; the independent spirit of this self-willed little beauty had met for the first time with defeat. When she had got over her womanly shock at the news of the sham baron's death, she had, I fear, only a selfish regret at his taking off —

believing that if living he would in some way show the world, which just then consisted of the headquarters and Major Van Zandt, that he had really made love to her, and possibly did honorably love her still, and might yet give her an opportunity to reject him. And now he was dead, and she was held up to the world as the conceited plaything of a fine gentleman's masquerading sport. That her father's cupidity and ambition made him sanction the imposture, in her bitterness she never doubted. No! lover, friend, father — all had been false to her, and the only kindness she had received was from the man she had wantonly insulted. Poor little Blossom! Indeed, a most premature Blossom; I fear a most unthankful Blossom, sitting there, shivering in the first chill wind of adversity, rocking backward and forward with the skirt of her dimity short gown over her shoulders, and her little buckled shoes and clocked stockings pathetically crossed before her.

But healthy youth is reactive, and in an hour or two Thankful was down at the cow-shed with her arms around the neck of her favorite heifer, to whom she poured out much of her woes, and from whom she won an intelligent sort of slobbering sympathy. And then she sharply scolded Cæsar for nothing at all, and a moment after returned to the house with the air and face of a deeply-injured angel, who had been disappointed in some celestial idea of setting this world right, but was still not above forgiveness. A spectacle that sank Major Van Zandt into the dark depths of remorse, and eventually sent him to smoke a pipe of Virginia with his men in the roadside camp. Seeing which, Thankful went early to bed and cried herself to sleep. And Nature, possibly, followed her example, for at sunset a great thaw set in, and by midnight the freed rivers and brooks were gurgling melodiously, and tree, and shrub, and fence were moist and dripping.

The red dawn at last struggled through the vaporous veil

that hid the landscape. Then occurred one of those magical changes peculiar to the climate, yet perhaps preëminently notable during that historic winter and spring. By ten o'clock on that 3d of May, 1780, a fervent June-like sun had rent that vaporous veil, and poured its direct rays upon the gaunt and haggard profile of the Jersey hills. The chilled soil responded but feebly to that kiss; perhaps a few of the willows that yellowed the river banks took on a deeper color. But the country folk were certain that spring had come at last, and even the correct and self-sustained Major Van Zandt came running in to announce to Mistress Thankful that one of his men had seen a violet in the meadow. In another moment Mistress Thankful had donned her cloak and pattens to view this firstling of the laggard summer. It was quite natural that Major Van Zandt should accompany her as she tripped on ; and so, without a thought of their past differences, they ran like very children down the moist and rocky slope that led to the quaggy meadow. Such was the influence of the vernal season.

But the violets were hidden. Mistress Thankful, regardless of the wet leaves and her new gown, groped with her fingers among the withered grasses. Major Van Zandt leaned against a boulder and watched her with admiring eyes.

"You 'll never find flowers that way," she said at last, looking up to him impatiently. "Go down on your knees like an honest man. There are some things in this world worth stooping for."

The major instantly dropped on his knees beside her. But at that moment Mistress Thankful found her posies and rose to her feet. "Stay where you are," she said mischievously, as she stooped down and placed a flower in the lappel of his coat. "That is to make amends for my rudeness. Now, get up."

But the major did not rise. He caught the two little hands that had seemed to flutter like birds against his breast, and, looking up into the laughing face above him, said, "Dear Mistress Thankful; dare I remind you of your own words that 'there be some things worth stooping for.' Think of my love, Mistress Thankful, as a flower — mayhap not as gracious to you as your violets, but as honest and — and — and — as" —

"Ready to spring up in a single night," laughed Thankful. "But, no; get up, Major! What would the fine ladies of Morristown say of your kneeling at the feet of a country girl, the play and sport of every fine gentleman? What if Mistress Bolton should see her own cavalier, the modish Major Van Zandt, proffering his affections to the disgraced sweetheart of a perjured traitor? Leave go my hand, I pray you, Major — if you respect" —

She was free, yet she faltered a moment beside him, with tears quivering on her long brown lashes. Then she said, tremulously, "Rise up, Major. Let us think no more of this. I pray you forgive me, if I have again been rude."

The major struggled to rise to his feet. But he could not. And then I regret to have to record that the fact became obvious that one of his shapely legs was in a bog-hole, and that he was perceptibly sinking out of sight. Whereat Mistress Thankful trilled out a three-syllabled laugh, looked demure and painfully concerned at his condition, and then laughed again. The major joined in her mirth, albeit his face was crimson. And then, with a little cry of alarm, she flew to his side, and put her arms around him.

"Keep away, keep away, for heaven's sake, Mistress Blossom," he said quickly, "or I shall plunge you into my mishap, and make you as ridiculous as myself."

But the quickwitted girl had already leaped to an adjacent boulder. "Take off your sash," she said quickly, "fasten it to your belt, and throw it to me." He did so. She straightened herself back on the rock. "Now, all together," she cried, with a preliminary strain on the sash, and then the cords of her well-trained muscles stood out on her rounded arms, and with a long pull, and a strong pull, and a pull all together, she landed the major upon the rock. And then she laughed. And then, inconsistent as it may appear, she became grave, and at once proceeded to scrape him off, and rub him down with dried leaves, with fern twigs, with her handkerchief, with the border of her mantle, as if he were a child, until he blushed with alternate shame and secret satisfaction.

They spoke but little on their return to the farmhouse, for Mistress Thankful had again become grave. And yet the sun shone cheerily above them; the landscape was filled with the joy of resurrection and new and awakened life; the breeze whispered gentle promises of hope and the fruition of their hopes in the summer to come. And these two fared on until they reached the porch with a half-pleased, half-frightened consciousness that they were not the same beings who had left it a half-hour before.

Nevertheless, at the porch Mistress Thankful regained something of her old audacity. As they stood together in the hall, she handed him back the sash she had kept with her. As she did so she could not help saying, "There are some things worth stooping for, Major Van Zandt."

But she had not calculated upon the audacity of the man, and as she turned to fly she was caught by his strong arm and pinioned to his side. She struggled, honestly, I think, and perhaps more frightened at her own feelings than at his strength, but it is to be recorded that he kissed her in a moment of comparative yielding, and then, frightened himself, released her quickly, whereat she fled to her room, and threw herself, panting and troubled, upon her bed.

For an hour or two she lay there, with flushed cheeks and conflicting thoughts. "He must never kiss me again," she said softly to herself, "unless" — but the interrupting thought said, "I shall die if he kiss me not again; and I never can kiss another." And then she was roused by a footstep upon the stair — which, in that brief time, she had learned to know and look for — and a knock at the door. She opened it to Major Van Zandt, white and so colorless as to bring out once more the faint red line made by her riding whip two days before, as if it had risen again in accusation. The blood dropped out of her cheeks as she gazed at him in silence.

"An escort of dragoons," said Major Van Zandt, slowly and with military precision, "has just arrived, bringing with them one Captain Allan Brewster, of the Connecticut Contingent, on his way to Morristown to be tried for mutiny and treason. A private note from Colonel Hamilton instructs me to allow him to have a private audience with you — if *you* so wish it."

With a woman's swift and too often hopeless intuition, Thankful knew that this was not the sole contents of the letter, and that her relations with Captain Brewster were known to the man before her. But she drew herself up a little proudly, and turning her truthful eyes upon the major, said, "I *do* so wish it."

"It shall be done as you desire, Mistress Blossom," returned the officer, with cold politeness, as he turned upon his heel.

"One moment, Major Van Zandt," said Thankful swiftly.

The major turned quickly. But Thankful's eyes were gazing thoughtfully forward, and scarcely glanced at him. "I would prefer," she said timidly and hesitatingly, "that this interview should not take place under the roof where — where — where my father lives. Half way down the meadow there is a barn, and before it a broken part of the wall, fronting on a sycamore tree. *He* will know where it is. Tell him I will see him there in half an hour."

A smile, which the major had tried to make a careless one, curled his lip satirically as he bowed in reply. "It is the first time," he said drily, "that I believe I have been honored with arranging a tryst for two lovers, but believe me, Mistress Thankful, I will do my best. In half an hour I will turn my prisoner over to you."

In half an hour the punctual Mistress Thankful, with a hood hiding her pale face, passed the officer in the hall on the way to her rendezvous. An hour later, Cæsar came with a message that Mistress Thankful would like to see him. When the major entered the sitting-room he was shocked to find her lying pale and motionless on the sofa, but as the door closed she rose to her feet and confronted him.

"I do not know," she said slowly, "whether you are aware that the man I just now parted from was, for a twelvemonth past, my sweetheart, and that I believed I loved him, and *knew* I was true to him. If you have not heard it I tell you now, for the time will come when you will hear part of it from the lips of others, and I would rather you should take the whole truth from mine. This man was false to me. He betrayed two friends of mine as spies. I could have forgiven it had it been only foolish jealousy, but it was, I have since learned from his own lips, only that he might gratify his spite against the Commander-in-Chief by procuring their arrest and making a serious difficulty in the American camp, by means of which he hoped to serve his own ends. He told me this, believing that I sympathized with him in his hatred of the Commander-in-Chief, and in his own wrongs and sufferings. I confess, to my shame, Major Van Zandt, that two days ago I did believe him, and that I looked upon you as a mere catchpoll or bailiff of the tyrant. That I found out how I was deceived when I saw the Commander-in-Chief, you, major, who know him so well, need not be told. Nor was it necessary for me to tell this man that he had deceived me — for I felt — that — that — was — not — the — only reason — why I could no longer return — his love."

She paused, as the major approached her earnestly, and waved him back with her hand. "He reproached me bitterly with my want of feeling for his misfortunes," she went on again; "he recalled my past protestations! he showed me my love letters — and he told me that if I were still his true sweetheart I ought to help him. I told him if he would never call me by that name again; if he would give up all claim to me; if he would never speak, write to me, or see me again; if he would hand me back my letters, I would help him." She stopped — the blood rushed into her pale face. "You will remember, major, that I accepted this man's love as a young, foolish, trustful girl; but when I made him this offer — he — he — accepted it."

"The dog!" said Major Van Zandt. "But in what way could you help this double traitor?"

"I *have* helped him," said Thankful quietly.

"But how?" said Major Van Zandt.

"By becoming a traitor myself," she said, turning upon him almost fiercely. "Hear me! While you were quietly pacing these halls, while your men were laughing and talking in the road, Cæsar was saddling my white mare, the fleetest in the country. He led her to the lane below. That mare is now two miles away, with Captain Brewster on her back. Why do you not start, major? Look at me. *I* am a traitor, and this is my bribe," and she drew a package of letters from her bosom, and flung them on the table.

She had been prepared for an outbreak or exclamation from the man before her, but not for his cold silence.

"Speak," she cried, at last, passionately, "speak. Open your lips if only to curse me! Order in your men to arrest me. I will proclaim myself guilty, and save your honor. But only speak!"

"May I ask," said Major Van Zandt coldly, "why you have twice honored me with a blow?"

"Because I loved you! Because when I first saw you I saw the only man that was my master, and I rebelled. Because when I found I could not help but love you, I knew I never had loved before, and I would wipe out with one stroke all the past that rose in judgment against me. Because I would not have you ever confronted with one endearing word of mine that was not meant for you!"

Major Van Zandt turned from the window where he had stood, and faced the girl with sad resignation. "If I have, in my foolishness, Mistress Thankful, shown you how great was your power over me, when you descended to this artifice to spare my feelings by confessing your own love for me, you should have remembered that you were doing that which forever kept me from wooing or winning you. If you had really loved me, your heart, as a woman's, would have warned you against that which my heart, as a gentleman's, has made a law of honor; when I tell you, as much for the sake of relieving your own conscience as for the sake of justifying mine, that if this man, a traitor, my prisoner, and your recognized lover, had escaped from my custody without your assistance, connivance, or even knowledge, I should have deemed it my duty to forsake you until I caught him, even if we had been standing before the altar."

Thankful heard him, but only as a strange voice in the distance, as she stood with fixed eyes and breathless, parted lips before him. Yet even then I fear that, woman-like, she did not comprehend his rhetoric of honor, but only caught here and there a dull, benumbing idea that he despised her, and that in her effort to win his love she had killed it, and ruined him forever.

"If you think it strange," continued the major, "that, believing as I do, I stand here only to utter moral axioms when my duty calls me to pursue your lover, I beg you to believe that it is only for your sake. I wish to allow a reasonable time between your interview with him and his escape, that shall save you from any suspicion of complicity. Do not think," he added, with a sad smile, as the girl made an impatient step towards him, "do not think I am running any risk. The man cannot escape. A cordon of pickets surrounds the camp for many miles. He has not the countersign, and his face and crime are known."

"Yes," said Thankful eagerly, "but a part of his own regiment guards the Baskingridge road."

"How know you this?" said the major, seizing her hand.

"He told me."

Before she could fall on her knees and beg his forgiveness, he had darted from the room, given an order, and returned with cheeks and eyes blazing.

"Hear me," he said rapidly, taking the girl's two hands, "you know not what you've done. I forgive you. But this is no longer a matter of duty, but of my personal honor. I shall pursue this man alone. I shall return with him, or not at all. Farewell; God bless you!"

But before he reached the door she caught him again. "Only say you have forgiven me once more."

"I do."

"Guert!"

There was something in the girl's voice more than this first utterance of his Christian name that made him pause.

"I told — a — lie — just — now. There is a fleeter horse in the stable than my mare; 't is the roan filly in the second stall."

"God bless you."

He was gone. She waited to hear the clatter of his horse's hoofs in the roadway. When Cæsar came in a few moments later to tell the news of Captain Brewster's escape, the room was empty. But it was soon filled again by a dozen turbulent troopers.

"Of course she's gone," said Sergeant Tibbitts; "the jade flew with the captain."

"Ay, 't is plain enough. Two horses are gone from the stable besides the major's," said Private Hicks.

Nor was this military criticism entirely a private one. When the courier arrived at headquarters the next morning, it was to bring the report that Mistress Thankful Blossom, after assisting her lover to escape, had fled with him. "The renegade is well off our hands," said General Sullivan gruffly. "He has saved us the public disgrace of a trial, but this is bad news of Major Van Zandt."

"What news of the major?" asked Washington quickly.

"He pursued the vagabond as far as Springfield, killing his horse, and falling himself insensible before Major Merton's quarters. Here he became speedily delirious, fever supervened, and the regimental surgeon, after a careful examination, pronounced his case one of smallpox."

A whisper of horror and pity went round the room. "Another gallant soldier who should have died leading a charge, laid by the heels by a beggar's filthy distemper," growled Sullivan; "where will it end?"

"God knows," said Hamilton. "Poor Van Zandt. But whither was he sent; to the hospital?"

"No. A special permit was granted in his case, and 't is said he was removed to the Blossom Farm — it being remote from neighbors, and the house was placed under quarantine. Abner Blossom has prudently absented himself from the chances of infection, and the daughter has fled. The sick man is attended only by a black servant and an ancient crone, so that if the poor major escapes with his life or without disfigurement, pretty Mistress Bolton of Morristown need not be scandalized or jealous."

PART V

The ancient crone alluded to in the last chapter had been standing behind the window-curtains of that bedroom which had been Thankful Blossom's in the weeks gone by. She did not move her head, but stood looking demurely, after the manner of ancient crones, over the summer landscape. For the summer had come before the tardy spring was scarce gone, and the elms before the window no longer lisped, but were eloquent in the softest zephyrs. There was the flash of birds in among the bushes, the occasional droning of bees in and out the open window, and a perpetually swinging censer of flower incense rising from below. The farm had put on its gayest bridal raiment, and, looking at the old farmhouse shadowed with foliage, and green with creeping vines, it was difficult to conceive that snow had ever lain on its porches or icicles swung from its mossy eaves.

"Thankful!" said a voice still tremulous with weakness.

The ancient crone turned, drew aside the curtains, and showed the sweet face of Thankful Blossom, more beautiful even in its paleness.

"Come here, darling," repeated the voice.

Thankful stepped to the sofa whereon lay the convalescent Major Van Zandt.

"Tell me, sweetheart," said the major, taking her hand in his, "when you married me, as you told the chaplain, that you might have the right to nurse me, did you never think that, if death had spared me, I might have been so disfigured that even you, dear love, would have turned from me with loathing?"

"That was why I did it, dear," said Thankful mischievously. "I know that the pride, and the sense of honor, and self-devotion of some people would have kept them from keeping their promises to a poor girl."

"But, darling," continued the major, raising her hand to his lips, "suppose the case had been reversed; suppose you had taken the disease; that I had recovered without disfigurement, but that this sweet face"—

"I thought of that too," interrupted Thankful.

"Well, what would you have done, dear," said the major, with his old mischievous smile.

"I should have died," said Thankful gravely.

"But how?"

"Somehow. But you are to go to sleep, and not ask impertinent and frivolous questions, for father is coming to-morrow."

"Thankful, dear, do you know what the trees and the birds said to me as I lay there tossing with the fever?"

"No, dear."

"Thankful Blossom! Thankful Blossom! Thankful Blossom is coming!"

"Do you know what I said, sweetheart, as I lifted your dear head from the ground when you reeled from your horse just as I overtook you at Springfield?"

"No, dear."

"There are some things in life worth stooping for."

And she winged this Parthian arrow home with a kiss.

A JERSEY CENTENARIAN.

I HAVE seen her at last. She is a hundred and seven years old, and remembers George Washington quite distinctly. It is somewhat confusing, however, that she also remembers a contemporaneous Josiah W. Perkins of Baskingridge, N. J., and, I think, has the impression that Perkins was the better man. Perkins, at the close of the last century, paid her some little attention. There are a few things that a really noble woman of a hundred and seven never forgets.

It was Perkins who said to her in 1795, in the streets of Philadelphia, "Shall I show thee Gen. Washington?" Then she said careless-like (for you know, child, at that time it was n't what it is now to see Gen. Washington), she said, "So do, Josiah, so do!" Then he pointed to a tall man who got out of a carriage, and went into a large house. He was larger than you be. He wore his own hair — not powdered; had a flowered chintz vest, with yellow breeches and blue stockings, and a broad-brimmed hat. In summer he wore a white straw hat, and at his farm at Baskingridge he always wore it. At this point, it became too evident that she was describing the clothes of the all-fascinating Perkins, so I gently but firmly led her back to Washington. Then it appeared that she did not remember exactly what he wore. To assist her, I sketched the general historic dress of that period. She said she thought he was dressed like that. Emboldened by my success, I added a hat of Charles II., and pointed shoes of the eleventh century. She indorsed these with such cheerful alacrity that I dropped the subject.

The house upon which I had stumbled, or, rather, to which my horse — a Jersey hack, accustomed to historic research — had brought me, was low and quaint. Like most old houses, it had the appearance of being encroached upon by the surrounding glebe, as if it were already half in the grave, with a sod or two in the shape of moss thrown on it, like ashes on ashes, and dust on dust. A wooden house, instead of acquiring dignity with age, is apt to lose its youth and respectability together. A porch, with scant, sloping seats, from which even the winter's snow must have slid uncomfortably, projected from a doorway that opened most unjustifiably into a small sitting-room. There was no vestibule, or *locus pœnitentiæ*, for the embarrassed or bashful visitor: he passed at once from the security of the public road into shameful privacy. And here, in the mellow autumnal sunlight, that, streaming through the maples and sumach on the opposite bank, flickered and danced upon the floor, she sat and discoursed of George Washington, and thought of Perkins. She was quite in keeping with the house and the season, albeit a little in advance of both; her skin being of a faded russet, and her hands so like dead November leaves, that I fancied they even rustled when she moved them.

For all that, she was quite bright and cheery; her faculties still quite vigorous, although performing irregularly and spasmodically. It was somewhat discomposing, I confess, to observe that at times her lower jaw would drop, leaving her speechless, until one of the family would notice it, and raise it smartly into place with a slight snap, — an operation always performed in such an habitual, perfunctory manner, generally in passing to and fro in their household duties, that it was very trying to the spectator. It was still more embarrassing to observe that the dear old lady had evidently no knowledge of this, but believed she was still talking, and that, on resuming her actual vocal utterance, she was often abrupt and incoherent, beginning always in the middle of a sentence, and often in the middle of a word. "Sometimes," said her daughter, a giddy, thoughtless young thing of eighty-five, — "sometimes just moving her head sort of unhitches her jaw; and, if we don't happen to see it, she 'll go on talking for hours without ever making a sound." Although I was convinced, after this, that during my interview I had lost several important revelations regarding George Washington through these peculiar lapses, I could not help reflecting how beneficent were these provisions of the Creator, — how, if properly studied and applied, they might be fraught with happiness to mankind, — how a slight jostle or jar at a dinner-party might make the post-prandial eloquence of garrulous senility satisfactory to itself, yet harmless to others, — how a more intimate knowledge of anatomy, introduced into the domestic circle, might make a home tolerable at least, if not happy, — how a long-suffering husband, under the pretence of a conjugal caress, might so unhook his wife's condyloid process as to allow the flow of expostulation, criticism, or denunciation to go on with gratification to her, and perfect immunity to himself.

But this was not getting back to George Washington and the early struggles of the Republic. So I returned to the commander-in-chief, but found, after one or two leading questions, that she was rather inclined to resent his re-appearance on the stage. Her reminiscences here were chiefly social and local, and more or less flavored with Perkins. We got back as far as the Revolutionary epoch, or, rather, her impressions of that epoch, when it was still fresh in the public mind. And here I came upon an incident, purely personal and local, but, withal, so novel, weird, and uncanny, that for a while I fear it quite displaced George Washington in my mind, and tinged the autumnal fields beyond with a red that was not of the sumach. I do not remember to have read of it in the books. I do not know that it is entirely authentic. It was attested to me by mother and daughter, as an uncontradicted tradition.

In the little field beyond, where the plough still turns up musket-balls and cartridge-boxes, took place one of those irregular skirmishes between the militiamen and Knyphausen's stragglers that made the retreat historical. A Hessian soldier, wounded in both legs and utterly helpless, dragged himself to the cover of a hazel-copse, and lay there hidden for two days. On the third day, maddened by thirst, he managed to creep to the rail-fence of an adjoining farmhouse, but found himself unable to mount it or pass through. There was no one in the house but a little girl of six or seven years. He called to her, and in a faint voice asked for water. She returned to the house, as if to comply with his request, but, mounting a chair, took from the chimney a heavily-loaded Queen Anne musket, and, going to the door, took deliberate aim at the helpless intruder, and fired. The man fell back dead, without a groan. She replaced the musket, and, returning to the fence, covered the body with boughs and leaves, until it was hidden. Two or three days after, she related the occurrence in a careless, casual way, and leading the way to the fence, with a piece of bread and butter in her guileless little fingers, pointed out the result of her simple, unsophisticated effort. The Hessian was decently buried, but I could not find out what became of the little girl. Nobody seemed to remember. I trust that, in after years, she was happily married; that no Jersey Lovelace attempted to trifle with a heart whose impulses were so prompt, and whose purposes were so sincere. They did not seem to know if she had married or not. Yet it does not seem probable that such simplicity of conception, frankness of expression, and deftness of execution were lost to posterity, or that they failed, in their time and season, to give flavor to the domestic felicity of the period. Beyond this, the story perhaps has little value, except as an offset to the usual anecdotes of Hessian atrocity.

They had their financial panics even in Jersey, in the old days. She remembered when Dr. White married your cousin Mary — or was it Susan? — yes, it was Susan. She remembers that your Uncle Harry brought in an armful of banknotes — paper money, you know — and threw them in the corner, saying they were no good to anybody. She remembered playing with them, and giving them to your Aunt Anna — no, child, it was your own mother, bless your heart! Some of them was marked as high as a hundred dollars. Everybody kept gold and silver in a stocking, or in a "chaney" vase, like that. You never used money to buy anything. When Josiah went to Springfield to buy anything, he took a cartload of things with him to exchange. That yaller picture frame was paid for in greenings. But then people knew jest what they had. They did n't fritter their substance away in unchristian trifles, like your father, Eliza Jane, who does n't know that there is a God who will smite him hip and thigh; for vengeance is mine, and those that believe in me. But here, singularly enough, the inferior maxillaries gave out, and her jaw dropped. (I noticed that her giddy daughter of eighty-five was sitting near her; but I do not pretend to connect this fact with the arrested flow of personal disclosure.) Howbeit, when she recovered her speech again, it appeared that she was complaining of the weather.

The seasons had changed very much since your father went to sea. The winters used to be terrible in those days. When she went over to Springfield, in June, she saw the snow still on Watson's Ridge. There were whole days when you could n't git over to William Henry's, their next neighbor, a quarter of a mile away. It was that dreffful winter that the Spanish sailor was found. You don't remember the Spanish sailor, Eliza Jane — it was before your time. There was a little personal skirmishing here, which I feared, at first, might end in a suspension of maxillary functions, and the loss of the story; but here it is. Ah, me! it is a pure white winter idyl: how shall I sing it this bright, gay autumnal day?

It was a terrible night, that winter's night, when she and the century were young together. The sun was lost at three o'clock; the snowy night came down like a white sheet, that flapped around the house, beat at the windows with its edges, and at last wrapped it in a close embrace. In the middle of the night they thought they heard above the wind a voice crying, "Christus, Christus!" in a foreign tongue. They opened the door, — no easy task in the north wind that pressed its strong shoulders against it, — but nothing was to be seen but the drifting snow. The next morning dawned on fences hidden, and a landscape changed and obliterated with drift. During the day, they again heard the cry of "Christus!" this time faint and hidden, like a child's voice. They searched in vain: the drifted snow hid its secret. On the third day they broke a path to the fence, and then they heard the cry distinctly. Digging down, they found the body of a man, — a Spanish sailor, dark and bearded, with ear-rings in his ears. As they stood gazing down at his cold and pulseless figure, the cry of "Christus!" again rose upon the wintry air; and they turned and fled in superstitious terror to the house. And then one of the children, bolder than the rest, knelt down, and opened the dead man's rough pea-jacket, and found — what think you? — a little blue-and-green parrot, nestling against his breast. It was the bird that had echoed mechanically the last despairing cry of the life that was given to save it. It was the bird, that ever after, amid outlandish oaths and wilder sailor-songs, that

I fear often shocked the pure ears of its gentle mistress, and brought scandal into the Jerseys, still retained that one weird and mournful cry.

The sun meanwhile was sinking behind the steadfast range beyond, and I could not help feeling that I must depart with my wants unsatisfied. I had brought away no historic fragment; I absolutely knew little or nothing new regarding George Washington. I had been addressed variously by the names of different members of the family who were dead and forgotten; I had stood for an hour in the past; yet I had not added to my historical knowledge, nor the practical benefit of your readers. I spoke once more of Washington, and she replied with a reminiscence of Perkins.

Stand forth, O Josiah W. Perkins of Baskingridge, N. J. Thou wast of little account in thy life, I warrant; thou didst not even feel the greatness of thy day and time; thou didst criticise thy superiors; thou wast small and narrow in thy ways; thy very name and grave are unknown and uncared for; but thou wast once kind to a woman who survived thee, and, lo! thy name is again spoken of men, and for a moment lifted up above thy betters.

EASTERN SKETCHES

PETER SCHROEDER

When we heard that Peter Schroeder had "struck it rich," or, to paraphrase the local idiom, had that morning taken fifty thousand dollars from a suddenly developed "pocket" in his claim, only one expression, that of sincere congratulation, went up from Spanish Gulch. It would, perhaps, be wrong to say that this feeling arose from any instinctive perception of his fitness for good fortune, or even of his practical deserts. Spanish Gulch was seldom moved by such delicate ethics. But he had always been a lovable figure in its rude life. His quaint, serious good nature; his touching belief in ourselves as representative Americans, and the legitimate results of those free institutions he admired so in theory; his innocent adoption of our slang, and often of our vices, which made even an oath or vulgarism from his lips as harmless and irresponsible as from a child's — all this gave "Dutch Pete," as he loved to be called, a certain place in our affections which no stroke of enviable good fortune could imperil. More than this, I think we took a great satisfaction in believing that in some way *we* were part of that Providence which had so blessed him. A few, I think, intimated as much. "I 'm so glad I allus told the old man to stick to that claim," said one, with an air of wearied well-doing; "I allus kept him up to the rack, and I reckon he now sees the benefit of my four years' experience in these parts." "Only yesterday," said another, "I lent him a pick, seein' his was rather shaky, — and they say thar 's luck in old tools in green hands."

A majority of the camp called upon him at once. The result of their visit satisfied them. Unchanged, unaltered by good fortune, Peter Schroeder welcomed them in his old simple way, and in that old simple, blundering slang which, to the delight of the camp, he was pleased to accept as idiomatic American speech. He stood beside a table covered with a vivid red blanket, which displayed from this vantage a huge fragment of decomposed quartz, dazzlingly streaked and honeycombed with the precious metal. Above it hung a placard — the gift of a native humorist — bearing the legend, "Welcome, little stranger."

"Come in, poys, and tondt pe pashful. Sits doun from de front! De elefant now goes round mit you. De pand pegins to play. Dare she ish — look at it, shentlemans! You dakes your money and you bays your schoice. Ha! ha! Vot for a strike ist dot? Eh? How high is dot, poys?"

When the laugh at his characteristic version of a slang phrase in the last sentence had subsided, some one asked him what he intended to do, now that he was a rich man.

"Well, poys, dot 's shoost it. I goes to Washington *first*. I looks round and maype I finds Dick Unterwoots, and I goes mit him mit de army — and I fights a little for de Union." The Dick Underwood here alluded to had recently exchanged his long-handled Californian shovel for the sword, and was now, in this last year of the Civil War, a colonel.

"But you 'll get killed, Pete, and what 's the good of your money then?"

"So! I sends it first to my fader and moder in Shermany."

"But it 's none of your funeral, Pete. You 're only a blank Dutchman."

"Eh — a Dootchman! Vell, vot 's Sigel, eh? Vot 's Rosenkrans, eh? Vot 's Heintzelmann? Vot 's Carl Schurz, eh?"

In vain did Spanish Gulch point out the egregious folly of a rich alien engaging in a domestic quarrel; Peter was firm in his determination. And Spanish Gulch, having by experience learned to respect his dull obstinacy in those matters of his private conscience which did not directly interfere with his duties to the camp, yielded the point gracefully, and gave him — in one farewell debauch — their half-maledictory valediction.

Peter Schroeder was as good as his word. Within three weeks he entered the Army of the Potomac, and served until the Richmond surrender. It is to be recorded that, although faithful, loyal, honest, and brave, only a sergeant's chevron marked his advancement. Perhaps he was not ambitious; possibly old habits of military servitude kept him out of the political manœuvrings of these citizen bayonets; perhaps he had no personal friends at Washington; perhaps he was a little dull. But it is to be also recorded that his dogged devotion to *his* theories of the great Republican principles for which he was contending never faltered amidst the free and outspoken criticism of superiors and general grumbling of these citizen camps. Malcontents feared him, even good patriots quite misunderstood his sentimental convictions; he was a confusion to his comrades as often as he was to the enemy. I close his brief military record with a story still extant, but until now imperfect in its details. A gallant Confederate officer, and a descendant of the Virginian founders of the Republic, found himself, after the shattered onset of a brave but unsuccessful charge, lying wounded and crippled before the earthwork of a battery, deserted by his men and confronted only by the guns of his adversary, and the flag his ancestors had created flaunting in his face! "I looked up, gentlemen," he said, "and the sergeant of the Yankee battery saw me, and at the risk of his life crept down and dragged me into the works. He was a German; so I felt thankful that I wasn't under obligations to a Yankee. But what did he do? Why, gentlemen, this d—d Dutchman — who couldn't speak the language plainly — who hadn't, I solemnly believe, been a fortnight in America, he looks down at me, and, pointing to my crippled leg, says, 'Aha! dot's wot you gets for fightin' against de *old flag!*' If a mule had kicked me I couldn't have felt meaner." The mule that had kicked this gallant gentleman was Peter Schroeder. But it was a Parthian kick. A few days later he was honorably discharged, drew his back-pay and bounty, and sailed for Germany.

. . . .

Fifteen years had elapsed. Peter Schroeder, much stouter and quite bald, sat in that inevitable latticed summer-house which is one of the sacred outdoor Penates of every Rhenish householder, and seriously sipped his Moselle wine. He was not thinking that his curiously wrought iron garden-chair was not as comfortable as an American rocker or armchair, — he was long past that grumbling; he was not thinking the table too high and insecure for his feet to rest on, for Frau Schroeder had in the first year of his married life interdicted that American attitude of reflection and bibulous enjoyment. He was not looking at the inevitable little fountain, whose stone basin suggested a hasty provision against a leak from some invisible water-cask, nor at the inevitable little grotto, — a child's playground of bright shells and pebbles artistically arranged by a grown-up player. None of these, nor even the statue of Germania looking like Lorelei with a helmet, nor of Lorelei looking like Germania with a harp, nor even of a bust of the good old Emperor, looking always like his own august self, and regarding reprehensible mythology with fatherly forbearance, attracted Peter's attention. His serious blue eyes were filmy and abstracted; the pinky red of his round cheeks was a little deeper for that digestive glow known in the rich vernacular of his analytical nation as "Essfieber;" his respiration was slightly stertorous, and his pipe had gone out idly in his hand; Peter was dreaming.

Of the Past. Of the fifteen long years that had flown since he arrived, almost a stranger, in his own land; of his reception by his few old friends, — a reception given to a new Peter whom they had evidently never known; of the joy of his old parents, — a joy tempered with a kind of awe at his fortune and his novel ideas and heresies; of the matchmaking of his parents that ended in his betrothal to the well-born but slightly dowered Fräulein Von Hummel; of the marriage that smoothed those parents' dying pillow, but left Peter's bridal couch lonelier than before; of his relegation to a new life to which he was stranger than ever.

Of the monotony of those days, of the monotony of all outward signs and symbols, band-playing, concert-singing, picture-viewing, troops parading night and morning before his window, of festivals, of fêtes, of celebrations of all conceivable things to celebrate, — all alike — uniform, theatrical, and unreal, and yet, too, all established with precedent, and often reinforced with the serene presence of hereditary greatness. Of the monotony of his home life; of the monotony of five meals a day seriously considered and dutifully performed; of betrothals and love-making under the parental and public eye; of sentimental handshakings and speech-makings to bride and bridegroom, and the pointed obtrusion of domestic and personal affairs before the world, as shown in the sentimental public advertisement of such conventionalities as births, deaths, and marriages.

Of the great war with France, which forever estopped his voluble reminiscences of his former transatlantic military career, by leaving him no longer an authority in slaughter and gunpowder, rekindled his old ardor for Das Vaterland, dragged him into its seething vortex, and left him at last stranded in his own town, with more parading, more rattle of drums, more celebrations to celebrate, more precedents, and, in fact, more settled convictions to combat than ever.

A clap of thunder recalled his wandering senses. Looking up, he saw above the lindens that stood in his garden a blue-black velvety cloud. It was the natural climax of a sultry summer's day; but Peter's thoughts were so dark that it seemed to be as ominous as the cloud that rose above the Arabian fisherman's jar when the awful seal of Solomon was broken. In such a mood Faust received a visit from Mephistopheles, and at this moment, at his elbow, a servant was presenting a card.

"Mr. John Folinsbee," read Peter aloud.

"A gentleman and four ladies," explained the servant.

Peter's mental processes were slowly evolving something.

"Strangers," suggested the maiden; "I think Americans."

The magical note of nationality sent the good-hearted Peter into his drawing-room, pleased, yet embarrassed as a schoolgirl.

Certainly no weakness of this kind was visible in his guests. Three of them, young ladies, were scattered about the room; one at the piano, one at the centre table, looking over a book of photographs, and another beside the jardinière, from which she had already extracted the rosebud suited to her complexion. On the sofa another, and possibly the elder, if a certain air of lassitude and ennui were a criterion of age, had gracefully composed herself. All were pretty, all were graceful, all were exceedingly well-dressed, and all were, to Peter's half pleasure, half embarrassment, very much at home!

They acknowledged his smile of welcome by an inquiring glance towards a gentleman who at that moment was engaged in examining a barometer at the window. He disengaged himself from his meteorological inquest, came forward with easy good-humor, and held out his hand. He was a tall, well-formed man, of Peter's own age, but looked, like the rest of his party, as if he were a thousand years younger.

"Peter Schroeder, I reckon?"

Peter's face beamed with delight as he shook the outstretched hand warmly.

"Ja! dot 's schoost it — Peter Schroeder."

"You don't remember *me?*" continued the stranger, with a slight smile. "I never saw you but once, and that was at Spanish Gulch, the day you made that strike! I came over from Dry Creek with the boys, and went up to your cabin. How are you, old man? You 're looking as if your grub agreed with you."

Peter, still shaking his hand, said in his half-forgotten English, that he knew him "from de voorst!"

"When I left California, a month ago, I promised the boys I 'd hunt you up," continued the stranger. "I stopped at Cologne yesterday. Heard you were here. Came up on a sort of pasear with the ladies. Let me introduce them. Rosey Tibbets, Grace Tibbets, Minnie Tibbets, Mrs. Johnson."

Peter, always a bashful man, under this presentation of bright eyes and Parisian toilettes could only stammer out his regrets that the Frau Schroeder was that day absent — visiting a soul-friend — and was not there to welcome them.

Mrs. Johnson, looking up from the sofa, would have *so* liked to see her; Miss Rosey, looking up from the photograph-book, would have *so* liked to see her; Miss Grace, at the piano, and Miss Minnie, with the delicate petals of a rose against her pink nostrils, would have both *so* liked to see her. Indeed, the only one present who might not have participated in this chorus was poor Peter himself, who, despite his previous polite assurance, felt a vague relief at his wife's absence. Conscious of this weakness, he insisted the more upon plying them with various refreshments, and "showing them the house."

Several American improvements which he had introduced, to the wonder and distrust of his neighbors, failed, however, to impress his visitors. The ladies regarded them languidly: "You 've got the old-fashioned kind. We use only the self-acting patent now," they said. "You 're behind the age, old man," was Folinsbee's less courteous comment. Peter, a trifle mortified, nevertheless kept up his unfailing good-humor, and finally stopped before the door of a small chamber with a confident air. "I shows you somedings now dot you can't imbrove on — ha! Somedings vot you and us fellus knows. Dot is mine own brivate abartment. Vot for Americans is dot?"

As he spoke he flung open the door, and disclosed a small room, with an American flag festooned over the window. On one side of the wall hung a portrait of Abraham Lincoln; on the other, the blue cap and blouse of a sergeant in the American army.

Peter paused to permit the patriotic feelings of his visitors their fullest vent. To his surprise, only a dead silence followed this national exhibition. Peter, doubtful of their eyesight, drew aside the window-curtains, and ostentatiously wiped the portrait of the martyred president.

"Dot is Lincoln."

"Chromo?" asked Folinsbee.

"I don't know," replied Peter, a little crestfallen.

"The engravings don't make him quite so ugly," said Mrs. Johnson, "although he was an ugly man."

"Awful," said Miss Rosey.

Peter smiled meekly. "He was n't bretty as a womans," he said, with an embarrassed attempt at gallantry, followed by an apoplectic blush.

"What 's that?" asked Folinsbee, indicating the cap and blouse with his cane. "Some of your mining duds from Spanish Gulch?"

"Dot?" gasped Peter. "Dot is mine uniforms!"

Folinsbee laughed. "I thought it might be some of that damaged clothing condemned by the War Department, and sold at auction there. The boys bought up a lot of it cheap to knock around in the tunnels with. Yes, I remember now. The fellers had a mighty good joke on your goin' into the War when you had n't any call to go."

"Which side were you on, Mr. Schroeder?" asked Mrs. Johnson, with a polite affectation of interest.

"Which side?" echoed Peter in vague astonishment. "I fights mit de Union."

"I had an uncle in the Federal army, and two cousins in the Confederate service," observed Miss Minnie languidly.

"Dey wos good fellers on the oder side too," hastily interpolated the kind-hearted Peter.

"They came home awfully sick of it — *all* of 'em," continued Miss Minnie. "I 'm sure it was dreadfully horrid."

"Awful," said Rosey.

Meanwhile they had backed out of the room listlessly, and were clearly indicating that they were awaiting Peter's further movements. He closed the door with an embarrassing laugh that was half a sigh, and led the way back to the drawing-room. On the way Miss Rosey stopped to admire the photograph of a stout, good-humored gentleman in a gorgeous hussar uniform.

"Who is this?"

"Dot is me — myself," said Peter — "wen I was in de war mit France," he added apologetically. To his surprise, the ladies gathered before it with an appearance of interest; and Mrs. Johnson remarked archly that the uniform was very becoming.

"Why did n't you show the girls that *first?*" asked Folinsbee, taking Peter aside. "Why did you trot out those old army rags of yours? Don't you know they 're just crazy after these foreign uniforms? Think there 's a count or baron inside of 'em always. By the way," he asked suddenly, "you ain't anything o' that sort now, are you?"

Peter shook his head blankly, but found himself blushing as he thought of his wife's uniformed relations.

"Did n't get anything of that kind for your services?" continued Folinsbee. "Nary ribbon — medals — eh?"

"I get de 'Iron Cross,'" said Peter mildly.

"Humph! *Iron* Cross! Could n't afford a gold one, eh? Not much of that lying round loose here in these parts?"

Too modest to explain further, too delicate to expose what he conceived to be the natural ignorance of his foreign visitor, but utterly oblivious of the mischief in that foreign visitor's eye, Peter endeavored to turn the subject by asking him to bring the ladies to dine with him the next day.

"I reckon not, old man," said Folinsbee. "I 'll be on my way to Berlin to-morrow, and I reckon the girls are headin' up the Rhine to tackle some of them ruined castles. But you might ask 'em, just for a flyer."

"Don't you all go mit yourselves together?" queried the astonished Peter.

Folinsbee smiled. "Not much, I reckon. We only met at Brussels, and we happened to travel in the same coupé to Cologne. We sorter passed the time o' day, swapped lies, and made ourselves sociable. I told 'em at Cologne I reckoned to run up yer to see you, and asked 'em to come along. It was a little pasear — that 's all. They 're all right, old man," he added, laughing at Peter's puzzled face, — "one of 'em a senator's daughter, I reckon. If they ain't right, I 'm responsible."

Peter laughed and blushed. Not that he saw anything in this escapade but an instance of that republican simplicity and social freedom which he admired in theory; but he was conscious that his new life had brought with it responsibilities to other customs. He was vaguely relieved that his wife was not present to hear Folinsbee's explanation, and, later, that the ladies politely declined his invitation.

Nevertheless, he parted with them reluctantly. When the smart landau drove up to his door, and they took their places, serene and self-possessed, under the wondering and critical fire of his neighbors' Spions, they seemed such a vision of happy, confident, graceful, beautiful, and fitly adorned youth, that, as he reëntered his house, he felt he had grown a hundred years older, and even his familiar surroundings appeared to belong to another epoch and planet. He mounted slowly to the little room which contained his treasures. He looked at them again carefully; inspected the grave melancholy of Lincoln's face, and lifted the blue blouse from its nail. Were those features "ugly"? was that blouse a "rag"? Peter pondered long and perplexedly. Gradually an explanation slowly evolved itself from its profundity. He placed his finger beside his nose, and a look of deep cunning shone in his eyes. "Dot 's it," he said to himself triumphantly, "dot 's shoost it! *Der rebooplicans don't got no memories. Ve don't got nodings else.*"

He did not, however, confide to his wife the full details of this visit. But one day, when she had returned from visiting a remote cousin at Kissingen, she asked him why he had never told her that Mrs. Johnson had called. The guilty blood flew to Peter's face, and he stammered out some half-intelligible excuse. To his infinite relief and astonishment, however, Frau Schroeder, far from noticing his confusion, spoke volubly of having met Mrs. Johnson at Kissingen, and dwelt at some length on the gentlemanly graces and breeding of Mr. Johnson.

"*He* did not call with her, then?" asked Mrs. Schroeder.

Peter, stammering and untruthful, really could not remember. There were half a dozen people, and they did not stop long.

"I forget if she said that her husband knew you," continued Frau Schroeder; "but you would remember him, of course. He 's not like the Americans, you know, — but like a — a gentleman and — an — officer."

Peter, not daring to allude to the informal character of Mrs. Johnson's escort, said nothing.

"They are coming here next week," added Frau Schroeder; "I have invited them."

As Peter seldom had a voice in the nomination of his visitors, he meekly acquiesced.

"But vot gets me," he communed with himself, "how dot bretty Mrs. Johnson, mit no cards, gets mine wife."

The next week brought Mrs. Johnson, who languidly remembered Peter, and at once made herself as much at home with Peter's wife as she had with him. It brought also Mr. Johnson, — a small, quiet, plain man.

"You would hardly remember me as a Californian, Mr. Schroeder?" he said, extending his hand.

Peter would hardly have recognized him even as an American. Certainly no one could be further from the type most familiar to Peter. He was unlike Folinsbee — unlike any of his old army comrades — unlike any other American he had known, and yet as certainly unlike any European with whom Peter was familiar. He was as confident and self-possessed as Folinsbee, and yet without Folinsbee's humorous familiarity; he was modest and unassuming, and yet Peter felt that he took possession of him as securely as Folinsbee had. He was inclined to resent this at first — inclined to watch Mr. Johnson's mouth — a peculiar mouth, with a latent apologetical smile — a smile as if humanity on all occasions presented a humorous aspect to him (Johnson) which nothing but his (Johnson's) thoughtful commiseration for humanity kept him from publicly noticing.

"Yet," continued Johnson, regarding Peter as a wayward, mirth-provoking child, "yet I have lived in California many years. I remember to have heard of you there; of your good fortune, of your subsequent career in the army, and of your return here. I have known many of your friends. Indeed, I feel as if we were old acquaintances."

That was what he *said*. His smiling commentary seemed to Peter to add as plainly, "And there are humorous depths in your career and character, Peter, which nobody knows better than myself; but we won't say anything about that, Peter, — not a word."

Considerably embarrassed, Peter asked him a few questions. But he was annoyed at the extent and variety of Mr. Johnson's knowledge of his affairs. Scarcely a person Peter had known — scarcely an incident in Peter's experience — but were as equally and humorously recognized by Mr. Johnson. Peter's first partner in the mines, the bugler in his regiment, his fellow-passenger and room-mate in the steamer, his banker and friend in Cologne, even his wife's relations, — yea, actually, a certain awe-inspiring general and forty-first cousin of Frau Schroeder's at Coblentz, were all familiar to Johnson. And all and each were, on the authority of his peculiar smile, more or less ridiculous, if he chose to say so. But he would n't.

Perhaps it was this appearance of restrained power, combined with great gentleness of manner, which made him so popular with the women, and particularly with Frau Schroeder. No American had before touched that formal, well-regulated woman's heart. Peter was astounded at the influence this stranger had gained in the Von Hummel family. Had he not intimated, by his peculiar smile, that he was sure that the Herr General Von Hummel drank too much, and that the family were more than once scandalized by his too susceptible weaknesses for the fair sex? Had he not suggested in the same way that the learned Herr Professor's last book on ethnology was ridiculous, — as, indeed, some critics had already said, — but insinuated that he was even capable of greater folly? Honest Peter could not understand it. Folinsbee, with his blunt familiarity and frivolity, would have been coldly repulsed by Frau Schroeder. Peter even now shuddered as he recalled the blank and even resentful amazement with which she had received the characteristic humor of an American tourist to whom he had once, in their earlier married life, rashly introduced her. Who was this Mr. T. Barker Johnson? Even the usual local caution regarding a stranger's social and financial standing was withheld. Frau Schroeder spoke of him as a Californian capitalist. His banker — Peter's banker too — knew him as a man of ample remittances. That was all.

For two weeks the stranger had held undoubted sway at the Schroeders'. Dinners and suppers had been given in his honor. General Von Hummel had sat late with him at table; the Herr Professor had presented him with his last volume and disclosed his future literary intentions.

Even Peter was conscious of being lifted into importance in his own family by his former residence in the country of this popular stranger and his familiarity with Americans. Little as he knew of the type represented by Johnson, he was compelled in sheer self-defense to assume a thorough knowledge of it; and I fear the poor fellow went even so far — when the praises of Johnson were being hymned in his ears — as to invent florid reminiscences of other Johnsons more extraordinary than this.

"Wunderschön!" gasped the apoplectic general.

"Man knows when man in that wonderful country has been," said Peter, shaking his head sententiously.

The Frau Schroeder did not indorse this sentiment.

"There are Americans — and Americans!" she said significantly; and Peter was fain to retire to his little room, and, in company with his pipe, contemplate the portrait of Lincoln and the faded trappings of his old military service.

He was sitting thus one evening, when there came a tap at his door. It opened to Johnson, — quiet, gentlemanly, and humorously sympathetic. Peter was a little embarrassed. Since the exhibition of his treasures to the Folinsbee party he had grown doubtful of their effect upon strangers, and had said nothing of them to Johnson. But that gentleman smiled on Lincoln's picture as on a brother humorist, and looked at Peter's blouse and cap with an evident instinctive foreknowledge of all that was laughable in his history.

"You knew dot Lincoln?" queried Peter timidly, pointing with his pipe at the picture.

Johnson smiled. It presently appeared that he not only knew all that contemporary history knew of the martyred President, but many facts yet unrecorded. To Mr. Lincoln's humor — as interpreted by Peter in one or two well-worn anecdotes — Mr. Johnson accorded the recognition of a thoughtful smile, while in Peter's clothes he detected evidently some kindred and latent folly. Emboldened by his sympathy, Peter confided to him the history of his life, his aims, his political theories and dreams, and even his recent disappointment at the conduct of Folinsbee and his friends.

"Yes," said Peter, "he called mine uniform 'rags;' dot was not an oopside ding to say, Mr. Johnson, and I says mit mineself, 'Der rebooplicans don't got no memories' — eh?"

Mr. Johnson smiled assentingly, patiently, expectantly — quite as if he were previously aware of all Peter had told him, but was too polite to interrupt him. Then, laying his hand on Peter's shoulder, he said softly, "You 're too good a republican, Peter, to brood over mere sentimental memories. Now, look here. I like you, and I want to be frank with you. I know you, and you 're not properly appreciated here — even by your own family. It is time, Peter, you should assert yourself. It is time they should know what you are. You are the stuff from which liberators and deliverers are made. I saw it when I first saw you, — long before you ever knew me."

The most modest and unassuming man has somewhere within him the germ of self-conscious merit, which needs only the sunshine of praise to bud and blossom into life. Poor Peter had never known praise before, — perhaps he had never missed it, — but, tasting the strange fruit, he found it good, and that, like other forbidden fruit, it made him a god like others, and, with his face glowing with pleasure, he seized and shook Johnson's hand warmly. He was still too unsophisticated to disguise his feelings. Perhaps, having already suffered from modesty, he did not care to simulate it.

"It rests with *you*, Peter, to make yourself what you should be, — what you *can* be," continued Johnson.

"What if I told you of another country, Peter, — newer and fresher than the one you once adopted; where the soil is virgin and the people are plastic, — a country to be moulded and fashioned into shape by men like you; a country with no predilections, few traditions, and *no* history; a republic wanting only ideas, and capital; a country that you might become president of — *as I am?*"

Peter, whose eyes had been growing wider and wider, shut them at this climax from sheer inability to face the astounding revelation. There was a dead silence. The voice of Mrs. Johnson at the piano came melodiously from the drawing-room; the voice of Mrs. Schroeder, inquiring for her missing lord, came potentially from the hall below; but Peter heeded them not. Johnson smiled, closed the door, and drawing a chair beside Peter, in a confidential whisper quietly took absorbing possession of his faculties for two mortal hours.

. . . .

I had arrived at Calais from Brussels near midnight, — an hour too early for the tidal boat, and in advance of the train from Paris. There was scarcely time to seek an hotel, — too much time to wait at the station, and the keeper of the "buffet" had informed me that his "establishment" could not be open for the receipt of custom until the arrival of the Paris train. Noticing a light in a cosy sitting-room adjoining, I made bold, in spite of his protestations, to enter, and was confronted by Jack Folinsbee, much to our mutual astonishment.

His greeting was hearty. "Come in. Don't mind that 'barkeep.' I'm running this yer concern until the train comes in. He tried to turn me off at first, too. But I asked him what he reckoned the rent of this old shebang would be for two hours. He tore round and thought I was crazy, I s'pose, until he saw I meant business, and he fixed his price. I paid him and took possession. Now, what 'll you take, old boy? Name your pizen. This is my treat. And I didn't think when I left Californy that I 'd be running a railroad restaurant in France."

It was true; he had, after his Californian fashion, gratified his present whim at a pretty price. The landlord, looking upon him as a spendthrift savage, was, I think, a little relieved when my appearance took some of the responsibility off his hands. By the light of the blazing fire, in a comfortable armchair, I did not propose to question the propriety of his impulses.

Our talk naturally fell upon old days and old friends. "You remember 'Dutch Pete,' don't you?" asked Folinsbee. I *did* remember Peter Schroeder. "You know," continued Jack, "how he took the money he made in that big strike, and, instead of getting away with it, goes off in a wildgoose chase to fight in the war?"

"Yes."

"Well, he had fool's luck then. Got off without a scratch; went back to Germany a rich man, married and settled down, and might have been all right now. But this yer last foolishness of his has fixed him, — sent him up the flume, sure!"

I begged Folinsbee to explain.

"Well, I reckon perhaps *I'm* a little to blame for it too. You remember Johnson, — T. Barker Johnson, — that old filibuster?"

"Yes."

"He failed, don't yer know, with Walker in Nicaragua, but came mighty near fixing things his own way in Costa Rica. Yes, sir," continued Jack, becoming excited, "it *was* a big thing he did down there. All alone, too. Got a canoe, by gum! and pulled out to a ship's yawl, and sorter revolutionizes the yawl's crew; then he takes that crew to the ship and raises a mutiny in the ship, takes command of the ship, and calls himself Admiral of the Ometepe Navy, and summons a fort to surrender! And it surrenders — blank it all! — the whole garrison and the Ometepe army surrenders. And he was such a quiet man — such a very qui-et man! You remember him, major, don't you? — such a qui-et man — just the faintest little snicker round his mouth, but allus so qui-et — just a lamb."

I ventured to remind Jack that we were talking of Peter Schroeder.

"That 's so. Well, Johnson got hisself made president or dictator of the Ometepe Confederacy — or at least one wing of it — and came over here incog., to negotiate bonds and get money. Well, it was jest my luck about that time to meet Mrs. Johnson and a party of nice girls, traveling, and I took 'em to see Peter just for a pasear. Peter was just about as big a fool as ever, and showed us his army duds, and spouted patriotic hog-wash; and I reckon Mrs. Johnson sorter took Peter's measure then and thar. But she says nothing, and it comes about in some way that she meets Mrs. Peter, who, I reckon, manages Peter and keeps him in bounds, and she captures her, and Johnson captures Peter, and the game is made. For in less than ten months — by gosh! — the Johnsons have got Peter made over, capital and all, to the Ometepe Confederacy. And, as if that was n't enough, d—n me! if they did n't rope in the whole Schroeder family generally, — old Frau Schroeder, aunts, uncles, cousins, and all. By Jingo! there was a whole German colony started out to Ometepe to settle, and Peter was made Secretary of the Treasury!"

"And then" —

Folinsbee looked at me in contemptuous surprise. "And then? Why, of course, the whole thing goes up. It might have been a month — I reckon it was n't more than three weeks — that they had a stable government in Ometepe. But it busted at the end of that time, — busted clean!"

"And Peter?"

"That 's just it! You see, all the Germans skedaddled except Peter. Even Johnson, I reckon, got clean away. But Peter — and that 's where his God-forsaken foolishness comes in — hangs round and gets captured. At least, you don't hear any more about *him.*"

. . . .

Folinsbee was wrong. More *was* heard of Peter Schroeder. For, when captured and led out to be shot as an insurgent, one of his comrades made an attempt to save him, on the plea of his being an innocent German emigrant. The general was inexorable; the firing party was waiting, but Peter's friend still pleaded.

"Let him step to the front!"

Peter stepped calmly before the loaded muskets. But his friend saw in dismay that he had changed his clothes, and wore his faded blouse and blue army cap of an American sergeant.

"Prisoner, to what nation do you claim to belong?"

Peter's blue eyes kindled. "Dot 's it! I claim to be an American citi—"

The officer's sword waved, there was a crackle of musketry and the rising of a pale blue smoke. And on its wings the soul of Peter Schroeder went in quest of his ideal republic.

MORNING ON THE AVENUES

I HAVE always been an early riser. The popular legend that "Early to bed and early to rise," invariably and rhythmically resulted in healthfulness, opulence, and wisdom, I beg here to solemnly protest against. As an "unhealthy" man, as an "unwealthy" man, and doubtless by virtue of this protest an "unwise" man, I am, I think, a glaring example of the untruth of the proposition.

For instance, it is my misfortune, as an early riser, to live upon a certain fashionable avenue, where the practice of early rising is confined exclusively to domestics. Consequently, when I issue forth on this broad, beautiful thoroughfare at 6 A. M., I cannot help thinking that I am to a certain extent desecrating its traditional customs. I have more than once detected the milkman winking at the maid with a diabolical suggestion that I was returning from a carouse, and Roundsman 9999 has once or twice followed me a block or two with the evident impression that I was a burglar returning from a successful evening out. Nevertheless, these various indiscretions have brought me into contact with a kind of character and phenomena whose existence I might otherwise have doubted.

First, let me speak of a large class of working people whose presence is, I think, unknown to many of those gentlemen who are in the habit of legislating or writing about them. A majority of these early risers in the neighborhood which I may call my "beat" carry with them unmistakable evidences of the American type. I have seen so little of that foreign element that is popularly supposed to be the real working class of the great metropolis that I have often been inclined to doubt statistics. The ground that my morning rambles cover extends from Twenty-third Street to Washington Park, and laterally from Sixth Avenue to Broadway. The early rising artisans that I meet here, crossing three avenues, the milkmen, the truck drivers, the workman, even the occasional tramp, — wherever they may come from or go to, or what their real habitat may be, — are invariably Americans. I give it as an honest record — whatever its significance or insignificance may be — that during the last year, between the hours of 6 and 8 A. M., in and about the locality I have mentioned I have met with but two unmistakable foreigners, — an Irishman and a German. Perhaps it may be necessary to add to this statement that the people I have met at those hours I have never seen at any other time in the same locality.

As to their quality, the artisans were always cleanly dressed, intelligent, and respectful. I remember, however, one morning, when the ice storm of the preceding night had made the sidewalks glistening, smiling, and impassable, to have journeyed down the middle of Twelfth Street with a mechanic so sooty as to absolutely leave a legible track in the snowy pathway. He was the fireman attending the engine in a noted manufactory, and in our brief conversation he told me many facts regarding his profession, which I fear interested me more than the after-dinner speeches of some distinguished gentlemen I had heard the preceding night. I remember that he spoke of his engine as "she," and related certain circumstances regarding her inconsistency, her aberrations, her pettishnesses, that seemed to justify the feminine gender. I have a grateful recollection of him as being one who introduced me to a restaurant where chicory, thinly disguised as coffee, was served with bread at five cents a cup, and that he honorably insisted on being the host, and paid his ten cents for our mutual entertainment with the grace of a Barmecide. I remember, in a more genial season — I think, early summer, — to have found upon the benches of Washington Park a gentleman who informed me that his profession was that of a "pigeon-catcher," that he contracted with certain parties in this city to furnish these birds for what he called their "pigeon shoots," and that in fulfilling this contract he often was obliged to go as far west as Minnesota. The details he gave, his methods of entrapping the birds, his study of their habits, his evident belief that the city pigeon, however well provided for by parties who fondly believed the bird to be their own, was really *feræ naturæ*, and consequently "game" for the pigeon-catcher, were all so interesting that I listened to him with undisguised delight. When he had finished, however, he said, "And now, sir, being a poor man with a large family, and work bein' rather slack this year, if ye could oblige me with the loan of a dollar and your address, until remittances what I 'm expecting come in from Chicago, you 'll be doin' me a great service, etc., etc." He got the dollar, of course (his information was worth twice the money), but I imagine he lost my address. Yet it is only fair to say that some days after, relating this experience to a prominent sporting man, he corroborated all its details, and satisfied me that my pigeon-catching friend, although unfortunate, was not an impostor.

And this leads me to speak of the birds. Of all early risers, my most importunate, aggressive, and obtrusive companions are the English sparrows. Between 7 and 8 A. M. they seem to possess the avenue and resent my intrusion. I remember, one chilly morning, when I came upon a flurry of them, chattering, quarreling, skimming, and alighting just before me, I stopped at last, fearful of stepping on the nearest. To my great surprise, instead of flying away, he contested the ground inch by inch before my advancing foot, with wings outspread and open bill outstretched, very much like that ridiculous burlesque of the American eagle which the common canary bird assumes, when teased. "Did you ever see 'em wash in the fountain in the square?" said Roundsman 9999, early one summer morning. I had not. "I guess they 're there yet. Come and see' em," he said, and complacently accompanied me two blocks. I don't know which was the finer sight; the thirty or forty winged sprites dashing in and out of the basin, each the very impersonation of a light-hearted, mischievous Puck, or this grave policeman, with badge and club and shield, looking on with delight. Perhaps my visible amusement, or the spectacle of a brother policeman just then going past with a couple of "drunk and disorderlies," recalled his official responsibility and duties. "They say them foreign sparrows drives all the other birds away," he added severely, and then walked off with a certain reserved manner, as if it were not impossible for him to be called upon some morning to take the entire feathered assembly into custody, and if so called upon he should do it.

Next, I think, in procession among the early risers, and surely next in fresh and innocent exterior, were the workwomen or shop girls. I have seen this beautiful avenue on its gala afternoon bright with the beauty and elegance of an opulent city, but I have seen no more beautiful faces than I have seen among these humbler sisters. As the mere habits of dress in America, except to a very acute critic, give no suggestion of the rank of the wearer, I can imagine an inexperienced foreigner utterly mystified and confounded by these girls, who perhaps work a sewing machine or walk the long floors of a fashionable dry-goods shop. I remember one face and figure, faultless and complete, — modestly yet most becomingly dressed, — indeed a figure that Compte-Calix might have taken for one of his exquisite studies, which, between 7 and 8 A. M., passed through Eleventh Street, between Sixth Avenue and Broadway. So exceptionally fine was her carriage, so chaste and virginal her presence, and so refined and even spiritual her features, that, as a literary man, I would have been justified in taking her for the heroine of a society novel. Indeed I had already woven a little romance about her, when one morning she overtook me accompanied by another girl — pretty, but of a different type — with whom she was earnestly conversing. As the two passed me there fell from her faultless lips the following astounding sentence: "And I told him if he did n't like it he might lump it, and he traveled off on his left ear, you bet." Heaven knows what indiscretion this speech saved me from, but the reader will understand what a sting the pain of rejection might have added to it by the above formula.

The "morning cocktail" men come next in my experience of early rising. I used to take my early cup of coffee in the café of a certain fashionable restaurant that had a bar attached. I could not help noticing that, unlike the usual social libations of my countrymen, the act of taking a morning cocktail was a solitary one. In the course of my experience I cannot recall the fact of two men taking an ante-breakfast cocktail together. On the contrary, I have observed the male animal rush savagely at the bar, demand his drink of the barkeeper, swallow it, and hasten from the scene of his early debauchery, or else take it in a languid, perfunctory manner, which, I think, must have been insulting to the barkeeper. I have observed two men whom I had seen drinking amicably together the preceding night, standing gloomily at the opposite corners of the bar, evidently trying not to see each other, and making the matter a confidential one with the barkeeper. I have seen even a thin disguise of simplicity assumed. I remember an elderly gentleman, of most respectable exterior, who used to enter the café as if he had strayed there accidentally. After looking around carefully, and yet unostentatiously, he would walk to the bar, and, with an air of affected carelessness, state that "not feeling well this morning, he guessed he would take — well, he would leave it to the barkeeper." The barkeeper invariably gave him a stiff brandy cocktail. When the old gentleman had done this half-a-dozen times, I think I lost faith in him. I tried afterward to glean from the barkeeper some facts regarding those experiences, but I am proud to say that he was honorably reticent. Indeed, I think it may be said, truthfully, that there is no record of a barkeeper who has been "interviewed." Clergymen and doctors have, but it is well for the weaknesses of humanity that the line should be drawn somewhere.

And this reminds me that one distressing phase of early rising is the incongruous and unpleasant contact of the preceding night. The social yesterday is not fairly over before 9 A. M., to-day, and there is always a humorous, sometimes a pathetic lapping over the edges. I remember one morning at six o'clock to have been overtaken by a carriage that drew up beside me. I recognized the coachman, who touched his hat apologetically, as if he wished me to understand that he was not at all responsible for the condition of his master, and I went to the door of the carriage. I was astonished to find two young friends of mine, in correct evening dress, reclining on each other's shoulders and sleeping the sleep of the justly inebriated. I stated this fact to the coachman. Not a muscle of his well-trained face answered to my smile. But he said, "You see, sir, we 've been out all night, and more than four blocks below they saw you, and wanted me to hail you, but you know you stopped to speak to a gentleman, and so I sorter lingered, and I drove round the block once or twice, and I guess I 've got 'em quiet again." I looked in the carriage door once more on these sons of Belial. They were sleeping quite unconsciously. A boutonnière in the lappel of the younger one's coat had shed its leaves, which were scattered over him with a ridiculous suggestion of the "babes in the wood," and I closed the carriage door softly. "I suppose I'd better take 'em home, sir?" queried the coachman gravely. "Well, yes, John, perhaps you had."

There is another picture in my early-rising experience that I wish were as simply and honestly ludicrous. It was at a time when the moral sentiment of the metropolis, expressed through ordinance and special legislation, had declared itself against a certain form of "variety" entertainment, and had, as usual, proceeded against the performers, and not the people who encouraged them. I remember, one frosty morning, to have encountered in Washington Park my honest friend, Sergeant X., and Roundsman 9999 conveying a party of these derelicts to the station. One of the women, evidently, had not had time to change her apparel, and had thinly disguised the flowing robe and loose cestus of Venus under a ragged "waterproof;" while the other, who had doubtless posed for Mercury, hid her shapely tights in a plaid shawl, and changed her winged sandals for a pair of "arctics." Their rouged faces were streaked and stained with tears. The man who was with them, the male of their species, had but hastily washed himself of his Ethiopian presentment, and was still black behind the ears; while an exaggerated shirt collar and frilled shirt made his occasional indignant profanity irresistibly ludicrous. So they fared on over the glittering snow, against the rosy sunlight of the square, the gray front of the University building, with a few twittering sparrows in the foreground, beside the two policemen, quiet and impassive as fate. I could not help thinking of the distinguished A, the most fashionable B, the wealthy and respectable C, the sentimental D, and the man of the world E, who were present at the performance, whose distinguished patronage had called it into life, and who were then resting quietly in their beds, while these haggard servants of their pleasaunce were haled over the snow to punishment and ignominy.

Let me finish by recalling one brighter picture of that same season. It was early, — so early that the cross of Grace Church had, when I looked up, just caught the morning sun, and for a moment flamed like a crusader's symbol. And then the grace and glory of that exquisite spire became slowly visible. Fret by fret the sunlight stole slowly down, quivering and dropping from each, until at last the whole church beamed in rosy radiance. Up and down the long avenue the street lay in shadow; by some strange trick of the atmosphere the sun seemed to have sought out only that graceful structure for its blessing. And then there was a dull rumble. It was the first omnibus, — the first throb in the great artery of the reviving city. I looked up. The church was again in shadow.

MY FRIEND THE TRAMP

I HAD been sauntering over the clover downs of a certain noted New England seaport. It was a Sabbath morning, so singularly reposeful and gracious, so replete with the significance of the seventh day of rest that even the Sabbath bells ringing a mile away over the salt marshes had little that was monitory, mandatory, or even supplicatory in their drowsy voices. Rather they seemed to call from their cloudy towers, like some renegade muezzin, "Sleep is better than prayer; sleep on, O sons of the Puritans! Slumber still, O deacons and vestrymen. Let, oh, let those feet that are swift to wickedness curl up beneath thee; those palms that are itching for the shekels of the ungodly, lie clasped beneath thy pillow. Sleep is better than prayer."

And, indeed, though it was high morning, sleep was still in the air. Wrought upon at last by the combined influences of sea and sky and atmosphere, I succumbed, and lay down on one of the boulders of a little stony slope that gave upon the sea. The great Atlantic lay before me, not yet quite awake, but slowly heaving with the rhythmical expiration of slumber. There was no sail visible in the misty horizon. There was nothing to do but to lie and stare at the unwinking ether.

Suddenly I became aware of the strong fumes of tobacco. Turning my head I saw a pale, blue smoke curling up from behind an adjacent boulder. Rising and climbing over the intervening granite, I came upon a little hollow in which, comfortably extended on the mosses and lichens, lay a

It was the tramp

powerfully built man. He was very ragged; he was very dirty; there was a strong suggestion about him of his having too much hair, too much nail, too much perspiration; too much of those superfluous excrescences and exudations that society and civilization strive to keep under. But it was noticeable that he had not much of anything else. It was The Tramp.

With that swift severity with which we always visit rebuke upon the person who happens to present any one of our vices offensively before us, in his own person, I was deeply indignant at his laziness. Perhaps I showed it in my manner, for he rose to a half-sitting attitude, returned my stare apologetically, and made a movement toward knocking the fire from his pipe against the granite.

"Shure, sur, and if I 'd belaved that I was trispassin' on yer honor's grounds it 's meself that would hev laid down on the say-shore and taken the salt waves for me blankits. But it 's sivinteen miles I 've walked this blessed noight, with nothin' to sustain me, and hevin' a mortal wakeness to fight wid in me bowels, by reason of starvation, and only a bit o' baccy that the Widdy Maloney giv me at the cross-roads, to kape me up entoirly. But it was the dark day I left me home in Milwaukee to walk to Boston, and if ye 'll oblige a lone man who has left a wife and six children in Milwaukee wid the loan of twenty-five cints, furninst the time he gits wurruk, God 'll be good to ye."

It instantly flashed through my mind that the man before me had the previous night partaken of the kitchen hospitality of my little cottage, two miles away. That he presented himself in the guise of a distressed fisherman, mulcted of his wages by an inhuman captain; that he had a wife lying sick of consumption in the next village, and two children, one of them a cripple, wandering in the streets of Boston. I remember that this tremendous indictment against Fortune touched the family, and that the distressed fisherman was provided with clothes, food, and some small change. The food and small change had disappeared, but the garments for the consumptive wife, where were they? He had been using them for a pillow.

I instantly pointed out this fact, and charged him with the deception. To my surprise he took it quietly and even a little complacently.

"Bedad, yer roight; ye see, sur (confidentially), ye see, sur, until I get wurruk — and it 's wurruk I 'm lukin' for — I have to desave now and thin to shute the locality. Ah, God save us, but on the say-coast thay 're that harrud upon thim that don't belong to the say."

I ventured to suggest that a strong, healthy man like him might have found work somewhere between Milwaukee and Boston.

"Ah, but ye see I got free passage on a freight train, and did n't sthop. It was in the Aist that I expicted to find wurruk."

"Have you any trade?"

"Trade, is it? I 'm a brickmaker, God knows, and many 's the lift I 've had at makin' bricks in Milwaukee. Sure, I 've as aisy a hand at it as any man. Maybe yer honor might know of a kill hereabout?"

Now, to my certain knowledge, there was not a brick-kiln within fifty miles of that spot, and of all unlikely places to find one would have been this sandy peninsula, given up to the summer residences of a few wealthy people. Yet I could not help admiring the assumption of the scamp, who knew this fact as well as myself. But I said, "I can give you work for a day or two," and, bidding him gather up his sick wife's apparel, led the way across the downs to my cottage.

At first I think the offer took him by surprise, and gave him some consternation, but he presently recovered his spirits, and almost instantly his speech. "Ah, wurruk, is it? God be praised; it 's meself that 's ready and willin', 'though maybe me hand is spoilt wid brickmaking."

I assured him that the work I would give him would require no delicate manipulation, and so we fared on over the sleepy downs. But I could not help noticing that, although an invalid, I was a much better pedestrian than my companion, frequently leaving him behind, and that, even as a "tramp," he was etymologically an impostor. He had a way of lingering beside the fences we had to climb over as if to continue more confidentially the history of his misfortunes and troubles, which he was delivering to me during our homeward walk, and I noticed that he could seldom resist the invitation of a mossy boulder or a tussock of salt grass. "Ye see, sur," he would say, suddenly sitting down, "it 's along uv me misfortunes beginning in Milwaukee that" — and it was not until I was out of hearing that he would languidly gather his traps again and saunter after me. When I reached my own garden gate he leaned for a moment over it, with both of his powerful arms extended downwards and said, "Ah, but it 's a blessin' that Sunday comes to give rest fur the wake and the weary, and thim as walks sivinteen miles to get it." Of course I took the hint. There was evidently no work to be had from my friend the Tramp that day. Yet his countenance brightened as he saw the limited extent of my domain, and observed that the garden, so-called, was only a flower bed about twenty-five by ten. As he had doubtless before this been utilized to the extent of his capacity in digging, he had probably expected that kind of work, and I dare say I discomfited him by pointing him to an almost leveled stone wall about twenty feet long, with the remark that his work would be the rebuilding of that stone wall with stone brought from the neighboring slopes. In a few moments he was comfortably provided for in the kitchen, where the cook, a woman of his own nativity, apparently "chaffed" him with a raillery that was to me quite unintelligible. Yet I noticed that when, at sunset, he accompanied Bridget to the spring for water, ostentatiously flourishing the empty bucket in his hand, when they returned in the gloaming Bridget was carrying the water, and my friend the Tramp was some paces behind her cheerfully "colloguing," and picking blackberries.

At seven the next morning he started in cheerfully to work. At 9 A. M. he had placed three large stones on the first course in position, an hour having been spent in looking for a pick and hammer, and in the intervals "chaffing" with Bridget. At ten o'clock I went to overlook his work; it was a rash action, as it caused him to respectfully doff his hat, discontinue his labors, and lean back against the fence in cheerful and easy conversation.

"Are ye fond uv blackberries, captain?"

I told him that the children were in the habit of getting them from the meadow beyond, hoping to estop the suggestion I knew was coming.

"Ah, but captain, it 's meself that with wandering and havin' nothin' to pass me lips but the berries I 'd pick from the hedges — it 's meself knows where to find thim. Shure, it 's yer childer, and foine boys they are, captain, that are besaching me to go wid 'em to the place, knownst only to meself."

It is unnecessary to say that he triumphed. After the manner of vagabonds of all degrees, he had enlisted the women and children on his side, and my friend the Tramp had his own way. He departed at 11 and returned at 4 P. M. with a tin dinner-pail half filled. On interrogating the boys, it appeared that they had had "a bully time," but on cross-examination it came out that *they* had picked the berries. From four to six three more stones were laid, and the arduous labors of the day were over.

As I stood looking at the first course of six stones, my friend the Tramp stretched his strong arms out to their fullest extent and said, "Ay, but it 's wurruk that 's good fur me; gin me wurruk, and it 's all I 'll be askin' fur."

I ventured to suggest that he had not yet accomplished much.

"Wait till to-morror. Ah, but ye 'll see thin. It 's me hand that 's yet onaisy wid brickmaking and sthrange to the shtones. Av ye 'll wait till to-morror?"

Unfortunately I did not wait. An engagement took me away at an early hour, and when I rode up to my cottage at noon my eyes were greeted with the astonishing spectacle of my two boys hard at work laying the courses of the stone wall, assisted by Bridget and Norah, who were dragging stones from the hillsides, while comfortably stretched on the top of the wall lay my friend the Tramp, quietly overseeing the operations with lazy and humorous comment. For an instant I was foolishly indignant, but he soon brought me to my senses.

"Shure, sur, it 's only larnin' the boys the habits uv industhry I was — and may they niver know, be the same token, what is it to wurruk for the bread betune their lips. Shure it 's but makin' 'em think it play, I was. As fur the colleens beyint in the kitchen, shure is n't it betther they was helping your honor here than colloguing with themselves inside?"

Nevertheless, I thought it expedient to forbid henceforth any interruption of servants or children with my friend's "wurruk." Perhaps it was the result of this embargo that the next morning early the Tramp wanted to see me.

"And it 's sorry I am to say it to ye, sur," he began, "but it 's the handlin' of this stun that 's desthroyin' me touch at the brickmakin', and it 's better I should lave ye and find wurruk at me own thrade. For it 's wurruk I 'm nadin'. It is n't meself, capt'in, to ate the bread of oidleness here. And so good-by to ye, and if it 's fifty cints ye can be givin' me ontil I 'll find a kill — it 's God that 'll repay ye."

He got the money. But he got also conditionally a note from me to my next neighbor, a wealthy retired physician, possessed of a large domain, — a man eminently practical and business-like in his management of it. He employed many laborers on the sterile waste he called his "farm," and it occurred to me that if there really was any work in my friend the Tramp, which my own indolence and preoccupation had failed to bring out, he was the man to do it.

I met him a week after. It was with some embarrassment that I inquired after my friend the Tramp. "Oh, yes," he said reflectively, "let 's see — he came Monday and left me Thursday. He was, I think, a stout, strong man, a well-meaning, good-humored fellow, but afflicted with a most singular variety of diseases. The first day I put him at work in the stables he developed chills and fever caught in the swamps of Louisiana" —

"Excuse me," I said hurriedly, "you mean in Milwaukee!"

"I know what I 'm talking about," returned the doctor testily; "he told me his whole wretched story; his escape from the Confederate service; the attack upon him by armed negroes; his concealment in the bayous and swamps" —

"Go on, doctor," I said feebly; "you were speaking of his work."

"Yes — well his system was full of malaria; the first day I had him wrapped up in blankets and dosed with quinine. The next day he was taken with all the symptoms of cholera morbus, and I had to keep him up on brandy and capsicum. Rheumatism set in on the following day and incapacitated him for work, and I concluded I had better give him a note to the director of the City Hospital than keep him here. As a pathological study he was good, but as I was looking for a man to help about the stable I could n't afford to keep him in both capacities."

As I never could really tell when the doctor was in joke or in earnest I dropped the subject. And so my friend the Tramp gradually faded from my memory, not, however, without leaving behind him in the barn, where he had slept, a lingering flavor of whisky, onions, and fluffiness. But in two weeks this had gone, and the "Shebang" (as my friends irreverently termed my habitation) knew him no more. Yet it was pleasant to think of him as having at last found a job at brickmaking, or having returned to his family at Milwaukee, or making his Louisiana home once more happy with his presence, or again tempting the fish-producing main, — this time with a noble and equitable captain.

It was a lovely August morning when I rode across the sandy peninsula to visit a certain noted family, whereof all the sons were valiant and the daughters beautiful. The front of the house was deserted, but on the rear veranda I heard the rustle of gowns, and above it arose what seemed to be the voice of Ulysses, reciting his wanderings. There was no mistaking that voice, — it was my friend the Tramp!

From what I could hastily gather from his speech, he had walked from St. John, N. B., to rejoin a distressed wife in New York, who was, however, living with opulent but objectionable relatives.

"An' shure, miss, I would n't be asking ye the loan of a cint if I could get wurruk at me trade of carpet-wavin' — and maybe ye know of some manufacthory where they wave carpets beyant here. Ah, miss, and if ye don't give me a cint, it 's enough for the loikes of me to know that me troubles has brought the tears in the most beautiful oiyes in the wurruld, and God bless ye for it, miss!"

Now I knew that the Most Beautiful Eyes in the World belonged to one of the most sympathetic and tenderest hearts in the world, and I felt that common justice demanded my interference between it and one of the biggest scamps in the world. So, without waiting to be announced by the servant, I opened the door and joined the group on the veranda.

If I expected to touch the conscience of my friend the Tramp by a dramatic entrance, I failed utterly! For no sooner did he see me than he instantly gave vent to a howl of delight, and, falling on his knees before me, grasped my hand and turned oratorically to the ladies.

"Oh, but it 's himself — himself that has come as a witness to me charackther! oh, but it 's himself that lifted me four wakes ago, when I was lyin' with a mortal wakeness on the say-coast and tuk me to his house. Oh, but it 's himself that shupported me over the faldes, and whin the chills and faver came on me and I shivered wid the cold, it was himself, God bless him, as sthripped the coat off his back, and giv it me, sayin', 'Tak it, Dinnis, it 's shtarved with the cowld say air ye 'll be entoirly.' Ah, but look at him — will ye, miss! Look at his swate, modist face — a-blushin' like your own, miss. Ah! look at him, will ye? He 'll be denyin' of it in a minit — may the blessin' uv God folly him. Look at him, miss! Ah, but it 's a swate pair ye 'd make! (The rascal knew I was a married man.) Ah, miss, if ye could see him wroightin' day and night with such an illigant hand of his own — (he had evidently believed from the gossip of my servants that I was a professor of chirography) — if ye could see him, miss, as I have, ye 'd be proud of him."

He stopped out of breath. I was so completely astounded I could say nothing; the tremendous indictment I had framed to utter as I opened the door vanished completely. And as the Most Beautiful Eyes in the Wurruld turned gratefully to mine — well —

I still retained enough principle to ask the ladies to withdraw, while I would take upon myself the duty of examining into the case of my friend the Tramp and giving him such relief as was required. (I did not know until afterward, however, that the rascal had already despoiled their scant purses of $3.50.) When the door was closed upon them I turned upon him.

"You infernal rascal!"

"Ah, capt'in, and would ye be refusin' *me* a carrakther and me givin' *ye* such a one as Oi did? God save us! but if ye 'd hav' seen the luk that the purty one give me. Well, before the chills and faver bruk me spirits entirely, when I was a young man, and makin' me tin dollars a week brickmakin', it 's meself that wud hav given" —

"I consider," I broke in, "that a dollar is a fair price for your story, and as I shall have to take it all back and expose you before the next twenty-four hours pass, I think you had better hasten to Milwaukee, New York, or Louisiana."

I handed him the dollar. "Mind, I don't want to see your face again."

"Ye wun't, capt'in."

And I did not.

But it so chanced that later in the season, when the migratory inhabitants had flown to their hot-air registers in Boston and Providence, I breakfasted with one who had lingered. It was a certain Boston lawyer, — replete with principle, honesty, self-discipline, statistics, æsthetics, and a perfect consciousness of possessing all these virtues, and a full recognition of their market values. I think he tolerated me as a kind of foreigner, gently but firmly waiving all argument on any topic, frequently distrusting my facts, generally my deductions, and always my ideas. In conversation he always appeared to descend only half-way down a long moral and intellectual staircase, and always delivered his conclusions over the balusters.

I had been speaking of my friend the Tramp. "There is but one way of treating that class of impostors; it is simply to recognize the fact that the law calls him a 'vagrant,' and makes his trade a misdemeanor. Any sentiment on the other side renders you *particeps criminis.* I don't know but an action would lie against you for encouraging tramps. Now, I have an efficacious way of dealing with these gentry." He rose and took a double-barreled fowling-piece from the chimney. "When a tramp appears on my property I warn him off. If he persists I fire on him — as I would on any criminal trespasser."

"Fire on him?" I echoed in alarm.

"Yes — *but with powder only!* Of course *he* does n't know that. But he does n't come back."

It struck me for the first time that possibly many other of my friend's arguments might be only blank cartridges, and used to frighten off other trespassing intellects.

"Of course, if the Tramp still persisted I would be justified in using shot. Last evening I had a visit from one. He was coming over the wall. My shotgun was efficacious; you should have seen him run!"

It was useless to argue with so positive a mind, and I dropped the subject. After breakfast I strolled over the downs, my friend promising to join me as soon as he had arranged some household business.

It was a lovely, peaceful morning, not unlike the day when I first met my friend the Tramp. The hush of a great benediction lay on land and sea. A few white sails twinkled afar, but sleepily; one or two large ships were creeping in lazily — like my friend the Tramp. A voice behind me startled me.

My host had rejoined me. His face, however, looked a little troubled.

"I just now learned something of importance," he began; "it appears that with all my precautions that Tramp has visited my kitchen and the servants have entertained him. Yesterday morning, it appears, while I was absent, he had the audacity to borrow my gun to go duck shooting. At the end of two or three hours he returned with two ducks and — the gun."

"That was, at least, honest."

"Yes; but — that fool of a girl says that, as he handed back the gun, he told her it was all right, and that he had loaded it up again to save the master trouble."

I think I showed my concern in my face, for he added hastily, "It was only duck shot, — a few would n't hurt him!"

Nevertheless we both walked on in silence for a moment.

"I thought the gun kicked a little," he said at last musingly; "but the idea of — Hallo! what 's this?"

He had stopped before the hollow where I had first seen my Tramp. It was deserted, but on the mosses there were spots of blood and fragments of an old gown, blood-stained, as if used for bandages. I looked at it closely; it was the gown intended for the consumptive wife of my friend the Tramp. But my host was already nervously tracking the bloodstains that on rock, moss, and boulder were steadily leading toward the sea. When I overtook him at last on the shore, he was standing before a flat rock, on which lay a bundle I recognized, tied up in a handkerchief, and a crooked grapevine stick.

"He may have come here to wash his wounds; salt is a styptic," said my host, who had recovered his correct precision of statement.

I said nothing, but looked toward the sea. Whatever secret lay hid in its breast, it kept it fast. Whatever its calm eyes had seen that summer night, it gave no reflection now. It lay there passive, imperturbable, and reticent. But my friend the Tramp was gone!

A SLEEPING-CAR EXPERIENCE

It was in a Pullman sleeping-car on a Western road. After that first plunge into unconsciousness which the weary traveler takes on getting into his berth, I awakened to the dreadful revelation that I had been asleep only two hours. The greater part of a long winter night was before me to face with staring eyes.

Finding it impossible to sleep, I lay there wondering a number of things: why, for instance, the Pullman sleeping-car blankets were unlike other blankets; why they were like squares cut out of cold buckwheat cakes, and why they clung to you when you turned over, and lay heavy on you without warmth; why the curtains before you could not have been made opaque, without being so thick and suffocating; why it would not be as well to sit up all night half asleep in an ordinary passenger car as to lie awake all night in a Pullman? But the snoring of my fellow-passengers answered this question in the negative.

With the recollection of last night's dinner weighing on me as heavily and coldly as the blankets, I began wondering why, over the whole extent of the continent, there was no local dish; why the bill of fare at restaurant and hotel was invariably only a weak reflex of the metropolitan hostelries; why the entrées were always the same, only more or less badly cooked; why the traveling American always was supposed to demand turkey and cold cranberry sauce; why the pretty waiter girl apparently shuffled your plates behind your back, and then dealt them over your shoulder in a semicircle, as if they were a hand at cards, and not always a good one? Why, having done this, she instantly retired to the nearest wall, and gazed at you scornfully, as one who would say, "Fair sir, though lowly, I am proud; if dost imagine that I would permit undue familiarity of speech, beware!" And then I began to think of and dread the coming breakfast; to wonder why the ham was always cut half an inch thick, and why the fried egg always resembled a glass eye that visibly winked at you with diabolical dyspeptic suggestions; to wonder if the buckwheat cakes, the eating of which requires a certain degree of artistic preparation and deliberation, would be brought in as usual one minute before the train started. And then I had a vivid recollection of a fellow-passenger who, at a certain breakfast station in Illinois, frantically enwrapped his portion of this national pastry in his red bandana handkerchief, took it into the smoking-car, and quietly devoured it en route.

Lying broad awake, I could not help making some observations which I think are not noticed by the day traveler. First, that the speed of a train is not equal or continuous. That at certain times the engine apparently starts up, and says to the baggage train behind it, "Come, come, this won't do! Why, it's nearly half-past two; how in h—ll shall we get through? Don't you talk to *me.* Pooh! pooh!" delivered in that rhythmical fashion which all meditation assumes on a railway train. *Exempli gratia:* One night, having raised my window curtain to look over a moonlit snowy landscape, as I pulled it down the lines of a popular comic song flashed across me. Fatal error! The train instantly took it up, and during the rest of the night I was haunted by this awful refrain: "Pull down the bel-lind, pull down the bel-lind; somebody 's klink klink. Oh, don't be shoo-shoo!" Naturally this differs on the different railways. On the New York Central, where the roadbed is quite perfect and the steel rails continuous, I have heard this irreverent train give the words of a certain popular revival hymn after this fashion: "Hold the fort, for I am Sankey, Moody slingers still, wave the swish swosh back from klinky, klinky klanky kill." On the New York and New Haven, where there are many switches, and the engine whistles at every cross-road, I have often heard, "Tommy, make room for your whoopy! that's a little clang, bumpity bumpity boopy, clikitty, clikitty, clang." Poetry, I fear, fared little better. One starlit night, coming from Quebec, as we slipped by a virgin forest, the opening lines of Evangeline flashed upon me. But all I could make of them was this: "This is the forest prim-eval-eval; the groves of the pines and the hem-locks-locks-locks-locks-loooock!" The train was only "slowing" or "braking" up at a station. Hence the jar in the metre.

I had noticed a peculiar Æolian-harp-like cry that ran through the whole train as we settled to rest at last after a long run, — an almost sigh of infinite relief, a musical sigh that began in *C* and ran gradually up to *F* natural, which I think most observant travelers have noticed day and night. No railway official has ever given me a satisfactory explanation of it. As the car, in a rapid run, is always slightly projected forward of its trucks, a practical friend once suggested to me that it was the gradual settling back of the car body to a state of inertia, which, of course, every poetical traveler would reject. Four o'clock — the sound of boot-blacking by the porter faintly apparent from the toilet room. Why not talk to him? But, fortunately, I remembered that any attempt at extended conversation with conductor or porter was always resented by them as implied disloyalty to the company they represented. I recalled that once I had endeavored to impress upon a conductor the absolute folly of a midnight inspection of tickets, and had been treated by him as an escaped lunatic. No, there was no relief from this suffocating and insupportable loneliness to be gained then. I raised the window blind and looked out. We were passing a farmhouse. A light, evidently the lantern of a farm hand, was swung beside a barn. Yes, the faintest tinge of rose in the far horizon. Morning, surely, at last.

We had stopped at a station. Two men had got into the car and had taken seats in the one vacant section, yawning occasionally, and conversing in a languid, perfunctory sort of way. They sat opposite each other, occasionally looking out of the window, but always giving the stray impression that they were tired of each other's company. As I looked out of my curtains at them, the One Man said with a feebly concealed yawn: —

"Yes, well, I reckon he was at one time as poplar an ondertaker ez I knew."

The Other Man (inventing a question rather than giving an answer, out of some languid social impulse): "But was he — this yer ondertaker — a Christian — hed he jined the church?"

The One Man (reflectively): "Well, I don't know ez you might call him a purfessin' Christian; but he hed — yes, he hed conviction. I think Dr. Wylie hed him under conviction. Et least that was the way I got it from *him.*"

A long, dreary pause.

The Other Man (feeling it was incumbent on him to say something): "But why was he popler ez an ondertaker?"

The One Man (lazily): "Well, he was kinder popler with widders and widderers — sorter soothen 'em a kinder keerless way; slung 'em suthin' here and there, sometimes outer the Book, sometimes outer himself, ez a man of experience az hed hed sorror. Hed, they say (*very cautiously*), lost three wives hisself, and five children by this yer new disease — dipthery — out in Wisconsin. I don't know the facts, but that 's what got round."

The Other Man: "But how did he lose his poplarity?"

The One Man: "Well, that 's the question. You see he introduced some things into ondertaking that waz new. He hed, for instance, a way, as he called it, of manniperlating the features of the deceased."

The Other Man (quietly): "How manniperlating?"

The One Man (struck with a bright and aggressive thought): "Look yer, did ye ever notiss how, generally speakin', onhandsome a corpse is?"

The Other Man had noticed this fact.

The One Man (returning to his fact): "Why, there was Mary Peebles, ez was daughter of my wife's bosom friend — a mighty pooty girl and a perfessing Christian — died of scarlet fever. Well, that gal — I was one of the mourners, being my wife's friend — well, that gal, though I hed n't, perhaps, oughter say — lying in that casket, fetched all the way from some A 1 establishment in Chicago, filled with flowers and furbelows — did n't really seem to be of much account. Well, although my wife's friend, and me a mourner — well, now, I was — disappointed and discouraged."

The Other Man (in palpably affected sympathy): "Sho! now!"

"Yes, *sir!* Well, you see, this yer ondertaker — this Wilkins — hed a way of correcting all thet. And just by manniperlation. He worked over the face of the deceased until he perduced what the survivin' relatives called a look of Resignation — you know, a sort of smile, like. When he wanted to put in any extrys, he produced what he called — hevin' reg'lar charges for this kind of work — a Christian's Hope."

The Other Man: "I want to know!"

"Yes. Well, I admit, at times it was a little startlin'.

And I 've allers said (a little confidentially) that I hed my doubts of its being Scriptooral or sacred, being, ez you know, worms of the yearth; and I relieved my mind to our pastor, but he did n't feel like interferin', ez long ez it was confined to church membership. But the other day, when Cy Dunham died — you disremember Cy Dunham?"

A long interval of silence. The Other Man was looking out of the window, and had apparently forgotten his companion completely. But as I stretched my head out of the curtain I saw four other heads as eagerly reached out from other berths to hear the conclusion of the story. One head, a female one, instantly disappeared on my looking around, but a certain tremulousness of her window curtain showed an unabated interest. The only two utterly disinterested men were the One Man and the Other Man.

The Other Man (detaching himself languidly from the window): "Cy Dunham?"

"Yes, Cy never hed hed either convictions or perfessions. Uster get drunk and go round with permiscous women. Sorter like the prodigal son, only a little more so, ez fur ez I kin judge from the facks ez stated to me. Well — Cy one day petered out down at Little Rock, and was sent up yer for interment. The fammerly, being proud-like, of course did n't spare any money on that funeral, and it waz — now between you and me — about ez shapely and first-class and prime-mess an affair ez I ever saw. Wilkins hed put in his extrys. He hed put onto that prodigal's face the A 1 touch — hed him fixed up with a Christian's Hope. Well — it waz about the turning-point, for thar waz some of the members and the pastor hisself thought that the line ort to be drawn somewhere, and thar waz some talk at Deacon Tibbet's about a reg'lar conference meetin' regardin' it. But it was n't thet which made him onpoplar."

Another silence — no expression nor reflection from the

face of the Other Man of the least desire to know what ultimately settled the unpopularity of the undertaker. But from the curtains of the various berths several eager and one or two even wrathful faces, anxious for the result.

The Other Man (lazily recurring to the lost topic): "Well, what made him onpoplar?"

The One Man (quietly): "Extrys, I think — that is, I suppose, — not knowin' (cautiously) all the facts. When Mrs. Widdecombe lost her husband — 'bout two months ago — though she 'd been through the valley of the shadder of death twice — this bein' her third marriage, hevin' been John Barker's widder" —

The Other Man (with an intense expression of interest): "No, you 're foolin' me!"

The One Man (solemnly): "Ef I was to appear before my Maker to-morrow, yes! she was the widder of Barker."

The Other Man: "Well, I swow."

The One Man: "Well, this widder Widdecombe, she put up a big funeral for the deceased. She hed Wilkins, and thet ondertaker just laid hisself out. Just spread himself. Onfort'nately — perhaps fort'natly in the ways of Providence — one of Widdecombe's old friends, a doctor up thar in Chicago, comes down to the funeral. He goes up with the friends to look at the deceased, smilin' a peaceful sort of heavinly smile, and everybody sayin' he 's gone to meet his reward, and this yer friend turns round, short and sudden, on the widder settin' in her pew, and kinder enjoyin', as wimen will, all the compliments paid the corpse, and he says, says he — 'What did you say your husband died of, marm?' 'Consumption,' she says, wiping her eyes, poor critter! — 'Consumption — gallopin' consumption.' 'Consumption be d—d,' sez he, bein' a profane kind of Chicago doctor, and not bein' ever under conviction. 'Thet man died of strychnine. Look at thet face. Look at thet contortion of them facial muscles. Thet 's strychnine. Thet 's *risers Sardonicus*' (thet 's what he said; he was always sorter profane). 'Why, doctor,' says the widder, 'thet — thet is his last smile. It 's a Christian's Resignation.' 'Thet be blowed; don't tell me,' sez he. 'Hell is full of thet kind of resignation. It 's pizon. And I 'll' — Why, dern my skin, yes we are; yes, it 's Joliet. Wall, now, who 'd hev thought we 'd been nigh onto an hour."

Two or three anxious passengers from their berths: "Say; look yer, stranger! Old Man! What became of" —

But the One Man and the Other Man had vanished.

THE MAN WHOSE YOKE WAS NOT EASY

He was a spare man, and, physically, an ill-conditioned man, but at first glance scarcely a seedy man. The indications of reduced circumstances in the male of the better class are, I fancy, first visible in the boots and shirt, the boots offensively exhibiting a degree of polish inconsistent with their dilapidated condition, and the shirt showing an extent of ostentatious surface that is invariably fatal to the threadbare waistcoat that it partially covers. He was a pale man, and I fancied still paler from his black clothes.

He handed me a note.

It was from a certain physician; a man of broad culture and broader experience; a man who had devoted the greater part of his active life to the alleviation of sorrow and suffering; a man who had lived up to the noble vows of a noble profession; a man who locked in his honorable breast the secrets of a hundred families, whose face was as kindly, whose touch was as gentle in the wards of the great public hospitals as it was beside the laced curtains of the dying Narcissa; a man who, through long contact with suffering, had acquired a universal tenderness and breadth of kindly philosophy; a man who, day and night, was at the beck and call of Anguish; a man who never asked the creed, belief, moral or worldly standing of the sufferer, or even his ability to pay the few coins that enabled him (the physician) to exist and practice his calling; in brief, a man who so nearly lived up to the example of the Great Master that it seems strange I am writing of him as a doctor of medicine and not of divinity.

The note was in pencil, characteristically brief, and ran thus: —

"Here is the man I spoke of. He ought to be good material for you."

For a moment I sat, looking from the note to the man, and sounding the "dim perilous depths" of my memory for the meaning of this mysterious communication. The "good material," however, soon relieved my embarrassment by putting his hand on his waistcoat, coming toward me, and saying, "It 's just here, you can feel it."

It was not necessary for me to do so. In a flash I remembered that my medical friend had told me of a certain poor patient, once a soldier, who, among his other trials and uncertainties, was afflicted with an aneurism caused by the buckle of his knapsack pressing upon the arch of the aorta. It was liable to burst at any shock or any moment. The poor fellow's yoke had indeed been too heavy.

In the presence of such a tremendous possibility I think for an instant I felt anxious only about myself. What *I* should do; how dispose of the body; how explain the circumstance of his taking off; how evade the ubiquitous reporter and the coroner's inquest; how a suspicion might arise that I had in some way, through negligence, or for some dark purpose, unknown to the jury, precipitated the catastrophe, all flashed before me. Even the note — with its darkly suggestive offer of "good material" for me — looked diabolically significant. What might not an intelligent lawyer make of it?

I tore it up instantly, and with feverish courtesy begged him to be seated.

"You don't care to feel it?" he asked a little anxiously.

"No."

"Nor see it?"

"No."

He sighed, a trifle sadly, as if I had rejected the only favor he could bestow. I saw at once that he had been under frequent exhibition to the doctors, and that he was, perhaps, a trifle vain of this attention. This perception was corroborated a moment later by his producing a copy of a medical magazine, with the remark that on the sixth page I would find a full statement of his case.

Could I serve him in any way? I asked.

It appeared that I could. If I could help him to any light employment, something that did not require any great physical exertion or mental excitement, he would be thankful. But he wanted me to understand that he was not, strictly speaking, a poor man; that some years before the discovery of his fatal complaint he had taken out a life insurance policy for five thousand dollars, and that he had raked and scraped enough together to pay it up, and that he would not leave his wife and four children destitute. "You see," he added, "if I could find some sort of light work to do, and kinder sled along you know — until" —

He stopped awkwardly.

I have heard several noted actors thrill their audiences with a single phrase. I think I never was as honestly moved by any spoken word as that "until" or the pause that followed it. He was evidently quite unconscious of its effect, for as I took a seat beside him on the sofa, and looked more closely in his waxen face, I could see that he was evidently embarrassed, and would have explained himself further if I had not stopped him.

Possibly it was the dramatic idea, or possibly chance, but a few days afterwards, meeting a certain kind-hearted theatrical manager, I asked him if he had any light employment for a man who was an invalid. "Can he walk?" "Yes." "Stand up for fifteen minutes?" "Yes." "Then I'll take him. He'll do for the last scene in the 'Destruction of Sennacherib;' it's a tremendous thing, you know; we 'll have two thousand people on the stage." I was a trifle alarmed at the title and ventured to suggest (without betraying my poor friend's secret) that he could not actively engage in the "Destruction of Sennacherib," and that even the spectacle of it might be too much for him. "Need n't see it at all," said my managerial friend; "put him in front; nothing to do but march in and march out, and dodge curtain."

He was engaged. I admit I was at times haunted by grave doubts as to whether I should not have informed the manager of his physical condition, and the possibility that he might some evening perpetrate a real tragedy on the mimic stage; but on the first performance of "The Destruction of Sennacherib," which I conscientiously attended, I was somewhat relieved. I had often been amused with the placid way in which the chorus in the opera invariably received the most astounding information, and witnessed the most appalling tragedies by poison or the block without anything more than a vocal protest or command always delivered to the audience, and never to the actors; but I think my poor friend's utter impassiveness to the wild carnage and the terrible exhibitions of incendiarism that were going on around him transcended even that. Dressed in a costume that seemed to be the very soul of anachronism, he stood a little outside the proscenium, holding a spear, the other hand pressed apparently upon the secret within his breast, calmly surveying, with his waxen face, the gay auditorium. I could not help thinking that there was a certain pride visible even in his placid features, as of one who was conscious that at any moment he might change this simulated catastrophe into real terror. I could not help saying this to the doctor, who was with me. "Yes," he said, with professional exactitude, "when it happens he 'll throw his arms up above his head, utter an ejaculation, and fall forward on his face, — it 's a singular thing, they always fall forward on their face, — and they 'll pick up the man as dead as Julius Caesar."

After that, I used to go night after night, with a certain hideous fascination; but, while it will be remembered the "Destruction of Sennacherib" had a tremendous run, it will also be remembered that not a single life was really lost during its representation.

It was only a few weeks after this modest first appearance on the boards of "The Man with an Aneurism" that, happening to be at a dinner party of practical business men, I sought to interest them with the details of the above story, delivered with such skill and pathos as I could command. I regret to say that, as a pathetic story, it for a moment seemed to be a dead failure. At last a prominent banker sitting next to me turned to me with the awful question, "Why don't your friend try to realize on his life insurance?" I begged his pardon; I did n't quite understand. "Oh, discount, sell out. Look here — (after a pause). Let him assign his policy to me — it 's not much of a risk, on your statement. Well — I 'll give him his five thousand dollars, clear."

And he did. Under the advice of this cool-headed — I think I may add warmhearted — banker, "The Man with an Aneurism" invested his money in the name of and for the benefit of his wife in certain securities that paid him a small but regular stipend. But he still continued upon the boards of the theatre.

By reason of some business engagements that called me away from the city, I did not see my friend the physician for three months afterward. When I did I asked tidings of the Man with the Aneurism. The doctor's kind face grew sad. "I 'm afraid — that is, I don't exactly know whether I 've good news or bad. Did you ever see his wife?"

I never had.

"Well, she was younger than he, and rather attractive, one of those doll-faced women. You remember, he settled that life insurance policy on her and the children; she might have waited. She did n't. The other day she eloped with some fellow, I don't remember his name, with the children and the five thousand dollars."

"And the shock killed him," I said, with poetic promptitude.

"No — that is — not yet; I saw him yesterday," said the doctor, with conscientious professional precision, looking over his list of calls.

"Well, where is the poor fellow now?"

"He 's still at the theatre. James, if these powders are called for, you 'll find them here in this envelope. Tell Mrs. Blank I 'll be there at seven — and she can give the baby this until I come. Say there 's no danger. These women are an awful bother! Yes, he 's at the theatre yet. Which way are you going? Down town? Why can't you step into my carriage, and I 'll give you a lift, and we 'll talk on the way down? Well — he 's at the theatre yet. And — and — do you remember the 'Destruction of Sennacherib'? No? Yes, you do. You remember that woman in pink, who pirouetted in the famous ballet scene! You don't? Why, yes, you do! Well, I imagine, of course I don't know — it 's only a summary diagnosis, but I imagine that our friend with the aneurism has attached himself to her."

"Doctor, you horrify me."

"There are more things, Mr. Poet, in heaven and earth than are yet dreamt of in your philosophy. Listen. My diagnosis may be wrong, but that woman called the other day at my office to ask about him, his health, and general condition. I told her the truth — and she *fainted.* It was about as dead a faint as I ever saw; I was nearly an hour in bringing her out of it. Of course it was the heat of the room, her exertions the preceding week, and I prescribed for her. Queer, was n't it? Now, if I were a writer, and had your faculty, I 'd make something of that."

"But how is his general health?"

"Oh, about the same. He can't evade what will come, you know, at any moment. He was up here the other day. Why, the pulsation was as plain — why, the entire arch of the aorta — What, you get out here? Good-by."

Of course no moralist, no man writing for a sensitive and strictly virtuous public, could further interest himself in this man. So I dismissed him at once from my mind, and returned to the literary contemplation of virtue that was clearly and positively defined, and of Sin that invariably commenced with a capital letter. That this man, in his awful condition, hovering on the verge of eternity, should allow himself to be attracted by — but it was horrible to contemplate.

Nevertheless, a month afterward I was returning from a festivity with my intimate friend Smith, my distinguished friend Jobling, my most respectable friend Robinson, and my wittiest friend Jones. It was a clear, starlit morning, and we seemed to hold the broad, beautiful avenue to ourselves, and I fear we acted as if it were so. As we hilariously passed the corner of Eighteenth Street, a coupé rolled by, and I suddenly heard my name called from its gloomy depths.

"I beg your pardon," said the doctor, as the driver drew up on the sidewalk, "but I 've some news for you. I 've just been to see our poor friend — Of course I was too late. He was gone in a flash."

"What, dead?"

"As Pharaoh! In an instant, just as I said. You see, the rupture took place in the descending arch of" —

"But, doctor!"

"It 's a queer story. Am I keeping you from your

friends? No? Well, you see she — that woman I spoke of — had written a note to him based on what I had told her. He got it, and dropped in his dressing-room, dead as a herring."

"How could she have been so cruel, knowing his condition; she might, with woman's tact, have rejected him less abruptly."

"Yes, but you 're all wrong. By Jove, she *accepted* him! — was willing to marry him!"

"What?"

"Yes — don't you see? It was joy that killed him. Gad, we never thought of *that!* Queer, ain't it. See here, don't you think you might make a story out of it?"

"But, doctor, it has n't got any moral."

"Humph! That 's so. Good-morning. Drive on, John."

THE OFFICE-SEEKER

He asked me if I had ever seen the "Remus Sentinel."

I replied that I had not, and would have added that I did not even know where Remus was, when he continued by saying it was strange the hotel proprietor did not keep the "Sentinel" on his files, and that he himself should write to the editor about it. He would not have spoken about it, but he himself had been a humble member of the profession to which I belonged, and had often written for its columns. Some friends of his — partial, no doubt — had said that his style somewhat resembled Junius's; but of course, you know — well, what he could say was that in the last campaign his articles were widely sought for. He did not know but he had a copy of one. Here his hand dived into the breast-pocket of his coat, with a certain deftness that indicated long habit, and after depositing on his lap a bundle of well-worn documents, every one of which was glaringly suggestive of certificates and signatures, he concluded he had left it in his trunk.

I breathed more freely. We were sitting in the rotunda of a famous Washington hotel, and only a few moments before had the speaker, an utter stranger to me, moved his chair beside mine and opened a conversation. I noticed that he had that timid, lonely, helpless air which invests the bucolic traveler who, for the first time, finds himself among strangers, and his identity lost, in a world so much larger, so much colder, so much more indifferent to him than he ever imagined. Indeed, I think that what we often attribute to the impertinent familiarity of countrymen and rustic travelers on railways or in cities is largely due to their awful loneliness and nostalgia. I remember to have once met in a smoking-car on a Kansas railway one of these lonely ones, who, after plying me with a thousand useless questions, finally elicited the fact that I knew slightly a man who had once dwelt in his native town in Illinois. During the rest of our journey the conversation turned chiefly upon this fellow-townsman, whom it afterwards appeared that my Illinois friend knew no better than I did. But he had established a link between himself and his far-off home through me, and was happy.

While this was passing through my mind I took a fair look at him. He was a spare young fellow, not more than thirty, with sandy hair and eyebrows, and eyelashes so white as to be almost imperceptible. He was dressed in black, somewhat to the "rearward o' the fashion," and I had an odd idea that it had been his wedding suit, and it afterwards appeared I was right. His manner had the precision and much of the dogmatism of the country schoolmaster, accustomed to wrestle with the feeblest intellects. From his history, which he presently gave me, it appeared I was right here also.

He was born and bred in a Western State, and, as schoolmaster of Remus and clerk of supervisors, had married one of his scholars, the daughter of a clergyman, and a man of some little property. He had attracted some attention by his powers of declamation, and was one of the principal members of the Remus Debating Society. The various questions then agitating Remus — "Is the doctrine of immortality consistent with an agricultural life?" and, "Are round dances morally wrong?" — afforded him an opportunity of bringing himself prominently before the country people. Perhaps I might have seen an extract copied from the "Remus Sentinel" in the "Christian Recorder" of May 7, 1875? No? He would get it for me. He had taken an active part in the last campaign. He did not like to say it, but it had been universally acknowledged that he had elected Gashwiler.

Who?

Gen. Pratt C. Gashwiler, member of Congress from our deestrict.

Oh!

A powerful man, sir, — a very powerful man; a man whose influence will presently be felt here, sir, — *here!* Well, he had come on with Gashwiler, and — well, he did not know why — Gashwiler did not know why he should not, you know (a feeble, half-apologetic laugh here), receive that reward, you know, for these services which, etc., etc.

I asked him if he had any particular or definite office in view.

Well, no. He had left that to Gashwiler. Gashwiler had said — he remembered his very words: "Leave it all to me; I'll look through the different departments, and see what can be done for a man of your talents."

And —

He's looking. I'm expecting him back here every minute. He's gone over to the Department of Tape to see what can be done there. Ah! here he comes.

A large man approached us. He was very heavy, very unwieldy, very unctuous and oppressive. He affected the "honest farmer," but so badly that the poorest husbandman would have resented it. There was a suggestion of a cheap lawyer about him that would have justified any self-respecting judge in throwing him over the bar at once. There was a military suspicion about him that would have entitled him to a court-martial on the spot. There was an introduction, from which I learned that my office-seeking friend's name was Expectant Dobbs. And then Gashwiler addressed me: —

"Our young friend here is waiting, waiting. Waiting, I may say, on the affairs of state. Youth," continued the Hon. Mr. Gashwiler, addressing an imaginary constituency, "is nothing but a season of waiting — of preparation — ha, ha!"

As he laid his hand in a fatherly manner — a fatherly manner that was as much of a sham as anything else about him — on Mr. Dobbs's shoulder, I don't know whether I was more incensed at him or his victim, who received it with evident pride and satisfaction. Nevertheless he ventured to falter out: —

"Has anything been done yet?"

"Well, no; I can't say that anything — that is, that anything has been *completed;* but I may say we are in excellent position for an advance — ha, ha! But we must wait, my young friend, wait. What is it the Latin philosopher says? 'Let us by all means hasten slowly' — ha, ha!" and he turned to me as if saying confidentially, "Observe the impatience of these boys!" "I met, a moment ago, my old friend and boyhood's companion, Jim McGlasher, chief of the Bureau for the Dissemination of Useless Information, and," lowering his voice to a mysterious but audible whisper, "I shall see him again to-morrow."

The "All aboard!" of the railway omnibus at this moment tore me from the presence of this gifted legislator and his protégé; but as we drove away I saw through the open window the powerful mind of Gashwiler operating, so to speak, upon the susceptibilities of Mr. Dobbs.

I did not meet him again for a week. The morning of my return I saw the two conversing together in the hall, but with the palpable distinction between this and their former interviews, that the gifted Gashwiler seemed to be anxious to get away from his friend. I heard him say something about "committees" and "to-morrow," and when

Dobbs turned his freckled face toward me I saw that he had got at last some expression into it, — disappointment.

I asked him pleasantly how he was getting on.

He had not lost his pride yet. He was doing well, although such was the value set upon his friend Gashwiler's abilities by his brother members that he was almost always occupied with committee business. I noticed that his clothes were not in as good case as before, and he told me that he had left the hotel, and taken lodgings in a by-street, where it was less expensive. Temporarily, of course.

A few days after this I had business in one of the great departments. From the various signs over the doors of its various offices and bureaus it always oddly reminded me of Stewart's or Arnold & Constable's. You could get pensions, patents, and plants. You could get land and the seeds to put in it, and the Indians to prowl round it, and what not. There was a perpetual clanging of office desk bells, and a running hither and thither of messengers strongly suggestive of "Cash 47."

As my business was with the manager of this Great National Fancy Shop, I managed to push by the sad-eyed, eager-faced crowd of men and women in the anteroom, and entered the secretary's room, conscious of having left behind me a great deal of envy and uncharitableness of spirit. As I opened the door I heard a monotonous flow of Western speech which I thought I recognized. There was no mistaking it. It was the voice of Gashwiler.

"The appointment of this man, Mr. Secretary, would be most acceptable to the people in my deestrict. His family are wealthy and influential, and it 's just as well in the fall elections to have the supervisors and county judge pledged to support the administration. Our delegates to the State Central Committee are to a man" — but here, perceiving from the wandering eye of Mr. Secretary that there was another man in the room, he whispered the rest with a familiarity that must have required all the politician in the official's breast to keep from resenting.

"You have some papers, I suppose?" asked the secretary wearily.

Gashwiler was provided with a pocketful, and produced them. The secretary threw them on the table among the other papers, where they seemed instantly to lose their identity, and looked as if they were ready to recommend anybody but the person they belonged to. Indeed, in one corner the entire Massachusetts delegation, with the Supreme Bench at their head, appeared to be earnestly advocating the manuring of Iowa waste lands; and to the inexperienced eye, a noted female reformer had apparently appended her signature to a request for a pension for wounds received in battle.

"By the way," said the secretary, "I think I have a letter here from somebody in your district asking an appointment, and referring to you? Do you withdraw it?"

"If anybody has been presuming to speculate upon my patronage," said the Hon. Mr. Gashwiler with rising rage.

"I 've got the letter somewhere here," said the secretary, looking dazedly at his table. He made a feeble movement among the papers, and then sank back hopelessly in his chair, and gazed out of the window as if he thought and rather hoped it might have flown away. "It was from a Mr. Globbs, or Gobbs, or Dobbs, of Remus," he said finally, after a superhuman effort of memory.

"Oh, that 's nothing, — a foolish fellow who has been boring me for the last month."

"Then I am to understand that this application is withdrawn?"

"As far as my patronage is concerned, certainly. In fact, such an appointment would not express the sentiments — indeed, I may say, would be calculated to raise active opposition in the deestrict."

The secretary uttered a sigh of relief, and the gifted Gashwiler passed out. I tried to get a good look at the honorable scamp's eye, but he evidently did not recognize me.

It was a question in my mind whether I ought not to expose the treachery of Dobbs's friend, but the next time I met Dobbs he was in such good spirits that I forebore. It appeared that his wife had written to him that she had discovered a second cousin in the person of the Assistant Superintendent of the Envelope Flap Moistening Bureau of the Department of Tape, and had asked his assistance; and Dobbs had seen him, and he had promised it. "You see," said Dobbs, "in the performance of his duties he is often very near the person of the secretary, frequently in the next room, and he is a powerful man, sir, — a powerful man to know, sir, — a *very* powerful man."

How long this continued I do not remember. Long enough, however, for Dobbs to become quite seedy, for the giving up of wrist-cuffs, for the neglect of shoes and beard, and for great hollows to form round his eyes, and a slight flush on his cheek-bones. I remember meeting him in all the departments, writing letters or waiting patiently in ante-rooms from morning till night. He had lost all his old dogmatism, but not his pride. "I might as well be here as anywhere, while I 'm waiting," he said, "and then I 'm getting some knowledge of the details of official life."

In the face of this mystery I was surprised at finding a note from him one day, inviting me to dine with him at a certain famous restaurant. I had scarce got over my amazement, when the writer himself overtook me at my hotel. For a moment I scarcely recognized him. A new suit of fashionably-cut clothes had changed him, without, however, entirely concealing his rustic angularity of figure and outline. He even affected a fashionable dilettante air, but so mildly and so innocently that it was not offensive.

"You see," he began, explanatory-wise, "I 've just found out the way to do it. None of these big fellows, these cabinet officers, know me except as an applicant. Now, the way to do this thing is to meet 'em fust sociably; wine 'em and dine 'em. Why, sir" — he dropped into the schoolmaster again here — "I had two cabinet ministers, two judges, and a general at my table last night."

"On *your* invitation?"

"Dear, no! all I did was to pay for it. Tom Soufflet gave the dinner and invited the people. Everybody knows Tom. You see, a friend of mine put me up to it, and said that Soufflet had fixed up no end of appointments and jobs in that way. You see, when these gentlemen get sociable over their wine, he says, carelessly, 'By the way, there 's So-and-so — a good fellow — wants something; give it to him.' And the first thing you know, or they know, he gets a promise from them. They get a dinner — and a good one — and he gets an appointment."

"But where did you get the money?"

"Oh" — he hesitated — "I wrote home, and Fanny's father raised fifteen hundred dollars some way, and sent it to me. I put it down to political expenses." He laughed a weak foolish laugh here, and added, "As the old man don't drink nor smoke, he 'd lift his eyebrows to know how the money goes. But I'll make it all right when the office comes — and she 's coming, sure pop."

His slang fitted as poorly on him as his clothes, and his familiarity was worse than his former awkward shyness. But I could not help asking him what had been the result of this expenditure.

"Nothing just yet. But the Secretary of Tape and the man at the head of the Inferior Department, both spoke to me, and one of them said he thought he 'd heard my name before. He might," he added with a forced laugh, "for I 've written him fifteen letters."

Three months passed. A heavy snowstorm stayed my chariot wheels on a Western railroad, ten miles from a nervous lecture committee and a waiting audience; there was nothing to do but to make the attempt to reach them in a sleigh. But the way was long and the drifts deep; and when at last four miles out we reached a little village, the driver declared his cattle could hold out no longer, and we must stop there. Bribes and threats were equally of no avail. I had to accept the fact.

"What place is this?"

"Remus."

"Remus, Remus,"—where had I heard that name before? But while I was reflecting he drove up before the door of the tavern. It was a dismal, sleep-forbidding place, and only nine o'clock, and here was the long winter's night before me. Failing to get the landlord to give me a team to go farther, I resigned myself to my fate and a cigar, behind the red-hot stove.

In a few moments one of the loungers approached me, calling me by name, and in a rough but hearty fashion condoled me for my mishap, advising me to stay at Remus all night, and added:—

"The quarters ain't the best in the world yer at this hotel. But thar 's an old man yer—the preacher that was—that for twenty years hez taken in such fellers as you and lodged 'em free gratis for nothing, and hez been proud to do it. The old man used to be rich; he ain't so now; sold his big house on the cross-roads, and lives in a little cottage with his darter right over yan. But ye could n't do him a better turn than to go over thar and stay, and if he thought I 'd let ye go out o' Remus without axing ye, he 'd give me h—ll. Stop, I 'll go with ye."

I might at least call on the old man, and I accompanied my guide through the still falling snow until we reached a little cottage. The door opened to my guide's knock, and with the brief and discomposing introduction, "Yer, ole man, I've brought you one of them snowbound lecturers," he left me on the threshold, as my host, a kindly-faced, white-haired man of seventy, came forward to greet me.

His frankness and simple courtesy overcame the embarrassment left by my guide's introduction, and I followed him passively as he entered the neat but plainly furnished sitting-room. At the same moment a pretty but faded young woman arose from the sofa and was introduced to me as his daughter. "Fanny and I live here quite alone, and if you knew how good it was to see somebody from the great outside world now and then, you would not apologize for what you call your intrusion."

During this speech I was vaguely trying to recall where and when and under what circumstances I had ever before seen the village, the house, the old man, or his daughter. Was it in a dream, or in one of those dim reveries of some previous existence to which the spirit of mankind is subject? I looked at them again. In the careworn lines around the once pretty girlish mouth of the young woman, in the furrowed seams over the forehead of the old man, in the ticking of the old-fashioned clock on the shelf, in the faint whisper of the falling snow outside, I read the legend "Patience, Patience; Wait and Hope."

The old man filled a pipe, and offering me one, continued, "Although I seldom drink myself, it was my custom to always keep some nourishing liquor in my house for passing guests, but to-night I find myself without any." I hastened to offer him my flask, which, after a moment's coyness, he accepted, and presently under its benign influence at least ten years dropped from his shoulders, and he sat up in his chair erect and loquacious.

"And how are affairs at the national capital, sir?" he began.

Now, if there was any subject of which I was profoundly ignorant, it was this. But the old man was evidently bent on having a good political talk. So I said vaguely, yet with a certain sense of security, that I guessed there was n't much being done.

"I see," said the old man, "in the matters of resumption of the sovereign rights of States and federal interference, you would imply that a certain conservative policy is not to be promulgated until after the electoral committee have given their verdict." I looked for help towards the lady, and observed feebly that he had very clearly expressed my views.

The old man, observing my looks, said, "Although my daughter's husband holds a federal position in Washington, the pressure of his business is so great that he has little time to give us mere gossip — I beg your pardon, did you speak?"

I had unconsciously uttered an exclamation. This, then, was Remus, — the home of Expectant Dobbs, — and these his wife and father; and the Washington banquet-table, ah me! had sparkled with the yearning heart's blood of this poor wife, and had been upheld by this tottering Caryatid of a father.

"Do you know what position he has?"

The old man did not know positively, but thought it was some general supervising position. He had been assured by Mr. Gashwiler that it was a first-class clerkship; yes, a *first*-class.

I did not tell him that in this, as in many other official regulations in Washington, they reckoned backward, but said: —

"I suppose that your M. C., Mr. — Mr. Gashwiler" —

"Don't mention his name," said the little woman, rising to her feet hastily; "he never brought Expectant anything but disappointment and sorrow. I hate, I despise, the man."

"Dear Fanny," expostulated the old man gently, "this is unchristian and unjust. Mr. Gashwiler is a powerful, a very powerful man! His work is a great one; his time is preoccupied with weightier matters."

"His time was not so preoccupied but he could make use of poor Expectant," said this wounded dove a little spitefully.

Nevertheless it was some satisfaction to know that Dobbs had at last got a place, no matter how unimportant, or who had given it to him; and when I went to bed that night in the room that had been evidently prepared for their conjugal chamber, I felt that Dobbs's worst trials were over. The walls were hung with souvenirs of their ante-nuptial days. There was a portrait of Dobbs, ætat. 25; there was a faded bouquet in a glass case, presented by Dobbs to Fanny on examination-day; there was a framed resolution of thanks to Dobbs from the Remus Debating Society; there was a certificate of Dobbs's election as President of the Remus Philomathean Society; there was his commission as captain in the Remus Independent Contingent of Home Guards; there was a Freemason's chart, in which Dobbs was addressed in epithets more fulsome and extravagant than any living monarch. And yet all these cheap glories of a narrow life and narrower brain were upheld and made sacred by the love of the devoted priestess who worshiped at this homely shrine, and kept the light burning through gloom and doubt and despair. The storm tore round the house, and shook its white fists in the windows. A dried wreath of laurel that Fanny had placed on Dobbs's head after his celebrated centennial address at the schoolhouse, July 4, 1876, swayed in the gusts, and sent a few of its dead leaves down on the floor, and I lay in Dobbs's bed and wondered what a first-class clerkship was.

I found out early the next summer. I was strolling

through the long corridors of a certain great department, when I came upon a man accurately yoked across the shoulders, and supporting two huge pails of ice on either side, from which he was replenishing the pitchers in the various offices. As I passed I turned to look at him again. It was Dobbs!

He did not set down his burden; it was against the rules, he said. But he gossiped cheerily, said he was beginning at the foot of the ladder, but expected soon to climb up. That it was Civil Service Reform, and of course he would be promoted soon.

Had Gashwiler procured the appointment?

No. He believed it was *me*. *I* had told his story to Assistant-Secretary Blank, who had in turn related it to Bureau-Director Dash — both good fellows — but this was all they could do. Yes, it was a foothold. But he must go now.

Nevertheless I followed him up and down, and cheered him with a rose-colored picture of his wife and family, and my visit there, and promising to come and see him the next time I came to Washington, I left him with his self-imposed yoke.

With a new administration Civil Service Reform came in, crude and ill-digested, as all sudden and sweeping reforms must be; cruel to the individual, as all crude reforms will ever be; and among the list of helpless men and women, incapaciated for other work by long service in the dull routine of federal office who were decapitated, the weak, foolish, emaciated head of Expectant Dobbs went to the block. It afterwards appeared that the gifted Gashwiler was responsible for the appointment of twenty clerks, and that the letter of poor Dobbs, in which he dared to refer to the now powerless Gashwiler, had sealed his fate. The country made an example of Gashwiler and — Dobbs.

From that moment he disappeared. I looked for him

in vain in anterooms, lobbies, and hotel corridors, and finally came to the conclusion that he had gone home.

How beautiful was that July Sabbath, when the morning train from Baltimore rolled into the Washington depot! How tenderly and chastely the morning sunlight lay on the east front of the Capitol until the whole building was hushed in a grand and awful repose! How difficult it was to think of a Gashwiler creeping in and out of those enfiling columns, or crawling beneath that portico, without wondering that yon majestic figure came not down with flat of sword to smite the fat rotundity of the intruder! How difficult to think that parricidal hands have ever been lifted against the Great Mother, typified here in the graceful white chastity of her garments, in the noble tranquillity of her face, in the gathering up her white-robed children within her shadow!

This led me to think of Dobbs, when, suddenly, a face flashed by my carriage window. I called to the driver to stop, and, looking again, saw that it was a woman standing bewildered and irresolute on the street corner. As she turned her anxious face toward me I saw that it was Mrs. Dobbs.

What was she doing here, and where was Expectant?

She began an incoherent apology, and then burst into explanatory tears. When I had got her in the carriage she said, between her sobs, that Expectant had not returned; that she had received a letter from a friend here saying he was sick, — oh, very, very sick, — and father could not come with her, so she came alone. She was so frightened, so lonely, so miserable.

Had she his address?

Yes, just here! It was on the outskirts of Washington, near Georgetown. Then I would take her there, if I could, for she knew nobody.

On our way I tried to cheer her up by pointing out some of the children of the Great Mother before alluded to, but she only shut her eyes as we rolled down the long avenues, and murmured, "Oh, these cruel, cruel distances!"

At last we reached the locality, a negro quarter, yet clean and neat in appearance. I saw the poor girl shudder slightly as we stopped at the door of a low, two-story frame house, from which the unwonted spectacle of a carriage brought a crowd of half-naked children and a comely, cleanly, kind-faced mulatto woman.

Yes, this was the house. He was upstairs, rather poorly, but asleep, she thought.

We went upstairs. In the first chamber, clean, though poorly furnished, lay Dobbs. On a pine table near his bed were letters and memorials to the various departments, and on the bed-quilt, unfinished, but just as the weary fingers had relaxed their grasp upon it, lay a letter to the Tape Department.

As we entered the room he lifted himself on his elbow. "Fanny!" he said quickly, and a shade of disappointment crossed his face. "I thought it was a message from the secretary," he added apologetically.

The poor woman had suffered too much already to shrink from this last crushing blow. But she walked quietly to his side without a word or cry, knelt, placed her loving arms around him, and I left them so together.

When I called again in the evening he was better; so much better that, against the doctor's orders, he had talked to her quite cheerfully and hopefully for an hour, until suddenly raising her bowed head in his two hands, he said, "Do you know, dear, that in looking for help and influence there was One, dear, I had forgotten; One who is very potent with kings and councilors; and I think, love, I shall ask Him to interest Himself in my behalf. It is not too late yet, darling, and I shall seek him to-morrow."

And before the morrow came he had sought and found Him, and I doubt not got a good place.

WITH THE ENTREES

"ONCE, when I was a pirate" —

The speaker was an elderly gentleman in correct evening dress, the room a tasteful one, the company of infinite respectability, the locality at once fashionable and exclusive, the occasion an unexceptionable dinner. To this should be added that the speaker was also the host.

With these conditions self-evident, all that good breeding could do was to receive the statement with a vague smile that might pass for good-humored incredulity or courteous acceptation of a simple fact. Indeed, I think we all rather tried to convey the impression that our host, when he *was* a pirate — if he ever really was one — was all that a self-respecting pirate should be, and never violated the canons of good society. This idea was, to some extent, crystallized by the youngest Miss Jones in the exclamation, "Oh, how nice!"

"It was, of course, many years ago, when I was quite a lad."

We all murmured "Certainly," as if piracy were a natural expression of the exuberance of youth.

"I ought, perhaps, to explain the circumstances that led me into this way of life."

Here Legrande, a courteous attaché of the Patagonian legation, interposed in French and an excess of politeness, "that it was not of a necessity," a statement to which his English neighbor hurriedly responded, "Oui, oui."

"There ess a boke," he continued, in a well-bred, rapid whisper, "from Captain Canot — a Frenchman — most eenteresting — he was — oh, a fine man of education — and what you call a 'slavair;'" but here he was quietly nudged into respectful silence.

"I ran away from home," continued our host. He paused, and then added, appealingly, to the two distinguished foreigners present, "I do not know if I can make you understand that this is a peculiarly American predilection. The exodus of the younger males of an American family against the parents' wishes does not, with us, necessarily carry any obloquy with it. To the average American the prospect of fortune and a better condition lies *outside* of his home; with you the home means the estate, the succession of honors or titles, the surety that the conditions of life shall all be kept intact. With us the children who do not expect, and generally succeed, in improving the fortunes of the house, are marked exceptions. Do I make myself clear?"

The French-Patagonian attaché thought it was "charming and progressif." The Baron Von Pretzel thought he had noticed a movement of that kind in Germany, which was expressed in a single word of seventeen syllables. Viscount Piccadilly said to his neighbor: "That, you know now, the younger sons, don't you see, go to Australia, you know, in some beastly trade — stock-raising or sheep — you know; but, by Jove! them fellahs" —

"My father always treated me well," continued our host. "I shared equally with my brothers the privileges and limitations of our New England home. Nevertheless, I ran away and went to sea" —

"To see — what?" asked Legrande.

"Aller sur mer," said his neighbor hastily.

"Go on with your piracy!" said Miss Jones.

The distinguished foreigners looked at each other and then at Miss Jones. Each made a mental note of the average cold-blooded ferocity of the young American female.

"I shipped on board of a Liverpool 'liner,'" continued our host.

"What ess a 'liner'?" interrupted Legrande, sotto voce, to his next neighbor, who pretended not to hear him.

"I need not say that these were the days when we had not lost our carrying trade, when American bottoms" —

"Qu'est ce 'bot toom'?" said Legrande imploringly to his other friend.

"When American bottoms still carried the bulk of freight, and the supremacy of our flag" —

Here Legrande recognized a patriotic sentiment, and responded to it with wild republican enthusiasm, nodding his head violently. Piccadilly noticed it too, and, seeing an opening for some general discussion on free trade, began half audibly to *his* neighbor: "Most extraordinary thing, you know, your American statesmen" —

"I deserted the ship at Liverpool" —

But here two perfunctory listeners suddenly turned toward the other end of the table, where another guest, our Nevada Bonanza lion, was evidently in the full flood of pioneer anecdote and narration. Calmly disregarding the defection, he went on: —

"I deserted the ship at Liverpool in consequence of my ill-treatment by the second mate — a man selected for his position by reason of his superior physical strength and recognized brutality. I have been since told that he graduated from the state prison. On the second day out I saw him strike a man senseless with a belaying pin for some trifling breach of discipline. I saw him repeatedly beat and kick sick men" —

"Did you ever read Dana's 'Two Years Before the Mast'?" asked Lightbody, our heavy literary man, turning to *his* neighbor, in a distinctly audible whisper. "Ah! there's a book! Got all this sort of thing in it. Dev'lishly well written, too."

The Patagonian (alive for information): "Who ess this Dana, eh?"

His left-hand neighbor (shortly): "Oh, that man!"

His right-hand neighbor (curtly): "The fellow who wrote the Encyclopædia and edits the 'Sun,' that was put up in Boston for the English mission and did n't get it."

The Patagonian (making a mental diplomatic note of the fact that the severe discipline of the editor of the "Sun," one of America's profoundest scholars, while acting from patriotic motives as the second mate of an American "bottom," had unfitted him for diplomatic service abroad): "Ah, ciel!"

"I wandered on the quays for a day or two, until I was picked up by a Portuguese sailor, who, interesting himself in my story, offered to procure me a passage to Fayal and Lisbon, where, he assured me, I could find more comfortable and profitable means of returning to my own land. Let me say here that this man, although I knew him afterward as one of the most unscrupulous and heartless of pirates — in fact, the typical buccaneer of the books — was to me always kind, considerate, and, at times, even tender. He was a capital seaman. I give this evidence in favor of a much-ridiculed race, who have been able seamen for centuries."

"Did you ever read that Portuguese Guidebook?" asked Lightbody of his neighbor; "it 's the most exquisitely ridiculous thing" —

"Will the great American pirate kindly go on, or resume his original functions," said Miss Jones, over the table, with a significant look in the direction of Lightbody. But her anxiety was instantly misinterpreted by the polite and fair-play-loving Englishman: "I say, now, don't you know that the fact is these Portuguese fellahs are always ahead of us in the discovery business? Why, you know" —

"I shipped with him on a brig, ostensibly bound to St.

Kitts and a market. We had scarcely left port before I discovered the true character of the vessel. I will not terrify you with useless details. Enough that all that tradition and romance has given you of the pirate's life was ours. Happily, through the kindness of my Portuguese friend, I was kept from being an active participant in scenes of which I was an unwilling witness. But I must always bear my testimony to one fact. Our discipline, our esprit de corps, if I may so term it, was perfect. No benevolent society, no moral organization, was ever so personally self-sacrificing, so honestly loyal to one virtuous purpose, as we were to our one vice. The individual was always merged in the purpose. When our captain blew out the brains of our quartermaster, one day" —

"That reminds me — *did* you read of that Georgia murder?" began Lightbody; "it was in all the papers, I think. Oh, I beg pardon" —

"For simply interrupting him in a conversation with our second officer," continued our host quietly, "the act, although harsh and perhaps unnecessarily final, was, I think, indorsed by the crew. James, pass the champagne to Mr. Lightbody."

He paused a moment for the usual casual interruption, but even the active Legrande was silent.

Alas! from the other end of the table came the voice of the Bonanza man: —

"The rope was around her neck. Well, gentlemen, that Mexican woman standing there, with that crowd around her, eager for her blood, dern my skin! if she did n't call out to the sheriff to hold on a minit. And what fer? Ye can't guess! Why, one of them long braids she wore was under the noose, and kinder in the way. I remember her raising her hand to her neck and givin' a spiteful sort of jerk to the braid that fetched it outside the slipknot, and then saying to the sheriff:

'There, d—n ye, go on.' There was a sort o' thoughtfulness in the act, a kind o' keerless, easy way, that jist fetched the boys — even them thet hed the rope in their hands, and they" — (suddenly recognizing the silence): "Oh, beg pardon, old man; did n't know I 'd chipped into your yarn — heave ahead; don't mind me."

"What I am trying to tell you is this: One night, in the Caribbean Sea, we ran into one of the Leeward Islands, that had been in olden time a rendezvous for our ship. We were piloted to our anchorage outside by my Portuguese friend, who knew the locality thoroughly, and on whose dexterity and skill we placed the greatest reliance. If anything more had been necessary to fix this circumstance in my mind, it would have been the fact that two or three days before he had assured me that I should presently have the means of honorable discharge from the pirate's crew, and a return to my native land. A launch was sent from the ship to communicate with our friends on the island, who supplied us with stores, provisions, and general information. The launch was manned by eight men, and officered by the first mate, — a grim, Puritanical, practical New Englander, if I may use such a term to describe a pirate, of great courage, experience, and physical strength. My Portuguese friend, acting as pilot, prevailed upon them to allow me to accompany the party as coxswain. I was naturally anxious, you can readily comprehend, to see" —

"Certainly," "Of course," "Why should n't you?" went round the table.

"Two trustworthy men were sent ashore with instructions. We, meanwhile, lay off the low, palm-fringed beach, our crew lying on their oars, or giving way just enough to keep the boat's head to the breakers. The mate and myself sat in the stern-sheets, looking shoreward for the signal. The night was intensely black. Perhaps for this reason never before had I seen the phosphorescence of a tropical sea so strongly marked. From the great open beyond, luminous crests and plumes of pale fire lifted themselves, ghost-like, at our bows, sank, swept by us with long, shimmering, undulating trails, broke on the beach in silvery crescents, or shattered their brightness on the black rocks of the promontory. The whole vast sea shone and twinkled like another firmament, against which the figures of our men, sitting with their faces toward us, were outlined darkly. The grim, set features of our first mate, sitting beside me, were faintly illuminated. There was no sound but the whisper of passing waves against our lapstreak, and the low, murmuring conversation of the men. I had my face toward the shore. As I looked over the glimmering expanse, I suddenly heard the whispered name of our first mate. As suddenly, by the phosphorescent light that surrounded it, I saw the long trailing hair and gleaming shoulders of a woman floating beside us. Legrande, you are positively drinking nothing! Lightbody, you are shirking the Burgundy, — you used to like it!"

He paused, but no one spoke.

"I — let me see! where was I? Oh, yes! Well, I saw the woman, and when I turned to call the attention of the first mate to this fact, I knew instantly, by some strange instinct, that he had seen and heard her too. So, from that moment to the conclusion of our little drama, we were silent but enforced spectators.

"She swam gracefully — silently. I remember noticing through that odd, half-weird, phosphorescent light which broke over her shoulders as she rose and fell with each quiet stroke of her splendidly rounded arms, that she was a mature, perfectly-formed woman. I remember, also, that when she reached the boat, and, supporting herself with one small hand on the gunwale, softly called the

That was a capital story

mate in a whisper by his Christian name, I had a boyish idea that she was — the — er — er — female of his species — his — er natural wife! I 'm boring you — am I not?"

Two or three heads shook violently and negatively. The youngest, and, I regret to say, the *oldest*, Miss Jones uttered together sympathetically, "Go on — please; do!"

"The — woman told him in a few rapid words that he had been betrayed; that the two men sent ashore were now in the hands of the authorities; that a force was being organized to capture the vessel; that instant flight was necessary, and that the betrayer and traitor was — my friend, the Portuguese, Fernandez!

"The mate raised the dripping little brown hand to his lips, and whispered some undistinguishable words in her ear. I remember seeing her turn a look of ineffable love and happiness upon his grim, set face, and then she was gone. She dove as a duck dives, and I saw her shapely head, after a moment's suspense, reappear a cable's length away toward the shore.

"I ventured to raise my eyes to the mate's face; it was cold and impassive. I turned my face toward the crew; they were conversing in whispers with each other, with their faces toward us, yet apparently utterly oblivious of the scene that had just taken place in the stern. There was a moment of silence, and then the mate's voice came out quite impassively, but distinctly: —

"'Fernandez!'

"'Ay, ay, sir!'

"'Come aft and — bring your oar with you.

"He did so, stumbling over the men, who, engaged in their whispered yarns, did n't seem to notice him.

"'See if you can find soundings here.'

"Fernandez leaned over the stern and dropped his oar to its shaft in the phosphorescent water. But he touched no bottom; the current brought the oar at right angles presently to the surface.

"'Send it down, man,' said the mate imperatively; 'down, down. Reach over there. What are you afraid of? So; steady there; I'll hold you.'

"Fernandez leaned over the stern and sent the oar and half of his bared brown arm into the water. In an instant the mate caught him with one tremendous potential grip at his elbows, and forced him and his oar head downward in the waters. The act was so sudden, yet so carefully premeditated, that no outcry escaped the doomed man. Even the launch scarcely dipped her stern to the act. In that awful moment I heard a light laugh from one of the men in response to a wanton yarn from his comrade. James, bring the Vichy to Mr. Lightbody! You'll find that a dash of cognac will improve it wonderfully.

"Well — to go on — a few bubbles arose to the surface. Fernandez seemed unreasonably passive, until I saw that when the mate had gripped his elbows with his hands he had also firmly locked the traitor's knees within his own. In a few moments — it seemed to me, then, a century — the mate's grasp relaxed; the body of Fernandez, a mere limp, leaden mass, slipped noiselessly and heavily into the sea. There was no splash. The ocean took it calmly and quietly to its depths. The mate turned to the men, without deigning to cast a glance on me.

"'Oars!'

"The men raised their oars apeak.

"'Let fall!'

"There was a splash in the water, encircling the boat in concentric lines of molten silver.

"'Give way!'

"Well, of course, that's all! *We* got away in time. I knew I bored you awfully! Eh? Oh, you want to know what became of the woman — really, I don't know.

And myself — oh, I got away at Havana! Eh? Certainly; James, you'll find some smelling salts in my bureau. Gentlemen, I fear we have kept the ladies too long."

But they had already risen, and were slowly filing out of the room. Only one lingered, — the youngest Miss Jones.

"That was a capital story," she said, pausing beside our host, with a special significance in her usual audacity. "Do you know you absolutely sent cold chills down my spine a moment ago? Really, now, you ought to write for the magazines."

Our host looked up at the pretty, audacious face. Then he said sotto voce: —

"I do!"

THE ARGONAUTS OF NORTH LIBERTY

PART I

CHAPTER I

The bell of the North Liberty Second Presbyterian Church had just ceased ringing. North Liberty, Connecticut, never on any day a cheerful town, was always bleaker and more cheerless on the seventh, when the Sabbath sun, after vainly trying to coax a smile of reciprocal kindliness from the drawn curtains and half-closed shutters of the austere dwellings and the equally sealed and hard-set church-going faces of the people, at last settled down into a blank stare of stony astonishment. On this chilly March evening of the year 1850, that stare had kindled into an offended sunset and an angry night that furiously spat sleet and hail in the faces of the worshipers, and made them fight their way to the church, step by step, with bent heads and fiercely compressed lips, until they seemed to be carrying its forbidding portals at the point of their umbrellas.

Within that sacred but graceless edifice, the rigors of the hour and occasion reached their climax. The shivering gas jets lit up the austere pallor of the bare walls, and the hollow, shell-like sweep of colorless vacuity behind the cold communion table. The chill of despair and hopeless renunciation was in the air, untempered by any glow from the sealed air-tight stove that seemed only to bring out a lukewarm exhalation of wet clothes and cheaply dyed umbrellas. Nor did the presence of the worshipers themselves impart any life to the dreary apartment. Scattered throughout the white pews, in dull, shapeless, neutral blotches, rigidly separated from each other, they seemed only to accent the colorless church and the emptiness of all things. A few children, who had huddled together for warmth in one of the back benches and who had become glutinous and adherent through moisture, were laboriously drawn out and painfully picked apart by a watchful deacon.

The dry, monotonous disturbance of the bell had given way to the strain of a bass viol, that had been apparently pitched to the key of the east wind without, and the crude complaint of a new harmonium that seemed to bewail its limited prospect of ever becoming seasoned or mellowed in its earthly tabernacle, and then the singing began. Here and there a human voice soared and struggled above the narrow text and the monotonous cadence with a cry of individual longing, but was borne down by the dull, trampling precision of the others' formal chant. This and a certain muffled raking of the stove by the sexton brought the temperature down still lower. A sermon, in keeping with the previous performance, in which the chill east wind of doctrine was not tempered to any shorn lamb within that dreary fold, followed. A spark of human and vulgar interest was momentarily kindled by the collection and the simultaneous movement of reluctant hands towards their owners' pockets; but the coins fell on the baize-covered plates with a dull thud, like clods on a coffin, and the dreariness returned. Then there was another hymn and a prolonged moan from the harmonium, to which mysterious suggestion the congregation rose and began slowly to file into the aisle. For a moment they mingled; there was the silent grasping of damp woolen mittens and cold black gloves, and the whispered interchange of each other's names with the prefix of "Brother" or "Sister," and an utter absence of fraternal geniality, and then the meeting slowly dispersed.

The few who had waited until the minister had resumed his hat, overcoat, and overshoes, and accompanied him to the door, had already passed out; the sexton was turning out the flickering gas jets one by one, when the cold and austere silence was broken by a sound, — the unmistakable echo of a kiss of human passion.

As the horror-stricken official turned angrily, the figure of a man glided from the shadow of the stairs below the organ loft, and vanished through the open door. Before the sexton could follow, the figure of a woman slipped out of the same portal, and with a hurried glance after the first retreating figure, turned in the opposite direction and was lost in the darkness. By the time the indignant and scandalized custodian had reached the portal, they had both melted in the troubled sea of tossing umbrellas already to the right and left of him, and pursuit and recognition were hopeless.

CHAPTER II

The male figure, however, after mingling with his fellow-worshipers to the corner of the block, stopped a moment under the lamp-post as if uncertain as to the turning, but really to cast a long, scrutinizing look towards the scattered umbrellas now almost lost in the opposite direction. He was still gazing and apparently hesitating whether to retrace his steps, when a horse and buggy rapidly driven down the side street passed him. In a brief glance he evidently recognized the driver, and stepping over the curbstone called in a brief authoritative voice: —

"Ned!"

The occupant of the vehicle pulled up suddenly, leaned from the buggy, and said in an astonished tone: —

"Dick Demorest! Well! I declare! Hold on, and I 'll drive up to the curb."

"No; stay where you are."

The speaker approached the buggy, jumped in beside the occupant, refastened the apron, and coolly taking the reins from his companion's hand, started the horse forward. The action was that of an habitually imperious man; and the only recognition he made of the other's ownership was the question: —

"Where were you going?"

"Home — to see Joan," replied the other. "Just drove over from Warensboro Station. But what on earth are *you* doing here?"

Without answering the question, Demorest turned to his companion with the same good-natured, half humorous authority. "Let your wife wait; take a drive with me. I want to talk to you. She 'll be just as glad to see you an hour later, and it 's her fault if I can't come home with you now."

"I know it," returned his companion, in a tone of half-annoyed apology. "She still sticks to her old compact when we first married, that she should n't be obliged to receive my old worldly friends. And, see here, Dick, I thought I 'd talked her out of it as regards *you* at least, but Parson Thomas has been raking up all the old stories about you — you know that affair of the Fall River widow, and that breaking off of Garry Spofferth's match — and about your horse-racing — until — you know, she 's more set than ever against knowing you."

"That 's not a bad sort of horse you 've got there," interrupted Demorest, who usually conducted conversation without reference to alien topics suggested by others. "Where did you get him? He 's good yet for a spin down the turnpike and over the bridge. We 'll do it, and I 'll bring you home safely to Mrs. Blandford inside the hour."

Blandford knew little of horseflesh, but like all men he was not superior to this implied compliment to his knowledge. He resigned himself to his companion as he had been in the habit of doing, and Demorest hurried the horse at a rapid gait down the street until they left the lamps behind, and were fully on the dark turnpike. The sleet rattled against the hood and leathern apron of the buggy, gusts of fierce wind filled the vehicle and seemed to hold it back, but Demorest did not appear to mind it. Blandford thrust his hands deeply into his pockets for warmth, and contracted his shoulders as if in dogged patience. Yet, in spite of the fact that he was tired, cold, and anxious to see his wife, he was conscious of a secret satisfaction in submitting to the caprices of this old friend of his boyhood. After all, Dick Demorest knew what he was about, and had never led him astray by his autocratic will. It was safe to let Dick have his way. It was true it was generally Dick's own way; but he made others think it was theirs too, or would have been theirs had they had the will and the knowledge to project it. He looked up comfortably at the handsome, resolute profile of the man who had taken selfish possession of him. Many women had done the same.

"Suppose if you were to tell your wife I was going to reform," said Demorest, "it might be different, eh? She 'd want to take me into the church — 'another sinner saved,' and all that, eh?"

"No," said Blandford earnestly. "Joan is n't as rigid as all that, Dick. What she 's got against you is the common report of your free way of living, and that — come now, you know yourself, Dick, that is n't exactly the thing a woman brought up in her style can stand. Why, she thinks I 'm unregenerate, and — well, a man can't carry on business always like a class meeting. But are you thinking of reforming?" he continued, trying to get a glimpse of his companion's eyes.

"Perhaps. It depends. Now — there 's a woman I know" —

"What, another? and you call this going to reform?" interrupted Blandford, yet not without a certain curiosity in his manner.

"Yes; that 's just why I think of reforming. For this one is n't exactly like any other — at least as far as I know."

"That means you don't know anything about her."

"Wait, and I 'll tell you." He drew the reins tightly to accelerate the horse's speed, and, half turning to his companion, without, however, moving his eyes from the darkness before him, spoke quickly between the blasts: "I 've seen her only half a dozen times. Met her first in 6.40 train out from Boston last fall. She sat next to me. Covered up with wraps and veils; never looked twice at her. She spoke first — kind of half bold, half frightened way. Then got more comfortable and unwound herself, you know, and I saw she was young and not bad-looking. Thought she was some school-girl out for a lark — but rather new at it. Inexperienced, you know, but quite able to take care of herself, by George! and although she looked and acted as if she 'd never spoken to a stranger all her life, did n't mind the kind of stuff I talked to her. Rather encouraged it; and laughed — such a pretty little odd laugh, as if laughing was n't in her usual line, either, and she did n't know how to manage it. Well, it ended in her slipping out at one end of the car when we arrived, while I was looking out for a cab for her at the other." He stopped to recover from a stronger gust of wind. "I — I thought it a good joke on me, and let the thing drop out of my mind, although, mind you, she 'd promised to meet me a month afterwards at the same time and place. Well, when the day came I happened to be in Boston, and went to the station. Don't know why I went, for I did n't for a moment think she 'd keep her appointment. First, I could n't find her in the train, but after we 'd started she came along out of some seat in the corner, prettier than ever, holding out her hand." He drew a long inspiration. "You can bet your life, Ned, I did n't let go that little hand the rest of the journey."

His passion, or what passed for it, seemed to impart its warmth to the vehicle, and even stirred the chilled pulses of the man beside him.

"Well, who and what was she?"

"Did n't find out; don't know now. For the first thing she made me promise was not to follow her, nor to try to know her name. In return she said she would meet me again on another train near Hartford. She did — and again and again — but always on the train for about an hour, going or coming. Then she missed an appointment. I was regularly cut up, I tell you, and swore as she had n't kept her word, I would n't keep mine, and began to hunt for her. In the midst of it I saw her accidentally; no matter where; I followed her to — well, that 's no matter to you, either. Enough that I saw her again — and, well, Ned, such is the influence of that girl over me that, by George! she made me make the same promise again."

Blandford, a little disappointed at his friend's dogmatic suppression of certain material facts, shrugged his shoulders.

"If that 's all your story," he said, "I must say I see no prospect of your reforming. It 's the old thing over again, only this time you are evidently the victim. She 's some designing creature who will have you if she has n't already got you completely in her power."

"You don't know what you 're talking about, Ned, and you 'd better quit," returned Demorest, with cheerful authoritativeness. "I tell you that that 's the sort of girl I 'm going to marry, if I can, and settle down upon. You can make a memorandum of that, old man, if you like."

"Then I don't really see why you want to talk to *me* about it. And if you are thinking that such a story would go down for a moment with Joan as an evidence of your reformation, you 're completely out, Dick. Was that your idea?"

"Yes — and I can tell you, you 're wrong again, Ned. You don't know anything about women. You do just as I say — do you understand? — and don't interfere with your own wrong-headed opinions of what other people will think, and I 'll take the risks of Mrs. Blandford giving me good advice. Your wife has got a heap more sense on these subjects than you have, you bet. You just tell her that I want to marry the girl and want her to help me — that I mean business this time — and you 'll see how quick she 'll come down. That 's all I want of you. Will you or won't you?"

With an outward expression of skeptical consideration and an inward suspicion of the peculiar force of this man's dogmatic insight, Blandford assented, with, I fear, the mental reservation of telling the story to his wife in his own way. He was surprised when his friend suddenly drew the horse up sharply, and after a moment's pause began to back him, cramp the wheels of the buggy, and then skillfully, in the almost profound darkness, turn the vehicle and horse completely round to the opposite direction.

"Then you are not going over the bridge?" said Blandford.

Demorest made an imperative gesture of silence. The tumultuous rush and roar of swollen and rapid water came from the darkness behind them. "There 's been another break-out somewhere, and I reckon the bridge has got all it can do to-night to keep itself out of water without taking us over. At least, as I promised to set you down at your wife's door inside of the hour, I don't propose to try." As the horse now traveled more easily with the wind behind him, Demorest, dismissing abruptly all other subjects, laid his hand with brusque familiarity on his companion's knee, and as if the hour for social and confidential greeting had only just then arrived, said: "Well, Neddy, old boy, how are you getting on?"

"So, so," said Blandford dubiously. "You see," he began, argumentatively, "in my business there 's a good deal of competition, and I was only saying this morning" —

But either Demorest was already familiar with his friend's arguments, or had as usual exhausted his topic, for without paying the slightest attention to him, he again demanded abruptly, "Why don't you go to California? Here everything 's played out. That 's the country for a young man like you — just starting into life, and without incumbrances. If I was free and fixed in my family affairs like you I 'd go to-morrow."

There was such an occult positivism in Demorest's manner that for an instant Blandford, who had been married two years, and was transacting a steady and fairly profitable manufacturing business in the adjacent town, actually believed he was more fitted for adventurous speculation than the grimly erratic man of energetic impulses and pleasures beside him. He managed to stammer hesitatingly: —

"But there 's Joan — she" —

"Nonsense! Let her stay with her mother; you sell out your interest in the business, put the money into an assorted cargo, and clap it and yourself into the first ship out of Boston — and there you are. You 've been married going on two years now, and a little separation until you 've built up a business out there won't do either of you any harm."

Blandford, who was very much in love with his wife,

was not, however, above putting the onus of embarrassing affection upon *her*.

"You don't know Joan, Dick," he replied. "She 'd never consent to a separation, even for a short time."

"Try her. She 's a sensible woman — a deuced sight more than you are. You don't understand women, Ned. That 's what 's the matter with you."

It required all of Blandford's fond memories of his wife's conservative habits, Puritan practicality, religious domesticity, and strong family attachments, to withstand Demorest's dogmatic convictions. He smiled, however, with a certain complacency, as he also recalled the previous autumn when the first news of the California gold discovery had penetrated North Liberty, and he had expressed to her his belief that it would offer an outlet to Demorest's adventurous energy. She had received it with ill-disguised satisfaction, and the remark that if this exodus of Mammon cleared the community of the godless and unregenerate it would only be another proof of God's mysterious providence.

With the tumultuous wind at their backs it was not long before the buggy rattled once more over the cobblestones of the town. Under the direction of his friend, Demorest, who still retained possession of the reins, drove briskly down a side street of more pretentious dwellings, where Blandford lived. One or two wayfarers looked up.

"Not so fast, Dick."

"Why? I want to bring you up to your door in style."

"Yes — but — it 's Sunday. That 's my house, the corner one."

They had stopped before a square, two-storied brick house, with an equally square wooden porch supported by two plain, rigid wooden columns, and a hollow sweep of dull concavity above the door, evidently of the same architectural order as the church. There was no corner or projection to break the force of the wind that swept its smooth glacial surface; there was no indication of light or warmth behind its six closed windows.

"There seems to be nobody at home," said Demorest briefly. "Come along with me to the hotel."

"Joan sits in the back parlor, Sundays," explained the husband.

"Shall I drive round to the barn and leave the horse and buggy there while you go in?" continued Demorest good-humoredly, pointing to the stable gate at the side.

"No, thank you," returned Blandford, "it 's locked, and I 'll have to open it from the other side after I go in. The horse will stand until then. I think I 'll have to say good-night, now," he added, with a sudden half-ashamed consciousness of the forbidding aspect of the house, and his own inhospitality. "I 'm sorry I can't ask you in — but you understand why."

"All right," returned Demorest stoutly, turning up his coat-collar, and unfurling his umbrella. "The hotel is only four blocks away — you 'll find me there to-morrow morning if you call. But mind you tell your wife just what I told you — and no meandering of your own — you hear! She 'll strike out some idea with her woman's wits, you bet. Good-night, old man!" He reached out his hand, pressed Blandford's strongly and potentially, and strode down the street.

Blandford hitched his steaming horse to a sleet-covered horse block with a quick sigh of impatient sympathy over the animal and himself, and after fumbling in his pocket for a latchkey, opened the front door. A vista of well-ordered obscurity with shadowy trestle-like objects against the walls, and an odor of chill decorum, as if of a damp but respectable funeral, greeted him on entering. A faint light, like a cold dawn, broke through the glass pane of a door leading to the kitchen. Blandford paused in the mid-darkness and hesitated. Should he first go to his wife in the back parlor, or pass silently through the kitchen, open the back gate, and mercifully bestow his sweating beast in the stable? With the reflection that an immediate conjugal greeting, while his horse was still exposed to the fury of the blast in the street, would necessarily be curtailed and limited, he compromised by quickly passing through the kitchen into the stable yard, opening the gate, and driving horse and vehicle under the shed to await later and more thorough ministration. As he entered the back door, a faint hope that his wife might have heard him and would be waiting for him in the hall for an instant thrilled him; but he remembered it was Sunday, and that she was probably engaged in some devotional reading or exercise. He hesitatingly opened the back-parlor door with a consciousness of committing some unreasonable trespass, and entered.

She was there, sitting quietly before a large, round, shining centre-table, whose sterile emptiness was relieved only by a shaded lamp and a large black and gilt open volume. A single picture on the opposite wall — the portrait of an elderly gentleman stiffened over a corresponding volume, which he held in invincible mortmain in his rigid hand, and apparently defied posterity to take from him — seemed to offer a not uncongenial companionship. Yet the greenish light of the shade fell upon a young and pretty face, despite the color it extracted from it, and the hand that supported her low white forehead over which her full hair was simply parted, like a brown curtain, was slim and gentlewomanly. In spite of her plain lustreless silk dress, in spite of the formal frame of sombre heavy horsehair and mahogany furniture that seemed to set her off, she diffused an atmosphere of cleanly grace and prim refinement through the apartment. The priestess of this ascetic temple, the femininity of her closely covered arms, her pink ears, and a little serviceable morocco house-shoe that was visible lower down, resting on the carved lion's paw that upheld the centre-table, appeared to be only the more accented. And the precisely rounded but softly heaving bosom, that was pressed upon the edges of the open book of sermons before her, seemed to assert itself triumphantly over the rigors of the volume.

At least so her husband and lover thought, as he moved tenderly towards her. She met his first kiss on her forehead; the second, a supererogatory one, based on some supposed inefficiency in the first, fell upon a shining band of her hair, beside her neck. She reached up her slim hands, caught his wrists firmly, and, slightly putting him aside, said: —

"There, Edward!"

"I drove out from Warensboro, so as to get here to-night, as I have to return to the city on Tuesday. I thought it would give me a little more time with you, Joan," he said, looking around him, and at last hesitatingly drawing an apparently reluctant chair from its formal position at the window. The remembrance that he had ever dared to occupy the same chair with her now seemed hardly possible of credence.

"If it was a question of your traveling on the Lord's Day, Edward, I would rather you should have waited until to-morrow," she said, with slow precision.

"But — I — I thought I'd get here in time for the meeting," he said weakly.

"And instead, you have driven through the town, I suppose, where everybody will see you and talk about it. But," she added, raising her dark eyes suddenly to his, "where else have you been? The train gets into Warensboro at six, and it's only half an hour's drive from there. What have you been doing, Edward?"

It was scarcely a felicitous moment for the introduction of Demorest's name, and he would have avoided it. But he reflected that he had been seen, and he was naturally truthful.

"I met Dick Demorest near the church, and as he had something to tell me, we drove down the turnpike a little way — so as to be out of the town, you know, Joan — and — and" —

He stopped. Her face had taken upon itself that appalling and exasperating calmness of very good people who never get angry, but drive others to frenzy by the simple occlusion of an adamantine veil between their own feelings and their opponents'.

"I 'll tell you all about it after I 've put up the horse," he said hurriedly, glad to escape until the veil was lifted again. "I suppose the hired man is out."

"I should hope he was in church, Edward, but I trust *you* won't delay taking care of that poor dumb brute who has been obliged to minister to your and Mr. Demorest's Sabbath pleasures."

Blandford did not wait for a further suggestion. When the door had closed behind him, Mrs. Blandford went to the mantel-shelf, where a grimly allegorical clock cut down the hours and minutes of men with a scythe, and consulted it with a slight knitting of her pretty eyebrows. Then she fell into a vague abstraction, standing before the open book on the centre-table. Then she closed it with a snap, and methodically putting it exactly in the middle of the top of a black cabinet in the corner, lifted the shaded lamp in her hand and passed slowly with it up the stairs to her bedroom, where her light steps were heard moving to and fro. In a few moments she reappeared, stopping for a moment in the hall with the lighted lamp as if to watch and listen for her husband's return. Seen in that favorable light, her cheeks had caught a delicate color, and her dark eyes shone softly. Putting the lamp down in exactly the same place as before, she returned to the cabinet for the book, brought it again to the table, opened it at the page where she had placed her perforated cardboard book-marker, sat down beside it, and with her hands in her lap and her eyes on the page began abstractedly to tear a small piece of paper into tiny fragments. When she had reduced it to the smallest shreds, she scraped the pieces out of her silk lap and again collected them in the pink hollow of her little hand, kneeling down on the scrupulously well-swept carpet to peck up with a birdlike action of her thumb and forefinger an escaped atom here and there. These and the contents of her hand she poured into the chilly cavity of a sepulchral-looking alabaster vase that stood on the étagère. Returning to her old seat, and making a nest for her clasped fingers in the lap of her dress, she remained in that attitude, her shoulders a little narrowed and bent forward, until her husband returned.

"I 've lit the fire in the bedroom for you to change your clothes by," she said, as he entered; then evading the caress which this wifely attention provoked, by bending still more primly over her book, she added, "Go at once. You 're making everything quite damp here."

He returned in a few moments in his slippers and jacket, but evidently found the same difficulty in securing a conjugal and confidential contiguity to his wife. There was no apparent social centre or nucleus of comfort in the apartment; its fireplace, sealed by an iron ornament like a monumental tablet over dead ashes, had its functions superseded by an air-tight drum in the corner, warmed at second-hand from the dining-room below, and offered no attractive seclusion; the sofa against the wall was immovable and formally repellent. He was obliged to draw a chair beside the table, whose every curve seemed to facilitate his wife's easy withdrawal from side-by-side familiarity.

"Demorest has been urging me very strongly to go to California, but, of course, I spoke of you," he said, stealing his hand into his wife's lap, and possessing himself of her fingers.

Mrs. Blandford slowly lifted her fingers inclosed in his clasping hand and placed them in shameless publicity on the volume before her. This implied desecration was too much for Blandford; he withdrew his hand.

"Does that man propose to go with you?" asked Mrs. Blandford coldly.

"No; he 's preoccupied with other matters that he wanted me to talk to you about," said her husband hesitatingly. "He is" —

"Because," continued Mrs. Blandford in the same measured tone, "if he does not add his own evil company to his advice, it is the best he has ever given yet. I think he might have taken another day than the Lord's to talk about it, but we must not despise the means nor the hour whence the truth comes. Father wanted me to take some reasonable moment to prepare you to consider it seriously, and I thought of talking to you about it to morrow. He thinks it would be a very judicious plan. Even Deacon Truesdail" —

"Having sold his invoice of damaged sugar kettles for mining purposes, is converted," said Blandford, goaded into momentary testiness by his wife's unexpected acquiescence and a sudden recollection of Demorest's prophecy. "You have changed your opinion, Joan, since last fall, when you could n't bear to think of my leaving you," he added reproachfully.

"I could n't bear to think of your joining the mob of lawless and sinful men who use that as an excuse for leaving their wives and families. As for my own feelings, Edward, I have never allowed them to stand between me and what I believed best for our home and your Christian welfare. Though I have no cause to admire the influence that I find this man, Demorest, still holds over you, I am willing to acquiesce, as you see, in what he advises for your good. You can hardly reproach *me*, Edward, for worldly or selfish motives."

Blandford felt keenly the bitter truth of his wife's speech. For the moment he would gladly have exchanged it for a more illogical and selfish affection, but he reflected that he had married this religious girl for the security of an affection which he felt was not subject to the temptations of the world — or even its own weakness — as was too often the case with the giddy maidens whom he had known through Demorest's companionship. It was, therefore, more with a sense of recalling this distinctive quality of his wife than any loyalty to Demorest that he suddenly resolved to confide to her the latter's fatuous folly.

"I know it, dear," he said apologetically, "and we 'll talk it over to-morrow, and it may be possible to arrange it so that you shall go with me. But, speaking of Demorest, I think you don't quite do *him* justice. He really respects *your* feelings and your knowledge of right and wrong more than you imagine. I actually believe he came here to-night merely to get me to interest you in an extraordinary love affair of his. I mean, Joan," he added hastily, seeing the same look of dull repression come over her face, "I mean, Joan, — that is, you know, from all I can judge, — it is something really serious this time. He intends to reform. And this is because he has become violently smitten with a young woman whom he has only seen half a dozen times, at long intervals, whom he first met in a railway train, and whose name and residence he don't even know."

There was an ominous silence — so hushed that the ticking of the allegorical clock came like a grim monitor.

"Then," said Mrs. Blandford, in a hard, dry voice that

her alarmed husband scarcely recognized, "he proposed to insult your wife by taking her into his shameful confidence."

"Good heavens! Joan, no — you don't understand. At the worst, this is some virtuous but silly schoolgirl, who, though she may be intending only an innocent flirtation with him, has made this man actually and deeply in love with her. Yes; it is a fact, Joan. I know Dick Demorest, and if ever there was a man honestly in love, it is he."

"Then you mean to say that this man — an utter stranger to me — a man whom I've never laid my eyes on — whom I would n't know if I met in the street — expects me to advise him — to — to" — She stopped. Blandford could scarcely believe his senses. There were tears in her eyes, — this woman who never cried; her voice trembled, — she who had always controlled her emotions.

He took advantage of this odd but opportune melting. He placed his arm around her shoulders. She tried to escape it, but with a coy, shy movement, half hysterical, half girlish, unlike her usual stony, moral precision.

"Yes, Joan," he repeated laughingly, "but whose fault is it? Not *his*, remember! And I firmly believe he thinks you can do him good."

"But he has never seen me," she continued, with a nervous little laugh, "and probably considers me some old Gorgon — like — like — Sister Jemima Skerret."

Blandford smiled with the complacency of far-reaching masculine intuition. Ah! that shrewd fellow, Demorest, was right. Joan, dear Joan, was only a woman after all.

"Then he'll be the more agreeably astonished," he returned gayly, "and I think *you* will, too, Joan. For Dick is n't a bad-looking fellow; most women like him. It's true," he continued, much amused at the novelty of the perfectly natural toss and grimace with which Mrs. Blandford received this statement.

"I think he 's been pointed out to me somewhere," she said thoughtfully; "he 's a tall, dark, dissipated-looking man."

"Nothing of the kind," laughed her husband. "He 's middle-sized and as blond as your cousin Joe, only he 's got a long yellow mustache, and has a quick, abrupt way of talking. He is n't at all fancy-looking; you 'd take him for an energetic business man or a doctor, if you did n't know him. So you see, Joan, this correct little wife of mine has been a little, just a little prejudiced."

He drew her again gently backwards and nearer his seat, but she caught his wrists in her slim hands, and rising from the chair at the same moment, dexterously slipped from his embrace with her back towards him.

"I do not know why I should be unprejudiced by anything you 've told me," she said, sharply closing the book of sermons, and with her back still to her husband, reinstating it formally in its place on the cabinet. "It 's probably one of his many scandalous pursuits of defenseless and believing women, and he, no doubt, goes off to Boston, laughing at you for thinking him in earnest, and as ready to tell his story to anybody else and boast of his double deceit." Her voice had a touch of human asperity in it now, which he had never before noticed, but recognizing, as he thought, the human cause, it was far from exciting his displeasure.

"Wrong again, Joan; he 's waiting here at the Independence House for me to see him to-morrow," he returned cheerfully. "And I believe him so much in earnest that I would be ready to swear that not another person will ever know the story but you and I and he. No, it is a real thing with him; he 's dead in love, and it 's your duty as a Christian to help him."

There was a moment of silence. Mrs. Blandford remained by the cabinet, methodically arranging some small articles displaced by the return of the book.

"Well," she said suddenly, "you don't tell me what mother had to say. Of course, as you came home earlier than you expected, you had time to stop *there* — only four doors from this house."

"Well, no, Joan," replied Blandford, in awkward discomfiture. "You see I met Dick first, and then — then I hurried here to you — and — and — I clean forgot it. I 'm very sorry," he added dejectedly.

"And *I* more deeply so," she returned, with her previous bloodless moral precision, "for she probably knows by this time, Edward, why you have omitted your usual Sabbath visit, and with *whom* you were."

"But I can pull on my boots again and run in there for a moment," he suggested dubiously, "if you think it necessary. It won't take me a moment."

"No," she said positively; "it is so late now that your visit would only show it to be a second thought. I will go myself, — it will be a call for us both."

"But shall I go with you to the door? It is dark and sleeting," suggested Blandford eagerly.

"No," she replied peremptorily. "Stay where you are, and when Ezekiel and Bridget come in send them to bed, for *I* have made everything fast in the kitchen. Don't wait up for me."

She left the room, and in a few moments returned, wrapped from head to foot in an enormous plaid shawl. A white woollen scarf thrown over her bare brown head, and twice rolled around her neck, almost concealed her face from view. When she had parted from her husband, and reached the darkened hall below, she drew from beneath the folds of her shawl a thick blue veil, with which she completely enveloped her features. As she opened the front door and peered out into the night, her own husband would have scarcely recognized her.

With her head lowered against the keen wind she walked rapidly down the street and stopped for an instant at the door of the fourth house. Glancing quickly back at the house she had left and then at the closed windows of the one she had halted before, she gathered her skirts with one hand and sped away from both, never stopping until she reached the door of the Independence Hotel.

CHAPTER III

Mrs. Blandford entered the side door boldly. Luckily for her, the austerities of the Sabbath were manifest even here; the bar-room was closed, and the usual loungers in the passages were absent. Without risking the recognition of her voice in an inquiry to the clerk, she slipped past the office, still muffled in her veil, and quickly mounted the narrow staircase. For an instant she hesitated before the public parlor, and glanced dubiously along the half-lit corridor. Chance befriended her; the door of a bedroom opened at that moment, and Richard Demorest, with his overcoat and hat on, stepped out in the hall.

With a quick and nervous gesture of her hand she beckoned him to approach. He came towards her leisurely, with an amused curiosity that suddenly changed to utter astonishment as she hurriedly lifted her veil, dropped it, turned, and glided down the staircase into the street again. He followed rapidly, but did not overtake her until she had reached the corner, when she slackened her pace an instant for him to join her.

"Lulu," he said eagerly; "is it you?"

"Not a word here," she said breathlessly. "Follow me at a distance."

She started forward again in the direction of her own house. He followed her at a sufficient interval to keep her faintly distinguishable figure in sight until she had crossed three streets, and near the end of the next block glided up the steps of a house not far from the one where he remembered to have left Blandford. As he joined her, she had just succeeded in opening the door with a pass-key, and was awaiting him. With a gesture of silence she took his hand in her cold fingers, and leading him softly through the dark hall and passage, quickly entered the kitchen. Here she lit a candle, turned, and faced him. He could see that the outside shutters were bolted, and the kitchen evidently closed for the night.

As she removed the veil from her face he made a movement as if to regain her hand again, but she drew it away.

"You have forced this upon me," she said hurriedly, "and it may be ruin to us both. Why have you betrayed me?"

"Betrayed you, Lulu — Good God! what do you mean?"

She looked him full in the eye, and then said slowly, "Do you mean to say that you have told no one of our meetings?"

"Only one — my old friend Blandford, who lives — Ah, yes! I see it now. You are neighbors. He has betrayed me. This house is" —

"My father's!" she replied boldly.

The momentary uneasiness passed from Demorest's resolute face. His old self-sufficiency returned.

"Good," he said, with a frank laugh, "that will do for me. Open the door there, Lulu, and take me to him. I 'm not ashamed of anything I 've done, my girl, nor need you be. I 'll tell him my real name is Dick Demorest, as I ought to have told you before, and that I want to marry you, fairly and squarely, and let him make the conditions.

I 'm not a vagabond nor a thief, Lulu, if I have met you on the sly. Come, dear, let us end this now. Come" —

But she had thrown herself before him and placed her hand upon his lips.

"Hush! are you mad? Listen to me, I tell you — please — oh, do — no you must not!" He had covered her hand with kisses and was drawing her face towards his own. "No — not again, it was wrong then, it is monstrous now. I implore you, listen; if you love me, stop."

He released her. She sank into a chair by the kitchen-table, and buried her flushed face in her hands.

He stood for a moment motionless before her.

"Lulu, if that is your name," he said slowly but gently, "tell me all now. Be frank with me, and trust me. If there is anything stands in the way, let me know what it is and I can overcome it. If it is my telling Ned Blandford, don't let that worry you, he 's as loyal a fellow as ever breathed, and I 'm a dog to ever think he willingly betrayed us. His wife, well, she 's one of those pious saints — but no, she would not be such a cursed hypocrite and bigot as this."

"Hush, I tell you! *Will* you hush," she said, in a frantic whisper, springing to her feet and grasping him convulsively by the lapels of his overcoat. "Not a word more, or I 'll kill myself. Listen! Do you know what I brought you here for? why I left my — this house and dragged you out of your hotel? Well, it was to tell you that you must leave me, leave *here* — go out of this house and out of this town at once, to-night! And never look on it or me again! There! you have said we must end this now. It is ended, as only it could and ever would end. And if you open that door except to go, or if you attempt to — to touch me again, I 'll do something desperate. There!"

She threw him off again and stepped back, strangely

beautiful in the loosened shackles of her long repressed human emotion. It was as if the passion-rent robes of the priestess had laid bare the flesh of the woman dazzling and victorious. Demorest was fascinated and frightened.

"Then you do not love me," he said with a constrained smile, "and I am a fool?"

"Love you!" she repeated. "Love you," she continued, bowing her brown head over her hanging arms and clasped hands, "what then has brought me to this? Oh," she said suddenly, again seizing him by his two arms, and holding him from her with a half-prudish, half-passionate gesture, "why could you not have left things as they were; why could we not have met in the same old way we used to meet, when I was so foolish and so happy? Why could you spoil that one dream I have clung to? Why did n't you leave me those few days of my wretched life when I was weak, silly, vain, but not the unhappy woman I am now. You were satisfied to sit beside me and talk to me then. You respected my secret, my reserve. My God! I used to think you loved me as I loved you — for *that!* Why did you break your promise and follow me here? I believed you the first day we met, when you said there was no wrong in my listening to you; that it should go no further; that you would never seek to renew it without my consent. You tell me I don't love you, and I tell you now that we must part, that, frightened as I was, foolish as I was, that day was the first day I had ever lived and felt as other women live and feel. If I ran away from you then it was because I was running away from my old self too. Don't you understand me? Could you not have trusted me as I trusted you?"

"I broke my promise only when you broke yours. When you would not meet me I followed you here, because I loved you."

"And that is why you must leave me now," she said,

starting from his outstretched arms again. "Do not ask me why, but go, I implore you. You must leave this town to-night; to-morrow will be too late."

He cast a hurried glance around him, as if seeking to gather some reason for this mysterious haste, or a clue for future identification. He saw only the Sabbath-sealed cupboards, the cold white china on the dresser, and the flicker of the candle on the partly-opened glass transom above the door.

"As you wish," he said, with quiet sadness. "I will go now, and leave the town to-night; but"—his voice struck its old imperative note—"this shall not end here, Lulu. There will be a next time, and I am bound to win you yet, in spite of all and everything."

She looked at him with a half-frightened, half-hysterical light in her eyes.

"God knows!"

"And you will be frank with me then, and tell me all?"

"Yes, yes, another time; but go now."

She had extinguished the candle, turned the handle of the door noiselessly, and was holding it open. A faint light stole through the dark passage. She drew back hastily.

"You have left the front door open," she said in a frightened voice.

"I thought you had shut it behind me," he returned quickly. "Good-night."

He drew her towards him. She resisted slightly. They were for an instant clasped in a passionate embrace; then there was a sudden collapse of the light and a dull jar. The front door had swung to.

With a desperate bound she darted into the passage and through the hall, dragging him by the hand, and threw the front door open. Without, the street was silent and empty.

"Go," she whispered frantically.

Demorest passed quickly down the steps and disappeared. At the same moment a voice came from the banisters of the landing above.

"Who 's there?"

"It 's I, mother."

"I thought so. And it 's like Edward to bring you and sneak off in that fashion."

Mrs. Blandford gave a quick sigh of relief. Demorest's flight had been mistaken for her husband's habitual evasion. Knowing that her mother would not refer to the subject again, she did not reply, but slowly mounted the dark staircase with an assumption of more than usual hesitating precaution, in order to recover her equanimity.

The clocks were striking eleven when she left her mother's house and reëntered her own. She was surprised to find a light burning in the kitchen, and Ezekiel, their hired man, awaiting her in a dominant and nasal key of religious and practical disapprobation.

"Pity you were n't tu hum afore, ma'am, considerin' the doin's that 's goin' on in perfessed Christians' houses arter meetin' on the Sabbath Day."

"What 's the difficulty now, Ezekiel?" said Mrs. Blandford, who had regained her rigorous precision once more under the decorous security of her own roof.

"Wa'al, here comes an entire stranger axin' for Squire Blandford. And when I tells he war n't tu hum" —

"Not at home?" interrupted Mrs. Blandford, with a slight start. "I left him here."

"Mebbee so, but folks nowadays don't 'pear to keer much whether they break the Sabbath or not, trapsen' raound town in and arter meetin' hours, ez if 't wor gin'ral trainin' day — and hez gone out agin."

"Go on," said Mrs. Blandford curtly

"Wa'al, the stranger sez, sez he, 'Show me the way to the stables,' sez he, and without takin' no for an answer, ups and meanders through the hall, outer the kitchen inter the yard, ez if he was justice of the peace; and when he gets there he sez, 'Fetch out his hoss and harness up, and be blamed quick about it, and tell Ned Blandford that Dick Demorest hez got to leave town to-night, and ez ther ain't a blamed puritanical shadbelly in this hull town ez would let a hoss go on hire Sunday night, he guesses he 'll hev to borry his.' And afore I could say Jack Robinson, he tackles the hoss up and drives outer the yard, flinging this two-dollar-and-a-half-piece behind him ez if I wur a Virginia slave and he was John C. Calhoun hisself. I 'd a chucked it after him if it had n't been the Lord's Day, and it mout hev provoked disturbance."

"Mr. Demorest is worldly, but one of Edward's old friends," said Mrs. Blandford, with a slight kindling of her eyes, "and he would not have refused to aid him in what might be an errand of grace or necessity. You can keep the money, Ezekiel, as a gift, not as a wage. And go to bed. I will sit up for Mr. Blandford."

She passed out and up the staircase into her bedroom, pausing on her way to glance into the empty back parlor and take the lamp from the table. Here she noticed that her husband had evidently changed his clothes again and taken a heavier overcoat from the closet. Removing her own wraps she again descended to the lower apartment, brought out the volume of sermons, placed it and the lamp in the old position, and with her abstracted eyes on the page fell into her former attitude. Every suggestion of the passionate, half-frenzied woman in the kitchen of the house only four doors away had vanished; one would scarcely believe she had ever stirred from the chair in which she had formally received her husband two hours before. And yet she was thinking of herself and Demorest in that kitchen.

His prompt and decisive response to her appeal, as shown in this last bold and characteristic action, relieved, while it half piqued her. But the overruling destiny which had enabled her to bring him from his hotel to her mother's house unnoticed, had protected them while there, had arrested a dangerous meeting between him and herself and her husband in her own house, impressed her more than all. It imparted to her a hideous tranquillity born of the doctrines of her youth — Predestination! She reflected with secret exultation that her moral resolution to fly from him and her conscientiously broken promise had been the direct means of bringing him there; that step by step circumstances not in themselves evil or to be combated had led her along; that even her husband and mother had felt it their duty to assist towards this fateful climax! If Edward had never kept up his worldly friendship, if she had never been restricted and compassed in her own; if she had ever known the freedom of other girls, — all this might not have happened. She had been elected to share with Demorest and her husband the effects of their ungodliness. She was no longer a free agent; what availed her resolutions? To Demorest's imperious hope, she had said, "God knows." What more could she say? Her small red lips grew white and compressed; her face rigid, her eyes hollow and abstracted; she looked like the genius of asceticism as she sat there, grimly formulating a dogmatic explanation of her lawless and unlicensed passion.

The wind had risen to a gale without, and stirred even the sealed sepulchre of the fireplace with dull rumblings and muffled moans. At times the hot-air drum in the corner seemed to expand as with some pent-up emotion. Strange currents of air crossed the empty room like the passage of unseen spirits, and she even fancied she heard whispers at the window. This caused her to rise and open it, when she found that the sleet had given way to a dry feathery snow that was swarming through the slits of the shutter; a faint reflection from the already whitened fences glimmered in the panes. She shut the window hastily, with a little shiver of cold. Where was Demorest in this storm? Would it stop him? She thought with pride now of the dominant energy that had frightened her, and knew it would not. But her husband? — what kept him? It was twelve o'clock; he had seldom stayed out so late before. During the first half-hour of her reflections she had been relieved by his absence; she had even believed that he had met Demorest in the town, and was not alarmed by it, for she knew that the latter would avoid any further confidence, and cut short any return to it. But why had not Edward returned? For an instant the terrible thought that something had happened, and that they might both return together, took possession of her, and she trembled. But no; Demorest, who had already taken such extreme measures, could not consistently listen to any suggestion for delay. As her only danger lay in Demorest's presence, the absence of her husband caused her more undefinable uneasiness than actual alarm.

The room had become cold with the dying out of the dining-room fire that warmed the drum. She would go to bed. She nevertheless arranged the room again with a singular impression that she was doing it for the last time in her present existing circumstances, and placing the lamp on the table in the hall, went up to her own room. By the light of a single candle she undressed herself hastily, said her prayers punctiliously, and got into bed, with an unexpected relief at finding herself still occupying it alone. Then she fell asleep and dreamed of Demorest.

CHAPTER IV

When Edward Blandford found himself alone after his wife had undertaken to fulfill his abandoned filial duty at her parents' house, he felt a slight twinge of self-reproach. He could not deny that this was not the first time he had evaded the sterile Sabbath evenings at his mother-in-law's, or that even at other times he was not in accord with the cold and colorless sanctity of the family. Yet he remembered that when he picked out from the budding womanhood of North Liberty this pure scentless blossom, he had endured the privations of its surroundings with a sense of security in inhaling the atmosphere in which it grew, and knowing the integrity of its descent. There was a certain pleasure also in invading this seclusion with human passion; the first pressure of her hand when they were kneeling together at family prayers had the zest without the sin of a forbidden pleasure; the first kiss he had given her with their heads over the family Bible had fairly intoxicated him in the thin, rarefied air of their surroundings. In transplanting this blossom to his own home with the fond belief that it would eventually borrow the hues and color of his own passion, he had no further interest in the house he had left behind. When he found, however, that the ancestral influence was stronger than he expected, that the young wife, instead of assimilating to his conditions, had imported into their little household the rigors of her youthful home, he had been chilled and disappointed. But he could not help also remembering that his own boyhood had been spent in an atmosphere like her own in everything but its sincerity and deep conviction. His father had recognized the business value of placating the narrow tyranny of the respectable well-to-do religious community, and had become a conscious hypocrite and a popular citizen. He had himself been under that influence, and it was partly a conviction of this that had drawn him towards her as something genuine and real. It occurred to him now for the first time, as he looked around upon that compromise of their two lives in this chilly artificial home, that it was only natural that she would prefer the more truthful austerities of her mother's house. Had she detected the sham, and did she despise him for it?

These were questions which seemed to bring another self-accusing doubt in his own mind, although, without his being conscious of it, they had been really the outcome of that doubt. He could not help dwelling on the singular human interest she had taken in Demorest's love affair, and the utterly unexpected emotion she had shown. He had never seen her as charmingly illogical, capricious, and bewitchingly feminine. Had he not made a radical mistake in not giving her a frequent provocation for this innocent emotion, — in fact, in not taking her out into a world of broader sympathies and experiences? What a household they might have had, — if necessary in some other town, — away from those cramped prejudices and limitations! What friends she might have been with Dick and his other worldly acquaintances; what social pleasures — guiltless amusements for her pure mind — in theatres, parties, and concerts! Would she have objected to them? — had he ever seriously proposed them to her? No! if she had objected there would have been time enough to have made this present compromise; she would have at least respected and understood his sacrifice — and his friends.

Even the artificial externals of his household had never before so visibly impressed him. Now that she was no longer in the room it did not even bear a trace of her habitation; it certainly bore no suggestion of his own. Why had he bought that hideous horsehair furniture? To remind her of the old provincial heirlooms of her father's sitting-room. Did it remind her of it? The stiff and stony emptiness of this room had been fashioned upon the decorous respectability of his own father's parlor, — in which his father, who usually spent his slippered leisure in the family sitting-room, never entered except on visits from the minister. It had chilled his own youthful soul; why had he perpetuated it here?

He could only answer these questions by moodily wandering about the house, and regretting he had not gone with her. After a vain attempt to establish social and domestic relations with the hot-air drum by putting his feet upon it, — after an equally futile attempt to extract interest from the book of sermons by opening its pages at random, — he glanced at the clock and suddenly resolved to go and fetch her. It would remind him of the old times when he used to accompany her from church, and, after her parents had retired, spend a blissful half-hour alone with her. With what a mingling of fear and childish curiosity she used to accept his equally timid caresses! Yes, he would go and fetch her; and he would recall it to her in a whisper while they were there. Filled with this idea, when he changed his clothes again he put on a certain heavy beaver overcoat, on whose shaggy sleeve her little hand had so often rested when he escorted her from meeting; and he even selected the gray muffler she had knit for him in the old antenuptial days. It was lying in the half-opened drawer from where she had not long before taken her disguising veil.

It was still blowing in sudden, capricious gusts; and when he opened the front door the wind charged fiercely upon him, as if to drive him back. When he had finally forced his way into the street, a return current closed the door as suddenly and sharply behind him as if it had ejected him from his home forever.

He reached the fourth house quickly, and as quickly

ran up the steps; his hand was upon the bell when his eye suddenly caught sight of his wife's pass-key still in the lock. She had evidently forgotten it. Here was a chance to mischievously banter that habitually careful little woman! He slipped it into his pocket and quietly entered the dark but perfectly familiar hall. He reached the staircase without a stumble and began to ascend softly. Halfway up he heard the sound of his wife's hurried voice and another that startled him. He ascended hastily two steps, which brought him to the level of the half-opened transom of the kitchen. A candle was burning on the kitchen table; he could see everything that passed in the room; he could hear distinctly every word that was uttered.

He did not utter a cry or sound; he did not even tremble. He remained so rigid and motionless, clutching the banisters with his stiffened fingers, that when he did attempt to move, all life, as well as all that had made life possible to him, seemed to have died from him forever. There was no nervous illusion, no dimming of his senses; he saw everything with a hideous clarity of perception. By some diabolical instantaneous photography of the brain, little actions, peculiarities, touches of gesture, expression and attitude never before noted by him in his wife, were clearly fixed and bitten in his consciousness. He saw the color of his friend's overcoat, the reddish tinge of his wife's brown hair, till then unnoticed; in that supreme moment he was aware of a sudden likeness to her mother; but more terrible than all, there seemed to be a nameless sympathetic resemblance that the guilty pair had to each other in gesture and movement as of some unhallowed relationship beyond his ken. He knew not how long he stood there without breath, without reflection, without one connected thought. He saw her suddenly put her hand on the handle of the door. He knew that in another moment they would pass almost before him. He made a convulsive effort to move, with an inward cry to God for support, and succeeded in staggering with outstretched palms against the wall, down the staircase, and blindly forward through the hall to the front door. As yet he had been able to formulate only one idea, — to escape before them, for it seemed to him that their contact meant the ruin of them both, of that house, of all that was near to him, — a catastrophe that struck blindly at his whole visible world. He had reached the door and opened it at the moment that the handle of the kitchen door was turned. He mechanically fell back behind the open door that hid him, while it let the cruel light glimmer for a moment on their clasped figures. The door slipped from his nerveless fingers and swung to with a dull sound. Crouching still in the corner, he heard the quick rush of hurrying feet in the darkness, saw the door open and Demorest glide out, — saw her glance hurriedly after him, close the door, and involve herself and him in the blackness of the hall. Her dress almost touched him in his corner; he could feel the near scent of her clothes, and the air stirred by her figure retreating towards the stairs; could hear the unlocking of a door above and the voice of her mother from the landing, his wife's reply, the slow fading of her footsteps on the stairs and overhead, the closing of a door, and all was quiet again. Still stooping, he groped for the handle of the door, opened it, and the next moment reeled like a drunken man down the steps into the street.

It was well for him that a fierce onset of wind and sleet at that instant caught him savagely, — stirred his stagnated blood into action, and beat thought once more into his brain. He had mechanically turned towards his own home; his first effort of recovering will hurried him furiously past it and into a side street. He walked rapidly but undeviatingly on to escape observation and secure some solitude for his returning thoughts. Almost before he knew it he was in the open fields.

The idea of vengeance had never crossed his mind. He was neither a physical nor a moral coward, but he had never felt the merely animal fury of disputed animal possession which the world has chosen to recognize as a proof of outraged sentiment, nor had North Liberty accepted the ethics that an exchange of shots equalized a transferred affection. His love had been too pure and too real to be moved like the beasts of the field, to seek in one brutal passion compensation for another. Killing — what was there to kill? All that he had to live for had been already slain. With the love that was in him — in them — already dead at his feet, what was it to him whether these two hollow lives moved on and passed him, or mingled their emptiness elsewhere. Only let them henceforth keep out of his way!

For in his first feverish flow of thought — the reaction to his benumbed will within and the beating sleet without — he believed Demorest as treacherous as his wife. He recalled his sudden and unexpected intrusion into the buggy only a few hours before, his mysterious confidences, his assurance of Joan's favorable reception of his secret, and her consent to the Californian trip. What had all this meant if not that Demorest was using him, the husband, to assist his intrigue, and carry the news of his presence in the town to her? And this boldness, this assurance, this audacity of conception was like Demorest! While only certain passages of the guilty meeting he had just seen and overheard were distinctly impressed on his mind, he remembered now, with hideous and terrible clearness, all that had gone before. It was part of the disturbed and unequal exaltation of his faculties that he dwelt more upon this and his wife's previous deceit and manifest hypocrisy, than upon the actual evidence he had witnessed of her unfaithfulness. The corroboration of the fact was stronger to him than the fact itself. He understood the coldness, the uncongeniality now ; the simulated increase of her aversion to Demorest; her journeys to Boston and Hartford to see her relatives; her acquiescence to his frequent absences; not an incident, not a characteristic of her married life was inconsistent with her guilt and her deceit. He went even back to her maidenhood: how did he know this was not the legitimate sequence of other secret schoolgirl escapades. The bitter worldly light that had been forced upon his simple ingenuous nature had dazzled and blinded him. He passed from fatuous credulity to equally fatuous distrust.

He stopped suddenly with the roaring of water before him. In the furious following of his rapid thought through storm and darkness he had come, he knew not how, upon the bank of the swollen river, whose endangered bridge Demorest had turned from that evening. A few steps more and he would have fallen into it. He drew nearer and looked at it with vague curiosity. Had he come there with any definite intention? The thought sobered without frightening him. There was always *that* culmination possible, and to be considered coolly.

He turned and began to retrace his steps. On his way thither he had been fighting the elements step by step; now they seemed to him to have taken possession of him and were hurrying him quickly away. But where? and to what? He was always thinking of the past. He had wandered he knew not how long, always thinking of that. It was the future he had to consider. What was to be done?

He had heard of such cases before; he had read of them in newspapers and talked of them with cold curiosity. But they were of worldly, sinful people, of dissolute men whose characters he could not conceive, — of silly, vain, frivolous, and abandoned women whom he had never even met. But Joan — O God! It was the first time since his mute prayer on the staircase that the Divine name had been wrested from his lips. It came with his wife's — and his first tears! But the wind swept the one away and dried the others upon his hot cheeks.

It had ceased to rain, and the wind, which was still high, had shifted more to the north and was bitterly cold. He could feel the roadway stiffening under his feet. When he reached the pavement of the outskirts once more he was obliged to take the middle of the street, to avoid the treacherous films of ice that were beginning to glaze the sidewalks. Yet this very inclemency, added to the usual Sabbath seclusion, had left the streets deserted. He was obliged to proceed more slowly, but he met no one and could pursue his bewildering thoughts unchecked. As he passed between the lines of cold, colorless houses, from which all light and life had vanished, it seemed to him that their occupants were dead as his love, or had fled their ruined houses as he had. Why should he remain? Yet what was his duty now as a man, — as a Christian? His eye fell on the hideous façade of the church he was passing, — her church! He gave a bitter laugh and stumbled on again.

With one of the gusts he fancied he heard a familiar sound, — the rattling of buggy wheels over the stiffening road. Or was it merely the fanciful echo of an idea that only at that moment sprang up in his mind? If it was real it came from the street parallel with the one he was in. Who could be driving out at this time? what other buggy than his own could be found to desecrate this Christian Sabbath? An irresistible thought impelled him at the risk of recognition to quicken his pace and turn the corner as Richard Demorest drove up to the Independence Hotel, sprang from his buggy, throwing the reins over the dashboard, and disappeared into the hotel!

Blandford stood still, but for an instant only. He had been wandering for an hour aimlessly, hopelessly, without consecutive idea, coherent thought, or plan of action; without the faintest inspiration or suggestion of escape from his bewildering torment, without — he had begun to fear — even the power to conceive or the will to execute; when a wild idea flashed upon him with the rattle of his buggy wheels. And even as Demorest disappeared into the hotel, he had conceived his plan and executed it. He crossed the street swiftly, leaped into his buggy, lifted the reins and brought down the whip simultaneously, and the next instant was dashing down the street in the direction of the Warensboro turnpike. So sudden was the action that by the time the astonished hall porter had rushed into the street, horse and buggy had already vanished in the darkness.

Presently it began to snow; so lightly at first, that it seemed a mere passing whisper to the ear, the brush of some viewless insect upon the cheek, or the soft tap of unseen fingers on the shoulders. But by the time the porter returned from his hopeless and invisible chase of the "runaway," he came in out of a swarming cloud of whirling flakes, blinded and whitened. There was a hurried consultation with the landlord, the exhibition of much imperious energy and some bank-notes from Demorest, and with a glance at the clock that marked the expiring limit of the Puritan Sabbath, the landlord at last consented. By the time the falling snow had muffled the street from the indiscreet clamor of Sabbath-breaking hoofs, the landlord's noiseless sledge was at the door and Demorest had departed.

The snow fell all that night; with fierce gusts of wind that moaned in the chimneys of North Liberty and sorely troubled the Sabbath sleep of its decorous citizens; with deep passionless silences, none the less fateful, that softly precipitated a spotless mantle of merciful obliteration equally over their precise or their straying footprints, that would have done them good to heed and to remember; and when morning broke upon a world of week-day labor, it was covered as far as their eyes could reach as with a clear and unwritten tablet, on which they might record their lives anew. Near the wreck of the broken bridge on the Warensboro turnpike an overturned buggy lay imbedded in the drift and débris of the river hurrying silently towards the sea, and a horse with fragments of broken and icy harness still clinging to him was found standing before the stable-door of Edward Blandford. But to any further knowledge of the fate of its owner North Liberty awoke never again.

PART II

CHAPTER I

THE last note of the Angelus had just rung out of the crumbling fissures in the tower of the mission chapel of San Buenaventura. The sun, which had beamed that day and indeed every day for the whole dry season over the red-tiled roofs of that old and happily ventured pueblo, seemed to broaden to a smile as it dipped below the horizon, as if in undiminished enjoyment of its old practical joke of suddenly plunging the Southern California coast in darkness without any preliminary twilight. The olive and fig trees at once lost their characteristic outlines in formless masses of shadow; only the twisted trunks of the old pear-trees in the mission garden retained their grotesque shapes and became gruesome in the gathering gloom. The encircling pines beyond closed up their serried files; a cool breeze swept down from the coast range, and, passing through them, sent their day-long heated spices through the town.

If there was any truth in the local belief that the pious incantation of the Angelus bell had the power of excluding all evil influence abroad at that perilous hour within its audible radius, and comfortably keeping all unbelieving wickedness at a distance, it was presumably ineffective as regarded the innovating stagecoach from Monterey that twice a week at that hour brought its question-asking, revolver-persuading, and fortune-seeking load of passengers through the sleepy Spanish town. On the night of the 3d of August, 1856, it had not only brought but set down at the posada one of those passengers. It was a Mr. Ezekiel Corwin, formerly known to these pages as "hired man" to the late Squire Blandford, of North Liberty, Connecticut, but now a shrewd, practical, self-sufficient, and self-asserting unit of the more cautious later Californian immigration. As the stage rattled away again with more or less humorous and open disparagement of the town and the posada from its "outsiders," he lounged with lazy but systematic deliberation towards Mateo Morez, the proprietor.

"I guess that some of your folks here could n't direct me to Dick Demorest's house, could ye?"

The Señor Mateo Morez was at once perplexed and pained. Pained at the ignorance thus forced upon him by a caballero; perplexed as to its intention. Between the two he smiled apologetically but gravely, and said, "No sabe, señor. I 'ave not understood."

"No more hev I," returned Ezekiel, with patronizing recognition of his obtuseness. "I guess ez heow you ain't much on American. You folks orter learn the language if you kalkilate to keep a hotel."

But the momentary vision of a waistless woman with a shawl gathered over her head and shoulders at the back door attracted his attention. She said something to Mateo in Spanish, and the yellowish white of Mateo's eyes glistened with intelligent comprehension.

"Ah, posiblemente; it is Don Ricardo Demorest you wish?"

Mr. Ezekiel's face and manner expressed a mingling of grateful curiosity and some scorn at the discovery.

"Wa'al," he said, looking around as if to take the entire posada into his confidence, "way up in North Liberty, where I kem from, he was allus known as Dick Demorest, and did n't tack any forrin titles to his name. Et would n't hev gone down there, I reckon, 'mongst free-born Merikin citizens, no more 'n *aliases* would in court — and I kinder guess for the same reason. But folks get peart and sassy when they 're way from hum, and put on ez many airs as a buck nigger. And so he calls hisself Don Ricardo here, does he?"

"The señor knows Don Ricardo?" said Mateo politely.

"Ef you mean me — wa'al, yes — I should say so. He was a partiklar friend of a man I 've known since he was knee-high to a grasshopper."

Ezekiel had actually never seen Demorest but once in his life. He would have scorned to lie, but strict accuracy was not essential with an ignorant foreign audience. He took up his carpetbag.

"I reckon I kin find his house, ef it 's anyway handy."

But the Señor Mateo was again politely troubled. The house of Don Ricardo was of a truth not more than a mile distant. It was even possible that the señor had observed it above a wall and vineyard as he came into the pueblo. But it was late — it was also dark, as the señor would himself perceive — and there was still to-morrow. To-morrow — ah, it was always there! Meanwhile there were beds of a miraculous quality at the posada, and a supper such as a caballero might order in his own house. Health, discretion, solicitude for one's self — all pointed clearly to to-morrow.

What part of this speech Ezekiel understood affected him only as an innkeeper's bid for custom, and as such to be steadily exposed and disposed of. With the remark that he guessed Dick Demorest's was "a good enough hotel for *him*," and that he 'd better be "getting along there," he walked down the steps, carpetbag in hand, and coolly departed, leaving Mateo pained, but smiling, on the door-step.

"An animal with a pig's head — without doubt," said Mateo sententiously.

"Clearly a brigand with the liver of a chicken," responded his wife.

The subject of this ambiguous criticism, happily oblivious, meantime walked doggedly back along the road the stagecoach had just brought him. It was badly paved and hollowed in the middle with the worn ruts of a century of slow undeviating ox-carts, and the passage of water during the rainy season. The low adobe houses on each side, with bright cinnamon-colored tiles relieving their dark brown walls, had the regular outlines of their doors and windows obliterated by the crumbling of years, until they looked as if they had been after-thoughts of the builder, rudely opened by pick and crowbar, and finished by the gentle auxiliary architecture of birds and squirrels. Yet these openings at times permitted glimpses of a picturesque past in the occasional view of a lace-edged pillow or silken counterpane, striped hangings, or dyed Indian rugs, the flitting of a flounced petticoat or flower-covered head, or the indolent leaning figure framed in a doorway of a man in wide velvet trousers and crimson-barred serape, whose brown face was partly hidden in a yellow nimbus of cigarette smoke. Even in the semi-darkness, Ezekiel's penetrating and impertinent eyes took eager note of these facts with superior complacency, quite unmindful, after the fashion of most critical travelers, of the hideous contrast of his own long shapeless nankeen duster, his stiff half-clerical brown straw hat, his wisp of gingham necktie, his dusty boots, his outrageous carpetbag, and his struggling goat-like beard. A few looked at him in grave, discreet wonder. Whether they recognized in him the advent of a civilization that was destined to supplant their own ignorant, sensuous, colorful life with austere intelligence and rigid practical improvement, did not appear. He walked steadily on. As he passed the low arched door of the mission church and saw a faint light glimmering from the side windows, he had indeed a weak human desire to go in and oppose in his own person a debased and idolatrous superstition with some happily chosen question that would necessarily make the officiating priest and his congregation exceedingly uncomfortable. But he resisted; partly in the hope of meeting some idolater on his way to Benediction, and, in the guise of a stranger seeking information, dropping a few unpalatable truths; and partly because he could unbosom himself later to Demorest, who he was not unwilling to believe had embraced Popery with his adoption of a Spanish surname and title.

It had become quite dark when he reached the long wall that inclosed Demorest's premises. The wall itself excited his resentment, not only as indicating an exclusiveness highly objectionable in a man who had emigrated from a free State, but because he, Ezekiel Corwin, had difficulty in discovering the entrance. When he succeeded, he found himself before an iron gate, happily open, but savoring offensively of feudalism and tyrannical proprietorship, and passed through and entered an avenue of trees scarcely distinguishable in the darkness, whose mysterious shapes and feathery plumes were unknown to him. Numberless odors equally vague and mysterious were heavy in the air; strange and delicate plants rose dimly on either hand; enormous blossoms, like ghostly faces, seemed to peer at him from the shadows. For an instant Ezekiel succumbed to an unprofitable sense of beauty, and acquiesced in this reckless extravagance of Nature that was so unlike North Liberty. But the next moment he recovered himself, with the reflection that it was probably unhealthy, and doggedly approached the house. It was a long, one-storied structure, apparently all roof, vine, and pillared veranda. Every window and door was open; the two or three grass hammocks swung emptily between the columns; the bamboo chairs and settees were vacant; his heavy footsteps on the floor had summoned no attendant; not even a dog had barked as he approached the house. It was shiftless, it was sinful, — it boded no good to the future of Demorest.

He put down his carpetbag on the veranda and entered the broad hall, where an old-fashioned lantern was burning on a stand. Here, too, the doors of the various apartments were open, and the rooms themselves empty of occupants. An opportunity not to be lost by Ezekiel's inquiring mind thus offered itself. He took the lantern and deliberately examined the several apartments, the furniture, the bedding, and even the small articles that were on the tables and mantles. When he had completed the round — including a corridor opening on a dark courtyard, which he did not penetrate — he returned to the hall, and set down the lantern again.

"Well," said a voice in his own familiar vernacular, "I hope you like it."

Ezekiel was surprised, but not disconcerted. What he had taken in the shadow for a bundle of serapes lying on the floor of the veranda, was the recumbent figure of a man who now raised himself to a sitting posture.

"Ez to that," drawled Ezekiel, with unshaken self-possession, "whether I like it or not ez only a question betwixt kempany manners and truth-telling. Beggars had n't oughter be choosers, and transient visitors like myself need n't allus speak their mind. But if you mean to signify that with every door and window open and universal shiftlessness lying round everywhere temptin' Providence, you ain't lucky in havin' a feller-citizen of yours drop in on ye instead of some Mexican thief, I don't agree with ye — that 's all."

The man laughed shortly and rose up. In spite of his careless yet picturesque Mexican dress, Ezekiel instantly recognized Demorest. With his usual instincts he was naturally pleased to observe that he looked older and more careworn. The softer, sensuous climate had perhaps imparted a heaviness to his figure and a deliberation to his manner that was quite unlike his own potential energy.

"That don't tell me who you are, and what you want," he said coldly.

"Wa'al then, I'm Ezekiel Corwin of North Liberty, ez used to live with my friend and *yours* too, I guess — seein' how the friendship was swapped into relationship — Squire Blandford."

A slight shade passed over Demorest's face.

"Well," he said impatiently, "I don't remember you; what then?"

"You don't remember me; that's likely," returned Ezekiel imperturbably, combing his straggling chin beard with three fingers, "but whether it's *nat'ral* or not, considerin' the sukumstances when we last met, ez a matter of op-pinion. You got me to harness up the hoss and buggy the night Squire Blandford left home, and never was heard of again. It's true that it kem out on inquiry that the hoss and buggy ran away from the hotel, and that you had to go out to Warensboro in a sleigh, and the theory is that poor Squire Blandford must have stopped the hoss and buggy somewhere, got in and got run away agin, and pitched over the bridge. But seein' your relationship to both Squire and Mrs. Blandford, and all the sukumstances, I reckoned you'd remember it."

"I heard of it in Boston a month afterwards," said Demorest dryly, "but I don't think I'd have recognized you. So you were the hired man who gave me the buggy. Well, I don't suppose they discharged you for it."

"No," said Ezekiel, with undisturbed equanimity. "I kalkilate Joan would have stopped that. Considerin', too, that I knew her when she was Deacon Salisbury's darter, and our fam'lies waz thick az peas. She knew me well enough when I met her in 'Frisco the other day."

"Have you seen Mrs. Demorest already?" said Demorest, with sudden vivacity. "Why did n't you say so before?" It was wonderful how quickly his face had lighted up with an earnestness that was not, however, without some undefinable uneasiness. The alert Ezekiel noticed it and observed that it was as totally unlike the irresistible dominance of the man of five years ago as it was different from the heavy abstraction of the man of five minutes before.

"I reckon you did n't ax me," he returned coolly. "She told me where you were, and as I had business down this way she guessed I might drop in."

"Yes, yes — it 's all right, Mr. Corwin; glad you did," said Demorest kindly but half nervously. "And you saw Mrs. Demorest? Where did you see her, and how did you think she was looking? As pretty as ever, eh?"

But the coldly literal Ezekiel was not to be beguiled into polite or ambiguous fiction. He even went to the extent of insulting deliberation before he replied: —

"I 've seen Joan Salisbury lookin' healthier, and ez far ez I kin judge doin' more credit to her stock and raisin' gin'rally," he said, thoughtfully combing his beard; "and I 've seen her when she was too poor to get the silks and satins, furbelows, fineries, and vanities she 's flauntin' in now, and that was in Squire Blandford's time, too, I reckon. Ez to her purtiness, that 's a matter of taste. You think her purty, and I guess them fellows ez was escortin' and squirin' her round 'Frisco thought so too, or *she* thought they did to hev allowed it."

"You are not very merciful to your townsfolk, Mr. Corwin," said Demorest, with a forced smile; "but what can I do for you?"

It was the turn for Ezekiel's face to brighten, or rather to break up, like a cold passionless mirror suddenly cracked, into various amusing but distorted reflections on the person before him.

"Townies ain't to be fooled by other townies, Mr. Demorest; at least that ain't my idea o' marcy, he-he! But see'n' you 're pressin', I don't mind tellen you *my* business. I 'm the only agent of Seventeen Patent Medicine Proprietors in Connecticut represented by the firm of Dilworth & Dusenberry, of San Francisco. Mebbe you heard of 'em afore — A 1 druggists and importers. Wa'al, I 'm openin' a field for 'em and spreadin' 'em gin'rally through these air benighted and onhealthy districts, havin' the contract for the hull State — especially for Wozun's Universal Injin Panacea ez cures everything — bein' had from a recipe given by a sachem to Dr. Wozun's gran'ther. That bag — leavin' out a dozen paper collars and socks — is all the rest samples. That 's me, Ezekiel Corwin — only agent for Californy, and that 's my mission."

"Very well; but look here, Corwin," said Demorest, with a slight return of his old off-hand manner, "I 'd advise you to adopt a little more caution, and a little less criticism in your speech to the people about here, or I 'm afraid you 'll need the Universal Panacea for yourself. Better men than you have been shot in my presence for half your freedom."

"I guess you 've just hit the bull's-eye there," replied Ezekiel coolly, "for it 's that *half* freedom and *half* truth that does n't pay. I kalkilate gin'rally to speak my hull mind — and I *do*. Wot 's the consequence? Why, when folks find I ain't afeard to speak my mind on their affairs, they kinder guess I 'm tellin' the truth about my own. Folks don't like the man that truckles to 'em, whether it 's in the sellin' of a box of pills or a principle. When they re-cognize Ezekiel Corwin ain't goin' to lie about 'em to curry favor with 'em, they 're ready to believe he ain't goin' to lie about Jones' Bitters, or Wozun's Panacea. And, wa'al, I 've been on the road just about a fortnit, and I have n't yet discovered that the original independent style introduced by Ezekiel Corwin ever broke anybody's bones or did n't pay."

And he told the truth. That remarkably unfair and unpleasant spoken man had actually frozen Hanley's Ford into icy astonishment at his audacity, and he had sold them an invoice of the Panacea before they had recovered; he had insulted Chipitas into giving an extensive order in bitters; he had left Hayward's Creek pledged to Burne's pills — with drawn revolvers still in their hands.

At another time Demorest might have been amused at his guest's audacity, or have combated it with his old imperiousness, but he only remained looking at him in a dull sort of way as if yielding to his influence. It was part of the phenomenon that the two men seemed to have changed character since they last met, and when Ezekiel said confidentially, "I reckon you 're goin' to show me what room I ken stow these duds o' mine in," Demorest replied hurriedly, "Yes, certainly," and taking up his guest's carpetbag preceded him through the hall to one of the apartments.

"I 'll send Manuel to you presently," he said, putting down the bag mechanically; "the servants are not back from church, it 's some saint's festival to-day."

"And so you keep a pack of lazy idolaters to leave your house to take care of itself, whilst they worship graven images," said Ezekiel, delighted at this opportunity to improve the occasion.

"If my memory is n't bad, Mr. Corwin," said Demorest dryly, "when I accompanied Mr. Blandford home the night he returned from his journey, we found *you* at church, and he had to put up his horse himself."

"But that was the Sabbath — the seventh day of the command," retorted Ezekiel.

"And here the Sabbath does n't consist of only *one* day to serve God in," said Demorest sententiously.

Ezekiel glanced under his white lashes at Demorest's thoughtful face. His fondest fears appeared to be confirmed; Demorest had evidently become a Papist. But that gentleman stopped any theological discussion by the abrupt inquiry: —

"Did Mrs. Demorest say when she thought of returning?"

"She allowed she mout kem to-morrow — but" — added Ezekiel dubiously.

"But what."

"Wa'al, wot with her enjyments of the vanities of this life and the kempany she keeps, I reckon she 's in no hurry," said Ezekiel cheerfully.

The entrance of Manuel here cut short any response from Demorest, who after a few directions in Spanish to the peon, left his guest to himself.

He walked to the veranda with the same dull preoccupation that Ezekiel had noticed as so different from his old decisive manner, and remained for a few moments abstractedly gazing into the dark garden. The strange and mystic shapes which had impressed even the practical Ezekiel had become even more weird and ghost-like in the faint radiance of a rising moon.

What memories evoked by his rude guest seemed to take form and outline in that dreamy and unreal expanse!

He saw his wife again, standing as she had stood that night in her mother's house, with the white muffler around her head, and white face, imploring him to fly; he saw himself again hurrying through the driving storm to Warensboro, and reaching the train that bore him swiftly and safely miles away — that same night when her husband was perishing in the swollen river. He remembered with what strangely mingled sensations he had read the account of Blandford's death in the newspapers, and how the loss of his old friend was forgotten in the associations conjured up by his singular meeting that very night with the mysterious woman he had loved. He remembered that he had never dreamed how near and fateful were these associations; and how he had kept his promise not to seek her without her permission, until six months after, when she appointed a meeting, and revealed to him the whole truth. He could see her now, as he had seen her then, more beautiful and fascinating than ever in her black dress, and the pensive grace of refined suffering and restrained passion in her delicate face. He remembered, too, how the shock of her disclosure, — the knowledge that she had been his old friend's wife, seemed only to accent her purity and suffering and his own willful recklessness, and how it had stirred all the chivalry, generosity, and affection of his easy nature to take the whole responsibility of this innocent but compromising intrigue on his own shoulders. He had had no self-accusing sense of disloyalty to Blandford in his practical nature; he had never suspected the shy, proper girl of being his wife; he was willing to believe now, that had he known it, even that night, he would never have seen her again; he had been very foolish; he had made this poor woman participate in his folly; but he had never been dishonest or treacherous in thought or action. If Blandford had lived, even he would have admitted it. Yet, he was guiltily conscious of a material satisfaction in Blandford's death, without his wife's religious conviction of the saving graces of predestination.

They had been married quietly when the two years of her widowhood had expired; his former relations with her husband and the straitened circumstances in which Blandford's death had left her having been deemed sufficient excuse in the eyes of North Liberty for her more worldly union. They had come to California at her suggestion "to begin life anew," for she had not hesitated to make this dislocation of all her antecedent surroundings a reason as well as a condition of this marriage. She wished to see the world of which he had been a passing glimpse; to expand under his protection beyond the limits of her fettered youth. He had bought this old Spanish estate, with its near vineyard and its outlying leagues covered with wild cattle, partly from that strange contradictory predilection for peaceful husbandry common to men who have led a roving life, and partly as a check to her growing and feverish desire for change and excitement. He had at first enjoyed with an almost parental affection her childish unsophisticated delight in that world he had already wearied of, and which he had been prepared to gladly resign for her. But as the months and even years had passed without any apparent diminution in her zest for these pleasures, he tried uneasily to resume his old interest in them, and spent ten months with her in the chaotic freedom of San Francisco hotel life. But to his discomfiture he found that they no longer diverted him; to his horror he discovered that those easy gallantries in which he had spent his youth, and in which he had seen no harm, were intolerable when exhibited to his wife, and he trembled between inquietude and indignation at the copies of his former self whom he met in hotel parlors, at theatres, and in public conveyances. The next time she visited some friends in San Francisco he did not accompany her. Though he fondly cherished his experience of her power to resist even stronger temptation, he was too practical to subject himself to the annoyance of witnessing it. In her absence he trusted her completely; his scant imagination conjured up no disturbing picture of possibilities beyond what he actually knew. In his recent questions of Ezekiel he did not expect to learn anything more. Even his guest's uncomfortable comments added no sting that he had not already felt.

With these thoughts called up by the unlooked-for

advent of Ezekiel under his roof, he continued to gaze moodily into the garden. Near the house were scattered several uncouth varieties of cacti which seemed to have lost all semblance of vegetable growth, and had taken rude likeness to beasts and human figures. One high-shouldered specimen, partly hidden in the shadow, had the appearance of a man with a cloak or serape thrown over his left shoulder. As Demorest's wandering eyes at last became fixed upon it, he fancied he could trace the faint outlines of a pale face, the lower part of which was hidden by the folds of the serape. There certainly was the forehead, the curve of the dark eyebrows, the shadow of a nose, and even, as he looked more steadily, a glistening of the eyes upturned to the moonlight. A sudden chill seized him. It was a horrible fancy, but it looked as might have looked the dead face of Edward Blandford! He started and ran quickly down the steps of the veranda. A slight wind at the same moment moved the long leaves and tendrils of a vine nearest him and sent a faint wave through the garden. He reached the cactus; its fantastic bulk stood plainly before him, but nothing more.

"Whar are ye runnin' to?" said the inquiring voice of Ezekiel from the veranda.

"I thought I saw some one in the garden," returned Demorest quietly, satisfied of the illusion of his senses, "but it was a mistake."

"It mout, and it mout n't," said Ezekiel dryly. "Thar 's nothin' to keep any one out. It 's only a wonder that you ain't overrun with thieves and sich like."

"There are usually servants about the place," said Demorest carelessly.

"Ef they 're the same breed ez that Manuel, I reckon I 'd almost as leave take my chances in the road. Ef it 's all the same to you I kalkilate to put a paytent fastener to my door and winder to-night. I allus travel with them."

Seeing that Demorest only shrugged his shoulders without replying, he continued, "Et ain't far from here that some folks allow is the headquarters of that cattle-stealing gang. The driver of the coach went ez far ez to say that some of these high and mighty Dons hereabouts knows more of it than they keer to tell."

"That 's simply a yarn for greenhorns," said Demorest contemptuously. "I know all the ranch proprietors for twenty leagues around, and they 've lost as many cattle and horses as I have."

"I wanter know," said Ezekiel, with grim interest. "Then you 've already had consid'ble losses, eh? I kalkilate them cattle are vallyble — about wot figger do you reckon yer out and injured?"

"Three or four thousand dollars, I suppose, altogether," replied Demorest shortly.

"Then you don't take any stock in them yer yarns about the gang being run and protected by some first-class men in 'Frisco?" said Ezekiel regretfully.

"Not much," responded Demorest dryly; "but if people choose to believe this bluff gotten up by the petty thieves themselves to increase their importance and secure their immunity — they can. But here 's Manuel to tell us supper is ready."

He led the way to the corridor and courtyard which Ezekiel had not penetrated on account of its obscurity and solitude, but which now seemed to be peopled with peons and household servants of both sexes. At the end of a long low-ceilinged room a table was spread with omelettes, chupa, cakes, chocolate, grapes, and melons, around which half a dozen attendants stood gravely in waiting. The size of the room, which to Ezekiel's eyes looked as large as the church at North Liberty, the profusion of the viands, the six attendants for the host and solitary guest, deeply impressed him. Morally rebelling against this feudal display and extravagance, he, who had disdained to even assist the Blandfords' servant in waiting at table and had always made his solitary meal on the kitchen dresser, was not above feeling a material satisfaction in sitting on equal terms with his master's friend and being served by these menials he despised. He did full justice to the victuals of which Demorest partook in sparing abstraction, and particularly to the fruit, which Demorest did not touch at all. Observant of his servants' eyes fixed in wonder on the strange guest who had just disposed of a second melon at supper, Demorest could not help remarking that he would lose credit as a *medico* with the natives unless he restrained a public exhibition of his tastes.

"Ez ha-aw?" queried Ezekiel.

"They have a proverb here that fruit is gold in the morning, silver at noon, and lead at night."

"That 'll do for lazy stomicks," said the unabashed Ezekiel. "When they 're once fortified by Jones' bitters and hard work, they 'll be able to tackle the Lord's nat'ral gifts of the airth at any time."

Declining the cigarettes offered him by Demorest for a quid of tobacco, which he gravely took from a tin box in his pocket, and to the astonished eyes of the servants apparently obliterated any further remembrance of the meal, he accompanied his host to the veranda again, where, tilting his chair back and putting his feet on the railing, he gave himself up to unwonted and silent rumination.

The silence was broken at last by Demorest, who, half reclining on a settee, had once or twice glanced towards the misshapen cactus.

"Was there any trace discovered of Blandford, other than we knew before we left the States?"

"Wa'al, no," said Ezekiel thoughtfully. "The last idea was that he 'd got control of the hoss after passin' the bridge, and had managed to turn him back, for there was marks of buggy wheels on the snow on the far side, and that, fearin' to trust the hoss on the bridge, he tried to lead him over, when the bridge gave way, and he was caught in the wreck and carried off down stream. That would account for his body not bein' found; they do tell that chunks of that bridge were picked up on the Sound beach near the mouth o' the river, nigh unto sixty miles away. That 's about the last idea they had of it at North Liberty." He paused, and then, cleverly directing a stream of tobacco juice at an accurate curve over the railing, wiped his lips with the back of his hand, and added, slowly, "Thar 's another idea — but I reckon it 's only mine. Leastways I ain't heard it argued by anybody."

"What is that?" asked Demorest.

"Wa'al, it ain't exakly complimentary to E. Blandford, Esq., and it mout be orkard for *you.*"

"I don't think you 're in the habit of letting such trifles interfere with your opinion," said Demorest, with a slightly forced laugh; "but what is your idea?"

"That thar was n't any accident."

"No accident?" replied Demorest, raising himself on his elbow.

"Nary accident," continued Ezekiel deliberately, "and, if it comes to that, not much of a dead body either."

"What the devil do you mean?" said Demorest, sitting up.

"I mean," said Ezekiel, with momentous deliberation, "that E. Blandford, of the Winnipeg Mills, was in March, '50, ez nigh bein' bust up ez any man kin be without actually failin'; that he 'd been down to Boston that day to get some extensions; that old Deacon Salisbury knew it, and had been pesterin' Mrs. Blandford to induce him to sell out and leave the place; and that the night he left he took about two hundred and fifty dollars in bank-bills that they allus kept in the house, and Mrs. Blandford was in the habit o' hidin' in the breast-pocket of one of his old overcoats hangin' up in the closet. I mean that that air money and that air overcoat went off with him, ez Mrs. Blandford knows, for I heard her tell her ma about it. And when his affairs were wound up and his debts paid, I reckon that the two hundred and fifty was all there was left — and he scooted with it. It 's orkard for you — ez I said afore — but I don't see wot on earth you need get riled for. Ef he ran off on account of only two hundred and fifty dollars he ain't goin' to run back again for the mere matter o' your marrying Joan. Ef he had — he 'd 'a' done it afore this. It 's orkard, ez I said — but the only orkardness is your feelin's. I reckon Joan 's got used to hers."

Demorest had risen angrily to his feet. But the next moment the utter impossibility of reaching this man's hidebound moral perception by even physical force hopelessly overcame him. It would only impress him with the effect of his own disturbing power, which to Ezekiel was equal to a proof of the truth of his opinions. It might even encourage him to repeat this absurd story elsewhere with his own construction upon his reception of it. After all it was only Ezekiel's opinion, — an opinion too preposterous for even a moment's serious consideration. Blandford alive, and a petty defaulter! Blandford above the earth and complacently abandoning his wife and home to another! Blandford — perhaps a sneaking, cowardly Nemesis — hiding in the shadow for future — impossible! It really was enough to make him laugh.

He did laugh, albeit with an uneasy sense that only a few years ago he would have struck down the man who had thus traduced his friend's memory.

"You 've been overtaxing your brain in patent medicine circulars, Corwin," he said in a roughly rallying manner, "and you 've got rather too much highfalutin and bitters mixed with your opinions. After that yarn of yours you must be dry. What 'll you take? I have n't got any New England rum, but I can give you some ten-year-old aguardiente made on the place."

As he spoke he lifted a decanter and glass from a small table which Manuel had placed in the veranda.

"I guess not," said Ezekiel dryly. "It 's now goin' on five years since I 've been a consistent temperance man."

"In everything but melons, and criticism of your neighbor, eh?" said Demorest, pouring out a glass of the liquor.

"I hev my convictions," said Ezekiel with affected meekness.

"And I have mine," said Demorest, tossing off the fiery liquor at a draught, "and it 's that this is devilish good stuff. Sorry you can't take some. I 'm afraid I 'll have to get you to excuse me for a while. I have to take a ride over the ranch before turning in, to see if everything 's right. The house is 'at your disposition,' as we say here. I 'll see you later."

He walked away with a slight exaggeration of unconcern. Ezekiel watched him narrowly with colorless eyes beneath his white lashes. When he had gone he examined the thoroughly emptied glass of aguardiente, and taking the decanter sniffed critically at its sharp and potent contents. A smile of gratified discernment followed. It was clear to him that Demorest was a heavy drinker.

Contrary to his prognostication, however, Mrs. Demorest *did* arrive the next day. But although he was to depart from Buenaventura by the same coach that had set her down at the gate of the casa, he had already left the house armed with some letters of introduction which Demorest had generously given him to certain small traders in the pueblo and along the route. Demorest was not displeased to part with him before the arrival of his wife, and thus spare her the awkwardness of a repetition of Ezekiel's effrontery in her presence. Nor was he willing to have the impediment of a guest in the house to any explanation he might have to seek from her, or to the confidences that hereafter must be fuller and more mutual. For with all his deep affection for his wife, Richard Demorest unconsciously feared her. The strong man whose dominance over men and women alike had been his salient characteristic, had begun to feel an undefinable sense of some unrecognized quality in the woman he loved. He had once or twice detected it in a tone of her voice, in a remembered and perhaps even once idolized gesture, or in the accidental lapse of some bewildering word. With the generosity of a large nature he had put the thought aside, referring it to some selfish weakness of his own, or — more fatuous than all — to a possible diminution of his own affection.

He was standing on the steps ready to receive her. Few of her appreciative sex could have remained indifferent to the tender and touching significance of his silent and subdued welcome. He had that piteous wistfulness of eye seen in some dogs and the husbands of many charming women, — the affection that pardons beforehand the indifference it has learned to expect. She approached him smiling in her turn, meeting the sublime patience of being unloved with the equally resigned patience of being loved, and feeling that comforting sense of virtue which might become a bore, but never a self-reproach. For the rest, she was prettier than ever; her five years of expanded life had slightly rounded the elongated oval of her face, filled up the ascetic hollows of her temples, and freed the repression of her mouth and chin. A more genial climate had quickened the circulation that North Liberty had arrested, and suffused the transparent beauty of her skin with eloquent life. It seemed as if the long protracted northern spring of her youth had suddenly burst into a summer of womanhood under those gentle skies; and yet enough of her puritan precision of manner, movement, and gesture remained to temper her fuller and more exuberant life and give it repose. In a community of pretty women more or less given to the license and extravagance of the epoch, she always looked like a lady.

He took her in his arms and half lifted her up the last step of the veranda. She resisted slightly with her characteristic action of catching his wrists in both her hands and holding him off with an awkward primness, and almost in the same tone that she had used to Edward Blandford five years before, said: —

"There, Dick, that will do."

CHAPTER II

Demorest's dream of a few days' conjugal seclusion and confidences with his wife was quickly dispelled by that lady.

"I came down with Rosita Pico, whose father, you know, once owned this property," she said. "She 's gone on to her cousins at Los Osos rancho to-night, but comes here to-morrow for a visit. She knows the place well; in fact, she once had a romantic love affair here. But she is very entertaining. It will be a little change for us," she added naïvely.

Demorest kept back a sigh, without changing his gentle smile.

"I 'm glad for your sake, dear. But is she not a little flighty and inclined to flirt a good deal? I think I 've heard so."

"She 's a young girl who has been severely tried, Richard, and perhaps is not to blame for endeavoring to forget it in such distraction as she can find," said Mrs. Demorest, with a slight return of her old manner. "*I* can understand her feelings perfectly."

She looked pointedly at her husband as she spoke, it being one of her late habits to openly refer to their antenuptial acquaintance as a natural reaction from the martyrdom of her first marriage, with a quiet indifference that seemed almost an indelicacy. But her husband only said, "As you like, dear," vaguely remembering Doña Rosita as the alleged heroine of a forgotten romance with some earlier American adventurer who had disappeared, and trying vainly to reconcile his wife's sentimental description of her with his own recollection of the buxom, pretty, laughing, but dangerous-eyed Spanish girl he had, however, seen but once.

She arrived the next day, flying into a protracted embrace of Joan, which included a smiling recognition of Demorest with an unoccupied blue eye, and a shake of her fan over his wife's shoulder. Then she drew back and seemed to take in the whole veranda and garden in another long caress of her eyes.

"Ah — yess! I have recog-nized it, mooch. It es ze same. Of no change — not even of a leetle. No, she ess always — esso."

She stopped, looked unutterable things at Joan, pressed her fan below a spray of roses on her full bodice as if to indicate some thrilling memory beneath it, shook her head again, suddenly caught sight of Demorest's serious face, said, "Ah, that brigand of our husband laughs himself at me," and then herself broke into a charming ripple of laughter.

"But I was not laughing, Doña Rosita," said Demorest, smiling sadly, however, in spite of himself.

She made a little grimace, and then raised her elbows, slightly lifting her shoulders.

"As it shall please you, señor. But he is gone — thees

passion. Yess — what you shall call thees sentiment of lof — zo — as he came!"

She threw her fingers in the air as if to illustrate the volatile and transitory passage of her affections, and then turned again to Joan with her back towards Demorest.

"Do please go on — Doña Rosita," said he. "I never heard the real story. If there is any romance about my house, I 'd like to know it," he added with a faint sigh.

Doña Rosita wheeled upon him with an inquiring little look.

"Ah, you have the sentiment, and *you*," she continued, taking Joan by the arms, "*you* have not. Eet ess good so. When a — the wife," she continued boldly, hazarding an extended English abstraction, "he has the sentimente and the hoosband he has nothing, eet is not good — for a-him — ze wife," she concluded triumphantly.

"But I have great appreciation and I am dying to hear it," said Demorest, trying to laugh.

"Well, poor one, you look so. But you shall lif till another time," said Doña Rosita, with a mock curtsy, gliding away with Joan.

The "other time" came that evening when chocolate was served on the veranda, where Doña Rosita, mantilla-draped against the dry, clear, moonlit air, sat at the feet of Joan on the lowest step. Demorest, uneasily observant of the influence of the giddy foreigner on his wife, and conscious of certain confidences between them from which he was excluded, leaned against a pillar of the porch in half abstracted resignation; Joan, under the tutelage of Rosita, lit a cigarette; Demorest gazed at her wonderingly, trying to recall, in her fuller and more animated face, some memory of the pale, refined profile of the Puritan girl he had first met in the Boston train, the faint aurora of whose cheek in that northern clime seemed to come and go with his words. Becoming conscious at last of the eyes of Doña Rosita watching him from below, with an effort he recalled his duty as her host and gallantly reminded her that moonlight and the hour seemed expressly fitted for her promised love story.

"Do tell it," said Joan, "I don't mind hearing it again."

"Then you know it already?" said Demorest, surprised.

Joan took the cigarette from her lips, laughed complacently, and exchanged a familiar glance with Rosita.

"She told it me a year ago, when we first knew each other," she replied. "Go on, dear," to Rosita.

Thus encouraged, Doña Rosita began, addressing herself first in Spanish to Demorest, who understood the language better than his wife, and lapsing into her characteristic English as she appealed to them both. It was really very little to interest Don Ricardo — this story of a silly mucha cha like herself and a strange caballero. He would go to sleep while she was talking, and to-night he would say to his wife, "Mother of God! why have you brought here this chattering parrot who speaks but of one thing?" But she would go on always like the windmill, whether there was grain to grind or no. "It was four years ago. Ah! Don Ricardo did not remember the country then — it was when the first Americans came — now it is different. Then there were no coaches — in truth one traveled very little, and always on horseback, only to see one's neighbors. And suddenly, as if in one day, it was changed; there were strange men on the roads, and one was frightened, and one shut the gates of the pateo and drove the horses into the corral. One did not know much of the Americans then — for why? They were always going, going — never stopping, hurrying on to the gold mines, hurrying away from the gold mines, hurrying to look for other gold mines; but always going on foot, on horseback, in queer wagons, hurrying, pushing everywhere. Ah, it took away the breath. All, except one American — he did not hurry, he did not go with the others, he came and stayed here at Buenaventura. He was very quiet, very civil, very sad, and very discreet. He was not like the others, and always kept aloof from them. He came to see Don Andreas Pico, and wanted to beg a piece of land and an old vaquero's hut near the road for a trifle. Don Andreas would have given it, or a better house, to him, or have had him live at the casa here; but he would not. He was very proud and shy, so he took the vaquero's hut, a mere adobe affair, and lived in it, though a caballero like yourself, with white hands that knew not labor, and small feet that had seldom walked. In good time he learned to ride like the best vaquero, and helped Don Andreas to find the lost mustangs, and showed him how to improve the old mill. And his pride and his shyness wore off, and he would come to the casa sometimes. And Don Andreas got to love him very much, and his daughter, Doña Rosita — ah, well, yes truly — a leetle.

"But he had strange moods and ways, this American, and at times they would have thought him a lunatico had they not believed it to be an American fashion. He would be very kind and gentle like one of the family, coming to the casa every day, playing with the children, advising Don Andreas and — yes — having a devotion — very discreet, very ceremonious, for Doña Rosita. And then, all in a moment, he would become as ill, without a word or gesture, until he would stalk out of the house, gallop away furiously, and for a week not be heard of. The first time it happened, Doña Rosita was piqued by his rudeness, Don Andreas was alarmed, for it was on an evening like the present, and Doña Rosita was teaching him a little song on the guitar when the fit came on him. And he snapped the guitar strings like thread and threw it down, and got up like a bear and walked away without a word."

"I see it all," said Demorest half seriously; "you were coquetting with him, and he was jealous."

But Doña Rosita shook her head and turned impetuously and said in English to Joan, "No, it was astutcia — a trick, a ruse. Because when my father have arrived at his house, he is agone. And so every time. When he have the fit he goes not to his house. No. And it ees not until after one time when he comes back never again, that we have comprehend what he do at these times. And what do you think? I shall tell to you."

She composed herself comfortably, with her plump elbows on her knees, and her fan crossed on the palm of her hand before her, and began again: —

"It is a year he has agone, and the stagecoach is attack of brigands. Tiburcio, our vaquero, have that night made himself a pasear on the road, and he have seen *him*. He have seen one, two, three men came from the wood with something on the face, and *he* is of them. He has nothing on his face, and Tiburcio have recognized him. We have laugh at Tiburcio. We believe him not. It is improbable that this Señor Huanson" —

"Señor who?" said Demorest.

"Huanson — eet is the name of him. Ah, Carr! — posiblemente it is nothing — a Don Fulano — or an apodo — Huanson."

"Oh, I see, *Johnson*, very likely."

"We have said it is not possible that this good man, who have come to the house and ride on his back the children, is a thief and a brigand. And one night my father have come from the Monterey in the coach, and it was stopped. And the brigands have take from the passengers the money, the rings from the finger, and the watch, — and my father was of the same. And my father, he have great dissatisfaction and anguish, for his watch is given to him of an old friend, and it is not like the other watch. But the watch he go all the same. And then when the robbers have make a finish comes to the window of the coach a mascara and have say, 'Who is the Don Andreas Pico?' And my father have say, 'It is I who am Don Andreas Pico.' And the mask have say, 'Behold, your watch is restore!' and he gif it to him. And my father say, 'To whom have I the distinguished honor to thank?' And the mask say" —

"Johnson," interrupted Demorest.

"No," said Doña Rosita in grave triumph, "he say Essmith. For this Essmith is like Huanson — an apodo — nothing."

"Then you really think this man was your old friend?" asked Demorest.

"I think."

"And that he was a robber even when living here — and that it was not your cruelty that really drove him to take the road?"

Doña Rosita shrugged her plump shoulders.

"You will not comprehend. It was because of his being a brigand that he stayed not with us. My father would not have object if he have present himself to me for marriage in these times. I would not have object, for I was young, and we have knew nothing. It was he who have object. For why? Inside of his heart he have feel he was a brigand."

"But you might have reformed him in time," said Demorest.

She again shrugged her shoulders.

"Quien sabe?"

After a pause she added with infinite gravity: —

"And before he have reform, it is bad for the ménage. I should invite to my house some friend. They arrive, and one say, 'I have not the watch of my pocket,' and another, 'The ring of my finger, he is gone,' and another,

'My earrings, she is loss.' And I am obliged to say, 'They reside now in the pocket of my hoosband; patience! a little while — perhaps to-morrow — he will restore.' No," she continued, with an air of infinite conviction, "it is not good for the ménage — the necessity of those explanation."

"You told me he was handsome," said Joan, passing her arm carelessly around Doña Rosita's comfortable waist. "How did he look?"

"As an angel! He have long curls to his back. His mustache was as silk, for he have had never a barber to his face. And his eyes — Santa Maria! — so soft and so — so melankoly. When he smile it is like the moonlight. But," she added, rising to her feet and tossing the end of her lace mantilla over her shoulder with a little laugh — "it is finish — Adelante! Dr-r-rive on!"

"I don't want to destroy your belief in the connection of your friend with the road agents," said Demorest grimly, "but if he belongs to their band it is in an inferior capacity. Most of them are known to the authorities, and I have heard it even said that their leader or organizer is a very unromantic speculator in San Francisco."

But this suggestion was received coldly by the ladies, who superciliously turned their backs upon it and the suggester. Joan dropped her voice to a lower tone and turned to Doña Rosita.

"And you have never seen him since?"

"Never."

"*I* should — at least, I would n't have let it end in *that* way," said Joan in a positive whisper.

"Eh?" said Doña Rosita, laughing. "So eet is *you*, Juanita, that have the romance — eh? Ah, bueno! 'you have the house — so I gif to you the lover also.' I place him at your disposition." She made a mock gesture of elaborate and complete abnegation. "But," she added in

Joan's ear, with a quick glance at Demorest, "do not let our hoosband eat him. Even now he have the look to strangle *me*. Make to him a little lof, quickly, when I shall walk in the garden." She turned away with a pretty wave of her fan to Demorest, and calling out, "I go to make an assignation with my memory," laughed again, and lazily passed into the shadow. An ominous silence on the veranda followed, broken finally by Mrs. Demorest.

"I don't think it was necessary for you to show your dislike to Doña Rosita quite so plainly," she said coldly, slightly accenting the Puritan stiffness, which any conjugal tête-à-tête lately revived in her manner.

"I show dislike of Doña Rosita?" stammered Demorest, in surprise. "Come, Joan," he added, with a forgiving smile, "you don't mean to imply that I dislike her because I could n't get up a thrilling interest in an old story I 've heard from every gossip in the pueblo since I can remember."

"It 's not an old story to *her*," said Joan dryly, "and even if it were, you might reflect that all people are not as anxious to forget the past as you are."

Demorest drew back to let the shaft glance by.

"The story is old enough, at least, for her to have had a dozen flirtations, as you know, since then," he returned gently, "and I don't think she herself seriously believes in it. But let that pass. I am sorry I offended her. I had no idea of doing so. As a rule, I think she is not so easily offended. But I shall apologize to her." He stopped and approached nearer his wife in a half-timid, half-tentative affection. "As to my forgetfulness of the past, Joan, even if it were true, I have had little cause to forget it lately. Your friend, Corwin" —

"I must insist upon your not calling him *my* friend, Richard," interrupted Joan sharply, "considering that it was through *your* indiscretion in coming to us for the buggy that night, that he suspected" —

She stopped suddenly, for at that moment a startled little shriek, quickly subdued, rang through the garden. Demorest ran hurriedly down the steps in the direction of the outcry. Joan followed more cautiously. At the first turning of the path Doña Rosita almost fell into his arms. She was breathless and trembling, but broke into a hysterical laugh.

"I have such a fear come to me — I cry out! I think I have seen a man; but it was nothing — nothing! I am a fool. It is no one here."

"But where did you see anything?" said Joan, coming up.

Rosita flew to her side. "Where? Oh, here! — everywhere! Ah, I am a fool!" She was laughing now, albeit there were tears glistening on her lashes when she laid her head on Joan's shoulder.

"It was some fancy — some resemblance you saw in that queer cactus," said Demorest gently. "It is quite natural; I was myself deceived the other night. But I'll look around to satisfy you. Take Doña Rosita back to the veranda, Joan. But don't be alarmed, dear, — it was only an illusion."

He turned away. When his figure was lost in the entwining foliage, Doña Rosita seized Joan's shoulder and dragged her face down to a level with her own.

"It was something!" she whispered quickly.

"Who?"

"It was — *Him!*"

"Nonsense," said Joan, nevertheless casting a hurried glance around her.

"Have no fear," said Doña Rosita quickly, "he is gone — I saw him pass away — so! But it was *He* — Huanson. I recognize him. I forget him never."

"Are you sure?"

"Have I the eyes? the memory? Madre de Dios!

Am I a lunatico too? Look! He have stood there — so."

"Then you think he knew you were here?"

"Quien sabe?"

"And that he came here to see you?"

Doña Rosita caught her again by the shoulders, and with her lips in Joan's ear, said with the intensest and most deliberate of emphasis: —

"NO!"

"What in Heaven's name brought him here then?"

"*You!*"

"Are you crazy?"

"You! you! *you!*" repeated Doña Rosita, with crescendo energy. "I have come upon him here; where he stood and look at the veranda, absorrrb of *you.* You move — he fly."

"Hush!"

"Ah, yes! I have said I give him to you. And he came, bueno," murmured Doña Rosita, with a half-resigned, half-superstitious gesture.

"*Will* you be quiet!"

It was the sound of Demorest's feet on the gravel path, returning from his fruitless search. He had seen nothing. It must have been Doña Rosita's fancy.

"She was just saying she thought she had been mistaken," said Joan quietly. "Let us go in; it is rather chilly here, and I begin to feel creepy too."

Nevertheless, as they entered the house again, and the light of the hall lantern fell upon her face, Demorest thought he had never but once before seen her look so nervously and animatedly beautiful.

CHAPTER III

The following day, when Mr. Ezekiel Corwin had delivered his letters of introduction, and thoroughly canvassed the scant mercantile community of San Buenaventura with considerable success, he deposited his carpetbag at the stage office in the posada, and found to his chagrin that he had still two hours to wait before the coach arrived. After a vain attempt to impart cheerful but disparaging criticism of the pueblo and its people to Señor Mateo and his wife, — whose external courtesy had been visibly increased by a line from Demorest, but whose confidence towards the stranger had not been extended in the same proportion, — he gave it up, and threw himself lazily on a wooden bench in the veranda, already hacked with the initials of his countrymen, and drawing a jack-knife from his pocket, he began to add to that emblazonry the trade-mark of the Panacea — as a casual advertisement. During its progress, however, he was struck by the fact that while no one seemed to enter the posada through the stage office, the number of voices in the adjoining room seemed to increase, and the ministrations of Mateo and his wife became more feverishly occupied with their invisible guests. It seemed to Ezekiel that consequently there must be a second entrance which he had not seen, and this added to the circumstance that one or two lounging figures who had been approaching unaccountably disappeared before reaching the veranda, induced him to rise and examine the locality. A few paces beyond was an alley, but it appeared to be already blocked by several cigarette-smoking, short-jacketed men who were leaning against its walls, and showed no inclination to make way for him. Checked, but not daunted, Ezekiel coolly returned to the stage office, and taking the first opportunity when Mateo passed through the rear door, followed him. As he expected, the innkeeper turned to the left and entered a large room filled with tobacco smoke and the local habitués of the posada. But Ezekiel, shrewdly surmising that the private entrance must be in the opposite direction, turned to the right along the passage until he came unexpectedly upon the corridor of the usual courtyard, or patio, of every Mexican hostelry, closed at one end by a low adobe wall, in which there was a door. The free passage around the corridor was interrupted by wide partitions, fitted up with tables and benches, like stalls, opening upon the courtyard where a few stunted fig and orange trees still grew. As the courtyard seemed to be the only communication between the passage he had left and the door in the wall, he was about to cross it, when the voices of two men in the compartment struck his ears. Although one was evidently an American's, Ezekiel was instinctively convinced that they were speaking in English only for greater security against being understood by the frequenters of the posada. It is unnecessary to say that this was an innocent challenge to the curiosity of Ezekiel that he instantly accepted. He drew back carefully into the shadow of the partition as one of the voices asked, —

"Was n't that Johnson just come in?"

There was a movement as if some one had risen to look over the compartment, but the gathering twilight completely hid Ezekiel.

"No!"

"He 's late. Suppose he don't come — or back out?"

The other man broke into a grim laugh.

"I reckon you don't know Johnson yet, or you 'd understand this yer little game o' his is just the one idea o' his life. He 's been two years on that man's track, and he ain't goin' to back out now that he 's got a dead sure thing on him."

"But why is he so keen about it, anyway? It don't seem nat'ral for a business man built after Johnson's style, and a rich man to boot, to go into this detective business. It ain't the reward, we know that. Is it an old grudge?"

"You bet!" The speaker paused, and then in a lower voice, which taxed Ezekiel's keen ear to the uttermost, resumed: "It 's said up in 'Frisco that Cherokee Bob knew suthin' agin Johnson way back in the States; anyhow, I believe it 's understood that they came across the plains together in '50 — and Bob hounded Johnson and blackmailed him here where he was livin', even to the point of makin' him help him on the road or give information, until one day Johnson bucked against it — kicked over the traces — and swore he 'd be revenged on Bob, and then just settled himself down to that business. Wotever he 'd been and done himself he made it all right with the sheriff here; and I 've heard ez it was n't anything criminal or that sort, but that it was o' some private trouble that he 'd confided to that hound Bob, and Bob had threatened to tell agen him. That 's the grudge they say Johnson has, and that 's why he 's allowed to be the head devil in this yer affair. It 's an understood thing, too, that the sheriff and the police ain't goin' to interfere if Johnson accidentally blows the top of Bob's head off in the scrimmage of a capter."

"And I reckon Bob would n't hesitate to do the same thing to him when he finds out that Johnson has given him away?"

"I reckon," said the other sententiously, "for it 's Johnson's knowledge of the country and the hoss-stealers that are in with Bob's gang of road agents that made it easy for him to buy up and win over Bob's friends here, so that they 'd help to trap him."

"It 's pretty rough on Bob to be sold out in that way," said the second speaker sympathizingly.

"If they were white men, p'rhaps," returned his companion contemptuously, "but this yer 's a case of Injin agen Injin, ez the men are Mexican half-breeds just as Bob's a half Cherokee. The sooner that kind o' cross cattle exterminate each other the better it 'll be for the country. It takes a white man like Johnson to set 'em by the ears."

A silence followed. Ezekiel, beginning to be slightly bored with his cheaply acquired but rather impractical information, was about to slip back into the passage again when he was arrested by a laugh from the first speaker.

"What 's the matter?" growled the other. "Do you want to bring the whole posada out here?"

"I was only thinkin' what a skeer them innocent greenhorn passengers will get just ez they 're snoozing off for the night, ten miles from here," responded his friend, with a chuckle. "Wonder ef anybody's goin' up from here besides that patent medicine softy."

Ezekiel stopped as if petrified.

"Ef the d—d fools keep quiet they won't be hurt, for our men will be ready to chip in the moment of the attack. But we 've got to let the attack be made for the sake of the evidence. And if we warn off the passengers from going this trip, and let the stage go up empty, Bob would suspect something and vamose. But here 's Johnson!"

The door in the adobe wall had suddenly opened, and a figure in a serape entered the patio. Ezekiel, whose curiosity was whetted with indignation at the ignominious part assigned to him in this comedy, forgot even his risk of detection by the new-comer, who advanced quickly towards the compartment. When he had reached it he said, in a tone of bitterness: —

"The game 's up, gentlemen, and the whole thing is blown. The scoundrel has got some confederate here — for he 's been seen openly on the road near Demorest's ranch, and the band have had warning and dispersed. We must find out the traitor, and take our precautions for the next time. Who is that there? I don't know him."

He was pointing to Ezekiel, who had started eagerly forward at the first sound of his voice. The two occupants of the compartment rose at the same moment, leaped into the courtyard, and confronted Ezekiel. Surrounded by the three menacing figures, he did not quail, but remained intently gazing upon the new-comer. Then his mouth opened, and he drawled lazily: —

"Wa'al, ef it ain't Squire Blandford, of North Liberty, Connecticut, I 'm a treed coon. Squire Blandford, how *do* you do?"

The stranger drew back in undisguised amazement; the two men glanced hurriedly at each other; Ezekiel alone remained cool, smiling, imperturbable, and triumphant.

"Who are *you*, sir? I do not know you," demanded the new-comer roughly.

"Like ez not," said Corwin dryly; "it 's a matter o' four year sense I lived in your house. Even Dick Demorest — you knew Dick? — did n't know me; but I reckon that Mrs. Blandford as used to be" —

"That 's enough," said Blandford — for it was he — suddenly mastering both himself and Corwin by a supreme emphasis of will and gesture. "Wait!" Then turning to the two others who were discreetly regarding the blank adobe wall before them, he said, "Excuse me for a few minutes, gentlemen. There is no hurry now. I will see you later;" and with an imperative wave of his hand motioned Ezekiel to precede him into the passage, and followed him.

He did not speak until they entered the stage office, when passing through it he said peremptorily, "Follow me." The few loungers, who seemed to recognize him, made way for him with a singular deference that impressed Ezekiel, already dominated by his manner. The first perception in his mind was that Blandford had in some strange way succeeded to Demorest's former imperious character. There was no trace left of the old gentle subjection to Joan's prim precision. Ezekiel followed him out of the office as unresistingly as he had followed Demorest into the stables on that eventful night. They passed down the narrow street until Blandford suddenly stopped short and turned into the crumbling doorway of one of the low adobe buildings and entered an apartment. It seemed to be the ordinary living-room of the house, made more domestic by the presence of a silk-counterpaned bed in one corner, a priedieu and crucifix, and one or two articles of bedchamber furniture. A woman was sitting in déshabillé by the window; a man was smoking on a lounge against the wall. Blandford, in the same peremptory manner, addressed a command in Spanish to the inmates, who immediately abandoned the apartment to the seeming trespasser.

Motioning his companion to a seat on the lounge just vacated, Blandford folded his arms and stood erect before him.

"Well," he said, with quick business conciseness, "what do you want?"

Ezekiel was staggered out of his complacency.

"Wa'al," he stammered, "I only reckoned to ask the news, ez we are old friends — I" —

"How much do you want?" repeated Blandford impatiently.

Ezekiel was mystified, yet expectant.

"I can't say ez I exakly understand," he began.

"How — much — money — do — you — want?" continued Blandford, with frigid accuracy, "to get up and get out of this place?"

"Wa'al, consideren ez I 'm travelin' here ez the only authorized agent of a first-class 'Frisco Drug House," said

Ezekiel, with a mingling of mortification, pride, and hopefulness, "unless you 're travelin' in the opposition business, I don't see what 's that to you."

Blandford regarded him searchingly for an instant.

"Who sent you here?"

"Dilworth & Dusenberry, Battery Street, San Francisco. Hev their card?" said Ezekiel, taking one from his waistcoat-pocket.

"Corwin," said Blandford sternly, "whatever your business is here, you 'll find it will pay you better, a d—d sight, to be frank with me and stop this Yankee shuffling. You say you have been with Demorest — what has *he* got to do with your business here?"

"Nothin'," said Ezekiel. "I reckon he wos ez astonished to see me ez you are."

"And did n't he send you here to seek me?" said Blandford impatiently.

"Considerin' he believes you a dead man, I reckon not."

Blandford gave a hard, constrained laugh. After a pause, still keeping his eyes fixed on Ezekiel, he said: —

"Then your recognition of me was accidental?"

"Wa'al, yes. And ez I never took much stock in the stories that you were washed off the Warensboro bridge, I ain't much astonished at finding you agin."

"What did you believe happened to me?" said Blandford, less brusquely.

Ezekiel noticed the softening; he felt his own turn coming.

"I kalkilated you had reasons for going off, leaving no address behind you," he drawled.

"What reasons?" asked Blandford, with a sudden relapse to his former harshness.

"Wa'al, Squire Blandford, sense you wanter know — I reckon your business was n't payin', and there was a matter of two hundred and fifty dollars ye took with ye, that your creditors would hev liked to hev back."

"Who dare say that?" demanded Blandford angrily.

"Your wife that was — Mrs. Demorest ez is — told it to her mother," returned Ezekiel lazily.

The blow struck deeper than even Ezekiel's dry malice imagined. For an instant Blandford remained stupefied. In the five years' retrospect of his resolution on that fatal night, whatever doubt of its wisdom might have obtruded itself upon him, he had never thought of *this*. He had been willing to believe that his wife had quietly forgotten him as well as her treachery to him; he had passively acquiesced in the results of that forgetfulness and his own silence; he had been conscious that his wound had healed sooner than he expected, but if this consciousness had enabled him to extend a certain passive forgiveness to his wife and Demorest, it was always with the conviction that his mysterious effacement had left an inexplicable shadow upon them which their consciences alone could explain. But for this unjust, vulgar, and degrading interpretation of his own act of expiation, he was totally unprepared. It completely crushed whatever sentiment remained of that act in the horrible irony of finding himself put upon his defense before the world, without being able now to offer the real cause. The anguish of that night had gone forever; but the ridiculous interpretation of it had survived, and would survive it. In the eyes of the man before him he was not a wronged husband, but an absconding petty defaulter, whom he had just detected!

His mind was quickly made up. In that instant he had resolved upon a step as fateful as his former one, and a fitting climax to its results. For five years he had clearly misunderstood his attitude towards his treacherous wife and perjured friend. Thanks to this practical, selfish machine before him, he knew it now.

"Look here, Corwin," he said, turning upon Ezekiel a colorless face, but a steady, merciless eye. "I can guess, without your telling me, what lies may be circulated about me by the man and woman who know that I have only to declare myself alive to convict them of infamy, — perhaps even of criminality before the law. You are not *my* friend, or you would not have believed them; if you are *theirs*, you have two courses open to you now. Keep this meeting to yourself and trust to my mercy to keep it a secret also; or, tell Mrs. Demorest that you have seen Mr. Johnson, who is not afraid to come forward at any moment and proclaim that he is Edward Blandford, her only lawful husband. Choose which course you like, — it is nothing more to me."

"Wa'al, I reckon that, as far as I know Mrs. Demorest," said Ezekiel dryly, "it don't make the least difference to her either; but if you want to know my opinion o' this matter, it is that neither you nor Demorest exactly understand that woman. I 've known Joan Salisbury since she was so high, but if ye expected me to tell you wot she was goin' to do next, I 'd be able to tell ye where the next flash o' lightnin' would strike. It 's wot you don't expect of Joan Salisbury that she does. And the best proof of it is that she filed papers for a divorce agin you in Chicago and got it by default a few weeks afore she married Demorest — and you don't know it."

Blandford recoiled. "Impossible," he said, but his voice too plainly showed how clearly its possibility struck him now.

"It 's so, but it was kept secret by Deacon Salisbury. I overheerd it. Wa'al, that 's a proof that *you* don't understand Joan, I reckon. And considerin' that Demorest *himself* don't know it, ez I found out only the other day in talking to him, I kalkilate I 'm safe in sayin' that you 're neither o' you quite up to Deacon Salisbury's darter in nat'ral cuteness. I don't like to obtrude my opinion, Squire Blandford, ez we 're old friends, but I do say that wot with Demorest's prematooriness and yer own hangfiredness, it 's a good thing that you two worldly men hev got Joan Salisbury to stand up for North Liberty and keep it from bein' scandalized by the ungodly. Ef it had n't been for her smartness whar y 'd both be landed now? There 's a heap in Christian bringin' up, and a power in grace, Squire Blandford."

His hard, dry face was for an instant transfigured by a grim fealty and the dull glow of some sectarian clannishness. Or was it possible that this woman's personality had in some mysterious way disturbed his rooted selfishness?

During his speech Blandford had walked to the window. When Corwin had ceased speaking, Blandford turned towards him with an equally changed face and cold imperturbability that astonished him, and held out his hand.

"Let bygones be bygones, Corwin — whether we ever meet again or not. Yet if I can do anything for you for the sake of old times, I am ready to do it. I have some power here and in San Francisco," he continued, with a slight touch of pride, "that is n't dependent upon the mere name I may travel under. I have a purpose in coming here."

"I know it," said Ezekiel dryly. "I heard it all from your two friends. You 're huntin' some man that did you an injury."

"I 'm hunting down a dog who, suspecting I had some secret in emigrating here, tried to blackmail and ruin me," said Blandford, with a sudden expression of hatred that seemed inconsistent with anything that Ezekiel had ever known of his old master's character, — "a scoundrel who tried to break up my new life as another had broken up the old." He stopped and recovered himself with a short laugh. "Well, Ezekiel, I don't know as his opinion of me was any worse than yours or *hers*. And until I catch *him* to clear my name again, I let the other slanderers go."

"Wa'al, I reckon you might lay hands on that devil yet, and not far away, either. I was up at Demorest's to-day, and I heard Joan and a skittish sort o' Mexican young lady talkin' about some tramp that had frightened her. And Miss Pico said" —

"What! Who did you say?" demanded Blandford, with a violent start.

"Wa'al, I reckoned I heerd the first name too — Rosita."

A quick flush crossed Blandford's face, and left it glowing like a boy's.

"Is *she* there?"

"Wa'al, I reckon she 's visitin' Joan," said Ezekiel, narrowly attentive of Blandford's strange excitement; "but wot of it?"

But Blandford had utterly forgotten Ezekiel's presence. He had remained speechless and flushed. And then, as if suddenly dazzled by an inspiration, he abruptly dashed from the room. Ezekiel heard him call to his passive host with a Spanish oath, but before he could follow, they had both hurriedly left the house.

Ezekiel glanced around him and contemplatively ran his fingers through his beard.

"It ain't Joan Salisbury nor Dick Demorest ez giv' him that start! Humph! Wa'al — I wanter know!"

CHAPTER IV

Mrs. Demorest was so fascinated by the company of Doña Rosita Pico and her romantic memories, that she prevailed upon that heart-broken but scarcely attenuated young lady to prolong her visit beyond the fortnight she had allotted to communion with the past. For a day or two following her singular experience in the garden, Mrs. Demorest plied her with questions regarding the apparition she had seen, and finally extorted from her the admission that she could not positively swear to its being the real Johnson, or even a perfectly consistent shade of that faithless man. When Joan pointed out to her that such masculine perfections as curling raven locks, long silken mustaches, and dark eyes, were attributes by no means exclusive to her lover, but were occasionally seen among other less favored and even equally dangerous Americans, Doña Rosita assented with less objection than Joan anticipated.

"Besides, dear," said Joan, eying her with feline watchfulness, "it is four years since you 've seen him, and surely the man has either shaved since, or else he took a ridiculous vow never to do it, and then he would be more fully bearded."

But Doña Rosita only shook her pretty head.

"Ah, but he have an air — a something I know not what you call — so."

She threw her shawl over her left shoulder, and as far as a pair of soft blue eyes and comfortably pacific features would admit, endeavored to convey an idea of wicked and gloomy abstraction.

"You child," said Joan, "that 's nothing; they all of them do that. Why, there was a stranger at the Oriental Hotel whom I met twice when I was there — just as mysterious, romantic, and wicked-looking. And in fact they hinted terrible things about him. Well! so much so, that Mr. Demorest was quite foolish about my being barely civil to him — you understand — and" — She stopped suddenly, with a heightened color under the fire of Rosita's laughing eyes.

"Ah — so — Doña Discretion! Tell to me all. Did our hoosband eat him?"

Joan's features suddenly tightened to their old Puritan rigidity.

"Mr. Demorest has reasons — abundant reasons — to thoroughly understand and trust me," she replied in an austere voice.

Rosita looked at her a moment in mystification, and then shrugged her shoulders. The conversation dropped. Nevertheless, it is worthy of being recorded that from that moment the usual familiar allusions, playful and serious, to Rosita's mysterious visitor began to diminish in frequency, and finally ceased. Even the news brought by Demorest of some vague rumor in the pueblo that an intended attack on the stagecoach had been frustrated by the authorities, and that the vicinity had been haunted by incognitos of both parties, failed to revive the discussion.

Meantime the slight excitement that had stirred the sluggish life of the pueblo of San Buenaventura had subsided. The posada of Señor Mateo had lost its feverish and perplexing dual life; the alley behind it no longer was congested by lounging cigarette smokers; the compartment looking upon the silent patio was unoccupied, and its chairs and tables were empty. The two deputy sheriffs, of whom Señor Mateo presumably knew very little, had fled; and the mysterious Señor Johnson, of whom he — still presumably — knew still less, had also disappeared. For Señor Mateo's knowledge of what transpired in and about his posada, and of the character and purposes of those who frequented it, was tinctured by grave and philosophical doubts. This courteous and dignified skepticism generally took the formula of "Quien sabe" to all frivolous and mundane inquiry. He would affirm with strict verity that his omelettes were unapproachable, his beds miraculous, his aguardiente supreme, his house was even as your own. Beyond these were questions with which the simply finite and always discreet human intellect declined to grapple.

The disturbing effect of Señor Corwin upon a mind thus gravely constituted may be easily imagined. Besides Ezekiel's inordinate capacity for useless or indiscreet information, it was undeniable that his patent medicines had effected a certain peaceful revolutionary movement in San Buenaventura. A simple and superstitious community that had steadily resisted the practical domestic and agricultural American improvements, succumbed to the occult healing influences of the Panacea and Jones's Bitters. The virtues of a mysterious balsam, more or less illuminated with a colored mythological label, deeply impressed them; and the exhibition of a circular, whereon a celestial visitant was represented as descending with a gross of Rogers's Pills to a suffering but admiring multitude, touched their religious sympathies to such an extent that the good Padre José was obliged to warn them from the pulpit of the diabolical character of their heresies of healing, — with the natural result of yet more dangerously advertising Ezekiel. There were those, too, who spoke under their breath of the miraculous efficacy of these nostrums. Had not Don Victor Arguello, whose respectable digestion, exhausted by continuous pepper and garlic, failed him suddenly, received an unexpected and pleasurable stimulus from the New England rum, which was the basis of the Jones Bitters? Had not the baker, tremulous from excessive aguardiente, been soothed and sustained by the invisible morphia, judiciously hidden in Blogg's Nerve

Tonic? Nor had the wily Ezekiel forgotten the weaker sex in their maiden and maternal requirements. Unguents, that made silken their black but somewhat coarsely fibrous tresses, opened charming possibilities to the señoritas; while soothing syrups lent a peaceful repose to many a distracted mother's household. The success of Ezekiel was so marked as to justify his return at the end of three weeks with a fresh assortment and an undiminished audacity.

It was on his second visit that the skeptical, non-committal policy of Señor Mateo was sorely tried. Arriving at the posada one night, Ezekiel became aware that his host was engaged in some mysterious conference with a visitor who had entered through the ordinary public room. The view which the acute Ezekiel managed to get of the stranger, however, was productive of no further discovery than that he bore a faint and disreputable resemblance to Blandford, and was handsome after a conscious, reckless fashion, with an air of mingled bravado and conceit. But an hour later, as Corwin was taking the cooler air of the veranda before retiring to one of the miraculous beds of the posada, he was amazed at seeing what was apparently Blandford himself emerge on horseback from the alley, and after a quick glance towards the veranda, canter rapidly up the street. Ezekiel's first impression was to call to him, but the sudden recollection that he parted from his old master on confidential terms only three days before in San Francisco, and that it was impossible for him to be in the pueblo, stopped him with his fingers meditatively in his beard. Then he turned in to the posada, and hastily summoned Mateo.

The gentleman presented himself in a state of such profound skepticism that it seemed to have already communicated itself to his shoulders, and gave him the appearance of having shrugged himself into the room.

"Ha'ow long ago did Mr. Johnson get here?" asked Corwin lazily.

"Ah — possibly — then there has been a Mr. Johnson?"

This is a polite doubt of his own perceptions and a courteous acceptance of his questioner's.

"Wa'al, I guess so. Considerin' I jest saw him with my own eyes," returned Ezekiel.

"Ah!" Mateo was relieved. Might he congratulate the Señor Corwin, who must be also relieved, and shake his respected hand. Bueno. And then he had met this Señor Johnson? doubtless a friend? And he was well? and all were happy?

"Look yer, Mattayo! What I wanter know ez *this*. When did that man, who has just ridden out of your alley, come here? Sabe that — it 's a plain question."

Ah, surely, of the clearest comprehension. Bueno. It may have been last week — or even this week — or perhaps yesterday — or of a possibility to-day. The Señor Corwin, who was wise and omniscient, would comprehend that the difficulty lay in deciding *who* was that man. Perhaps a friend of the Señor Corwin — perhaps only one who *looked* like him. There existed — might Mateo point out — a doubt.

Ezekiel regarded Mateo with a certain grim appreciation.

"Wa'al, is there anybody here who looks like Johnson?"

Again there was the difficulty of ascertaining perfectly how the Señor Johnson looked. If the Señor Johnson was Americano, doubtless there were other Americanos who had resembled him. It was possible. The Señor Corwin had doubtless observed for a little space a caballero who was here, as it were, in the instant of the appearance of Señor Johnson? Possibly there was a resemblance, and yet —

Corwin had certainly noticed this resemblance, but it did not suit his cautious intellect to fall in with any prevailing skepticism of his host. Satisfied in his mind that Mateo was concealing something from him, and equally satisfied that he would sooner or later find it out, he grinned diabolically in the face of that worthy man, and sought the meditation of his miraculous couch. When he had departed, the skeptic turned to his wife: —

"This animal has been sniffing at the trail."

"Truly — but Mother of God — where is the discretion of our friend. If he will continue to haunt the pueblo like a love-sick chicken, he will get his neck wrung yet."

Following out an ingenious idea of his own, Ezekiel called the next day on the Demorests, and in some occult fashion obtained an invitation to stay under their hospitable roof during his sojourn in Buenaventura. Perfectly aware that he owed this courtesy more to Joan than to her husband, it is probable that his grim enjoyment was not diminished by the fact; while Joan, for reasons of her own, preferred the constraint which the presence of another visitor put upon Demorest's uxoriousness. Of late, too, there were times when Doña Rosita's naïve intelligence, which was not unlike the embarrassing perceptions of a bright and half-spoiled child, was in her way, and she would willingly have shared the young lady's company with her husband had Demorest shown any sympathy for the girl. It was in the faint hope that Ezekiel might in some way beguile Rosita's wandering attention that she had invited him. The only difficulty lay in his uncouthness, and in presenting to the heiress of the Picos a man who had been formerly her own servant. Had she attempted to conceal that fact, she was satisfied that Ezekiel's independence and natural predilection for embarrassing situations would have inevitably revealed it. She had even gone so far as to consider the propriety of investing him with a poor relationship to her family, when Doña Rosita herself happily stopped all further trouble. On her very first introduction to him, that charming young lady at once accepted him as a lunatic whose brains were turned by occult, scientific, and medical study! Ah! she, Rosita, had heard of such cases before. Had not a paternal ancestor of hers, one Don Diego Castro, believed he had discovered the elixir of youth! Had he not to that end refused even to wash him the hand, to cut him the nail of the finger and the hair of the head! Exalted by that discovery, had he not been unsparingly uncomplimentary to all humanity, especially to the weaker sex? Even as the Señor Corwin!

Far from being offended at this ingenious interpretation of his character, Ezekiel exhibited a dry gratification over it, and even conceived an unwholesome admiration of the fair critic; he haunted her presence and preoccupied her society far beyond Joan's most sanguine expectations. He sat in open-mouthed enjoyment of her at the table, he waylaid her in the garden, he attempted to teach her English. Doña Rosita received these extraordinary advances in a no less extraordinary manner. In the scant masculine atmosphere of the house, and the somewhat rigid New England reserve that still pervaded it, perhaps she languished a little, and was not averse to a slight flirtation, even with a madman. Besides, she assumed the attitude of exercising a wholesome restraint over him.

"If we are not found dead in our bed one morning, and extracted of our blood for a cordial, you shall thank to me for it," she said to Joan. "Also for the not empoisoning of the coffee!"

So she permitted him to carry a chair or hammock for her into the garden, to fetch the various articles which she was continually losing, and which he found with his usual penetration; and to supply her with information, in which, however, he exercised an unwonted caution. On the other hand, certain naïve recollections and admissions, which in the quality of a voluble child she occasionally imparted to this "madman" in return, were in the proportion of three to one.

It had been a hot day, and even the usual sunset breeze had failed that evening to rock the tops of the outlying pine-trees or cool the heated tiles of the pueblo roofs. There was a hush and latent expectancy in the air that reacted upon the people with feverish unrest and uneasiness; even a lull in the faintly whispering garden around the Demorests' casa had affected the spirits of its inmates, causing them to wander about in vague restlessness. Joan had disappeared; Doña Rosita, under an olive-tree in one of the deserted paths, and attended by the faithful Ezekiel, had said it was "earthquake weather," and recalled, with a sign of the cross, a certain dreadful day of her childhood, when el temblor had shaken down one of the mission towers.

"You shall see it now; as he have left it so it has remain always," she added with superstitious gravity.

"That 's just the lazy shiftlessness of your folks," responded Ezekiel with prompt ungallantry. "It ain't no wonder the Lord Almighty hez to stir you up now and then to keep you goin'."

Doña Rosita gazed at him with simple childish pity.

"Poor man; it have affect you also in the head, this weather. So! It was even so with the uncle of my father. Hush up yourself, and bring to me the box of chocolates of my table. I will gif to you one. You shall for one time have something pleasant on the end of your tongue, even if you must swallow him after."

Ezekiel grinned.

"Ye ain't afraid o' bein' left alone with the ghost that haunts the garden, Miss Rosita?"

"After *you* — never-r-r."

"I'll find Mrs. Demorest and send her to ye," said Ezekiel hesitatingly.

"Eh, to attract here the ghost? Thank you, no, very mooch."

Ezekiel's face contracted until nothing but his bright peering gray eyes could be seen.

"Attract the ghost!" he echoed. "Then you kalkilate that it's" — he stopped, insinuatingly.

Rosita brought her fan sharply over his knuckles, and immediately opened it again over her half embarrassed face.

"I comprehend not anything to 'ekalkilate.' *Will* you go, Don Fantastico; or is it for me to bring to you?"

Ezekiel flew. He quickly found the chocolates and returned, but was disconcerted on arriving under the olive-tree to find Doña Rosita no longer in the hammock. He turned into a bypath, where an extraordinary circumstance attracted his attention. The air was perfectly still, but the leaves of a manzanita bush near the misshapen cactus were slightly agitated. Presently Ezekiel saw the stealthy figure of a man emerge from behind it and approach the cactus. Reaching his hand cautiously towards the plant, the stranger detached something from one of its thorns, and instantly disappeared. The quick eyes of Ezekiel had seen that it was a letter, his unerring perception of faces recognized at the same moment that the intruder was none other than the handsome, reckless-looking man he had seen the other day in conference with Mateo.

But Ezekiel was not the only witness of this strange intrusion. A few paces from him, Doña Rosita, unconscious of his return, was gazing in a half-frightened breathless absorption in the direction of the stranger's flight.

"Wa'al!" drawled Ezekiel lazily.

She started and turned towards him. Her face was pale and alarmed, and yet to the critical eye of Ezekiel it seemed to wear an expression of gratified relief. She laughed faintly.

"Ef that 's the kind o' ghost you hev about yer, it 's a healthy one," drawled Ezekiel. He turned and fixed his keen eyes on Rosita's face. "I wonder what kind o' fruit grows on the cactus that he 's so fond of?"

Either she had not seen the abstraction of the letter, or her acting was perfect, for she returned his look unwaveringly.

"The fruit, eh? I have not comprehend."

"Wa'al, I reckon I will," said Ezekiel. He walked towards the cactus; there was nothing to be seen but its thorny spikes. He was confronted, however, by the sudden apparition of Joan from behind the manzanita at its side. She looked up and glanced from Ezekiel to Doña Rosita with an agitated air.

"Oh, you saw him too?" she said eagerly.

"I reckon," answered Ezekiel, with his eyes still on Rosita. "I was wondering what on airth he was so taken with that air cactus for."

Rosita had become slightly pale again in the presence of her friend. Joan quietly pushed Ezekiel aside and put her arm around her.

"Are you frightened again?" she asked, in a low whisper.

"Not mooch," returned Rosita, without lifting her eyes.

"It was only some peon, trespassing to pick blossoms for his sweetheart," she said significantly, with a glance towards Ezekiel. "Let us go in."

She passed her hand through Rosita's passive arm and led her towards the house, Ezekiel's penetrating eyes still following Rosita with an expression of gratified doubt.

For once, however, that astute observer was wrong. When Mrs. Demorest had reached the house she slipped into her own room, and, bolting the door, drew from her bosom a letter which *she* had picked from the cactus thorn, and read it with a flushed face and eager eyes.

It may have been the effect of the phenomenal weather, but the next day a malign influence seemed to pervade the Demorest household. Doña Rosita was confined to her room by an attack of languid nerves, superinduced, as she was still voluble enough to declare, by the narcotic effect of some unknown herb which the lunatic Ezekiel had no doubt mysteriously administered to her with a view of experimenting on its properties. She even avowed that she must speedily return to Los Osos, before Ezekiel should further compromise her reputation by putting her on a colored label in place of the usual Celestial Distributer of the Panacea. Ezekiel himself, who had been singularly abstracted and reticent, and had absolutely foregone one or two opportunities of disagreeable criticism, had gone to the pueblo early that morning. The house was comparatively silent and deserted when Demorest walked into his wife's boudoir.

It was a pretty room, looking upon the garden, furnished with a singular mingling of her own inherited formal tastes and the more sensuous coloring and abandon of her new life. There were a great many rugs and hangings scattered in disorder around the room, and apparently purposeless, except for color; there was a bamboo lounge as large as a divan, with two or three cushions disposed on it, and a low chair that seemed the incarnation of indolence. Opposed to this, on the wall, was the rigid picture of her grandfather, who had apparently retired with his volume further into the canvas before the spectacle of this ungodly opulence; a large Bible on a funereal trestle-like stand, and the primmest and barest of writing-tables, before which she was standing as at a sacrificial altar. With an almost mechanical movement she closed her portfolio as her husband entered, and also shut the lid of a small box with a slight snap. This suggested exclusion of him from her previous occupation, whatever it might have been, caused a faint shadow of pain to pass across his loving eyes. He cast a glance at his wife as if mutely asking her to sit beside him, but she drew a chair to the table, and with her elbow resting on the box, resignedly awaited his speech.

"I don't mean to disturb you, darling," he said gently, "but as we were alone, I thought we might have one of our old-fashioned talks, and" —

"Don't let it be so old-fashioned as to include North Liberty again," she interrupted wearily. "We 've had quite enough of that since I returned."

"I thought you found fault with me then for forgetting the past. But let that pass, dear; it is not *our* affairs I wanted to talk to you about now," he said, stifling a sigh, "it 's about your friend. Please don't misunderstand what I am going to say; nor that I interpose except from necessity."

She turned her dark brown eyes in his direction, but her glance passed abstractedly over his head into the garden.

"It 's a matter perfectly well known to me — and, I fear, to all our servants also — that somebody is making clandestine visits to our garden. I would not trouble you before, until I ascertained the object of these visits. It is quite plain to me now that Doña Rosita is that object, and that communications are secretly carried on between her and some unknown stranger. He has been here once or twice before; he was here again yesterday. Ezekiel saw him and saw her."

"Together?" asked Mrs. Demorest sharply.

"No; but it was evident that there was some understanding, and that some communication passed between them."

"Well?" said Mrs. Demorest, with repressed impatience.

"It is equally evident, Joan, that this stranger is a man who does not dare to approach your friend in her own house, nor more openly in this; but who, with her connivance, uses us to carry on an intrigue which may be perfectly innocent, but is certainly compromising to all concerned. I am quite willing to believe that Doña Rosita is only romantic and reckless, but that will not prevent her from becoming a dupe of some rascal who dare not face us openly, and who certainly does not act as her equal."

"Well, Rosita is no chicken, and you are not her guardian."

There was a vague heartlessness, more in her voice than in her words, that touched him as her cold indifference to himself had never done, and for an instant stung his crushed spirit to revolt.

"No," he said sternly, "but I am her father's *friend*, and I shall not allow his daughter to be compromised under my roof."

Her eyes sprang up to meet his in hatred as promptly as they once had met in love.

"And since when, Richard Demorest, have you become so particular?" she began, with dry asperity. "Since you lured *me* from the side of my wedded husband? Since you met *me* clandestinely in trains and made love to *me* under an assumed name? Since you followed *me* to my house under the pretext of being my husband's friend, and forced me — yes, forced me — to see you secretly under my mother's roof? Did you think of compromising *me* then? Did you think of ruining my reputation, of driving my husband from his home in despair? Did you call yourself a rascal then? Did you" —

"Stop!" he said, in a voice that shook the rafters; "I command you, stop!"

She had gradually worked herself from a deliberately insulting precision into an hysterical, and it is to be feared a virtuous, conviction of her wrongs. Beginning only with the instinct to taunt and wound the man before her, she had been led by a secret consciousness of something else he did not know to anticipate his reproach and justify herself in a wild feminine abandonment of emotion. But she stopped at his words. For a moment she was even thrilled again by the strength and imperiousness she had loved.

They were facing each other after five years of mistaken passion, even as they had faced each other that night in her mother's kitchen. But the grave of that dead passion yawned between them. It was Joan who broke the silence, that after her single outburst seemed to fill and oppress the room.

"As far as Rosita is concerned," she said, with affected calmness, "she is going to-night. And you probably will not be troubled any longer by your mysterious visitor."

Whether he heeded the sarcastic significance of her last sentence, or even heard her at all, he did not reply. For a moment he turned his blazing eyes full upon her, and then without a word strode from the room.

She walked to the door and stood uneasily listening in the passage until she heard the clatter of hoofs in the paved patio, and knew that he had ordered his horse. Then she turned back relieved to her room.

It was already sunset when Demorest drew rein again at the entrance of the corral, and the last stroke of the Angelus was ringing from the mission tower. He looked haggard and exhausted, and his horse was flecked with foam and dirt. Wherever he had been, or for what object, or whether, objectless and dazed, he had simply sought to lose himself in aimlessly wandering over the dry yellow hills or in careering furiously among his own wild cattle on the arid, brittle plain; whether he had beaten all thought from his brain with the jarring leap of his horse, or whether he had pursued some vague and elusive determination to his own door, is not essential to this brief chronicle. Enough that when he dismounted he drew a pistol from his holster and replaced it in his pocket.

He had just pushed open the gate of the corral as he led in his horse by the bridle, when he noticed another horse tethered among some cottonwoods that shaded the outer wall of his garden. As he gazed, the figure of a man swung lightly from one of the upper boughs of a cottonwood on the wall and disappeared on the other side. It was evidently the clandestine visitor. Demorest was in no mood for trifling. Hurriedly driving his horse into the inclosure with a sharp cut of his riata, he closed the gate upon him, slipped past the intervening space into the patio, and then unnoticed into the upper part of the garden. Taking a narrow by-path in the direction of the cottonwoods that could be seen above the wall, he presently came in sight of the object of his search moving stealthily towards the house. It was the work of a moment only to dash forward and seize him, to find himself engaged in a sharp wrestle, to half draw his pistol as he struggled with his captive in the open. But once in the clearer light, he started, his grasp of the stranger relaxed, and he fell back in bewildered terror.

"Edward Blandford! Good God!"

The pistol had dropped from his hand as he leaned breathless against a tree. The stranger kicked the weapon contemptuously aside. Then quietly adjusting his disordered dress, and picking the brambles from his sleeve, he said with the same air of disdain, —

"Yes! Edward Blandford, whom you thought dead! There! I 'm not a ghost — though you tried to make me one this time," he said, pointing to the pistol.

Demorest passed his hand across his white face.

"Then it 's you — and you have come here for — for — Joan?"

"For Joan?" echoed Blandford, with a quick scornful laugh, that made the blood flow back into Demorest's face as from a blow, and recalled his scattered senses. "For Joan?" he repeated. "Not much!"

The two men were facing each other in irreconcilable yet confused antagonism. Both were still excited and combative from their late physical struggle, but with feelings so widely different that it would have been impossible for either to have comprehended the other. In the figure that had apparently risen from the dead to confront him, Demorest only saw the man he had unconsciously wronged — the man who had it in his power to claim Joan and exact a terrible retribution! But it was part of this monstrous and irreconcilable situation that Blandford had ceased to contemplate it, and in his preoccupation only saw the actual interference of a man whom he no longer hated but had begun to pity and despise.

He glanced coolly around him.

"Whatever we 've got to say to each other," he said deliberately, "had better not be overheard. At least what *I* have got to say to you."

CHAPTER V

Demorest, now as self-possessed as his adversary, haughtily waved his hand towards the path. They walked on in silence, without even looking at each other, until they reached a small summer-house that stood in the angle of the wall. Demorest entered.

"We cannot be heard here," he said curtly.

"And we can see what is going on. Good," said Blandford, coolly following him.

The summer-house contained a bench and a table. Blandford seated himself on the bench. Demorest remained standing beside the table. There was a moment's silence.

"I came here with no desire to see you or avoid you," said Blandford, with cold indifference. "A few weeks ago I might perhaps have avoided you, for your own sake. But since then I have learned that among the many things I owe to — to your wife is the fact that five years ago she secretly *divorced me*, and that consequently my living presence could neither be a danger nor a menace to you. I see," he added dryly, with a quick glance at Demorest's horror-stricken face, "that I was also told the truth when they said you were as ignorant of the divorce as I was."

He stopped, half in pity of his adversary's shame, half in surprise of his own calmness. Five years before, in the tumultuous consciousness of his wrongs, he would have scarcely trusted himself face to face with the cooler and more self-controlled Demorest. He wondered at and partly admired his own coolness now, in the presence of his enemy's confusion.

"As your mind is at rest on that point," he continued sarcastically, "I don't suppose you care to know what became of *me* when I left North Liberty. But as it happens to have something to do with my being here to-night, and is a part of my business with you, you 'll have to listen to it. Sit down! Very well, then — stand up! It 's your own house."

His half cynical, wholly contemptuous ignoring of the real issue between them was more crushing to Demorest than the keenest reproach or most tragic outburst. He did not lift his eyes as Blandford resumed in a dry, business-like way: —

"When I came across the plains to California, I fell in with a man about my own age, — an emigrant also. I suppose I looked and acted like a crazy fool through all the journey, for he satisfied himself that I had some secret reason for leaving the States, and suspected that I was, like himself — a criminal. I afterwards learned that he was an escaped thief and assassin. Well, he played upon me all the way here, for I didn't care to reveal my real trouble to him, lest it should get back to North Liberty" — he interrupted himself with a sarcastic laugh. "Of course, you understand that all this while Joan was getting her divorce unknown to me, and you were marrying her — yet as *I* didn't know anything about it I let him compromise me to save her. But" — he stopped, his eye kindled, and, losing his self-control in what to Demorest seemed some incoherent passion, went on excitedly, "that man continued his persecution *here* — yes, *here*, in this very house, where I was a trusted and honored guest, and threatened to expose me to a pure, innocent, simple girl who had taken pity on me — unless I helped him in a conspiracy of cattle-stealers and road agents, of which he was chief. I was such a cursed sentimental fool then, that, believing him capable of doing this, believing myself still the husband of that woman, your wife, and to spare that innocent girl the shame of thinking me a villain, I purchased his silence by consenting. May God curse me for it!"

He had started to his feet with flashing eyes, and the indication of an overmastering passion that to Demorest, absorbed only in the stupefying revelation of his wife's divorce and the horrible doubt it implied, seemed utterly vacant and unmeaning. He had often dreamed of Blandford as standing before him, reproachful, indignant, and even desperate over his wife's unfaithfulness; but this insane folly and fury over some trivial wrong done to that plump, baby-faced, flirting Doña Rosita, crushed him by its unconscious but degrading obliteration of Joan and himself more than the most violent denunciation. Dazed and bewildered, yet with the instinct of a helpless man, he clung only to that part of Blandford's story which indicated that he had come there for Rosita, and *not* to separate him from Joan, and even turned to his former friend with a half-embarrassed gesture of apology as he stammered, —

"Then it was *you* who were Rosita's lover, and you who have been here to see her. Forgive me, Ned — if I had only known it."

He stopped and timidly extended his hand. But Blandford put it aside with a cold gesture and folded his arms.

"You have forgotten all you ever knew of me, Demorest! *I* am not in the habit of making clandestine appointments with helpless women whose natural protectors I dare not face. *I* have never pursued an innocent girl to the house I dared not enter. When I found that I could not honorably retain Doña Rosita's affection, I fled her roof. When I believed that even if I broke with this scoundrel — as I did — I was still legally if not morally tied to your wife, and could not marry Rosita, I left her never to return. And I tore my heart out to do it."

The tears were standing in his eyes. Demorest regarded him again with vacant wonder. Tears! — not for Joan's unfaithfulness to him — but for this silly girl's transitory sentimentalism. It was horrible!

And yet what was Joan to Blandford now? Why should he weep for the woman who had never loved him, — whom he loved no longer? The woman who had deceived him, — who had deceived them *both*. Yes! for Joan must have suspected that Blandford was living to have sought her secret divorce — and yet she had never told him — *him* — the man for whom she got it. Ah! he must not forget *that!* It was to marry him that she had taken that step. It was perhaps a foolish caution, — a mistaken reservation; but it was the folly — the mistake of a loving woman. He hugged this belief the closer, albeit he was conscious at the same time of following Blandford's story of his alienated affection with a feeling of wonder and envy.

"And what was the result of this touching sacrifice?" continued Blandford, trying to resume his former cynical indifference. "I 'll tell you. This scoundrel set himself about to supplant me. Taking advantage of my absence, his knowledge that her affection for me was heightened by the mystery of my life, and trusting to profit by a personal resemblance he is said to bear to me, he began to haunt her. Lately he has grown bolder, and he dared even to communicate with her here. For it is he," he continued, again giving way to his passion, "this dog, this sneaking coward, who visits the place unknown to you, and thinks to entrap the poor girl through her memory of me. And it is he that I came here to prevent, to expose — if necessary, to kill! Don't misunderstand me. I have made myself a deputy of the law for that purpose. I 've a warrant in my pocket, and I shall take him, this mongrel, half-breed Cherokee Bob, by fair means or foul!"

The energy and presence of his passion was so infectious that it momentarily swept away Demorest's doubts of the past.

"And I will help you, before God, Blandford," he said eagerly. "And Joan shall, too. She will find out from Rosita how far" —

"Thank you," interrupted Blandford dryly; "but your wife has already interfered in this matter, to my cost. It is to her, I believe, I owe this wretch's following Rosita here. She already knows this man — has met him twice in San Francisco; he even boasts of *your* jealousy. You know best how far he lied."

But Demorest had braced himself against the chill sensation that had begun to creep over him as Blandford spoke. He nerved himself and said, proudly, —

"I forbade her knowing him on account of his reputation solely. I have no reason to believe she has ever even wished to disobey me."

A smile of scorn that had kindled in Blandford's eyes darkened with a swift shadow of compassion as he glanced at Demorest's hard, ashen face. He held out his hand with a sudden impulse.

"Enough; I accept your offer, and shall put it to the test this very night. I know — if you do not — that Rosita is to leave here for Los Osos an hour from now in a private carriage, which your wife has ordered especially for her. The same information tells me that this villain and another of his gang will be in wait for the carriage three miles out of the pueblo to attack it and carry off the young girl."

"Are you mad?" said Demorest, in unfeigned amazement. "Do you believe them capable of attacking a private carriage and carrying off a solitary, defenseless woman? Come, Blandford, this is a schoolgirl romance, — not an act of mercenary highwaymen, — least of all Cherokee Bob and his gang. This is some madness of Rosita's, surely," he continued with a forced laugh.

"Does this mean that you think better of your promise?" asked Blandford dryly.

"I said I was at your service," said Demorest reproachfully.

"Then hear my plan to prevent it, and yet take that dog in the act," said Blandford. "But we must first wait here till the last moment to ascertain if he makes any signal to show that his plan is altered, or that he has discovered he is watched."

He turned, and in his preoccupation laid his hand for an instant upon Demorest's shoulder with the absent familiarity of old days. Unconscious as the action was, it thrilled them both, — from its very unconsciousness, — and impelled them to throw themselves into the new alliance with such feverish and excited activity in order to preclude any dangerous alien reflection, that when they rose a few moments later and cautiously left the garden arm-in-arm through the outer gates, no one would have believed they had ever been estranged, least of all the clever woman who had separated them.

It was nearly nine o'clock when the two friends, accompanied by the sheriff of the county, left San Buenaventura turnpike and turned into a thicket of alders to wait the coming of the carriage they were to henceforth follow cautiously and unseen in a parallel trail to the main road. The moon had risen, and with it the long withheld wind that now swept over the distant stretch of gleaming road and partly veiled it at times with flying dust unchecked by any dew from the clear cold sky. Demorest shivered even with his ready hand on his revolver. Suddenly the sheriff uttered an exclamation of disgust.

"Blasted if thar ain't some one in the road between us and their ambush."

"It 's one of their gang — scouting. Lie close."

"Scout be darned. Look at him bucking round there in the dust. He can't even ride! It 's some blasted greenhorn taking a pasear on a hoss for the first time. Damnation! he 's ruined everything. They 'll take the alarm."

"I 'll push on and clear him out," said Blandford excitedly. "Even if they 're off, I may yet get a shot at the Cherokee."

"Quick, then," said Demorest, "for here comes the carriage."

He pointed to a dark spot on the road occasionally emerging from the driven dust clouds.

In another moment Blandford was at the heels of the awkward horseman, who wheeled clumsily at his approach and revealed the lank figure of Ezekiel Corwin!

"You here!" said Blandford, in stupefied fury.

"Wa'al, yes, squire," said Ezekiel lazily, in spite of his uneasy seat. "I kalkilated ef there was suthin' goin' on, I 'd like to see it."

"You cursed prying fool! you 've spoiled all. There!" he shouted despairingly, as the quick clatter of hoofs rang from the arroyo behind them, "there they go! That 's your work, blockhead! Out of my way, or by God" — but the sentence was left unfinished, as joined by the sheriff, who had galloped up at the sound of the robbers' flight, he darted past the unconcerned Ezekiel. Demorest would have followed, but Blandford, with a warning cry to him to remain and protect the carriage, halted him at the side of Corwin as the vehicle now rapidly approached.

But Ezekiel was before him even then, and as the driver pulled up, that inquiring man tumbled from his horse, ran to the door, and opened it. Demorest rode up, glanced into the carriage, and fell back in blank amazement.

It was his wife who was sitting there alone, pale, erect, and beautiful. By some illusion of the moonlight, her face and figure, covered with soft white wrappings for a journey, looked as he remembered to have seen her the first night they had met in the Boston train. The picture was completed by the traveling bag and rug that lay on the seat before her. Another terrible foreboding seized him; his brain reeled. Was he going mad?

"Joan!" he stammered. "*You?* What is the meaning of this?"

Ezekiel — whom but for his dazed condition he might have seen violently contorting his features in Joan's face, presumably in equal astonishment — broke into a series of discordant chuckles.

"Wa'al, ef that ain't Deacon Salisbury's darter all over. Ha! Here are ye two men folks makin' no end o' fuss to save that Mexican gal with pistols and ambushes and plots and counterplots, and yer 's Joan Salisbury shows ye the way ha'ow to do it. And so, ma'am, you succeeded in fixin' it up with Doña Rosita to take her place and just sell them robbers cheap? Wa'al, ma'am, yer sold this yer party, too — for" — he advanced his face close to hers — "I never let on a word, though *I* knew it, and although they nearly knocked me off my hoss in their fuss and fury. Ha! ha! They wanted to know what *I* was doin' here! he-he! Tell 'em, Joan, tell 'em."

Demorest gazed from one to another with a troubled face, yet one on which a faint relief was breaking.

"What does he mean, Joan? Speak," he said, almost imploringly.

Joan, whose color was slightly returning, drew herself up with her old cold Puritan precision.

"After the scene you made this morning, Richard, when you chose to accuse your wife of unfaithfulness to her friend, her guest, and even your reputation, I resolved to go myself with Doña Rosita to Los Osos and explain the matter to her father. Some rumor of the ridiculous farce I have just witnessed reached us through Ezekiel, and frightened the poor girl so that she declined — and properly, too — to face the hoax which you and some nameless impersonator of a disgraced fugitive have gotten up for purposes of your own! I wish you joy of your work! If the play is over now, I presume I may be allowed to proceed on my journey?"

"Not yet," said Demorest slowly, with a face over which the chasing doubts had at last settled in a grayish pallor. "Believe what you like, misunderstand me if you will, laugh at the danger you perhaps comprehend better than I do, but upon this road, *wherever or to whatever it was leading you* — to-night you go no further!"

"Then I suppose I may return home," she said coldly. "Ezekiel will accompany me back to protect me from — *robbers.* Come, Ezekiel. Mr. Demorest and his friends can be safely trusted to take care of — your horse."

And as the grinning Ezekiel sprang into the carriage beside her, she pulled up the glass in the fateful and set face of her once trusting husband; the carriage turned and drove off, leaving him like a statue in the road.

. . . .

The bell of the North Liberty Second Presbyterian Church had just ceased ringing. But in the last five years it had rung out the bass viol and harmonium, and rung in an organ and choir; and the old austere interior had been subjected at the hands of the rising generation to an invasion of youthful warmth and color. Nowhere was this more apparent than in the choir itself, where the bright spring sunshine, piercing a newly-opened stained-glass window, picked out the new spring bonnet of Mrs. Demorest and settled upon it during the singing of the hymn. Perhaps that was the reason why a few eyes were curiously directed in that direction, and that even the minister himself strayed from the precise path of doctrine to allude with ecclesiastical vagueness to certain shining examples of the Christian virtues that were "again in our midst." The shrewd face and white eyelashes of Ezekiel Corwin, junior partner in the firm of Dilworth & Dusenberry, of San Francisco, were momentarily raised towards the choir, and then relapsed into an expression of fatigued self-righteousness.

When the service was over a few worshipers lingered near the choir staircase, mindful of the spring bonnet.

"It looks quite nat'ral," said Deacon Fairchild, "ter see Joan Salisbury attendin' the ministration of the Word agin. And I ain't sorry she did n't bring that second husband of hers with her. It kinder looks like old times — afore Edward Blandford was gathered to the Lord."

"That 's so," replied his auditor meekly, "and they *do* say ez ha'ow Demorest got more powerful worldly and unregenerate in that heathen country, and that Joan ez a professin' Christian had to leave him. I 've heerd tell thet he 'd got mixed up, out thar, with some half-breed outlaw, of the name o' Johnson, ez hez a purty, high-flyin' Mexican wife. It was fort'nit for Joan that she found a friend in grace in Brother Corwin to look arter her share in the property and bring her back tu hum."

"She 's lookin' peart," said Sister Bradley, "though to my mind that bonnet savors still o' heathen vanities."

"Et 's the new idees — crept in with that organ," groaned Deacon Fairchild; "but — sho — thar she comes."

She shone for an instant — a charming vision — out of the shadow of the choir stairs, and then glided primly into the street.

The old sexton, still in waiting with his hand on the half-closed door, paused and looked after her with a troubled brow. A singular and utterly incomprehensible recollection and resemblance had just crossed his mind.

THEIR UNCLE FROM CALIFORNIA

PART I

It was bitterly cold. When night fell over Lakeville, Wisconsin, the sunset, which had flickered rather than glowed in the western sky, took upon itself a still more boreal tremulousness, until at last it seemed to fade away in cold blue shivers to the zenith. Nothing else stirred; in the crisp still air the evening smoke of chimneys rose threadlike and vanished. The stars were early, pale, and pitiless; when the later moonlight fell, it appeared only to whiten the stiffened earth like snow, except where it made a dull, pewter-like film over the three frozen lakes which encompassed the town.

The site of the town itself was rarely beautiful, and its pioneers and founders had carried out the suggestions they had found there with loving taste and intelligence. Themselves old voyageurs, trappers, and traders, they still loved Nature too well to exclude her from the restful homes they had achieved after years of toiling face to face with her. So a strip of primeval forest on the one side, and rolling level prairie on the other, still came up to the base of the hill, whereon they had built certain solid houses, which a second generation had beautified and improved with modern taste, but which still retained their old honesty of foundation and wholesome rustic space. These yet stood among the old trees, military squares, and broad sloping avenues of the town. Seen from the railway by day, the regularity of streets and blocks was hidden by environing trees; there remained only a picturesque lifting of rustic gardens, brown roofs, gables, spires, and cupolas above the mirroring lake; seen from the railway this bitter night, the invisible terraces and streets were now pricked out by symmetrical lines and curves of sparkling lights, which glittered through the leafless boughs and seemed to encircle the hill like a diadem.

Central in the chiefest square, and yet preserving its old lordly isolation in a wooded garden, the homestead of Enoch Lane stood with all its modern additions and improvements. Already these included not only the latest phases of decoration, but various treasures brought by the second generation from Europe, which they were wont to visit, but from which they always contentedly returned to their little provincial town. Whether there was some instinctive yearning, like the stirred sap of great forests, in their wholesome pioneer blood, or whether there was some occult fascination in the pretty town-crested hill itself, it was still certain that the richest inhabitants always preferred to live in Lakeville. Even the young, who left it to seek their fortune elsewhere, came back to enjoy their success under the sylvan vaults of this vast ancestral roof. And that was why, this 22d of December, 1870, the whole household of Gabriel Lane was awaiting the arrival from California of his brother, Sylvester Lane, at the old homestead which he had left twenty-five years ago.

"And you don't know how he looks?" said Kitty Lane to her father.

"I do, perfectly; rather chubby, with blue eyes, curly hair, fair skin, and blushes when you speak to him."

"Papa!"

"Eh?—Oh, well, he *used* to. You see that was twenty-five years ago, when he left here for boarding-school. He ran away from there, as I told you; went to sea, and finally brought up at San Francisco."

"And you haven't had any picture, or photograph of him, since?"

"No — that is — I say! — you have n't, any of you, got a picture of Sylvester, have you?" he turned in a vague parenthetical appeal to the company of relatives and friends collected in the drawing-room after dinner.

"Cousin Jane has; she knows all about him!"

But it appeared that Cousin Jane had only heard Susan Marckland say that Edward Bingham had told her that he was in California when "Uncle Sylvester" had been nearly hanged by a Vigilance Committee for protecting a horse thief or a gambler, or some such person. This was felt to be ineffective as a personal description.

"He 's sure to wear a big beard; they all do when they first come back," said Amos Gunn, with metropolitan oraculousness.

"He has a big curling mustache, long silken hair, and broad shoulders," said Marie du Page.

There was such piquant conviction in the manner of the speaker, who was also a very pretty girl, that they all turned towards her, and Kitty quickly said, —

"But *you 've* never seen him?"

"No — but" — She stopped, and, lifting one shoulder, threw her spirited head sideways, in a pretty deprecatory way, with elevated eyebrows and an expression intended to show the otherwise untranslatable character of her impression. But it showed quite as pleasantly the other fact, that she was the daughter of a foreigner, an old French military explorer, and that she had retained even in Anglo-Saxon Lakeville some of the Gallic animation.

"Well, how many of you girls are going with me to meet him at the station?" said Gabriel, dismissing with masculine promptness the lesser question. "It 's time to be off."

"I 'd like to go," said Kitty, "and so would Cousin Jane; but really, papa, you see if *you* don't know him, and *we* don't either, and you 've got to satisfy yourself that it 's the right man, and then introduce *yourself* and then us — and all this on the platform before everybody — it makes it rather embarrassing for us. And then, as he 's your younger brother and we 're supposed to be his affectionate nieces, you know, it would make *him* feel *so* ridiculous!"

"And if he were to *kiss* you," said Marie tragically, "and then turn out not to be him!"

"So," continued Kitty, "you 'd better take Cousin John, who was more in Uncle Sylvester's time, to represent the past of the family, and perhaps Mr. Gunn" —

"To represent the future, I suppose?" interrupted Gabriel in a wicked whisper.

"To represent a name that most men of the world in New York and San Francisco know," went on Kitty, without a blush. "It would make recognition and introduction easier. And take an extra fur with you, dear — not for *him* but for yourself. I suppose he 's lived so much in the open air as to laugh at our coddling."

"I don't know about that," said her father thoughtfully; "the last telegram I have from him, en route, says he 's half frozen, and wants a close carriage sent to the station."

"Of course," said Marie impatiently; "you forget the poor creature comes from burning cañons and hot golden sands and perpetual sunshine."

"Very well; but come along, Marie, and see how I 've prepared his room," and as her father left the drawing-room Kitty carried off her old schoolfellow upstairs.

The room selected for the coming Sylvester had been one of the elaborate guest-chambers, but was now stripped of its more luxurious furniture and arranged with picturesque yet rural extravagance. A few rare buffalo, bear, and panther skins were disposed over the bare floor, and even displayed gracefully over some elaborately rustic chairs. The handsome French bedstead had been displaced for a small wrought-iron ascetic-looking couch covered with a gorgeously striped Mexican blanket. The fireplace had been dismantled of its steel grate, and the hearth extended so as to allow a pile of symmetrically heaped moss-covered hickory logs to take its place. The walls were covered with trophies of the chase, buck-horns and deer-heads, and a number of Indian arrows stood in a sheaf in the corners beside a few modern guns and rifles.

"Perfectly lovely," said Marie, "but" — with a slight shiver of her expressive shoulders — "a little cold and out-doorish, eh?"

"Nonsense," returned Kitty dictatorially, "and if he *is* cold, he can easily light those logs. They always build their open fires under a tree. Why, even Mr. Gunn used to do that when he was camping out in the Adirondacks last summer. I call it perfectly comfortable and *so* natural." Nevertheless, they had both tucked their chilly hands under the fleecy shawls they had snatched from the hall for this hyperborean expedition.

"You have taken much pains for him, Kaitee," said Marie, with her faintest foreign intonation. "You will like this strange uncle — you?"

"He is a wonderful man, Marie; he 's been everywhere, seen everything, and done everything out there. He 's fought duels, been captured by Indians, and tied to a stake to be tortured. He 's been leader of a Vigilance Committee, and they say that he has often shot and killed men himself. I 'm afraid he 's been rather wicked, you know. He 's lived alone in the woods like a hermit without seeing a soul, and then, again, he 's been a chief among the Indians, with Heaven knows how many Indian wives! They called him 'The Pale-faced Thunderbolt,' my dear, and 'The Young Man who Swallows the Lightning,' or something like that."

"And what can he want here?" asked Marie.

"To see us, my dear," said Kitty loftily; "and then, too, he has to settle something about *his* share of the property; for you know grandpa left a share of it to him. Not that he's ever bothered himself about it, for he's rich, — a kind of Monte Cristo, you know, — with a gold mine and an island off the coast, to say nothing of a whole county that he owns, that is called after him, and millions of wild cattle that he rides among and lassoes! It's dreadfully hard to do. You know you take a long rope with a slip-knot, and you throw it around your head so, and" —

"Hark!" said Marie, with a dramatic start, and her finger on her small mouth, "he comes!"

There was the clear roll of wheels along the smooth, frozen carriage sweep towards the house, the sharp crisp click of hoofs on stone, the opening of heavy doors, the sudden sparkling invasion of frigid air, the uplifting of voices in greeting, — but all familiar! There were Gabriel Lane's cheery, hopeful tones, the soprano of Cousin Jane and Cousin Emma, the baritone of Mr. Gunn, and the grave measured oratorical utterance of Parson Dexter, who had joined the party at the station; but certainly the accents of no *stranger*. Had he come? Yes, for his name was just then called, and the quick ear of Marie had detected a light, lounging, alien footstep cross the cold strip of marble vestibule. The two girls exchanged a rapid glance; each looked into the mirror, and then interrogatively at the other, nodded their heads affirmatively, and descended to the drawing-room. A group had already drawn round the fire, and a small central figure, who, with its back turned towards them, was still enwrapped in an enormous overcoat of rich fur, was engaged in presenting an alternate small varnished leather boot to the warmth of the grate. As they entered the room the heavy fur was yielded up with apparent reluctance, and revealed to the astonished girls a man of ordinary stature with a slight and elegant figure set off by a traveling suit of irreproachable cut. His light reddish-yellow hair, mustache, and sunburned cheek, which seemed all of one color and outline, made it impossible to detect the gray of the one or the hollowness of the other, and gave no indication of his age. Yet there was clearly no mistake. Here was Gabriel Lane seizing their nervously cold fingers and presenting them to their "Uncle Sylvester."

Far from attempting to kiss Kitty, the stranger for an instant seemed oblivious of the little hand she offered him in the half-preoccupied bow he gave her. But Marie was not so easily passed over, and, with her audacious face challenging his, he abstractedly imparted to the shake of her hand something of the fervor that he should have shown his relative. And then, still warming his feet on the fender, he seemed to have forgotten them both.

"Accustomed as you have been, sir," said the Reverend Mr. Dexter, seizing upon an awkward silence, and accenting it laboriously, — "perhaps I should say *inured* as you have been to the exciting and stirring incidents of a lawless and adventurous community, you doubtless find in a pastoral, yet cultivated and refined seclusion like Lakeville a degree of" —

"Oh, several degrees," said Uncle Sylvester, blandly flicking bits of buffalo hair from his well-fitting trousers; "it 's colder, you know — much colder."

"I was referring to a less material contrast," continued Mr. Dexter, with a resigned smile; "yet, as to the mere question of cold, I am told, sir, that in California there are certain severe regions of altitude, — although the mean temperature" —

"I suppose out in California you fellows would say our temperature was a darned sight *meaner*, eh?" broke in Amos Gunn, with a confidential glance at the others, as if offering a humorous diversion suited to the Californian taste.

Uncle Sylvester did not, however, smile. Gazing critically at Gunn, he said thoughtfully: —

"I think not; I 've even known men killed for saying less than that," — and turned to the clergyman. "You are quite right; some of the higher passes are very cold. I was lost in one of them in '56 with a small party. We were seventy miles from any settlement; we had had nothing to eat for thirty-six hours; our camp-fire, melting the snow, sank twelve feet below the surface." The circle closed eagerly around him, Marie, Kitty, and Cousin Jane pressing forward with excited faces; even the clergyman assumed an expression of profound interest. "A man by the name of Thompson, I think," continued Uncle Sylvester, thoughtfully gazing at the fire, "was frozen a few yards away. Towards morning, having been fifty-eight hours without food, our last drop of whiskey exhausted, and the fire extinguished, we found" —

"Yes, yes!" said half a dozen voices.

"We found," continued Uncle Sylvester, rubbing his hands cheerfully, "we found it — exceedingly cold. Yes — *exceedingly* cold!"

There was a dead silence.

"But you escaped!" said Kitty breathlessly.

"I think so. I think we all escaped — that is, except Thompson, if his name *was* Thompson; it might have been Parker," continued Uncle Sylvester, gazing with a certain languid astonishment on the eager faces around him.

"But *how* did you escape?"

"Oh, somehow! I don't remember exactly. I don't think," he went on reflectively, "that we had to eat Thompson — if it was *him* — at least not then. No" — with a faint effort of recollection — "that would have been another affair. Yes," assuringly to the eager, frightened eyes of Cousin Jane, "you are quite right, that was something altogether different. Dear me; one quite mixes up these things. Eh?"

A servant had entered, and after a hurried colloquy with Gabriel, the latter turned to Uncle Sylvester, —

"Excuse me, but I think there must be some mistake! We brought up your luggage with you — two trunks — in the station wagon. A man has just arrived with three more, which he says are yours."

"There should be five in all, I think," said Uncle Sylvester thoughtfully.

"Maybe there are, sir, I did n't count exactly," said the servant.

"All right," said Uncle Sylvester cheerfully, turning to his brother. "You can put them in my room or on the landing, except two marked 'L' in a triangle. They contain some things I picked up for you and the girls. We 'll look them over in the morning. And, if you don't mind, I 'll excuse myself now and go to bed."

"But it 's only half past ten," said Gabriel remonstratingly. "You don't, surely, go to bed at half past ten?"

"I do when I travel. Travel is *so* exhausting. Good-night! Don't let anybody disturb themselves to come with me."

He bowed languidly to the company, and disappeared with a yawn gracefully disguised into a parting smile.

"Well!" said Cousin Jane, drawing a long breath.

"I don't believe it 's your Uncle Sylvester at all!" said Marie vivaciously. "It 's some trick that Gabriel is playing upon us. And he 's not even a good actor — he forgets his part."

"And, then, five trunks for one single man! Heavens! what can he have in them?" said Cousin Emma.

"Perhaps his confederates, to spring out upon us at night, after everybody 's asleep."

"Are you sure you remembered him, papa?" said Kitty sotto voce.

"Certainly. And, my dear child, he knows all the family history as well as you do; and" — continued her father with a slight laugh that did not, however, conceal a certain seriousness that was new to him — "I only wish I understood as much about the property as he does. By the way, Amos," he broke off suddenly, turning to the young man, "he seemed to know your people."

"Most men in the financial world do," said Gunn a little superciliously.

"Yes; but he asked me if you had n't a relative of some kind in Southern California or Mexico."

A slight flush — so slight that only the keen, vivaciously observant eyes of Marie noticed it — passed over the young man's face.

"I believe it is a known fact that our branch of the family never emigrated from their native town," he said emphatically. "The Gunns were rather peculiar and particular in that respect."

"Then there were no offshoots from the old *stock*," said Gabriel.

Nevertheless, this pet joke of Gabriel's did not dissipate the constraint and disappointment left upon the company by Uncle Sylvester's unsatisfying performance and early withdrawal, and they separated soon after, Kitty and Marie being glad to escape upstairs together. On the landing they met two of the Irish housemaids in a state of agitated exhaustion. It appeared that the "sthrange gintleman" had requested that his bed be remade from bedclothes and bedding *always carried with him in his trunk!* From their apologetic tone it was evident that he had liberally rewarded them. "Shure, Miss," protested Norah, in deprecation of Kitty's flashing eye, "there 's thim that 's lived among shnakes and poysin riptiles and faverous disayses that 's particklar av the beds and sheets they lie on. Hisht! Howly Mother! it 's something else he 's wanting now!"

The door of Uncle Sylvester's room had slowly opened, and a blue pajama'd sleeve appeared, carefully depositing the sheaf of bows and arrows outside the door.

"I say, Norah, or Bridget there, some of you take those infernal things away. And look out, will you, for the arrowheads are deadly poison. The fool who got 'em did n't know they were African, and not Indian at all! And hold on!" The hand vanished, and presently reappeared holding two rifles. "And take these away, too! They 're loaded, capped, and *not* on the half-cock! A jar, a fall, the slightest shock is enough to send them off!"

"I 'm dreadfully sorry that you should find it so uncomfortable in our house, Uncle Sylvester," said Kitty, with a flushed cheek and vibrating voice.

"Oh, it 's you — is it?" said Uncle Sylvester's voice cheerfully. "I thought it was Bridget out there. No, I don't intend to find it uncomfortable. That 's why I 'm putting these things outside. But, for Heaven's sake, don't *you* touch them. Leave that to the ineffable ass who put them there. Good-night!"

The door closed; the whispering voices of the girls faded from the corridor; the lights were lowered in the central hall, only the red Cyclopean eye of an enormous columnar stove, like a lighthouse, gleamed through the darkness. Outside, the silent night sparkled, glistened, and finally paled. Towards morning, having invested the sturdy wooden outer walls of the house and filmed with delicate tracery every available inch of windowpane, it seemed stealthily to invade the house itself, stilling and chilling it as it drew closer around its central heart of warmth and life. Only once the frigid stillness was broken by the opening of a door and steps along the corridor. This was preceded by an acrid smell of burning bark.

It was subtle enough to permeate the upper floor and the bedroom of Marie du Page, who was that night a light and nervous sleeper. Peering from her door, she could see, on the lower corridor, the extraordinary spectacle of Uncle Sylvester, robed in a gorgeous Japanese dressing-gown of quilted satin trimmed with the fur of the blue fox, candle in hand, leisurely examining the wall of the passage. Presently, drawing out a foot-rule from his pocket, he actually began to measure it! Miss Du Page saw no more. Hurriedly closing her door, she locked and bolted it, firmly convinced that Gabriel Lane was harboring in the guise of Uncle Sylvester a somnambulist, a maniac, or an impostor.

PART II

"It does n't seem as if Uncle Sylvester was any the more comfortable for having his own private bedding with him," said Kitty Lane, entering Marie's room early the next morning. "Bridget found him curled up in his furs like a cat asleep on the drawing-room sofa this morning."

Marie started; she remembered her last night's vision. But some instinct — she knew not what — kept her from revealing it at this moment. She only said a little ironically: —

"Perhaps he missed the wild freedom of his barbaric life in a small bedroom."

"No. Bridget says he said something about being smoked out of his room by a ridiculous wood fire. The idea! As if a man brought up in the woods could n't stand a little smoke. No — that 's his excuse! Marie! — do you know what I firmly believe?"

"No," said Marie quickly.

"I firmly believe that poor man is ashamed of his past rough life, and does everything he can to forget it. That 's why he affects those ultra-civilized and effeminate ways, and goes to the other extreme, as people always do."

"Then you think he 's really reformed, and is n't likely to take an impulse to rob and murder anybody again?"

"Why, Marie, what nonsense!"

Nevertheless, Uncle Sylvester appeared quite fresh and cheerful at breakfast. It seemed that he had lit the fire before undressing, but the green logs were piled so far into the room that the smoke nearly suffocated him. Fearful of alarming the house by letting the smoke escape through the door, he opened the window, and when it had partly dispersed, sought refuge himself from the arctic air of his bedroom in the drawing-room. So far the act did not seem inconsistent with his sanity, or even intelligence and consideration for others. But Marie fixed upon him a pair of black, audacious eyes.

"Did you ever walk in your sleep, Mr. Lane?"

"No; but" — thoughtfully breaking an egg — "I have ridden, I think."

"In your sleep? Oh, do tell us all about it!" said cousins Jane and Emma in chorus.

Uncle Sylvester cast a resigned glance out of the window. "Oh, yes — certainly; it is n't much. You see at one time I was in the habit of making long monotonous journeys, and they were often exhausting, and," he added, becoming wearied as if at the recollection, "always dreadfully tiresome. As the trail was sometimes very uncertain and dangerous, I rode a very sure-footed mule that could go anywhere where there was space big enough to set her small hoofs upon. One night I was coming down the slope of a mountain towards a narrow valley and river that were crossed by an old, abandoned flume, of which nothing was now left but the upright trestle-work and long horizontal string-piece. As the trail was very difficult and the mule's pace was slow, I found myself dozing at times, and at last I must have fallen asleep. I think I must have been awakened by a singular regularity in the movement of the mule, — or else it was the monotony of step that had put me to sleep and the cessation of it awakened me. You see, at first I was not certain that I was n't really dreaming. For the trail seemed to have disappeared; the wall of rock on one side had vanished also, and there appeared to be nothing ahead of me but the opposite hillside."

Uncle Sylvester stopped to look out of the window at a passing carriage. Then he went on.

"The moon came out, and I saw what had happened. The mule, either of her own free will, or obeying some movement I had given the reins in my sleep, had swerved from the trail, got on top of the flume, and was actually walking across the valley on the narrow string-piece, a foot wide, half a mile long, and sixty feet from the ground. I knew," he continued, examining his napkin thoughtfully, "that she was perfectly sure-footed, and that if I kept quiet she could make the passage; but I suddenly remembered that midway there was a break and gap of twenty feet in the continuous line, and that the string-piece was too narrow to allow her to turn round and retrace her steps."

"Good heavens!" said Cousin Jane.

"I beg your pardon?" said Uncle Sylvester politely.

"I only said, 'Good heavens!' Well?" she added impatiently.

"Well?" repeated Uncle Sylvester vaguely. "Oh, that 's all. I only wanted to explain what I meant by saying I had ridden in my sleep."

"But," said Cousin Jane, leaning across the table with grim deliberation and emphasizing each word with the handle of her knife, "how — did — you — and — that — mule get down?"

"Oh, with slings and ropes, you know — so," demonstrating by placing his napkin-ring in a sling made of his napkin.

"And I suppose you carried the slings and ropes with you in your five trunks?" gasped Cousin Jane.

"No. Fellows on the river brought 'em in the morning. Mighty spry chaps, those river miners."

"Very!" said Cousin Jane.

Breakfast over, they were not surprised that their sybaritic guest excused himself from an inspection of the town in the frigid morning air, and declined joining a skating party to the lake, on the ground that he could keep warmer indoors with half the exertion. An hour later found him standing before the fire in Gabriel Lane's study, looking languidly down on his elder brother.

"Then, as far as I can see," he said quietly, "you have made ducks and drakes of your share of the property, and that virtually you are in the hands of this man Gunn and his father."

"You 're putting it too strongly," said Gabriel deprecatingly. "In the first place, my investments with Gunn's firm are by no means failures, and they only hold as security a mortgage on the forest land below the hill. It 's scarcely worth the money. I would have sold it long ago, but it had been a fancy of father's to keep it wild land for the sake of old times and the healthiness of the town."

"There used to be a log cabin there, where the old man had a habit of camping out whenever he felt cramped by civilization up here, was n't there?" said Uncle Sylvester meditatively.

"Yes," said Gabriel impatiently; "it 's still there — but to return to Mr. Gunn. He has taken a fancy to Kitty, and even if *I* could not lift the mortgage, there 's some possibility that the land would still remain in the family."

"I think I 'll drive over this afternoon and take a look at the old shanty if this infernal weather lets up."

"Yes; but just now, my dear Sylvester, let us attend to business. I want to show you those investments."

"Oh, certainly; trot 'em out," said his brother, plucking up a simulation of interest as he took a seat at the table.

From a drawer of his desk Gabriel brought out a bundle of prospectuses and laid them before Uncle Sylvester.

A languid smile of recognition lit up the latter's face.

"Ah! yes," he said, glancing at them. "The old lot: 'Carmelita,' 'Santa Maria,' and 'Preciosa!' Just as I imagined — and yet who 'd have thought of seeing them *here!* A good deal rouged and powdered, Miss Carmelita, since I first knew you! Considerably bolstered up by miraculous testimony to your powers, my dear Santa Maria, since the day I found you out, to my cost! And you too, Preciosa! — a precious lot of money I dropped on you in the old days!"

"You are joking," said Gabriel, with an uneasy smile. "You don't mean to imply that this stock is old and worthless?"

"There is n't a capital in America or Europe where for the last five years it has n't been floated with a new character each time. My dear Gabriel, that stock is n't worth the paper it is printed on."

"But it is impossible that an experienced financier like Gunn could be deceived!"

"I 'm sorry to hear *that.*"

"Come, Sylvester! confess you 've taken a prejudice against Gunn from your sudden dislike of his son! And what have you against him?"

"I could n't say exactly," said Uncle Sylvester reflectively. "It may be his eyes, or only his cravat! But," rising cheerfully and placing his hand lightly on his brother's shoulder, "don't *you* worry yourself about that stock, old man; *I'll* see that somebody else has the worry and you the cash. And as to the land and — Kitty — well, you hold on to them both until you find out which the young man is really after."

"And then?" said Gabriel, with a smile.

"Don't give him either! But, I say, have n't we had enough business this morning? Let 's talk of something else. Who 's the French girl?"

"Marie? She 's the daughter of Jules du Page — don't you remember? — father's friend. When Jules died, it was always thought that father, who had half adopted her as a child, would leave her some legacy. But you know that father died without making a will, and that — rich as he was — his actual assets were far less than we had reason to expect. Kitty, who felt the disappointment as keenly as her friend, I believe would have divided her own share with her. It 's odd, by the way, that father could have been so deceived in the amount of his capital, or how he got rid of his money in a way that we knew nothing of. Do you know, Sylvester, I 've sometimes suspected" —

"What?" said Uncle Sylvester suddenly.

The bored languor of his face had abruptly vanished. Every muscle was alert; his gray eyes glittered.

"That he advanced money to Du Page, who lost it, or that they speculated together," returned Gabriel, who, following Uncle Sylvester's voice only, had not noticed the change of expression.

"That would seem to be a weakness of the Lane family," said Uncle Sylvester grimly, with a return of his former carelessness. "But that is not *your* own opinion — that 's a suggestion of some one else?"

"Well," said Gabriel, with a laugh and a slight addition of color, "it *was* Gunn's theory. As a man of the world and a practical financier, you know."

"And you 've talked with *him* about it?"

"Yes. It was a matter of general wonder years ago."

"Very likely; but, just now, don't you think we 've had enough financial talk?" said Uncle Sylvester, with a bored contraction of his eyebrows. "Come," looking around the room, "you 've changed the interior of the old house."

"Yes. Unfortunately, just after father's death it was put in the hands of a local architect or builder, one of father's old friends, but not a very skillful workman, who made changes while the family were away. That 's why your present bedroom, which was father's old study, had a slice taken off it to make the corridor larger, and why the big chimney and hearthstone are still there, although the fireplace is modernized. That was Flint's stupidity."

"Whose stupidity?" asked Uncle Sylvester, trimming his nails.

"Flint's — the old architect."

"Why did n't you make him change it back again?"

"He left Lakeville shortly after, and I brought an architect from St. Louis after I returned from Europe. But nothing could be done to your room without taking down the chimney, so it remained as Flint left it."

"That reminds me, Gabriel, I 'm afraid I spoke rather cavalierly to Kitty, last night, about the arrangements of the room. The fact is, I 've taken a fancy to it, and should like to fit it up myself. Have I your permission?"

"Certainly, my dear Sylvester."

"I 've some knickknacks in my trunks, and I 'll do it at once."

"As you like."

"And you 'll see that I am not disturbed; and you 'll explain it to Kitty, with my apologies?"

"Yes."

"Then I 'm off.

Gabriel glanced at his brother with a perplexed smile. Here was the bored traveler, explorer, gold-seeker, soldier of fortune, actually as pleased as a girl over the prospect of arranging his room! He called after him, "Sylvester!"

"Yes."

"I say, if you could, you know, just try to interest these people to-night with some of your adventures — something told *seriously*, you know, as if you really were in earnest — I 'd be awfully obliged to you. The fact is, — you 'll excuse me, — but they think you don't come up to your reputation."

"They want a story?"

"Yes, — one of your experiences."

"I 'll give them one. Ta-ta!"

For the rest of the day Uncle Sylvester was invisible, although his active presence in his room was betrayed by the sound of hammering and moving of furniture. As the remainder of the party were skating on the lake, this eccentricity was not remarked except by one, — Marie du Page, — who on pretense of a slight cold had stayed at home. But with her suspicions of the former night, she had determined to watch the singular relative of her friend. Added to a natural loyalty to the Lanes, she was moved by a certain curiosity and fascination towards this incomprehensible man.

The house was very quiet when she stole out of her room and passed softly along the corridor; she examined the wall carefully to discover anything that might have excited the visitor's attention. There were a few large engravings hanging there; could he have designed to replace them by some others? Suddenly she was struck with the distinct conviction that the wall of the corridor did not coincide with the wall of his room as represented by the line of the door. There was certainly a space between the two walls unaccounted for. This was undoubtedly what had attracted *his* attention; but what *business* was it of his?

She reflected that she had seen in the wall of the conservatory an old closed staircase, now used as shelves for dried herbs and seeds, which she had been told was the old-time communication between the garden and Grandfather Lane's study, — the room now occupied by the stranger. Perhaps it led still farther, and thus accounted for the space. Determined to satisfy herself, she noiselessly descended to the conservatory. There, surely, was the staircase, — a narrow flight of wooden steps encumbered with packages of herbs, — losing itself in upper darkness. By the aid of a candle she managed to grope and pick her way up step by step. Then she paused. The staircase had abruptly ended on the level of the study, now cut off from it by the new partition. She was in a stifling inclosure, formed by the walls, scarcely eighteen inches wide. It was made narrower by a singular excrescence on the old wall, which seemed to have been a bricked closet, now half destroyed and in ruins. She turned to descend, when a strange sound from Uncle Sylvester's room struck her ear. It was the sound of tapping on the floor close to the partition, within a foot of where she was standing. At the same moment there was a decided movement of the plank of the flooring beneath the partition: it began to slide slowly, and then was gradually withdrawn into the room. With prompt presence of mind, she instantly extinguished her candle and drew herself breathlessly against the partition.

When the plank was entirely withdrawn, a ray of light slipped through the opening, revealing the bare rafters of the floor, and a hand and arm inserted under the partition, groping as if towards the bricked closet. As the fingers of the exploring hand were widely extended, Marie had no difficulty in recognizing on one of them a peculiar signet ring which Uncle Sylvester wore. A swift impulse seized her. To the audacious Marie impulse and action were the same thing. Bending stealthily over the aperture, she suddenly snatched the ring from the extended finger. The hand was quickly withdrawn with a start and uncontrolled exclamation, and she availed herself of that instant to glide rapidly down the stairs.

She regained her room stealthily, having the satisfaction a moment later of hearing Uncle Sylvester's door open and the sound of his footsteps in the corridor. But he was evidently unable to discover any outer ingress to the inclosure, or believed the loss of his ring an accident, for he presently returned. Meantime, what was she to do? Tell Kitty of her discovery, and show the ring? No — not yet! Oddly enough, now that she had the ring, taken from his wicked finger in the very act, she found it as difficult as ever to believe in his burglarious design. She must wait. The mischief — if there had been mischief — was done; the breaking in of the bricked closet was, from the appearance of the ruins, a bygone act. Could it have been some youthful escapade of Uncle Sylvester's, the scene of which he was revisiting as criminals are compelled to do? And had there been anything taken from the closet, or was its destruction a part of the changes in the old house? How could she find out without asking Kitty? There was one way. She remembered that Mr. Gunn had once shown a great deal of interest to Kitty about the old homestead, and even of old Mr. Lane's woodland cabin. She would ask *him*. It was a friendly act, for Kitty had not of late been very kind to him.

The opportunity presented itself at dusk, as Mr. Gunn, somewhat abstracted, stood apart at the drawing-room window. Marie hoped he had enjoyed himself while skating; her stupid cold had kept her indoors. She had amused herself rambling about the old homestead; it was such a queer place, so full of old nooks and corners and unaccountable spaces. Just the place, she would think, where old treasures might have been stored. Eh?

Mr. Gunn had not spoken — he had only coughed. But in the darkness his eyes were fixed angrily on her face. Without observing it, she went on. She knew he was interested in the old house; she had heard him talk to Kitty about it; had Kitty ever said anything about some old secret hoarding place?

No, certainly not! And she was mistaken, he never was interested in the house! He could not understand what had put that idea in her head! Unless it was this ridiculous, shady stranger in the guise of an uncle whom they had got there. It was like his affectation!

"Oh, dear, no," said Marie, with unmistakable truthfulness, "*he* did not say anything. But," with sudden inconsistent aggression, "is *that* the way you speak to Kitty of her uncle?"

Really he did n't know — he was joking only, and he was afraid he must just now ask her to excuse him. He had received letters that made it possible that he might be called suddenly to New York at any moment. Marie stared. It was evident that he had proposed to Kitty and been rejected! But she was no nearer her discovery.

Nor was there the least revelation in the calm, half-bored, yet good-humored presence of the wicked uncle at dinner. So indifferent did he seem, not only to his own villainy but even to the loss it had entailed, that she had a wild impulse to take the ring from her pocket and display it on her own finger before him then and there. But the conviction that he would in some way be equal to the occasion prevented her. The dinner passed off with some constraint, no doubt emanating from the conscious Kitty and Gunn. Nevertheless, when they had returned to the drawing-room, Gabriel rubbed his hands expectantly.

"I prevailed on Sylvester this morning to promise to tell us some of his experiences, — something *complete* and satisfactory this time. Eh?"

Uncle Sylvester, warming his cold blood before the fire, looked momentarily forgetful and — disappointing. Cousins Jane and Emma shrugged their shoulders.

"Eh," said Uncle Sylvester absently, "er — er — oh yes! Well" (more cheerfully), "about what, eh?"

"Let it be," said Marie pointedly, fixing her black magnetic eyes on the wicked stranger, "let it be something about the *discovery* of gold, or a buried *treasure hoard*, or a robbery."

To her intense disgust Uncle Sylvester, far from being discomfited or confused, actually looked pleased, and his gray eyes thawed slightly.

"Certainly," he said. "Well, then! Down on the San Joaquin River there was an old chap — one of the earliest settlers — in fact, he 'd come on from Oregon before the gold discovery. His name, dear me!" — continued Uncle Sylvester, with an effort of memory and apparently beginning already to lose his interest in the story — "was — er — Flint."

As Uncle Sylvester paused here, Cousin Jane broke in impatiently.

"Well, that 's not an uncommon name. There was an old carpenter here in your father's time who was called Flint."

"Yes," said Uncle Sylvester languidly. "But there is, or was, something uncommon about it — and that 's the point of the story, for in the old time Flint and Gunn were of the same stock."

"Is this a Californian joke?" said Gunn, with a forced smile on his flushed face. "If so, spare me, for it 's an old one."

"It 's much older *history*, Mr. Gunn," said Uncle Sylvester blandly, "which I remember from a boy. When the first Flint traded near Sault Sainte Marie, the Canadian voyageurs literally translated his name into Pierre à Fusil, and he went by that name always. But when the English superseded the French in numbers and language the name was literally translated back again into 'Peter Gunn,' which his descendants bear."

"A labored form of the old joke," said Gunn, turning contemptuously away.

"But the story," said cousins Jane and Emma. "The story of the gold discovery — never mind the names."

"Excuse me," said Uncle Sylvester, placing his hand in the breast of his coat with a delightful exaggeration of offended dignity. "But, doubts having been cast upon my preliminary statement, I fear I must decline proceeding further." Nevertheless, he smiled unblushingly at Miss Du Page as he followed Gunn from the room.

The next morning those who had noticed the strained relations of Miss Kitty and Mr. Gunn were not surprised that the latter was recalled on pressing business to New York by the first train; but it was a matter of some astonishment to Gabriel Lane and Marie du Page that Uncle Sylvester should have been up early, and actually accompanied that gentleman as far as the station! Indeed, the languid explorer and gold-seeker exhibited remarkable activity, and, clad in a rough tourist suit, announced, over the breakfast-table, his intention of taking a long tramp through the woods, which he had not revisited since a boy. To this end he had even provided himself with a small knapsack, and for once realized Kitty's ideal of his character.

"Don't go too far," said Gabriel, "for, although the cold has moderated, the barometer is falling fast, and there is every appearance of snow. Take care you are not caught in one of our blizzards."

"But *you* are all going on the lake to skate!" protested Uncle Sylvester.

"Yes; for the very reason that it may be our last chance; but should it snow we shall be nearer home than you may be."

Nevertheless, when it came on to snow, as Gabriel had predicted, the skating party was by no means so near home as he had imagined. A shrewd keenness and some stimulating electric condition of the atmosphere had tempted the young people far out on the lake, and they had ignored the first fall of fine grayish granulations that swept along the icy surface like little puffs of dust or smoke. Then the fall grew thicker, the gray sky contracted, the hurrying flakes, dashed against them by a fierce northwester, were larger, heavier, and seemed an almost palpable force that held them back. Their skates, already clogged with drift, were beginning to be useless. The bare wind-swept spaces were becoming rarer; they could only stumble on blindly towards the nearest shore. Nor when they reached it were they yet safe; they could scarcely stand against the still increasing storm that was fast obliterating the banks and stretch of meadow beyond. Their only hope of shelter was the range of woods that joined the hill. Holding hands in single file, the little party, consisting of Kitty, Marie, and cousins Jane and Emma — stout-hearted Gabriel leading and Cousin John bringing up the rear — at last succeeded in reaching it, and were rejoiced to find themselves near old Lane's half-ruined cabin. To their added joy and astonishment, whiffs of whirling smoke were issuing from the crumbling chimney. They ran to the crazy door, pushed aside its weak fastening, and found — Uncle Sylvester calmly enjoying a pipe before a blazing fire. A small pickaxe and crowbar were lying upon a mound of freshly turned earth beside the chimney, where the rotten flooring had been torn up.

The tumultuous entrance of the skating party required no explanation; but when congratulations had been exchanged, the wet snow shaken off, and they had drawn round the fire, curious eyes were cast upon the solitary occupant and the pile of earth and débris before him.

"I believe," said Gabriel laughingly, "that you have been so bored here that you have actually played at gold-hunting for amusement."

Uncle Sylvester took the pipe from his mouth and nodded.

"It 's a common diversion of yours," said Marie audaciously.

Uncle Sylvester smiled sweetly.

"And have you been successful *this time?*" asked Marie.

"I got the color."

"Eh?"

Uncle Sylvester rose and placed himself with his back to the fire, gently surveying the assembled group.

"I was interrupted in a story of gold-digging last evening," he said blandly. "How far had I got?"

"You were down on the San Joaquin River in the spring of '50, with a chap named Flint," chorused cousins Jane and Emma promptly.

"Ah! yes," said Uncle Sylvester. "Well, in those days there was a scarcity of money in the diggings. Gold dust there was in plenty, but no *coin.* You can fancy it was a bother to weigh out a pinch of dust every time you wanted a drink of whiskey or a pound of flour; but there was no other legal tender. Pretty soon, however, a lot of gold and silver pieces found their way into circulation in our camp and the camps around us. They were foreign — old French and English coins. Here 's one of them that I kept."

He took from his pocket a gold coin and handed it to Gabriel.

Lane rose to his feet with an exclamation: —

"Why, this is like the louis-d'or that grandfather saved through the war and gave to father."

Uncle Sylvester took the coin back, placed it in his left eye, like a monocle, and winked gravely at the company.

"It is the *same!*" he went on quietly. "I was interested, for I had a good memory, and I remembered that, as a boy, grandfather had shown me one of those coins and told me he was keeping them for old Jules du Page, who did n't believe in banks and bank-notes. Well, I traced them to a trader called Flint, who was shipping gold dust from Stockton to Peter Gunn & Sons, in New York."

"To whom?" asked Gabriel quickly.

"Old Gunn — the father of your friend!" said Uncle Sylvester blandly. "We talked the matter over on our way to the station this morning. Well, to return. Flint only said that he had got them from a man called Thompson, who had got them from somebody else in exchange for goods. A year or two afterwards this same Thompson happened to be frozen up with me in Starvation Camp. When he thought he was dying he confessed that he had been bribed by Flint to say what he had said, but that he believed the coins were stolen. Meantime, Flint had disappeared. Other things claimed my attention. I had quite forgotten him, until one night, five years afterwards, I blundered into a deserted mining camp, by falling asleep on my mule, who carried me across a broken flume, but — I think I told you that story already."

"You never finished it," said Cousin Jane sharply.

"Let me do so now, then. I was really saved by some Indians, who took me for a spirit up aloft there in the moonlight and spread the alarm. The first white man they brought me was a wretched drunkard known to the boys as 'Old Fusil,' or 'Fusel Oil,' who went into delirium tremens at the sight of me. Well, who do you suppose he turned out to be? Flint! Flint played out and ruined! Cast off and discarded by his relations in New York — the foundation of whose fortunes he had laid by the villainy they had accepted and condoned. For Flint, as the carpenter of the old homestead, had discovered the existence of a bricked closet in the wall of father's study, partitioned it off so that he could break into it without detection and rifle it at his leisure, and who had thus carried off that part of grandfather's hoard which father had concealed there. He knew it could never be missed by the descendants. But, through haste or ignorance, he *did not touch the papers* and documents also hidden there. And *they* told of the existence of grandfather's second cache, or hiding-place, beneath this hearth, and were left for me to discover."

He coolly relit his pipe, fixed his eyes on Marie without apparently paying attention to the breathless scrutiny of the others, and went on: —

"Flint, *alias* Pierre à Fusil, *alias* Gunn, died a maniac. I resolved to test the truth of his story. I came here. I knew the old homestead, as a boy who had wandered over every part of it, far better than you, Gabriel, or any one. The elder Gunn had only heard of it through the criminal disclosure of his relative, and only wished to absorb it through his son in time, and thus obliterate all trace of Flint's outrage. I recognized the room perfectly — thanks to our dear Kitty, who had taken up the carpet, which thus disclosed the loose plank before the closet that was hidden by the partition. Under pretext of rearranging the room — for which Kitty will forgive me — I spent the day behind a locked door, making my way through the partition. There I found the rifled closet, but the papers intact. They contained a full description of the sum taken by Flint, and also of a larger sum buried in a cask beside this chimney. I had just finished unearthing it a few moments before you came. I had at first hoped to offer it to the family as a Christmas gift to-morrow, but" —

He stopped and sucked slowly at his pipe.

"We anticipated you," said Gabriel, laughing.

"No," said Uncle Sylvester coolly. "But because it don't happen to belong to *you* at all! According to the paper I have in my pocket, which is about as legal a document as I ever saw, it is father's free gift to Miss Marie du Page."

Kitty threw her arms around her white and breathless friend with a joyful cry, and honest Gabriel's face shone with unselfish gratification.

"For yourself, my dear Gabriel, you must be satisfied with the fact that Messrs. Peter Gunn & Sons will take back your wild-cat stock at the price you paid for it. It is the price they pay for their share in this little transaction, as I had the honor of pointing out to Mr. Gunn on our way to the station this morning."

"Then you think that young Mr. Gunn knew that Flint was his relation, and that he had stolen father's money," said Kitty, "and that Mr. Gunn only wanted to" — She stopped, with flashing eyes.

"I think he would have liked to make an arrangement, my dear, that would keep the secret and the property in the family," said Uncle Sylvester. "But I don't think he suspected the existence of the second treasure here."

"And then, sir," said Cousin Jane, "it appears that all these wretched, unsatisfactory scraps of stories you were telling us were nothing after all but" —

"My way of telling *this* one," said Uncle Sylvester.

As the others were eagerly gathering around the unearthed treasure, Marie approached him timidly, all her audacity gone, tears in her eyes, and his ring held hesitatingly between her fingers. "How can I thank you — and how *can* you ever forgive me?"

"Well," said Uncle Sylvester, gazing at her critically, "you might keep the ring to think over it."

THE GHOSTS OF STUKELEY CASTLE

There should have been snow on the ground to make the picture seasonable and complete, but the Western Barbarian had lived long enough in England to know that, except in the pages of a holiday supplement, this was rarely the accompaniment of a Christmas landscape, and he cheerfully accepted, on the 24th of December, the background of a low, brooding sky, on which the delicate tracery of leafless sprays and blacker chevaux de frise of pine was faintly etched, as a consistent setting to the turrets and peacefully stacked chimneys of Stukeley Castle. Yet, even in this disastrous eclipse of color and distance, the harmonious outlines of the long, gray, irregular pile seemed to him as wonderful as ever. It still dominated the whole landscape, and, as he had often fancied, carried this subjection even to the human beings who had created it, lived in it, but which it seemed to have in some dull, senile way dozed over and forgotten. He vividly recalled the previous sunshine of an autumnal house party within its walls, where some descendants of its old castellans, encountered in long galleries or at the very door of their bedrooms, looked as alien to the house as the Barbarian himself.

For the rest, it may be found described in the local guide-books, with a view of its "South Front," "West Front," and "Great Quadrangle." It was alleged to be based on an encampment of the Romans — that highly apocryphal race who seemed to have spent their time in getting up picnics on tessellated pavements, where, after hilariously emptying their pockets of their loose coin and throwing round their dishes, they instantly built a road to escape by, leaving no other record of their existence. Stow and Dugdale had recorded the date when a Norman favorite obtained the royal license to "embattle it;" it had done duty on Christmas cards with the questionable snow already referred to laid on thickly in crystal; it had been lovingly portrayed by a fair countrywoman — the vivacious correspondent of the "East Machias Sentinel" — in a combination of the most delightful feminine disregard of facts with the highest feminine respect for titles. It was rich in a real and spiritual estate of tapestries, paintings, armor, legends, and ghosts. Everything the poet could wish for, and indeed some things that decent prose might have possibly wished out of it, were there.

Yet, from the day that it had been forcibly seized by a Parliamentary General, until more recently, when it had passed by the no less desperate conveyance of marriage into the hands of a Friendly Nobleman known to the Western Barbarian, it had been supposed to suggest something or other more remarkable than itself. "Few spectators," said the guide-book, "even the most unimpassioned, can stand in the courtyard and gaze upon those historic walls without feeling a thrill of awe," etc. The Western Barbarian had stood there, gazed, and felt no thrill. "The privileged guest," said the grave historian, "passing in review the lineaments of the illustrious owners of Stukeley, as he slowly paces the sombre gallery, must be conscious of emotions of no ordinary character," etc., etc. The Barbarian had been conscious of no such emotions. And it was for this reason, and believing he *might* experience them if left there in solitude, with no distracting or extraneous humanity around him, it had been agreed between him and the Friendly Nobleman, who had fine Barbarian instincts, that as he — the Friendly Nobleman

— and his family were to spend their holidays abroad, the Barbarian should be allowed, on the eve and day of Christmas, to stay at Stukeley alone. "But," added his host, "you 'll find it beastly lonely, and although I 've told the housekeeper to look after you, you 'd better go over to dine at Audley Friars, where there 's a big party, and they know you, and it will be a deuced deal more amusing. And — er — I say — you know — you 're really *not* looking out for ghosts, and that sort of thing, are you? You know you fellows don't believe in them — over there." And the Barbarian, assuring him that this was a part of his deficient emotions, it was settled then and there that he should come. And that was why, on the 24th of December, the Barbarian found himself gazing hopefully on the landscape with his portmanteau at his feet, as he drove up the avenue.

The ravens did *not* croak ominously from the battlements as he entered. And the housekeeper, although neither "stately" nor "tall," nor full of reminiscences of "his late lordship, the present Earl's father," was very sensible and practical. The Barbarian could, of course, have his choice of rooms — but — she had thought — remembering his tastes the last time, that the long blue room? Exactly! The long, low-arched room, with the faded blue tapestry, looking upon the gallery — capital! He had always liked that room. From purely negative evidence he had every reason to believe that it was the one formidable-looking room in England that Queen Elizabeth had *not* slept in.

When the footman had laid out his clothes, and his step grew fainter along the passage, until it was suddenly swallowed up with the closing of a red baize door in the turret staircase, like a trap in an oubliette, the whole building seemed to sink back into repose. Quiet it certainly was, but not more so, he remembered, than when the chambers on either side were filled with guests, and floating voices in the corridor were lost in those all-absorbing walls. So far, certainly, this was no new experience. It was past four. He waited for the shadows to gather. Light thickened beyond his windows; gradually the outflanking wall and part of a projecting terrace crumbled away in the darkness, as if Night were slowly reducing the castle. The figures on the tapestry in his room stood out faintly. The gallery, seen through his open door, barred with black spaces between the mullioned windows, presently became obliterated, as if invaded by a dull smoke from without. But nothing moved, nothing glimmered. Really this might become in time very stupid.

He was startled, however, while dressing, to see from his windows that the great banqueting-hall was illuminated, but on coming down was amused to find his dinner served on a small table in its oaken solitude lit by the large electric chandelier — for Stukeley Castle under its present lord had all the modern improvements — shining on the tattered banners and glancing mail above him. It was evidently the housekeeper's reading of some written suggestion of her noble master. The Barbarian, in a flash of instinct, imagined the passage: —

"Humor him as a harmless lunatic; the plate is quite safe."

Declining the further offer of an illumination of the picture gallery, grand drawing-room, ball-room, and chapel, a few hours later he found himself wandering in the corridor with a single candle and a growing conviction of the hopelessness of his experiment. The castle had as yet yielded to him nothing that he had not seen before in the distraction of company and the garishness of day. It was becoming a trifle monotonous. Yet fine — exceedingly; and now that a change of wind had lifted the fog, and the full moon shone on the lower half of the pictures of the gallery, starting into the most artificial simulation of life a number of Van Dyke legs, farthingales, and fingers that would have deceived nobody, it seemed gracious, gentle, and innocent beyond expression. Wandering down the gallery, conscious of being more like a ghost than any of the painted figures, and that they might reasonably object to him, he wished he could meet the original of one of those pictured gallants and secretly compare his fingers with the copy. He remembered an embroidered pair of gloves in a cabinet and a suit of armor on the wall that, in measurement, did not seem to bear out the delicacy of the one nor the majesty of the other. It occurred to him also to satisfy a yearning he had once felt to try on a certain breastplate and steel cap that hung over an oaken settle. It will be perceived that he was getting a good deal bored. For thus caparisoned he listlessly, and, as will be seen, imprudently, allowed himself to sink back into a very modern chair, and give way to a dreamy cogitation.

What possible interest could the dead have in anything that was here? Admitting that they had any, and that it was not the *living*, whom the Barbarian had always found most inclined to haunt the past, would not a ghost of any decided convictions object to such a collection as his descendant had gathered in this gallery? Yonder idiot in silk and steel had blunderingly and cruelly persecuted his kinsman in leather and steel only a few panels distant. Would they care to meet here? And if their human weaknesses had died with them, what would bring them here at all? And if not *them* — who then? He stopped short. The door at the lower end of the gallery had opened! Not stealthily, not noiselessly, but in an ordinary fashion, and a number of figures, dressed in the habiliments of a bygone age, came trooping in. They did not glide in nor float in, but trampled in awkwardly, clumsily, and unfamiliarly, gaping about them as they walked. At the head was apparently a steward in a kind of livery, who stopped once or twice and seemed to be pointing out and explaining certain objects in the room. A flash of indignant intelligence filled the brain of the Barbarian! It seemed absurd! — impossible! — but it was true! It was a holiday excursion party of ghosts, being shown over Stukeley Castle by a ghostly cicerone! And as his measured, monotonous voice rose on the Christmas morning air, it could be heard that he was actually showing off, not the antiquities of the Castle, but the *modern improvements!*

"This 'ere, gossips," — the Barbarian instantly detected the fallacy of all the so-called mediæval jargon he had read, — "is the Helectric Bell, which does away with our hold, hordinary 'orn blowin', and the hattendant waitin' in the 'all for the usual 'Without there, who waits?' which all of us was accustomed to in mortal flesh. You hobserve this button. I press it so, and it instantly rings a bell in the kitchen 'all, and shows in fair letters the name of this 'ere gallery, — as we will see later. Will hany good dame or gaffer press the button? Will *you*, mistress?" said the cicerone to a giggling, kerchief-coifed lass.

"Oi soy, Maudlin! — look out — will yer! — It 's the soime old gag as them bloomin' knobs you ketched hold of when yer was 'ere las' Whitsuntide," called out the mediæval 'Arry of the party.

"It is *not* the Galvanic-Magnetic machine in 'is lordship's library," said the cicerone severely, "which is a mere toy for infants, and hold-fashioned. And we have 'ere a much later invention. I open this little door, I turn this 'andle — called a switch — and, has you perceive, the gallery is hinstantly hilluminated."

There was a hoarse cry of astonishment from the assem-

A number of figures . . . came trooping in

blage. The Barbarian felt an awful thrill as this searching, insufferable light of the nineteenth century streamed suddenly upon the up-turned, vacant-eyed, and dull faces of those sightseers of the past. But there was no responsive gleam in their eyes.

"It be the sun," gasped an old woman in a gray cloak.

"Toime to rouse out, Myryan, and make the foire," said the mediæval 'Arry. The custodian smiled with superior toleration.

"But what do 'ee want o' my old lanthorne," asked a yellow-jerkined stable boy, pointing to an old-fashioned horned lantern, *tempus* Edward III., "with this brave loight?"

"You know," said the custodian, with condescending familiarity, "these mortals worship what they call 'curios' and the 'antique,' and 'is lordship gave a matter of fifty pounds for that same lanthern. That 's what the modern folk come 'ere to see — like as ye."

"Oi 've an old three-legged stool in Whitechapel oi 'll let his lordship 'ave cheap — for five quid," suggested the humorist.

"The 'prentice wight knows not that he speaks truly. For 'ere is a braver jest than 'is. Good folks, wilt please ye to examine yon coffer?" pointing to an oaken chest.

"'T is but poor stuff, marry," said Maudlin.

"'T is a coffer — the same being made in Wardour Street last year — 'is lordship gave one hundred pounds for it. Look at these would-be wormholes, — but they were made with an *auger*. Marry, *we* know what wormholes are!"

A ghastly grin spread over the faces of the spectral assembly as they gathered around the chest with silent laughter.

"Wilt walk 'ere and see the phonograph in the lib'ry, made by Hedison, an Hamerican, which bottles up the voice and preserves it fresh for a hundred years? 'T is a rare new fancy."

"Rot," said 'Arry. Then turning to the giggling Maudlin, he whispered: "Saw it las' toime. 'Is lordship got a piece o' moy moind that oi reeled off into it about this 'ere swindle. Fawncy that old bloke there charging a tanner apiece to us for chaffin' a bit of a barrel."

"Have you no last new braveries to show us of the gallants and their mistresses, as you were wont?" said Maudlin to the cicerone. "'T was a rare show last time — the modish silk gowns and farthingales in the closets."

"But there be no company this Christmas," said the custodian, "and 'is lordship does not entertain, unless it be the new fool 'is lordship sent down 'ere to-day, who has been mopin' and moonin' in the corridors, as is ever the way of these wittol creatures when they are not heeded. He was 'ere in a rare motley of his own choosing, with which he thinks to raise a laugh, a moment ago. Ye see him not — not 'avin' the gift that belongs by right to my dread office. 'T is a weird privilege I have — and may not be imparted to others — save" —

"Save what, good man steward? Prithee, speak," said Marian earnestly.

"'T is ever a shillin' extra."

There was no response. A few of the more bashful ghosts thrust their hands in their pockets and looked awkwardly another way. The Barbarian felt a momentary relief followed by a slight pang of mortified vanity. He was a little afraid of them. The price was an extortion, certainly, but surely he was worth the extra shilling!

"He has brought but little braveries of attire into the Castle," continued the cicerone, "but I 'ave something 'ere which was found on the top of his portmanteau. I wot ye know not the use of this." To the Barbarian's intense indignation, the cicerone produced, from under his, his (the Barbarian's) own opera hat. "Marry, what should be this? Read me this riddle! To it — and unyoke!"

A dozen vacant guesses were made as the showman held it aloft. Then with a conjuror's gesture he suddenly placed his thumbs within the rim, released the spring and extended the hat. The assembly laughed again silently as before.

"'T is a hat," said the cicerone, with a superior air.

"Nay," said Maudlin, "give it here." She took it curiously, examined it, and then with a sudden coquettish movement lifted it towards her own coifed head, as if to try it on. The cicerone suddenly sprang forward with a despairing gesture to prevent her. And here the Barbarian was conscious of a more startling revelation. How and why he could not tell, but he *knew* that the putting on of that article of his own dress would affect the young girl as the assumption of the steel cap and corselet had evidently affected him, and that he would instantly become as visible to her as she and her companions had been to him. He attempted to rise, but was too late; she had evaded the cicerone by ducking, and, facing in the direction of the Barbarian, clapped the hat on her head. He saw the swift light of consciousness, of astonishment, of sudden fear spring into her eyes! She shrieked, he started, struggled, and awoke!

But what was this! He was alone in the moonlit gallery, certainly; the ghastly figures in their outlandish garb were gone; he was awake and in his senses, but, in this first flash of real consciousness, he could have sworn that something remained! Something terror-stricken, and retreating even then before him, — something of the world, modern, — and, even as he gazed, vanishing through the gallery door with the material flash and rustle of silk.

He walked quietly to the door. It was open. Ah! no doubt he had forgotten to shut it fast; a current of air or a sudden draught had opened it. That noise had awakened him. More than that, remembering the lightning flash of dream consciousness, it had been the *cause* of his dream. Yet, for a few moments he listened attentively.

What might have been the dull reverberation of a closing door in the direction of the housekeeper's room, on the lower story, was all he heard. He smiled, for even that, natural as it might be, was less distinct and real than his absurd vision.

Nevertheless the next afternoon he concluded to walk over to Audley Friars for his Christmas dinner. Its hospitable master greeted him cordially.

"But do you know, my dear fellow," he said, when they were alone for a moment, "if you had n't come by yourself I 'd have sent over there for you. The fact is that A—— wrote to us that you were down at Stukeley alone, ghost-hunting or something of that sort, and I 'm afraid it leaked out among the young people of our party. Two of our girls — I shan't tell you which — stole over there last night to give you a start of some kind. They did n't see you at all, but, by Jove, it seems they got the biggest kind of a fright *themselves*, for they declare that something dreadful in armor, you know, was sitting in the gallery. Awfully good joke, was n't it? Of course *you* did n't see anything, — did you?"

"No," said the Barbarian discreetly.

A ROSE OF GLENBOGIE

The American consul at St. Kentigern stepped gloomily from the train at Whistlecrankie station. For the last twenty minutes his spirits had been slowly sinking before the drifting procession past the carriage windows of dull gray and brown hills — mammiform in shape, but so cold and sterile in expression that the swathes of yellow mist which lay in their hollows, like soiled guipure, seemed a gratuitous affectation of modesty. And when the train moved away, mingling its escaping steam with the slower mists of the mountain, he found himself alone on the platform, — the only passenger and apparently the sole occupant of the station. He was gazing disconsolately at his trunk, which had taken upon itself a human loneliness in the emptiness of the place, when a railway porter stepped out of the solitary signal-box, where he had evidently been performing a double function, and lounged with exasperating deliberation towards him. He was a hard-featured man, with a thin fringe of yellow-gray whiskers that met under his chin like dirty strings to tie his cap on with.

"Ye 'll be goin' to Glenbogie House, I 'm thinkin'?" he said moodily

The consul said that he was.

"I kenned it. Ye 'll no be gettin' any machine to tak' ye there. They 'll be sending a carriage for ye — if ye 're *expected.*" He glanced half doubtfully at the consul as if he was not quite so sure of it. But the consul believed he *was* expected, and felt relieved at the certain prospect of a conveyance. The porter meanwhile surveyed him moodily.

"Ye 'll be seein' Mistress MacSpadden there!"

The consul was surprised into a little over-consciousness. Mrs. MacSpadden was a vivacious acquaintance at St. Kentigern, whom he certainly — and not without some satisfaction — expected to meet at Glenbogie House. He raised his eyes inquiringly to the porter's.

"Ye 'll no be rememberin' me. I had a machine in St. Kentigern and drove ye to MacSpadden's ferry often. Far, far too often! She 's a strange flagrantitious creature; her husband 's but a puir fule, I 'm thinkin', and ye did yersel' nae guid gaunin' there."

It was a besetting weakness of the consul's that his sense of the ludicrous was too often reached before his more serious perceptions. The absurd combination of the bleak, inhospitable desolation before him, and the sepulchral complacency of his self-elected monitor, quite upset his gravity.

"Ay, ye 'll be laughin' *the noo*," returned the porter with gloomy significance.

The consul wiped his eyes. "Still," he said demurely, "I trust you won't object to my giving you sixpence to carry my box to the carriage when it comes, and let the morality of this transaction devolve entirely upon me. Unless," he continued, even more gravely, as a spick and span brougham, drawn by two thoroughbreds, dashed out of the mist up to the platform, "unless you prefer to state the case to those two gentlemen" — pointing to the smart coachman and footman on the box — "and take *their* opinion as to the propriety of my proceeding any further. It seems to me that their consciences ought to be consulted as well as yours. I 'm only a stranger here, and am willing to do anything to conform to the local custom."

"It 's a saxpence ye 'll be payin' anyway," said the porter, grimly shouldering the trunk, "but I 'll be no takin' any other mon's opinion on matters of my ain dooty and conscience."

"Ah," said the consul gravely, "then you'll perhaps be allowing *me* the same privilege."

The porter's face relaxed, and a gleam of approval — purely intellectual, however — came into his eyes.

"Ye were always a smooth deevel wi' your tongue, Mr. Consul," he said, shouldering the box and walking off to the carriage.

Nevertheless, as soon as he was fairly seated and rattling away from the station, the consul had a flashing conviction that he had not only been grievously insulted but also that he had allowed the wife of an acquaintance to be spoken of disrespectfully in his presence. And he had done nothing! Yes — it was like him! — he had *laughed* at the absurdity of the impertinence without resenting it! Another man would have slapped the porter's face! For an instant he hung out of the carriage window, intent upon ordering the coachman to drive back to the station, but the reflection — again a ludicrous one — that he would now be only bringing witnesses to a scene which might provoke a scandal more invidious to his acquaintance, checked him in time. But his spirits, momentarily diverted by the porter's effrontery, sunk to a lower ebb than before.

The clattering of his horses' hoofs echoed back from the rocky walls that occasionally hemmed in the road was not enlivening, but was less depressing than the recurring monotony of the open. The scenery did not suggest wildness to his alien eyes so much as it affected him with a vague sense of scorbutic impoverishment. It was not the loneliness of unfrequented nature, for there was a well-kept carriage road traversing its dreariness; and even when the hillside was clothed with scanty verdure, there were "outcrops" of smooth glistening weather-worn rocks showing like bare brown knees under the all too imperfectly kilted slopes. And at a little distance, lifting above a black drift of firs, were the square rigid sky-lines of Glenbogie House, standing starkly against the cold, lingering northern twilight. As the vehicle turned, and rolled between two square stone gateposts, the long avenue before him, though as well kept as the road, was but a slight improvement upon the outer sterility, and the dark iron-gray rectangular mansion beyond, guiltless of external decoration, even to the outlines of its small lustreless windows, opposed the grim inhospitable prospect with an equally grim inhospitable front. There were a few moments more of rapid driving, a swift swishing over soft gravel, the opening of a heavy door into a narrow vestibule, and then — a sudden sense of exquisitely diffused light and warmth from an arched and galleried central hall, the sounds of light laughter and subdued voices half lost in the airy space between the lofty pictured walls; the luxury of color in trophies, armor, and hangings; one or two careless groups before the recessed hearth or at the centre table, and the halted figure of a pretty woman on the broad, slow staircase. The contrast was sharp, ironical, and bewildering.

So much so that the consul, when he had followed the servant to his room, was impelled to draw aside the heavy window-curtains and look out again upon the bleak prospect it had half obliterated. The wing in which he was placed overhung a dark ravine or gully choked with shrubs and brambles that grew in a new luxuriance. As he gazed a large black bird floated upwards slowly from its depths, circled around the house with a few quick strokes of its wing, and then sped away — a black bolt — in one straight undeviating line towards the paling north. He still gazed into the abyss — half expecting another, even fancying he heard the occasional stir and flutter of obscure life below, and the melancholy call of night-fowl. A long-forgotten fragment of old English verse began to haunt him: —

Hark! the raven flaps hys wing
  In the briered dell belowe,
Hark! the dethe owl loude doth synge
  To the night maers as thaie goe.

"Now, what put that stuff in my head?" he said as he turned impatiently from the window. "And why does this house, with all its interior luxury, hypocritically oppose such a forbidding front to its neighbors?" Then it occurred to him that perhaps the architect instinctively felt that a more opulent and elaborate exterior would only bring the poverty of surrounding nature into greater relief. But he was not in the habit of troubling himself with abstruse problems. A nearer recollection of the pretty frock he had seen on the staircase — in whose wearer he had just recognized his vivacious friend — turned his thoughts to her. He remembered how at their first meeting he had been interested in her bright audacity, unconventionality, and high spirits, which did not, however, amuse him as greatly as his later suspicion that she was playing a self-elected rôle, often with difficulty, opposition, and feverishness, rather than spontaneity. He remembered how he had watched her in the obtrusive assumption of a new fashion, in some reckless departure from an old one, or in some ostentatious disregard of certain hard and set rules of St. Kentigern; but that it never seemed to him that she was the happier for it. He even fancied that her mirth at such times had an undue nervousness; that her pluck — which was undoubted — had something of the defiance of despair, and that her persistence often had the grimness of duty rather than the thoughtlessness of pure amusement. What was she trying to do? — what was she trying to *undo* or forget? Her married life was apparently happy and even congenial. Her young husband was clever, complaisant, yet honestly devoted to her, even to the extension of a certain camaraderie to her admirers and a chivalrous protection by half participation in her maddest freaks. Nor could he honestly say that her attitude towards his own sex — although marked by a freedom that often reached the verge of indiscretion — conveyed the least suggestion of passion or sentiment. The consul, more perceptive than analytical, found her a puzzle — who was, perhaps, the least mystifying to others who were content to sum up her eccentricities under the single vague epithet "fast." Most women disliked her; she had a few associates among them, but no confidante, and even these were so unlike her, again, as to puzzle him still more. And yet he believed himself strictly impartial.

He walked to the window again, and looked down upon the ravine from which the darkness now seemed to be slowly welling up and obliterating the landscape, and then, taking a book from his valise, settled himself in the easy-chair by the fire. He was in no hurry to join the party below, whom he had duly recognized and greeted as he passed through. They or their prototypes were familiar friends. There was the recently created baronet, whose "bloody hand" had apparently wiped out the stains of his earlier Radicalism, and whose former provincial self-righteousness had been supplanted by an equally provincial skepticism; there was his wife, who through all the difficulties of her changed position had kept the stalwart virtues of the Scotch bourgeoisie, and was — "decent;" there were the two native lairds that reminded him of "parts of speech," one being distinctly alluded to as a definite article, and the other being "of" something, and apparently governed always by that possessive case. There were two or three "workers," — men of power and ability in their several vocations; indeed, there was the general over-proportion of intellect, characteristic of such Scotch gatherings, and often in excess of minor social qualities. There was the usual foreigner, with Latin quickness, eagerness, and misapprehending adaptability. And there was the solitary Englishman — perhaps less generously equipped than the others — whom everybody differed from, ridiculed, and then looked up to and imitated. There were the half-dozen smartly frocked women, who, far from being the females of the foregoing species, were quite indistinctive, with the single exception of an American wife, who was infinitely more Scotch than her Scotch husband.

Suddenly he became aware of a faint rustling at his door, and what seemed to be a slight tap on the panel. He rose and opened it — the long passage was dark and apparently empty, but he fancied he could detect the quick swish of a skirt in the distance. As he reëntered his room, his eye fell for the first time on a rose whose stalk was thrust through the keyhole of his door. The consul smiled at this amiable solution of a mystery. It was undoubtedly the playful mischievousness of the vivacious MacSpadden. He placed it in water — intending to wear it in his coat at dinner as a gentle recognition of the fair donor's courtesy.

Night had thickened suddenly as from a passing cloud. He lit the two candles on his dressing-table, gave a glance into the now scarcely distinguishable abyss below his window, as he drew the curtains, and by the more diffused light for the first time surveyed his room critically. It was a larger apartment than that usually set aside for bachelors; the heavy four-poster had a conjugal reserve about it, and a tall cheval glass and certain minor details of the furniture suggested that it had been used for a married couple. He knew that the guest-rooms in country houses, as in hotels, carried no suggestion or flavor of the last tenant, and therefore lacked color and originality, and he was consequently surprised to find himself impressed with some distinctly novel atmosphere. He was puzzling himself to discover what it might be, when he again became aware of cautious footsteps apparently halting outside his door. This time he was prepared. With a half smile he stepped softly to the door and opened it suddenly. To his intense surprise he was face to face with a man.

But his discomfiture was as nothing compared to that of the stranger, whom he at once recognized as one of his fellow-guests, — the youthful Laird of Whistlecrankie. The young fellow's healthy color at once paled, then flushed a deep crimson, and a forced smile stiffened his mouth.

"I — beg your par-r-rdon," he said with a nervous brusqueness that brought out his accent. "I couldna find ma room. It 'll be changed, and I" —

"Perhaps I have got it," interrupted the consul smilingly. "I 've only just come, and they 've put me in here."

"Nae! Nae!" said the young man hurriedly, "it 's no' thiss. That is, it 's no' mine noo."

"Won't you come in?" suggested the consul politely, holding open the door.

The young man entered the room with the quick strides but the mechanical purposelessness of embarrassment. Then he stiffened and stood erect. Yet in spite of all this he was strikingly picturesque and unconventional in his Highland dress, worn with the freedom of long custom and a certain lithe, barbaric grace. As the consul continued to gaze at him encouragingly, the quick resentful pride of a shy man suddenly mantled his high cheekbones, and with an abrupt "I 'll not deesturb ye longer," he strode out of the room.

The consul watched the easy swing of his figure down the passage, and then closed the door. "Delightful creature," he said musingly, "and not so very unlike an Apache chief either! But what was he doing outside my door? And was it *he* who left that rose — not as a delicate Highland attention to an utter stranger, but" — the consul's mouth suddenly expanded — "to some fair previous occupant? Or was it really *his* room — he looked as if he were lying — and" — here the consul's mouth expanded even more wickedly — "and Mrs. MacSpadden had put the flower there for him?" This implied snub to his vanity was, however, more than compensated by his wicked anticipation of the pretty perplexity of his fair friend when *he* should appear at dinner with the flower in his own buttonhole. It would serve her right, the arrant flirt! But here he was interrupted by the entrance of a tall housemaid with his hot water.

"I am afraid I 've dispossessed Mr. — Mr. — Kilcraithie rather prematurely," said the consul lightly.

To his infinite surprise the girl answered with grim decision, "Nane too soon."

The consul stared. "I mean," he explained, "that I found him hesitating here in the passage, looking for his room."

"Ay, he 's always hoaverin' and glowerin' in the passages — but it 's no' for his *room!* And it 's a deesgrace to decent Christian folk his carryin' on wi' married weemen — mebbee they 're nae better than he!"

"That will do," said the consul curtly. He had no desire to encourage a repetition of the railway porter's freedom.

"Ye 'll no fash yoursel' aboot *him*," continued the girl, without heeding the rebuff. "It 's no' the meestreess' wish that he 's keepit here in the wing reserved for married folk, and she 's no' sorry for the excuse to pit ye in his place. Ye 'll be married yoursel', I 'm hearin'. But, I ken ye 's nae mair to be lippened tae for *that.*"

This was too much for the consul's gravity. "I 'm afraid," he said with diplomatic gayety, "that although I am married, as I have n't my wife with me, I 've no right to this superior accommodation and comfort. But you can assure your mistress that I 'll try to deserve them."

"Ay," said the girl, but with no great confidence in her voice, as she grimly quitted the room.

"When our foot 's upon our native heath, whether our name 's Macgregor or Kilcraithie, it would seem that we must tread warily," mused the consul as he began to dress. "But I 'm glad she did n't see that rose, or *my* reputation would have been ruined." Here another knock at the door arrested him. He opened it impatiently to a tall gillie, who instantly strode into the room. There was such another suggestion of Kilcraithie in the man and his manner that the consul instantly divined that he was Kilcraithie's servant.

"I 'll be takin' some bit things that yon Whistlecrankie left," said the gillie gravely, with a stolid glance around the room.

"Certainly," said the consul; "help yourself." He continued his dressing as the man began to rummage in the empty drawers. The consul had his back towards him, but, looking in the glass of the dressing-table, he saw that the gillie was stealthily watching him. Suddenly he passed before the mantelpiece and quickly slipped the rose from its glass into his hand.

"I 'll trouble you to put that back," said the consul quietly, without turning round. The gillie slid a quick glance towards the door, but the consul was before him. "I don't think *that* was left by your master," he said in an ostentatiously calm voice, for he was conscious of an absurd and inexplicable tumult in his blood, "and perhaps you 'd better put it back."

The man looked at the flower with an attention that might have been merely ostentatious, and replaced it in the glass.

"A thocht it was hiss."

"And I think it is n't," said the consul, opening the door.

Yet when the man had passed out he was by no means certain that the flower was not Kilcraithie's. He was even conscious that if the young Laird had approached him with a reasonable explanation or appeal he would have yielded it up. Yet here he was — looking angrily pale in the glass, his eyes darker than they should be, and with an unmistakable instinct to do battle for this idiotic gage! Was there some morbid disturbance in the air that was affecting him as it had Kilcraithie? He tried to laugh, but catching sight of its sardonic reflection in the glass became grave again. He wondered if the gillie had been really looking for anything his master had left — he had certainly *taken* nothing. He opened one or two of the drawers, and found only a woman's tortoise-shell hairpin — overlooked by the footman when he had emptied them for the consul's clothes. It had been probably forgotten by some fair tenant previous to Kilcraithie. The consul looked at his watch; it was time to go down. He grimly pinned the fateful flower in his buttonhole, and half defiantly descended to the drawing-room.

Here, however, he was inclined to relax when, from a group of pretty women, the bright gray eyes of Mrs. MacSpadden caught his, were suddenly diverted to the lapel of his coat, and then leaped up to his again with a sparkle of mischief. But the guests were already pairing off in dinner couples, and as they passed out of the room, he saw that she was on the arm of Kilcraithie. Yet, as she passed him, she audaciously turned her head, and in a mischievous affectation of jealous reproach, murmured: —

"So soon!"

At dinner she was too far removed for any conversation with him, although from his seat by his hostess he could plainly see her saucy profile midway up the table. But, to his surprise, her companion, Kilcraithie, did not seem to be responding to her gayety. By turns abstracted and feverish, his glances occasionally wandered towards the end of the table where the consul was sitting. For a few moments he believed that the affair of the flower, combined, perhaps, with the overhearing of Mrs. MacSpadden's mischievous sentence, rankled in the Laird's barbaric soul. But he became presently aware that Kilcraithie's eyes eventually rested upon a quiet-looking blonde near the hostess. Yet the lady not only did not seem to be aware of it, but her face was more often turned towards the consul, and their eyes had once or twice met. He had been struck by the fact that they were half-veiled but singularly unimpassioned eyes, with a certain expression of cold wonderment and criticism quite inconsistent with their veiling. Nor was he surprised when, after a preliminary whispering over the plates, his hostess presented him. The lady was the young wife of the middle-aged dignitary who, seated further down the table, opposite Mrs. MacSpadden, was apparently enjoying that lady's wildest levities. The consul bowed, the lady leaned a little forward.

"We were saying what a lovely rose you had."

The consul's inward response was "Hang that flower!" His outward expression was the modest query: —

"Is it *so* peculiar?"

"No; but it's very pretty. Would you allow me to see it?"

Disengaging the flower from his buttonhole he handed it to her. Oddly enough, it seemed to him that half the table was watching and listening to them. Suddenly the lady uttered a little cry. "Dear me! it's full of thorns; of course you picked and arranged it yourself, for any lady would have wrapped something around the stalk!"

But here there was a burlesque outcry and a good-humored protest from the gentlemen around her against this manifestly leading question. "It 's no fair! Ye 'll not answer her — for the dignity of our sex." Yet in the midst of it it suddenly occurred to the consul that there *had* been a slip of paper wrapped around it, which had come off and remained in the keyhole. The blue eyes of the lady were meanwhile sounding his, but he only smiled and said: —

"Then it seems it *is* peculiar?"

When the conversation became more general he had time to observe other features of the lady than her placid eyes. Her light hair was very long, and grew low down the base of her neck. Her mouth was firm, the upper lip slightly compressed in a thin red line, but the lower one, although equally precise at the corners, became fuller in the centre and turned over like a scarlet leaf, or, as it struck him suddenly, like the telltale drop of blood on the mouth of a vampire. Yet she was very composed, practical, and decorous, and as the talk grew more animated — and in the vicinity of Mrs. MacSpadden, more audacious — she kept a smiling reserve of expression, — which did not, however, prevent her from following that lively lady, whom she evidently knew, with a kind of encouraging attention.

"Kate is in full fling to-night," she said to the hostess. Lady Macquoich smiled ambiguously, — so ambiguously that the consul thought it necessary to interfere for his friend. "She seems to say what most of us think, but I am afraid very few of us could voice as innocently," he smilingly suggested.

"She is a great friend of yours," returned the lady, looking at him through her half-veiled lids. "She has made us quite envy her."

"And I am afraid made it impossible for *me* to either sufficiently thank her or justify her taste," he said quietly. Yet he was vexed at an unaccountable resentment which had taken possession of him — who but a few hours before had only laughed at the porter's criticism.

After the ladies had risen, the consul with an instinct of sympathy was moving up towards "Jock" MacSpadden, who sat nearer the host, when he was stopped midway of the table by the dignitary who had sat opposite to Mrs. MacSpadden. "Your frien' is maist amusing wi' her audacious tongue, — ay, and her audacious ways," he said with large official patronage; "and we 've enjoyed her here immensely, but I hae mae doots if mae Leddy Macquoich taks as kindly to them. You and I — men of the wurrld, I may say — we understand them for a' their worth; ay! — ma wife too, with whom I observed ye speakin' — is maist tolerant of her, but man! it 's extraordinar' " — he lowered his voice slightly — "that yon husband of hers does na' check her freedoms with Kilcraithie. I wadna' say anythin' was wrong, ye ken, but is he no' over confident and conceited aboot his wife?"

"I see you don't know him," said the consul smilingly, "and I 'd be delighted to make you acquainted. Jock," he continued, raising his voice as he turned towards MacSpadden, "let me introduce you to Sir Alan Deeside, who don't know *you*, although he 's a great admirer of your wife;" and unheeding the embarrassed protestations of Sir Alan and the laughing assertions of Jock that they were already acquainted, he moved on beside his host. That hospitable knight, who had been airing his knowledge of London smart society to his English guest with a singular mixture of assertion and obsequiousness, here stopped short. "Ay, sit down, laddie, it was so guid of ye to come, but I 'm thinkin' at your end of the table ye lost the bit fun of Mistress MacSpadden. Eh, but she was unco' lively to-night. 'T was all Kilcraithie could do to keep her from proposin' your health with Hieland honors, and offerin' to lead off with her ain foot on the table!

Ay, and she 'd ha' done it. And that 's a braw rose she 's been givin' ye — and ye got out of it claverly wi' Lady Deeside."

When he left the table with the others to join the ladies, the same unaccountable feeling of mingled shyness and nervous irascibility still kept possession of him. He felt that in his present mood he could not listen to any further criticisms of his friend without betraying some unwonted heat, and as his companions filed into the drawing-room he slipped aside in the hope of recovering his equanimity by a few moments' reflection in his own room. He glided quickly up the staircase and entered the corridor. The passage that led to his apartment was quite dark, especially before his door, which was in a bay that really ended the passage. He was consequently surprised and somewhat alarmed at seeing a shadowy female figure hovering before it. He instinctively halted; the figure became more distinct from some luminous halo that seemed to encompass it. It struck him that this was only the light of his fire thrown through his open door, and that the figure was probably that of a servant before it, who had been arranging his room. He started forward again, but at the sound of his advancing footsteps the figure and the luminous glow vanished, and he arrived blankly face to face with his own closed door. He looked around the dim bay; it was absolutely vacant. It was equally impossible for any one to have escaped without passing him. There was only his room left. A half-nervous, half-superstitious thrill crept over him as he suddenly grasped the handle of the door and threw it open. The leaping light of his fire revealed its emptiness: no one was there! He lit the candle and peered behind the curtains and furniture and under the bed; the room was as vacant and undisturbed as when he left it.

Had it been a trick of his senses or a bona-fide apparition? He had never heard of a ghost at Glenbogie — the house dated back some fifty years; Sir John Macquoich's tardy knighthood carried no such impedimenta. He looked down wonderingly on the flower in his buttonhole. Was there something uncanny in that innocent blossom? But here he was struck by another recollection, and examined the keyhole of his door. With the aid of the tortoise-shell hairpin he dislodged the paper he had forgotten. It was only a thin spiral strip, apparently the white outer edge of some newspaper, and it certainly seemed to be of little service as a protection against the thorns of the rose-stalk. He was holding it over the fire, about to drop it into the blaze, when the flame revealed some pencil-marks upon it. Taking it to the candle he read, deeply bitten into the paper by a hard pencil-point: "At half-past one." There was nothing else — no signature; but the handwriting was *not* Mrs. MacSpadden's!

Then whose? Was it that of the mysterious figure whom he had just seen? Had he been selected as the medium of some spiritual communication, and, perhaps, a ghostly visitation later on? Or was he the victim of some clever trick? He had once witnessed such dubious attempts to relieve the monotony of a country house. He again examined the room carefully, but without avail. Well! the mystery or trick would be revealed at half-past one. It was a somewhat inconvenient hour, certainly. He looked down at the baleful gift in his buttonhole, and for a moment felt inclined to toss it in the fire. But this was quickly followed by his former revulsion of resentment and defiance. No! he would wear it, no matter what happened, until its material or spiritual owner came for it. He closed the door and returned to the drawing-room.

Midway of the staircase he heard the droning of pipes. There was dancing in the drawing-room to the music of the gorgeous piper who had marshaled them to dinner.

He was not sorry, as he had no inclination to talk, and the one confidence he had anticipated with Mrs. MacSpadden was out of the question now. He had no right to reveal his later discovery. He lingered a few moments in the hall. The buzzing of the piper's drones gave him that impression of confused and blindly aggressive intoxication which he had often before noticed in this barbaric instrument, and had always seemed to him as the origin of its martial inspiration. From this he was startled by voices and steps in the gallery he had just quitted, but which came from the opposite direction to his room. It was Kilcraithie and Mrs. MacSpadden. As she caught sight of him, he fancied she turned slightly and aggressively pale, with a certain hardening of her mischievous eyes. Nevertheless, she descended the staircase more deliberately than her companion, who brushed past him with an embarrassed self-consciousness, quite in advance of her. She lingered for an instant.

"You are not dancing?" she said.

"No."

"Perhaps you are more agreeably employed?"

"At this exact moment, certainly."

She cast a disdainful glance at him, crossed the hall, and followed Kilcraithie.

"Hang me, if I understand it all!" mused the consul, by no means good-humoredly. "Does she think I have been spying upon her and her noble chieftain? But it 's just as well that I did n't tell her anything."

He turned to follow them. In the vestibule he came upon a figure which had halted before a large pier-glass. He recognized M. Delfosse, the French visitor, complacently twisting the peak of his Henri Quatre beard. He would have passed without speaking, but the Frenchman glanced smilingly at the consul and his buttonhole. Again the flower!

"Monsieur is décoré," he said gallantly.

The consul assented, but added, not so gallantly, that though they were not in France he might still be unworthy of it. The baleful flower had not improved his temper. Nor did the fact that, as he entered the room, he thought the people stared at him — until he saw that their attention was directed to Lady Deeside, who had entered almost behind him. From his hostess, who had offered him a seat beside her, he gathered that M. Delfosse and Kilcraithie had each temporarily occupied his room, but that they had been transferred to the other wing, apart from the married couples and young ladies, because when they came upstairs from the billiard and card room late, they sometimes disturbed the fair occupants. No! — there were no ghosts at Glenbogie. Mysterious footsteps had sometimes been heard in the ladies' corridor, but — with peculiar significance — she was *afraid* they could be easily accounted for. Sir Alan, whose room was next to the MacSpaddens', had been disturbed by them.

He was glad when it was time to escape to the billiard-room and tobacco. For a while he forgot the evening's adventure, but eventually found himself listening to a discussion — carried on over steaming tumblers of toddy — in regard to certain predispositions of the always debatable sex.

"Ye 'll not always judge by appearances," said Sir Alan. "Ye 'll mind the story o' the meenester's wife of Aiblinnoch. It was thocht that she was ower free wi' one o' the parishioners — ay! it was the claish o' the whole kirk, while none dare tell the meenester hisself — bein' a bookish, simple, unsuspectin' creeter. At last one o' the elders bethocht him of a bit plan of bringing it home to the wife, through the gospel lips of her ain husband! So he intimated to the meenester his suspicions of grievous laxity amang the female flock, and of the necessity of a special sermon on the Seventh Command. The puir man consented — although he dinna ken why and wherefore — and preached a gran' sermon! Ay, man! it was crammed wi' denunciation and an emptyin' o' the vials o' wrath! The congregation sat dumb as huddled sheep — when they were no' starin' and gowpin' at the meenester's wife settin' bolt upright in her place. And then, when the air was blue wi' sulphur frae tae pit, the meenester's wife uprises! Man! Ivry eye was spearin' her — ivry lug was prickt towards her! And she goes out in the aisle facin' the meenester, and" —

Sir Alan paused.

"And what?" demanded the eager auditory.

"She pickit up the elder's wife, sobbin' and tearin' her hair in strong hysterics."

At the end of a relieved pause Sir Alan slowly concluded: "It was said that the elder removed frae Aiblinnoch wi' his wife, but no' till he had effected a change of meenesters."

It was already past midnight, and the party had dropped off one by one, with the exception of Deeside, Macquoich, the young Englishman, and a Scotch laird, who were playing poker, — an amusement which he understood they frequently protracted until three in the morning. It was nearly time for him to expect his mysterious visitant. Before he went upstairs he thought he would take a breath of the outer evening air, and throwing a mackintosh over his shoulders, passed out of the garden door of the billiard-room. To his surprise it gave immediately upon the fringe of laurel that hung over the chasm.

It was quite dark; the few far-spread stars gave scarcely any light, and the slight auroral glow towards the north was all that outlined the fringe of the abyss, which might have proved dangerous to any unfamiliar wanderer. A damp breath of sodden leaves came from its depths. Beside him stretched the long dark façade of the wing he inhabited, his own window the only one that showed a faint light. A few paces beyond, a singular structure of rustic wood and glass, combining the peculiarities of a sentry-box, a summer-house, and a shelter, was built against the blank wall of the wing. He imagined the monotonous prospect from its windows of the tufted chasm, the coldly profiled northern hills beyond, — and shivered. A little further on, sunk in the wall like a postern, was a small door that evidently gave easy egress to seekers of this stern retreat. In the still air a faint grating sound like the passage of a foot across gravel came to him as from the distance. He paused, thinking he had been followed by one of the card-players, but saw no one, and the sound was not repeated.

It was past one. He reëntered the billiard-room, passed the unchanged group of card-players, and, taking a candle-stick from the hall, ascended the dark and silent staircase into the corridor. The light of his candle cast a flickering halo around him, but did not penetrate the gloomy distance. He at last halted before his door, gave a scrutinizing glance around the embayed recess, and opened the door half expectantly. But the room was empty as he had left it.

It was a quarter past one. He threw himself on the bed without undressing, and fixed his eyes alternately on the door and his watch. Perhaps the unwonted seriousness of his attitude struck him, but a sudden sense of the preposterousness of the whole situation, of his solemnly ridiculous acceptance of a series of mere coincidences as a foregone conclusion, overcame him, and he laughed. But in the same breath he stopped.

There *were* footsteps approaching — cautious footsteps — but not at his door! They were *in the room* — no! in the *wall* just behind him! They were descending some staircase at the back of his bed — he could hear the regular tap of a light slipper from step to step and the rustle of a skirt seemingly in his very ear. They were becoming less and less distinct — they were gone! He sprang to his feet, but almost at the same instant he was conscious of a sudden chill — that seemed to him as physical as it was mental. The room was slowly suffused with a cool sodden breath and the dank odor of rotten leaves. He looked at the candle — its flame was actually deflecting in this mysterious blast. It seemed to come from a recess for hanging clothes topped by a heavy cornice and curtain. He had examined it before, but he drew the curtain once more aside. The cold current certainly seemed to be more perceptible there. He felt the red-clothed backing of the interior, and his hand suddenly grasped a doorknob. It turned, and the whole structure — cornice and curtains — swung inwards towards him with *the door on which it was hung!* Behind it was a dark staircase leading from the floor above to some outer door below, whose opening had given ingress to the chill humid current from the ravine. This was the staircase where he had just heard the footsteps — and this was, no doubt, the door through which the mysterious figure had vanished from his room a few hours before!

Taking his candle, he cautiously ascended the stairs until he found himself on the landing of the suites of the married couples and directly opposite to the rooms of the MacSpaddens and Deesidos. He was about to descend again when he heard a far-off shout, a scuffling sound on the outer gravel, and the frenzied shaking of the handle of the lower door. He had hardly time to blow out his candle and flatten himself against the wall, when the door was flung open and a woman frantically flew up the staircase. His own door was still open; from within its depths the light of his fire projected a flickering beam across the steps. As she rushed past it the light revealed her face; it needed not the peculiar perfume of her garments as she swept by his concealed figure to make him recognize — Lady Deeside!

Amazed and confounded, he was about to descend, when he heard the lower door again open. But here a sudden instinct made him pause, turn, and reascend to the upper landing. There he calmly relit his candle, and made his way down to the corridor that overlooked the central hall. The sound of suppressed voices — speaking with the exhausted pauses that come from spent excitement — made him cautious again, and he halted. It was the card party slowly passing from the billiard-room to the hall.

"Ye owe it yoursel' — to your wife — not to pit up with it a day longer," said the subdued voice of Sir Alan. "Man! ye war in an ace o' havin' a braw scandal."

"Could ye no' get your wife to speak till her," responded Macquoich, "to gie her a hint that she 's better awa' out of this? Lady Deeside has some influence wi' her."

The consul ostentatiously dropped the extinguisher from his candlestick. The party looked up quickly. Their faces were still flushed and agitated, but a new restraint seemed to come upon them on seeing him.

"I thought I heard a row outside," said the consul explanatorily.

They each looked at their host without speaking.

"Oh, ay," said Macquoich, with simulated heartiness, "a bit fuss between the Kilcraithie and yon Frenchman; but they 're baith goin' in the mornin'."

"I thought I heard MacSpadden's voice," said the consul quietly.

There was a dead silence. Then Macquoich said hurriedly: —

"Is he no' in his room — in bed — asleep, —man?"

"I really don't know; I did n't inquire," said the consul with a slight yawn. "Good-night!"

He turned, not without hearing them eagerly whispering again, and entered the passage leading to his own room. As he opened the door he was startled to find the subject of his inquiry — Jock MacSpadden — quietly seated in his armchair by his fire.

"Jock!"

"Don't be alarmed, old man; I came up by that staircase and saw the door open, and guessed you 'd be returning soon. But it seemed you went *round by the corridor*," he said, glancing curiously at the consul's face. "Did you meet the crowd?"

"Yes, Jock! *What* does it all mean?"

MacSpadden laughed. "It means that I was just in time to keep Kilcraithie from chucking Delfosse down that ravine; but they both scooted when they saw me. By Jove! I don't know which was the most frightened."

"But," said the consul slowly, "what was it all about, Jock?"

"Some gallantry of that d—d Frenchman, who 's trying to do some woman-stalking up here, and jealousy of Kilcraithie's, who 's just got enough of his forbears' blood in him to think nothing of sticking three inches of his dirk in the wame of the man that crosses him. But I say," continued Jock, leaning easily back in his chair, "*you* ought to know something of all this. This room, old man, was used as a sort of rendezvous, having two outlets, don't you see, when they could n't get at the summer-house below. By Jove! they both had it in turns — Kilcraithie and the Frenchman — until Lady Macquoich got wind of something, swept them out, and put *you* in it."

The consul rose and approached his friend with a grave face. "Jock, I *do* know something about it — more about it than any one thinks. You and I are old friends. Shall I tell you *what* I know?"

Jock's handsome face became a trifle paler, but his frank, clear eyes rested steadily on the consul's.

"Go on!" he said.

"I know that this flower which I am wearing was the signal for the rendezvous this evening," said the consul slowly, "and this paper," taking it from his pocket, "contained the time of the meeting, written in the lady's own hand. I know who she was, for I saw her face as plainly as I see yours now, by the light of the same fire; it was as pale, but not as frank as yours, old man. That is what I know. But I know also what people *think* they know, and for that reason I put that paper in *your* hand. It is yours — your vindication — your *revenge*, if you choose. Do with it what you like."

Jock, with unchanged features and undimmed eyes, took the paper from the consul's hand, without looking at it.

"I may do with it what I like?" he repeated.

"Yes."

He was about to drop it into the fire, but the consul stayed his hand.

"Are you not going to *look* at the handwriting first?"

There was a moment of silence. Jock raised his eyes with a sudden flash of pride in them and said, "No!"

The friends stood side by side, grasping each other's hands, as the burning paper leaped up the chimney in a vanishing flame.

"Do you think you have done quite right, Jock, in view of any scandal you may hear?"

"Quite! You see, old man, I know *my wife* — but I don't think that Deeside *knows his.*"

THE HEIR OF THE M^{c}HULISHES

I

The consul for the United States of America at the port of St. Kentigern was sitting alone in the settled gloom of his private office. Yet it was only high noon, of a "seasonable" winter's day, by the face of the clock that hung like a pallid moon on the murky wall opposite to him. What else could be seen of the apartment by the faint light that struggled through the pall of fog outside the lustreless windows presented the ordinary aspect of a business sanctum. There were a shelf of fog-bound admiralty law, one or two colored prints of ocean steamships under full steam, bow on, tremendously foreshortened, and seeming to force themselves through shadowy partitions; there were engravings of Lincoln and Washington, as unsubstantial and shadowy as the dead themselves. Outside, against the window, which was almost level with the street, an occasional procession of black silhouetted figures of men and women, with prayer-books in their hands and gloom on their faces, seemed to be born of the fog, and prematurely to return to it. At which a conviction of sin overcame the consul. He remembered that it was the Sabbath day, and that he had no business to be at the consulate at all.

Unfortunately, with this shameful conviction came the sound of a bell ringing somewhere in the depths of the building, and the shuffling of feet on the outer steps. The light of his fire had evidently been seen, and like a beacon had attracted some wandering and possibly intoxicated mariner with American papers. The consul walked into the hall with a sudden righteous frigidity of manner. It was one thing to be lounging in one's own office on the Sabbath day, and quite another to be deliberately calling there on business.

He opened the front door, and a middle-aged man entered, accompanying and partly shoving forward a more diffident and younger one. Neither appeared to be a sailor, although both were dressed in that dingy respectability and remoteness of fashion affected by second and third mates when ashore. They were already well in the hall, and making their way toward the private office, when the elder man said, with an air of casual explanation, "Lookin' for the American consul; I reckon this yer 's the consulate?"

"It is the consulate," said the official dryly, "and I am the consul; but"—

"That 's all right," interrupted the stranger, pushing past him, and opening the door of the private office, into which he shoved his companion. "Thar now!" he continued to the diffident youth, pointing to a chair, and quite ignoring the presence of the consul; "thar 's a bit of America. Sit down thar. You 're under the flag now, and can do as you darn please." Nevertheless, he looked a little disappointed as he glanced around him, as if he had expected a different environment and possibly a different climate.

"I presume," said the consul suavely, "you wish to see me on some urgent matter; for you probably know that the consulate is closed on Sunday to ordinary business. I am here myself quite accidentally."

"Then you don't live here?" said the visitor disappointedly.

"No."

"I reckon that 's the reason why we did n't see no flag a-flyin' when we was a-huntin' this place yesterday. We were directed here, but I says to Malcolm, says I, 'No; it ain't here, or you 'd see the Stars and Stripes afore you 'd see anythin' else.' But I reckon you float it over your house, eh?"

The consul here explained smilingly that he did *not* fly a flag over his lodgings, and that except on national holidays it was not customary to display the national ensign on the consulate.

"Then you can't do here — and you a *consul* — what any nigger can do in the States, eh? That 's about how it pans out, don't it? But I did n't think *you* 'd tumble to it quite so quick, Jack."

At this mention of his Christian name, the consul turned sharply on the speaker. A closer scrutiny of the face before him ended with a flash of reminiscence. The fog without and within seemed to melt away; he was standing once more on a Western hillside with this man; a hundred miles of sparkling sunshine and crisp, dry air stretching around him, and above a blue and arched sky that roofed the third of a continent with six months' summer. And then the fog seemed to come back heavier and thicker to his consciousness. He emotionally stretched out his hand to the stranger. But it was the fog and his personal surroundings which now seemed to be unreal.

"Why, it 's Harry Custer!" he said with a laugh that, however, ended in a sigh. "I did n't recognize you in this half light." He then glanced curiously toward the diffident young man, as if to identify another possible old acquaintance.

"Well, I spotted you from the first," said Custer, "though I ain't seen you since we were in Scott's Camp together. That 's ten years ago. You 're lookin' at *him*," he continued, following the consul's wandering eye. "Well, it 's about him that I came to see you. This yer 's a McHulish, — a genuine McHulish!"

He paused, as if to give effect to this statement. But the name apparently offered no thrilling suggestion to the consul, who regarded the young man closely for further explanation. He was a fair-faced youth of about twenty years, with pale reddish-brown eyes, dark hair reddish at the roots, and a singular white and pink waxiness of oval cheek, which, however, narrowed suddenly at the angle of the jaw, and fell away with the retreating chin.

"Yes," continued Custer; "I oughter say the *only* McHulish. He is the direct heir — and of royal descent! He 's one of them McHulishes whose name in them old history times was enough to whoop up the boys and make 'em paint the town red. A regular campaign boomer — the old McHulish was. Stump speeches and brass-bands war n't in it with the boys when *he* was around. They 'd go their bottom dollar and last cartridge — if they 'd had cartridges in them days — on him. That was the regular McHulish gait. And Malcolm there 's the last of 'em — got the same style of features, too."

Ludicrous as the situation was, it struck the consul dimly, as through fog and darkness, that the features of the young man were not unfamiliar, and indeed had looked out upon him dimly and vaguely at various times, from various historic canvases. It was the face of complacent fatuity, incompetency, and inconstancy, which had dragged down strength, competency, and constancy to its own idiotic fate and levels, — a face for whose weaknesses valor and beauty had not only sacrificed themselves, but made things equally unpleasant to a great many minor virtues. Nevertheless, the consul, with an amused sense of its ridiculous incongruity to the grim Scottish Sabbath procession in the street, and the fog-bound volumes of admiralty law in the room, smiled affably.

"Of course our young friend has no desire to test the magic of his name here, in these degenerate days."

"No," said Custer complacently; "though between you and me, old man, there 's always no tellin' what might turn up over in this yer monarchy. Things of course are different over our way. But jest now Malcolm will be satisfied to take the title and property to which he 's rightful heir."

The consul's face fell. Alas! it was only the old, old story. Its endless repetitions and variations had been familiar to him even in his youth and in his own land. "Ef that man had his rights," had once been pointed out to him in a wild Western camp, "he 'd be now sittin' in scarlet on the right of the Queen of England!" The gentleman who was indicated in this apocalyptical vision, it appeared, simply bore a singular likeness to a reigning Hanoverian family, which for some unexplained reason he had contented himself with bearing with fortitude and patience. But it was in his official capacity that the consul's experience had been the most trying. At times it had seemed to him that much of the real property and peerage of Great Britain was the inherited right of penniless American republicans who had hitherto refrained from presenting their legal claims, and that the habitual first duty of generations of British noblemen on coming into their estates and titles was to ship their heirs and next of kin to America, and then forget all about them. He had listened patiently to claims to positions more or less exalted, — claims often presented with ingenuous sophistry or pathetic simplicity, prosecuted with great good humor, and abandoned with invincible cheerfulness; but they seldom culminated more seriously than in the disbursement of a few dollars by the consul to enable the rightful owner of millions to procure a steerage passage back to his previous democratic retirement. There had been others, less sincere but more pretentious in quality, to whom, however, a letter to the Heralds' College in London was all sufficient, and who, on payment of various fees and emoluments, were enabled to stagger back to New York or Boston with certain unclaimed and forgotten luggage which a more gallant ancestor had scorned to bring with him into the new life, or had thrown aside in his undue haste to make them citizens of the republic. Still, all this had grown monotonous and wearisome, and was disappointing as coming through the intervention of an old friend who ought to know better.

"Of course you have already had legal opinion on the subject over there," said the consul, with a sigh, "but here, you know, you ought first to get some professional advice from those acquainted with Scotch procedure. But perhaps you have that too."

"No," said Custer cheerfully. "Why, it ain't only two months ago that I first saw Malcolm. Tumbled over him on his own farm jest out of MacCorkleville, Kentucky, where he and his fathers before him had been livin' nigh a hundred years — yes, *a hundred years*, by Jove! ever since they first emigrated to the country. Had a talk over it; saw an old Bible about as big and as used up as that," — lifting the well-worn consular Bible, — "with dates in it, and heard the whole story. And here we are."

"And you have consulted no lawyer?" gasped the consul.

"The McHulishes," said an unexpected voice that sounded thin and feminine, "never took any legal decision. From the craggy summits of Glen Crankie he lifted the banner of his forefathers, or raised the war-cry, 'Hulish dhu, ieroe!' from the battlements of Craigiedurrach. And the clan gathered round him with shouts that rent the air. That was the way of it in old times. And the boys whooped him up and stood by him." It was the diffident young man who had half spoken, half recited, with an odd enthusiasm that even the culminating slang could not make conventional.

"That 's about the size of it," said Custer, leaning back in his chair easily with an approving glance at the young man. "And I don't know if that ain't the way to work the thing now."

The consul stared hopelessly from the one to the other. It had always seemed possible that this dreadful mania might develop into actual insanity, and he had little doubt but that the younger man's brain was slightly affected. But this did not account for the delusion and expectations of the elder. Harry Custer, as the consul remembered him, was a level-headed, practical miner, whose leaning to adventure and excitement had not prevented him from being a cool speculator, and he had amassed more than a competency by reason of his judicious foresight and prompt action. Yet he was evidently under the glamour of this madman, although outwardly as lazily self-contained as ever.

"Do you mean to tell me," said the consul in a suppressed voice, "that you two have come here equipped only with a statement of facts and a family Bible, and that you expect to take advantage of a feudal enthusiasm which no longer exists — and perhaps never did exist out of the pages of romance — as a means of claiming estates whose titles have long since been settled by law, and can be claimed only under that tenure? Surely I have misunderstood you. You cannot be in earnest."

"Honest Injun," said Custer, nodding his head lazily. "We mean it, but not jest that way you 've put it. F'r instance, it ain't only us two. This yer thing, ole pard, we 're runnin' as a syndicate."

"A syndicate?" echoed the consul.

"A syndicate," repeated Custer. "Half the boys that were at Eagle Camp are in it, and two of Malcolm's neighbors from Kentucky, — the regular old Scotch breed like himself; for you know that MacCorkle County was settled by them old Scotch Covenanters, and the folks are Scotch Presbyterians to this day. And for the matter of that, the Eagle boys that are in it are of Scotch descent, or a kind of blend, you know; in fact, I 'm half Scotch myself — or Irish," he added thoughtfully. "So you see that settles your argument about any local opinion, for if them Scots don't know their own people, who does?"

"May I ask," said the consul, with a desperate attempt to preserve his composure, "what you are proposing to do?"

"Well," said Custer, settling himself comfortably back in his chair again, "that depends. Do you remember the time that we jumped them Mexican claims on the North Fork — the time them greasers wanted to take in the whole river-bank because they 'd found gold on one of the upper bars? Seems to me we jest went peaceful-like over there one moonshiny night, and took up *their* stakes and set down *ours*. Seems to me *you* were one of the party."

"That was in our own country," returned the consul hastily, "and was an indefensible act, even in a lawless frontier civilization. But you are surely not mad enough even to conceive of such a thing *here!*"

"Keep your hair on, Jack," said Custer lazily. "What 's the matter with constitutional methods, eh? Do you remember the time when we did n't like Pueblo rules, and we laid out Eureka City on their lines, and whooped up the Mexicans and diggers to elect mayor and aldermen, and put the city front on Juanita Creek, and then corraled it for water lots? Seems to me you were county clerk then. Now who 's to keep Dick Macgregor and Joe Hamilton, that are both up the Nile now, from droppin' in over here to see Malcolm in his own house? Who 's goin' to object to Wallace or Baird, who are on this side, doin' the Eytalian lakes, from comin' here on their way home; or Watson and Moore and Timley, that are livin' over in

Paris, from joinin' the boys in givin' Malcolm a house-warmin' in his old home? What 's to keep the whole syndicate from gatherin' at Kelpie Island up here off the west coast, among the tombs of Malcolm's ancestors, and fixin' up things generally with the clan?"

"Only one thing," said the consul, with a gravity which he nevertheless felt might be a mistaken attitude. "You should n't have told *me* about it. For if, as your old friend, I cannot keep you from committing an inconceivable folly, as the American consul here it will be my first duty to give notice to our legation, and perhaps warn the authorities. And you may be sure I will do it."

To his surprise Custer leaned forward and pressed his hand with an expression of cheerful relief. "That 's so, old pard; I reckoned on it. In fact, I told Malcolm that that would be about your gait. Of course you could n't do otherwise. And it would have been playin' it rather low down on you to have left you out in the cold — without even *that* show in the game. For what you will do in warnin' the other fellows, don't you see, will just waken up the clan. It 's better than a campaign circular."

"Don't be too sure of that," said the consul, with a half-hysterical laugh. "But we won't consider so lamentable a contingency. Come and dine with me, both of you, and we 'll discuss the only thing worth discussing, — your *legal* rights, — and you can tell me your whole story, which, by the way, I have n't heard."

"Sorry, Jack, but it can't be done," said Custer, with his first approach to seriousness of manner. "You see, we 'd made up our mind not to come here again after this first call. We ain't goin' to compromise you."

"I am the best judge of that," returned the consul dryly. Then suddenly changing his manner, he grasped Custer's hands with both his own. "Come, Harry," he said earnestly, "I will not believe that this is not a joke, but I beg of you to promise me one thing, — do not move a step further in this matter without legal counsel. I will give you a letter to a legal friend of mine, — a man of affairs, a man of the world, and a Scot as typical, perhaps, as any you have mentioned. State your *legal* case to him, — only that; but his opinion will show you also, if I am not mistaken, the folly of your depending upon any sectional or historical sentiment in this matter."

Without waiting for a reply, he sat down and hastily wrote a few lines to a friendly local magnate. When he had handed the note to Custer, the latter looked at the address, and showed it to his young companion.

"Same name, is n't it?" he asked.

"Yes," responded Mr. McHulish.

"Do you know him?" asked the consul, evidently surprised.

"We don't; but he 's a friend of one of the Eagle boys. I reckon we would have seen him anyhow; but we 'll agree with you to hold on until we do. It 's a go. Good-by, old pard! So long."

They both shook the consul's hand, and departed, leaving him staring at the fog into which they had melted as if they were unreal shadows of the past.

II

The next morning the fog had given way to a palpable, horizontally driving rain, which wet the inside as well as the outside of umbrellas, and caused them to be presented at every conceivable angle as they drifted past the windows of the consulate. There was a tap at the door, and a clerk entered.

"Ye will be in to Sir James MacFen?"

The consul nodded and added, "Show him in here."

It was the magnate to whom he had sent the note the

previous day, a man of large yet slow and cautious nature, learned and even pedantic, yet far-sighted and practical; very human and hearty in social intercourse, which, however, left him as it found him, — with no sentimental or unbusiness-like entanglements. The consul had known him sensible and sturdy at board meetings and executive councils; logical and convincing at political gatherings; decorous and grave in the kirk; and humorous and jovial at festivities, where perhaps later in the evening, in company with others, hands were clasped over a libation lyrically defined as a "right guid williewaught." On one of these occasions they had walked home together, not without some ostentation of steadiness; yet when MacFen's eminently respectable front door had closed upon him, the consul was perfectly satisfied that a distinctly proper and unswerving man of business would issue from it the next morning.

"Ay, but it 's a soft day," said Sir James, removing his gloves. "Ye 'll not be gadding about in this weather."

"You got my note of introduction, I suppose?" said the consul, when the momentous topic of the weather was exhausted.

"Oh, ay."

"And you saw the gentlemen?"

"Ay."

"And what 's your opinion of — his claims?"

"He 's a fine lad — that Malcolm — a fine type of a lad," said Sir James, with an almost too effusive confidence. "Ye 'll be thinking so yourself no doubt? Ay, it 's wonderful to consider the preservation of type so long after its dispersal in other lands. And it 's a strange and wonderful country that of yours, with its plantations — as one might say — of homogeneity unimpaired for so many years, and keeping the old faith too — and all its strange survivals. Ay, and that Kentucky, where his land is — it will be a rich State! It 's very instructing and interesting to hear his account of that remarkable region they call 'the blue grass country,' and the stock they raise there. I 'm obliged to ye, my friend, for a most edifying and improving evening."

"But his claim — did he not speak of that?"

"Oh, ay. And that Mr. Custer — he 's a grand man, and an amusing one. Ye 'll be great comrades, you and he! Man! it was delightful to hear him tell of the rare doings and the bit fun ye two had in the old times. Eh, sir, but who 'd think that of the proper American consul at St. Kentigern!" And Sir James leaned back in his chair, and bestowed an admiring smile on that official.

The consul thought he began to understand this evasion. "Then you don't think much of Mr. McHulish's claim?" he said.

"I 'm not saying that."

"But do you really think a claim based upon a family Bible and a family likeness a subject for serious consideration?"

"I 'm not saying *that* either, laddie."

"Perhaps he has confided to you more fully than he has to me, or possibly you yourself knew something in corroboration of his facts."

"No."

His companion had evidently no desire to be communicative. But the consul had heard enough to feel that he was justified in leaving the matter in his hands. He had given him fair warning. Yet, nevertheless, he would be even more explicit.

"I do not know," he began, "whether this young McHulish confided to you his great reliance upon some peculiar effect of his presence among the tenants, and of establishing his claim to the property by exciting the enthusiasm of the clan. It certainly struck me that he had some rather exaggerated ideas, borrowed, perhaps, from romances he 'd read, like Don Quixote his books of chivalry. He seems to believe in the existence of a clan loyalty, and the actual survival of old feudal instincts and of old feudal methods in the Highlands. He appears to look upon himself as a kind of local Prince Charlie, and, by Jove! I 've an idea he 's almost as crazy."

"And why should he na believe in his own kith and kin?" said Sir James, quickly, with a sudden ring in his voice, and a dialectical freedom quite distinct from his former deliberate and cautious utterance. "The McHulishes were chieftains before America was discovered, and many 's the time they overran the border before they went as far as that. If there 's anything in blood and loyalty, it would be strange if they did na respond. And I can tell ye, ma frien', there 's more in the Hielands than any 'romancer,' as ye call them, — ay, even Scott hissel', and he was but an Edinboro' man, — ever dreamed of. Don't fash yoursel' about that. And you and me 'll not agree about Prince Charlie. Some day I 'll tell ye, ma frien', mair aboot that bonnie laddie than ye 'll gather from your partisan historians. Until then ye 'll be wise when ye 'll be talking to Scotchmen not to be expressing your Southern prejudices."

Intensely surprised and amused at this sudden outbreak of enthusiasm on the part of the usually cautious lawyer, the consul could not refrain from accenting it by a marked return to practical business.

"I shall be delighted to learn more about Prince Charlie," he said, smiling, "but just now his prototype — if you 'll allow me to call him so — is a nearer topic, and for the present, at least until he assume his new titles and dignities, has a right to claim my protection, and I am responsible for him as an American citizen. Now, my dear friend, is there really any property, land, or title of any importance involved in his claim, and what and where, in Heaven's name, is it? For I assure you I know nothing practical about it, and cannot make head or tail of it."

Sir James resumed his slow serenity, and gathered up his gloves. "Ay, there 's a great deer-forest in Ballochbrinkie, and there 's part of Loch Phillibeg in Cairngormshire, and there 's Kelpie Island off Moreovershire. Ay, there 's enough land when the crofters are cleared off, and the small sheep-tenants evicted. It will be a grand property then."

The consul stared. "The crofters and tenants evicted!" he repeated. "Are they not part of the clan, and loyal to the McHulish?"

"The McHulish," said Sir James with great deliberation, "has n't set foot there for years. They 'd be burning him in effigy."

"But," said the astonished consul, "that 's rather bad for the expectant heir — and the magic of the McHulish presence."

"I 'm not saying that," returned Sir James cautiously. "Ye see he can be making better arrangements with the family on account of it."

"With the family?" repeated the consul. "Then does he talk of compromising?"

"I mean they would be more likely to sell for a fair consideration, and he 'd be better paying money to them than the lawyers. The syndicate will be rich, eh? And I 'm not saying the McHulish would n't take Kentucky lands in exchange. It 's a fine country, that blue grass district."

The consul stared at Sir James so long that a faint smile came into the latter's shrewd eyes; at which the consul smiled, too. A vague air of relief and understanding seemed to fill the apartment.

"Oh, ay," continued Sir James, drawing on his gloves with easy deliberation, "he 's a fine lad that Malcolm, and it 's a praiseworthy instinct in him to wish to return to the land of his forbears, and take his place again among them. And I 'm noticing, Mr. Consul, that a great many of your countrymen are doing the same. Eh, yours is a gran' country of progress and ceevel and religious liberty, but for a' that, as Burns says, it 's in your blood to turn to the auld home again. And it 's a fine thing to have the money to do it — and, I 'm thinking, money well spent all around. Good-morning. Eh, but I 'm forgetting that I wanted to ask you to dine with me and Malcolm, and your Mr. Custer, and Mr. Watson, who will be one of your syndicate, and whom I once met abroad. But ye 'll get a bit note of invitation, with the day, from me later."

The consul remembered that Custer had said that one of the "Eagle boys" had known Sir James. This was evidently Watson. He smiled again, but this time Sir James responded only in a general sort of way, as he genially bowed himself out of the room.

The consul watched his solid and eminently respectable figure as it passed the window, and then returned to his desk, still smiling. First of all he was relieved. What had seemed to him a wild and reckless enterprise, with possibly some grim international complications on the part of his compatriots, had simply resolved itself into an ordinary business speculation, — the ethics of which they had pretty equally divided with the local operators. If anything, it seemed that the Scotchman would get the best of the bargain, and that, for once at least, his countrymen were deficient in foresight. But that was a matter between the parties, and Custer himself would probably be the first to resent any suggestion of the kind from the consul. The vision of the McHulish burned in effigy by his devoted tenants and retainers, and the thought that the prosaic dollars of his countrymen would be substituted for the potent presence of the heir, tickled, it is to be feared, the saturnine humor of the consul. He had taken an invincible dislike to the callow representative of the McHulish, who he felt had in some extraordinary way imposed upon Custer's credulity. But then he had apparently imposed equally upon the practical Sir James. The thought of this sham ideal of feudal and privileged incompetency being elevated to actual position by the combined efforts of American republicans and hard-headed Scotch dissenters, on whom the soft Scotch mists fell from above with equal impartiality, struck him as being very amusing, and for some time thereafter lightened the respectable gloom of his office. Other engagements prevented his attendance at Sir James's dinner, although he was informed afterward that it had passed off with great *éclat*, the later singing of "Auld lang Syne," and the drinking of the health of Custer and Malcolm with "Hieland honors." He learned also that Sir James had invited Custer and Malcolm to his lacustrine country-seat in the early spring. But he learned nothing more of the progress of Malcolm's claim, its details, or the manner in which it was prosecuted. No one else seemed to know anything about it; it found no echo in the gossip of the clubs, or in the newspapers of St. Kentigern. In the absence of the parties connected with it, it began to assume to him the aspect of a half-humorous romance. He often found himself wondering if there had been any other purpose in this quest or speculation than what had appeared on the surface, it seemed so inadequate in result. It would have been so perfectly easy for a wealthy syndicate to buy up a much more valuable estate. He disbelieved utterly in the sincerity of Malcolm's sentimental attitude. There must be some other reason, — perhaps not known even to the syndicate.

One day he thought that he had found it. He had

received a note addressed from one of the principal hotels, but bearing a large personal crest on paper and envelope. A Miss Kirkby, passing through St. Kentigern on her way to Edinburgh, desired to see the consul the next day, if he would appoint an hour at the consulate; or, as her time was limited, she would take it as a great favor if he would call at her hotel. Although a countrywoman, her name might not be so well known to him as those of her "old friends" Harry Custer, Esq., and Sir Malcolm McHulish. The consul was a little surprised; the use of the title — unless it referred to some other McHulish — would seem to indicate that Malcolm's claim was successful. He had, however, no previous knowledge of the title of "Sir" in connection with the estate, and it was probable that his fair correspondent — like most of her countrywomen — was more appreciative than correct in her bestowal of dignities. He determined to waive his ordinary business rules, and to call upon her at once, accepting, as became his patriotism, that charming tyranny which the American woman usually reserves exclusively for her devoted countrymen.

She received him with an affectation of patronage, as if she had lately become uneasily conscious of being in a country where there were distinctions of class. She was young, pretty, and tastefully dressed; the national feminine adaptability had not, however, extended to her voice and accent. Both were strongly Southwestern, and as she began to speak she seemed to lose her momentary affectation.

"It was mighty good of you to come and see me, for the fact is, I did n't admire going to your consulate — not one bit. You see, I 'm a Southern girl, and never was 'reconstructed' either. I don't hanker after your Gov'ment. I have n't recognized it, and don't want to. I reckon I ain't been under the flag since the wah. So you see, I have n't any papers to get authenticated, nor any certificates to ask for, and ain't wanting any advice or protection. I thought I 'd be fair and square with you from the word 'go.'"

Nothing could be more fascinating and infectious than the mirthful ingenuousness which accompanied and seemed to mitigate this ungracious speech, and the consul was greatly amused, albeit conscious that it was only an attitude, and perhaps somewhat worn in sentiment. He knew that during the war of the Rebellion, and directly after it, Great Britain was the resort of certain Americans from the West as well as from the South who sought social distinction by the affectation of dissatisfaction with their own government or the ostentatious simulation of enforced exile; but he was quite unprepared for this senseless protraction of dead and gone issues. He ventured to point out with good-humored practicality that several years had elapsed since the war, that the South and North were honorably reconciled, and that he was legally supposed to represent Kentucky as well as New York. "Your friends," he added smilingly, "Mr. Custer and Mr. McHulish, seemed to accept the fact without any posthumous sentiment."

"I don't go much on that," she said with a laugh. "I 've been living in Paris till maw — who 's lying down upstairs — came over and brought me across to England for a look around. And I reckon Malcolm 's got to keep touch with you on account of his property."

The consul smiled. "Ah, then I hope you can tell me something about *that*, for I really don't know whether he has established his claim or not."

"Why," returned the girl with naïve astonishment, "that was just what I was going to ask *you*. He reckoned you 'd know all about it."

"I have n't heard anything of the claim for two

months," said the consul; "but from your reference to him as 'Sir Malcolm' I presumed you considered it settled. Though, of course, even then he would n't be 'Sir Malcolm,' and you might have meant somebody else."

"Well, then, Lord Malcolm — I can't get the hang of those titles yet."

"Neither 'Lord' nor 'Sir'; you know the estate carries no title whatever with it," said the consul smilingly.

"But would n't he be the laird of something or other, you know?"

"Yes; but that is only a Scotch description, not a title. It 's not the same as Lord."

The young girl looked at him with undisguised astonishment. A half laugh twitched the corners of her mouth. "Are you sure?" she said.

"Perfectly," returned the consul, a little impatiently; "but do I understand that you really know nothing more of the progress of the claim?"

Miss Kirkby, still abstracted by some humorous astonishment, said quickly: "Wait a minute. I 'll just run up and see if maw 's coming down. She 'd admire to see you." Then she stopped, hesitated, and as she rose added, "Then a laird's wife would n't be Lady anything, anyway, would she?"

"She certainly would acquire no title merely through her marriage."

The young girl laughed again, nodded, and disappeared. The consul, amused yet somewhat perplexed over the naïve brusqueness of the interview, waited patiently. Presently she returned, a little out of breath, but apparently still enjoying some facetious retrospect, and said, "Maw will be down soon." After a pause, fixing her bright eyes mischievously on the consul, she continued: —

"Did you see much of Malcolm?"

"I saw him only once."

"What did you think of him?"

The consul in so brief a period had been unable to judge.

"You would n't think I was half engaged to him, would you?"

The consul was obliged again to protest that in so short an interview he had been unable to conceive of Malcolm's good fortune.

"I know what you mean," said the girl lightly. "You think he 's a crank. But it 's all over now; the engagement 's off."

"I trust that this does not mean that you doubt his success?"

The lady shrugged her shoulders disdainfully. "That 's all right enough, I reckon. There 's a hundred thousand dollars in the syndicate. Maw put in twenty thousand, and Custer 's bound to make it go, — particularly as there 's some talk of a compromise. But Malcolm 's a crank, and I reckon if it was n't for the compromise the syndicate would n't have much show. Why, he did n't even know that the McHulishes had no title."

"Do you think he has been suffering under a delusion in regard to his relationship?"

"No; he was only a fool in the way he wanted to prove it. He actually got these boys to think it could be filibustered into his possession. Had a sort of idea of 'a rising in the Highlands,' you know, like that poem or picture — which is it? And those fool boys, and Custer among them, thought it would be great fun and a great spree. Luckily, maw had the gumption to get Watson to write over about it to one of his friends, a Mr. — Mr. — MacFen, a very prominent man."

"Perhaps you mean Sir James MacFen," suggested the consul. "He 's a knight. And what did *he* say?" he added eagerly.

"Oh, he wrote a most sensible letter," returned the lady, apparently mollified by the title of Watson's adviser, "saying that there was little doubt, if any, that if the American McHulishes wanted the old estate they could get it by the expenditure of a little capital. He offered to make the trial; that was the compromise they're talking about. But he did n't say anything about there being no 'Lord' McHulish."

"Perhaps he thought, as you were Americans, you did n't care for *that*," said the consul dryly.

"That's no reason why we should n't have it if it belonged to us, or we chose to pay for it," said the lady pertly.

"Then your changed personal relation with Mr. McHulish is the reason why you hear so little of his progress or his expectations?"

"Yes; but he don't know that they are changed, for we have n't seen him since we've been here, although they say he's here, and hiding somewhere about."

"Why should he be hiding?"

The young girl lifted her pretty brows. "Maybe he thinks it's mysterious. Did n't I tell you he was a crank?" Yet she laughed so naïvely, and with such sublime unconsciousness of any reflection on herself, that the consul was obliged to smile too.

"You certainly do not seem to be breaking your heart as well as your engagement," he said.

"Not much — but here comes maw. Look here," she said, turning suddenly and coaxingly upon him, "if she asks you to come along with us up north, you'll come, won't you? Do! It will be such fun!"

"Up north?" repeated the consul interrogatively.

"Yes; to see the property. Here's maw."

A more languid but equally well-appointed woman had entered the room. When the ceremony of introduction was over, she turned to her daughter and said, "Run away, dear, while I talk business with — er — this gentleman," and, as the girl withdrew laughingly, she half stifled a reminiscent yawn, and raised her heavy lids to the consul.

"You 've had a talk with my Elsie?"

The consul confessed to having had that pleasure.

"She speaks her mind," said Mrs. Kirkby wearily, "but she means well, and for all her flightiness her head 's level. And since her father died she runs me," she continued with a slight laugh. After a pause, she added abstractedly, "I suppose she told you of her engagement to young McHulish?"

"Yes; but she said she had broken it."

Mrs. Kirkby lifted her eyebrows with an expression of relief. "It was a piece of girl and boy foolishness, anyway," she said. "Elsie and he were children together at MacCorkleville, — second cousins, in fact, — and I reckon he got her fancy excited over his nobility, and his being the chief of the McHulishes. Of course Custer will manage to get something for the shareholders out of it, — I never knew him to fail in a money speculation yet, — but I think that 's about all. I had an idea of going up with Elsie to take a look at the property, and I thought of asking you to join us. Did Elsie tell you? I know she 'd like it — and so would I."

For all her indolent, purposeless manner, there was enough latent sincerity and earnestness in her request to interest the consul. Besides, his own curiosity in regard to this singularly supported claim was excited, and here seemed to be an opportunity of satisfying it. He was not quite sure, either, that his previous antagonism to his fair countrywoman's apparent selfishness and snobbery was entirely just. He had been absent from America a long time; perhaps it was he himself who had changed, and lost touch with his compatriots. And yet the demonstrative independence and recklessness of men like Custer were less objectionable to, and less inconsistent with, his American ideas than the snobbishness and almost servile adaptability of the women. Or was it possible that it was only a weakness of the sex, which no republican nativity or education could eliminate? Nevertheless he looked up smilingly.

"But the property is, I understand, scattered about in various places," he said.

"Oh, but we mean to go only to Kelpie Island, where there is the ruin of an old castle. Elsie must see that."

The consul thought it might be amusing. "By all means, let us see that. I shall be delighted to go with you."

His ready and unqualified assent appeared to relieve and dissipate the lady's abstraction. She became more natural and confiding; spoke freely of Malcolm's mania, which she seemed to accept as a hallucination or a conviction with equal cheerfulness, and, in brief, convinced the consul that her connection with the scheme was only the caprice of inexperienced and unaccustomed idleness. He left her, promising to return the next day and arrange for their early departure.

His way home lay through one of the public squares of St. Kentigern, at an hour of the afternoon when it was crossed by working men and women returning to their quarters from the docks and factories. Never in any light a picturesque or even cheery procession, there were days when its unwholesome, monotonous poverty and dull hopelessness of prospect impressed him more forcibly. He remembered how at first the spectacle of barefooted girls and women slipping through fog and mist across the greasy pavement had offended his fresh New World conception of a more tenderly nurtured sex, until his susceptibilities seemed to have grown as callous and hardened as the flesh he looked upon, and he had begun to regard them from the easy local standpoint of a distinct and differently equipped class.

It chanced, also, that this afternoon some of the male workers had added to their usual stolidity a singular trance-like intoxication. It had often struck him before as a form of drunkenness peculiar to the St. Kentigern laborers. Men passed him singly and silently, as if following some vague alcoholic dream, or moving through some Scotch mist of whiskey and water. Others clung unsteadily but as silently together, with no trace of convivial fellowship or hilarity in their dull fixed features and mechanically moving limbs. There was something weird in this mirthless companionship, and the appalling loneliness of those fixed or abstracted eyes. Suddenly he was aware of two men who were reeling toward him under the influence of this drug-like intoxication, and he was startled by a likeness which one of them bore to some one he had seen; but where, and under what circumstances, he could not determine. The fatuous eye, the features of complacent vanity and self-satisfied reverie were there, either intensified by drink, or perhaps suggesting it through some other equally hopeless form of hallucination. He turned and followed the man, trying to identify him through his companion, who appeared to be a petty tradesman of a shrewder, more material type. But in vain, and as the pair turned into a side street the consul slowly retraced his steps. But he had not proceeded far before the recollection that had escaped him returned, and he knew that the likeness suggested by the face he had seen was that of Malcolm McHulish.

III

A journey to Kelpie Island consisted of a series of consecutive episodes by rail, by coach, and by steamboat. The consul was already familiar with them, as indeed were most of the civilized world, for it seemed that all roads at certain seasons led out of and returned to St. Kentigern as a point in a vast circle wherein travelers were sure to meet one another again, coming or going, at certain depots and caravansaries with more or less superiority or envy. Tourists on the road to the historic crags of Wateffa came sharply upon other tourists returning from them, and glared suspiciously at them, as if to wrest the dread secret from their souls, — a scrutiny which the others returned with half-humorous pity or superior calm.

The consul knew, also, that the service by boat and rail was admirable and skillful; for were not the righteous St. Kentigerners of the tribe of Tubal-cain, great artificers in steel and iron, and a mighty race of engineers before the Lord, who had carried their calling and accent beyond the seas? He knew, too, that the land of these delightful caravansaries overflowed with marmalade and honey, and that the manna of delicious scones and cakes fell even upon deserted waters of crag and heather. He knew that their way would lie through much scenery whose rude barrenness, and grim economy of vegetation had been usually accepted by cockney tourists for sublimity and grandeur; but he knew, also, that its severity was mitigated by low land glimpses of sylvan luxuriance and tangled delicacy utterly unlike the complacent snugness of an English pastoral landscape, with which it was often confounded and misunderstood, as being tame and civilized.

It rained the day they left St. Kentigern, and the next, and the day after that, spasmodically, as regarded local effort, sporadically, as seen through the filmed windows of railway carriages or from the shining decks of steamboats. There was always a shower being sown somewhere along the valley, or reluctantly tearing itself from a mountain-top, or being pulled into long threads from the leaden bosom of a lake; the coach swept in and out of them to the folding and unfolding of umbrellas and mackintoshes, accompanied by flying beams of sunlight that raced with the vehicle on long hillsides, and vanished at the turn of the road. There were hat-lifting scurries of wind down the mountain-side, small tumults in little lakes below, hysteric ebullitions on mild, melancholy inland seas, boisterous passages of nearly half an hour with landings on tempestuous miniature quays. All this seen through wonderful aqueous vapor, against a background of sky darkened at times to the depths of an India ink washed sketch, but more usually blurred and confused on the surface like the gray silhouette of a child's slate-pencil drawing, half rubbed from the slate by soft palms. Occasionally a rare glinting of real sunshine on a distant fringe of dripping larches made some frowning crest appear to smile as through wet lashes.

Miss Elsie tucked her little feet under the mackintosh.

"I know," she said sadly, "I should get web-footed if I stayed here long. Why, it 's like coming down from Ararat just after the deluge cleared up."

Mrs. Kirkby suggested that if the sun would only shine squarely and decently, like a Christian, for a few moments, they could see the prospect better.

The consul here pointed out that the admirers of Scotch scenery thought that this was its greatest charm. It was this misty effect which made it so superior to what they called the vulgar chromos and sun-pictures of less favored lands.

"You mean because it prevents folks from seeing how poor the view really is."

The consul remarked that perhaps distance was lacking. As to the sun shining in a Christian way, this might depend upon the local idea of Christianity.

"Well, I don't call the scenery giddy or frivolous, certainly. And I reckon I begin to understand the kind of sermons Malcolm's folks brought over to MacCorkleville. I guess they didn't know much of the heaven they saw only once a year. Why, even the highest hills — which they call mountains here — ain't big enough to get above the fogs of their own creating."

Feminine wit is not apt to be abstract. It struck the consul that in Miss Elsie's sprightliness there was the usual ulterior and personal object, and he glanced around at his fellow-passengers. The object evidently was sitting at the end of the opposite seat, an amused but well-behaved listener. For the rest, he was still young and reserved, but in face, figure, and dress utterly unlike his companions, — an Englishman of a pronounced and distinct type, the man of society and clubs. While there was more or less hinting of local influence in the apparel of the others, — there was a kilt, and bare, unweather-beaten knees from Birmingham, and even the American Elsie wore a bewitching tam-o'-shanter, — the stranger carried easy distinction, from his tweed traveling-cap to his well-made shoes and gaiters, as an unmistakable Southerner. His deep and pleasantly level voice had been heard only once or twice, and then only in answering questions, and his quiet, composed eyes alone had responded to the young girl's provocation.

They were passing a brown glen, in the cheerless depths of which a brown watercourse, a shade lighter, was running, and occasionally foaming like brown beer. Beyond it heaved an arid bulk of hillside, the scant vegetation of which, scattered like patches of hair, made it look like the decaying hide of some huge antediluvian ruminant. On the dreariest part of the dreary slope rose the ruins of a tower, and crumbling walls and battlements.

"Whatever possessed folks to build there?" said Miss Elsie. "If they were poor, it might be some excuse; but that those old swells, or chiefs, should put up a castle in such a God-forsaken place gets *me*."

"But don't you know, they *were* poor, according to our modern ideas, and I fancy they built these things more for defense than show, and really more to gather in cattle — like one of your Texan ranches — after a raid. That is, I have heard so; I rather fancy that was the idea, was n't it?" It was the Englishman who had spoken, and was now looking around at the other passengers as if in easy deference to local opinion.

"What raid?" said Miss Elsie animatedly. "Oh, yes; I see — one of their old border raids — moss-troopers. I used to like to read about them."

"I fancy, don't you know," said the Englishman slowly, "that it was n't exactly *that* sort of thing, you know, for it 's a good way from the border; but it was one of their raids upon their neighbors, to lift their cattle — steal 'em, in fact. That 's the way those chaps had. But of course you 've read all about that. You Americans, don't you know, are all up in these historical matters."

"Eh, but they were often reprisals," said a Scotch passenger.

"I don't suppose they took much trouble to inquire if the beasts belonged to an enemy," said the Englishman.

But here Miss Elsie spoke of castles generally, and averred that the dearest wish of her life was to see Macbeth's castle at Glamis, where Duncan was murdered. At which the Englishman, still deferentially, mistrusted the fact that the murder had been committed there, and thought that the castle to which Shakespeare probably referred, if he had n't invented the murder, too, was farther north, at Cawdor. "You know," he added playfully, "over there in America you've discovered that Shakespeare himself was an invention."

This led to some retaliating brilliancy from the young lady, and when the coach stopped at the next station their conversation had presumably become interesting enough to justify him in securing a seat nearer to her. The talk returning to ruins, Miss Elsie informed him that they were going to see some on Kelpie Island. The consul, from some instinctive impulse, — perhaps a recollection of Custer's peculiar methods, — gave her a sign of warning. But the Englishman only lifted his eyebrows in a kind of half-humorous concern.

"I don't think you'd like it, you know. It's a beastly place, — rocks and sea, — worse than this, and half the time you can't see the mainland, only a mile away. Really, you know, they ought n't to have induced you to take tickets there — those excursion-ticket chaps. They're jolly frauds. It's no place for a stranger to go to."

"But there are the rnins of an old castle, the old seat of" — began the astonished Miss Elsie; but she was again stopped by a significant glance from the consul.

"I believe there was something of the kind there once — something like your friends the cattle-stealers' castle over on that hillside," returned the Englishman; "but the stones were taken by the fishermen for their cabins, and the walls were quite pulled down."

"How darod they do that?" said the young lady indignantly. "I call it not only sacrilege, but stealing."

"It was defrauding the owner of the property; they might as well take his money," said Mrs. Kirkby, in languid protest.

The smile which this outburst of proprietorial indignation brought to the face of the consul lingered with the Englishman's reply.

"But it was only robbing the old robbers, don't you know, and they put their spoils to better use than their old masters did; certainly to more practical use than the owners do now, for the ruins are good for nothing."

"But the hallowed associations — the picturesqueness!" continued Mrs. Kirkby, with languid interest.

"The associations would n't be anything except to the family, you know; and I should fancy they would n't be either hallowed or pleasant. As for picturesqueness, the ruins are beastly ugly; weather-beaten instead of being mellowed by time, you know, and bare where they ought to be hidden by vines and moss. I can't make out why anybody sent you there, for you Americans are rather particular about your sight-seeing."

"We heard of them through a friend," said the consul, with assumed carelessness. "Perhaps it 's as good an excuse as any for a pleasant journey."

"And very likely your friend mistook it for something else, or was himself imposed upon," said the Englishman politely. "But you might not think it so, and, after all," he added thoughtfully, "it 's years since I 've seen it. I only meant that I could show you something better a few miles from my place in Gloucestershire, and not quite so far from a railway as this. If," he added with a pleasant deliberation which was the real courtesy of his conventionally worded speech, "you ever happened at any time to be anywhere near Audrey Edge, and would look me up, I should be glad to show it to you and your friends." An hour later, when he left them at a railway station where their paths diverged, Miss Elsie recovered a fluency that she had lately checked. "Well, I like that! He never told us his name, or offered a card. I wonder if they call that an invitation over here. Does he suppose anybody 's going to look up his old Audrey Edge — perhaps it 's named after his wife — to find out who *he* is? He might have been civil enough to have left his name, if he — meant anything."

"But I assure you he was perfectly sincere, and meant an invitation," returned the consul smilingly. "Audrey Edge is evidently a well-known place, and he a man of some position. That is why he did n't specify either."

"Well, you won't catch me going there," said Miss Elsie.

"You would be quite right in either going or staying away," said the consul simply.

Miss Elsie tossed her head slightly. Nevertheless, before they left the station, she informed him that she had been told that the station-master had addressed the stranger as "my lord," and that another passenger had said he was Lord Duncaster.

"And that proves" —

"That I 'm right," said the young lady decisively, "and that his invitation was a mere form."

It was after sundown when they reached the picturesque and well-appointed hotel that lifted itself above the little fishing-village which fronted Kelpie Island. The hotel was in as strong contrast to the narrow, curving street of dull, comfortless-looking stone cottages below it, as were the smart tourists who had just landed from the steamer to the hard-visaged, roughly clad villagers who watched them with a certain mingling of critical independence and superior self-righteousness. As the new arrivals walked down the main street, half beach, half thoroughfare, their baggage following them in low trolleys drawn by porters at their heels, like a decorous funeral, the joyless faces of the lookers-on added to the resemblance. Beyond them, in the prolonged northern twilight, the waters of the bay took on a peculiar pewtery brightness, but with the usual mourning-edged border of Scotch seacoast scenery. Low banks of cloud lay on the chill sea; the outlines of Kelpie Island were hidden.

But the interior of the hotel, bright with the latest fastidiousness in modern decoration and art-furniture, and gay with pictured canvases and color, seemed to mock the sullen landscape and the sterile crags amid which the building was set. An attempt to make a pleasance in this barren waste had resulted only in empty vases, bleak statuary, and iron settees, as cold and slippery to the touch as the sides of their steamer.

"It 'll be a fine morning to-morra, and ther' 'll be a boat going away to Kelpie for a peekneek in the ruins," said the porter, as the consul and his fair companions looked doubtfully from the windows of the cheerful hall.

A picnic in the sacred ruins of Kelpie! The consul saw the ladies stiffening with indignation at this trespass upon their possible rights and probable privileges, and glanced at them warningly.

"Do you mean to say that it is common property, and *anybody* can go there?" demanded Miss Elsie scornfully.

"No; it 's only the hotel that owns the boat and gives the tickets — a half-crown the passage."

"And do the owners, the McHulishes, permit this?"

The porter looked at them with a puzzled, half-pitying politeness. He was a handsome, tall, broad-shouldered young fellow, with a certain naïve and gentle courtesy of manner that relieved his strong accent. "Oh, ay," he said, with a reassuring smile; "ye 'll no be troubled by *them*. I 'll just gang away noo, and see if I can secure the teekets."

An elderly guest, who was examining a time-table on the wall, turned to them as the porter disappeared.

"Ye 'll be strangers noo, and not knowing that Tonalt the porter is a McHulish hissel'?" he said deliberately.

"A what?" said the astonished Miss Elsie.

"A McHulish. Ay, one of the family. The McHulishes of Kelpie were his own forbears. Eh, but he 's a fine lad, and doin' well for the hotel."

Miss Elsie extinguished a sudden smile with her handkerchief as her mother anxiously inquired, "And are the family as poor as that?"

"But I am not saying he 's *poor*, ma'am, no," replied the stranger, with native caution. "What wi' tips and gratooities and percentages on the teekets, it 's a bit of money he 'll be having in the bank noo."

The prophecy of Donald McHulish as to the weather came true. The next morning was bright and sunny, and the boat to Kelpie Island — a large yawl — duly received its complement of passengers and provision hampers. The ladies had apparently become more tolerant of their fellow pleasure-seekers, and it appeared that Miss Elsie had even overcome her hilarity at the discovery of what "might have been" a relative in the person of the porter Donald. "I had a long talk with him before breakfast this morning," she said gayly, "and I know all about him. It appears that there are hundreds of him — all McHulishes — all along the coast and elsewhere — only none of them ever lived *on* the island, and don't want to. But he looks more like a 'laird' and a chief than Malcolm, and if it comes to choosing a head of the family, remember, maw, I shall vote solid for him."

"How can you go on so, Elsie?" said Mrs. Kirkby, with languid protest. "Only I trust you did n't say anything to him of the syndicate. And, thank Heaven! the property is n't here."

"No; the waiter tells me all the lovely things we had for breakfast came from miles away. And they don't seem to have ever raised anything on the island, from its looks. Think of having to row three miles for the morning's milk!"

There was certainly very little appearance of vegetation on the sterile crags that soon began to lift themselves above the steely waves ahead. A few scraggy trees and bushes, which twisted and writhed like vines around the square tower and crumbling walls of an irregular but angular building, looked in their brown shadows like part of the débris.

"It 's just like a burnt-down bone-boiling factory," said Miss Elsie critically; "and I should n't wonder if that really was old McHulish's business. They could n't have it on the mainland for its being a nuisance."

Nevertheless, she was one of the first to leap ashore when the yawl's bow grated in a pebbly cove, and carried her pretty but incongruous little slippers through the seaweed, wet sand, and slimy cobbles with a heroism that redeemed her vanity. A scrambling ascent of a few moments brought them to a wall with a gap in it, which gave easy ingress to the interior of the ruins. This was merely a little curving hollow from which the outlines of the plan had long since faded. It was kept green by the brown walls, which, like the crags of the mainland valleys, sheltered it from the incessant strife of the Atlantic gales. A few pale flowers that might have grown in a damp cellar shivered against the stones. Scraps of newspapers, soda-water and beer bottles, highly decorated old provision tins, and spent cartridge cases, — the remains of chilly picnics and damp shooting luncheons, — had at first sight lent color to the foreground by mere contrast; but the corrosion of time and weather had blackened rather than mellowed the walls in a way which forcibly reminded the consul of Miss Elsie's simile of the "burnt-down factory." The view from the square tower — a mere roost for unclean sea-fowl, from the sides of which rags of peeling moss and vine hung like tattered clothing — was equally depressing. The few fishermen's huts along the shore were built of stones taken from the ruin, and roofed in with sodden beams and timbers in the last stages of deliquescence. The thick smoke of smouldering peat-fires came from the low chimneys, and drifted across the ruins with the odors of drying fish.

"I 've just seen a sort of ground-plan of the castle," said Miss Elsie cheerfully. "It never had a room in it as big as our bedroom in the hotel, and there were n't windows enough to go round. A slit in the wall, about two inches wide by two feet long, was considered dazzling extravagance to Malcolm's ancestors. I don't wonder some of 'em broke out and swam over to America. That reminds me. Who do you suppose is here — came over from the hotel in a boat of his own, just to see maw?"

"Not Malcolm, surely."

"Not much," replied Miss Elsie, setting her small lips together. "It 's Mr. Custer. He 's talking business with her now down on the beach. They 'll be here when lunch is ready."

The consul remembered the romantic plan which the enthusiastic Custer had imparted to him in the foggy consulate at St. Kentigern, and then thought of the matter-of-fact tourists, the few stolid fishermen, and the prosaic ruins around them, and smiled. He looked up, and saw that Miss Elsie was watching him.

"You know Mr. Custer, don't you?"

"We are old Californian friends."

"I thought so; but I think he looked a little upset when he heard you were here, too."

He certainly was a little awkward, as if struggling with some half-humorous embarrassment, as he came forward a few moments later with Mrs. Kirkby. But the stimulation of the keen sea air triumphed over the infelicities of the situation and surroundings, and the little party were presently enjoying their well-selected luncheon with the wholesome appetite of travel and change. The chill damp made limp the napkins and tablecloth, and invaded the victuals; the wind, which was rising, whistled round the walls, and made miniature cyclones of the torn paper and dried twigs around them; but they ate, drank, and were merry. At the end of the repast the two gentlemen rose to light their cigars in the lee of the wall.

"I suppose you know all about Malcolm?" said Custer, after an awkward pause.

"My dear fellow," said the consul, somewhat impatiently, "I know nothing about him, and you ought to know that by this time."

"I thought *your friend*, Sir James, might have told you," continued Custer, with significant emphasis.

"I have not seen Sir James for two months."

"Well, Malcolm 's a crank — always was one, I reckon, and is reg'larly off his head now. Yes, sir; Scotch whiskey and your friend Sir James finished him. After that dinner at MacFen's he was done for, — went wild. Danced a sword-dance, or a strathspey, or some other blamed thing, on the table, and yelled louder than the pipes. So they all did. Jack, I 've painted the town red once myself; I thought I knew what a first-class jamboree was; but they were prayer-meetings to that show. Everybody was blind drunk; but they all got over it except *him*. *They* were a different lot of men the next day, as cool and cautious as you please, but *he* was shut up for a week, and came out crazy."

"But what 's that to do with his claim?"

"Well, there ain't much use 'whooping up the boys' when only the whooper gets wild."

"Still, that does not affect any right he may have in the property."

"But it affects the syndicate," said Custer gloomily; "and when we found that he was whooping up some shopkeepers and factory hands who claimed to belong to the clan, — and you can't heave a stone at a dog around here without hitting a McHulish, — we concluded we had n't much use for him ornamentally. So we shipped him home last steamer."

"And the property?"

"Oh, that 's all right," said Custer, still gloomily. "We 've effected an amicable compromise, as Sir James calls it. That means we 've taken a lot of land somewhere north, that you can shoot over — that is, you need n't be afraid of hitting a house, or a tree, or a man anywhere; and we 've got a strip more of the same sort on the seashore somewhere off here, occupied only by some gay galoots called crofters, and you can raise a lawsuit and an imprecation on every acre. Then there 's this soul-subduing, sequestered spot, and what 's left of the old bone-boiling establishment, and the rights of fishing and peat-burning, and otherwise creating a nuisance off the mainland. It cost the syndicate only a hundred thousand dollars, half cash and half in Texan and Kentucky grass lands. But we 've carried the thing through."

"I congratulate you," said the consul.

"Thanks." Custer puffed at his cigar for a few moments. "That Sir James MacFen is a fine man."

"He is."

"A large, broad, all-round man. Knows everything and everybody, don't he?"

"I think so."

"Big man in the church, I should say? No slouch at a party canvass, or ward politics, eh? As a board director, or president, just takes the cake, don't he?"

"I believe so."

"Nothing mean about Jimmy as an advocate or an arbitrator, either, is there? Rings the bell every time, don't he? Financiers take a back seat when he 's around? Owns half of Scotland by this time, I reckon."

The consul believed that Sir James had the reputation of being exceedingly sagacious in financial and mercantile matters, and that he was a man of some wealth.

"Naturally. I wonder what he 'd take to come over to America, and give the boys points," continued Custer, in meditative admiration. "There were two or three men on Scott's River, and one Chinaman, that we used to think smart, but they were doddering ijuts to *him*. And as for me — I say, Jack, you did n't see any hayseed in my hair that day I walked inter your consulate, did you?"

The consul smilingly admitted that he had not noticed these signs of rustic innocence in his friend.

"Nor any flies? Well, for all that, when I get home I 'm going to resign. No more foreign investments for *me*. When anybody calls at the consulate and asks for H. J. Custer, say you don't know me. And you don't. And I say, Jack, try to smooth things over for me with *her*."

"With Miss Elsie?"

Custer cast a glance of profound pity upon the consul. "No; with Mrs. Kirkby, of course. See?"

The consul thought he did see, and that he had at last found a clue to Custer's extraordinary speculation. But, like most theorists who argue from a single fact, a few months later he might have doubted his deduction.

He was staying at a large country-house many miles distant from the scene of his late experiences. Already they had faded from his memory with the departure of his compatriots from St. Kentigern. He was smoking by the fire in the billiard-room late one night when a fellow-guest approached him.

"Saw you did n't remember me at dinner."

The voice was hesitating, pleasant, and not quite unfamiliar. The consul looked up, and identified the figure before him as one of the new arrivals that day, whom, in the informal and easy courtesy of the house, he had met with no further introduction than a vague smile. He remembered, too, that the stranger had glanced at him once or twice at dinner, with shy but engaging reserve.

"You must see such a lot of people, and the way things are arranged and settled here everybody expects to look and act like everybody else, don't you know, so you can't tell one chap from another. Deuced annoying, eh? That 's where you Americans are different, and that 's why those countrywomen of yours were so charming, don't you know, so original. We were all together on the top of a coach in Scotland, don't you remember? Had such a jolly time in the beastly rain. You did n't catch my name. It 's Duncaster."

The consul at once recalled his former fellow-traveler. The two men shook hands. The Englishman took a pipe from his smoking-jacket, and drew a chair beside the consul.

"Yes," he continued, comfortably filling his pipe, "the daughter, Miss Kirkby, was awfully good fun; so fresh, so perfectly natural and innocent, don't you know, and yet so extraordinarily sharp and clever. She had some awfully good chaff over that Scotch scenery before those Scotch tourists, do you remember? And it was all so beastly true, too. Perhaps she 's with you here?"

There was so much unexpected and unaffected interest in the young Englishman's eyes that the consul was quite serious in his regrets that the ladies had gone back to Paris.

"I 'd like to have taken them over to Audrey Edge from here. It 's no distance by train. I did ask them in Scotland, but I suppose they had something better to do. But you might tell them I 've got some sisters there, and that it is an old place and not half bad, don't you know, when you write to them. You might give me their address."

The consul did so, and added a few pleasant words regarding their position, — barring the syndicate, — which he had gathered from Custer. Lord Duncaster's look of interest, far from abating, became gently confidential.

"I suppose you must see a good deal of your countrymen in your business, and I suppose, just like Englishmen, they differ, by Jove! Some of them, don't you know, are rather pushing and anxious for position, and all that sort of thing; and some of 'em, like your friends, are quite independent and natural."

He stopped, and puffed slowly at his pipe. Presently he took it from his mouth, with a little laugh. "I 've a mind to tell you a rather queer experience of mine. It 's nothing against your people generally, you know, nor do I fancy it 's even an American type; so you won't mind my speaking of it. I 've got some property in Scotland, — rather poor stuff you 'd call it, — but, by Jove! some Americans have been laying claim to it under some obscure plea of relationship. There might have been something in it, although not all they claim, but my business man, a clever chap up in your place, — perhaps you may have heard of him, Sir James MacFen, — wrote to me that what they really wanted were some ancestral lands with the right to use the family name and privileges. The oddest part of the affair was that tho claimant was an impossible sort of lunatic, and the whole thing was run by a syndicate of shrewd Western men. As I don't care for the property, which has only been dropping a lot of money every year for upkeep and litigation, Sir James, who is an awfully far-sighted chap at managing, thought he could effect a compromise, and get rid of the property at a fair valuation. And, by Jove! he did. But what your countrymen can get out of it, — for the shooting is n't half as good as what they can get in their own country, — or what use the privileges are to them, I can't fancy."

"I think I know the story," said the consul, eying his fellow-guest attentively; "but if I remember rightly, the young man claimed to be the rightful and only surviving heir."

The Englishman rose, and, bending over the hearth, slowly knocked the ashes from his pipe. "That 's quite impossible, don't you know. For," he added, as he stood up in front of the fire in face, figure, and careless repose more decidedly English than ever, "you see my title of Duncaster only came to me through an uncle, but I am the direct and sole heir of the old family, and the Scotch property. I don't perhaps look like a Scot, — we 've been settled in England some time, — but," he continued with an invincible English drawling deliberation, "*I* — am — really — you — know — what they call The McHulish."

YOUNG ROBIN GRAY

THE good American bark Skyscraper was swinging at her moorings in the Clyde, off Bannock, ready for sea. But that good American bark — although owned in Baltimore — had not a plank of American timber in her hulk, nor a native American in her crew, and even her nautical "goodness" had been called into serious question by divers of that crew during her voyage, and answered more or less inconclusively with belaying-pins, marline spikes, and ropes' ends at the hands of an Irish-American captain and a Dutch and Danish mate. So much so, that the mysterious powers of the American consul at St. Kentigern had been evoked to punish mutiny on the one hand, and battery and starvation on the other; both equally attested by manifestly false witness and subornation on each side. In the exercise of his functions the consul had opened and shut some jail doors, and otherwise effected the usual sullen and deceitful compromise, and his flag was now flying, on a final visit, from the stern-sheets of a smart boat alongside. It was with a feeling of relief at the end of the interview that he at last lifted his head above an atmosphere of perjury and bilge-water and came on deck. The sun and wind were ruffling and glinting on the broadening river beyond the "measured mile;" a few gulls were wavering and dipping near the lee scuppers, and the sound of Sabbath bells, mellowed by a distance that secured immunity of conscience, came peacefully to his ear.

"Now that job 's over ye 'll be takin' a partin' dhrink," suggested the captain.

The consul thought not. Certain incidents of "the job" were fresh in his memory, and he proposed to limit himself to his strict duty.

"You have some passengers, I see," he said, pointing to a group of two men and a young girl, who had apparently just come aboard.

"Only wan; an engineer going out to Rio. Them 's just his friends seein' him off, I 'm thinkin'," returned the captain, surveying them somewhat contemptuously.

The consul was a little disturbed. He wondered if the passenger knew anything of the quality and reputation of the ship to which he was intrusting his fortunes. But he was only a *passenger*, and the consul's functions — like those of the aloft-sitting cherub of nautical song — were restricted exclusively to looking after "Poor Jack." However, he asked a few further questions, eliciting the fact that the stranger had already visited the ship with letters from the eminently respectable consignees at St. Kentigern, and contented himself with lingering near them. The young girl was accompanied by her father, a respectably rigid-looking middle-class tradesman, who, however, seemed to be more interested in the novelty of his surroundings than in the movements of his daughter and their departing friend. So it chanced that the consul reëntered the cabin — ostensibly in search of a missing glove, but really with the intention of seeing how the passenger was bestowed — just behind them. But to his great embarrassment he at once perceived that, owing to the obscurity of the apartment, they had not noticed him, and before he could withdraw, the man had passed his arm around the young girl's half stiffened, yet half yielding figure.

"Only one, Ailsa," he pleaded in a slow, serious voice, pathetic from the very absence of any youthful passion in it; "just one now. It 'll be gey lang before we meet again. Ye 'll not refuse me now."

The young girl's lips seemed to murmur some protest that, however, was lost in the beginning of a long and silent kiss.

The consul slipped out softly. His smile had died away. That unlooked-for touch of human weakness seemed to purify the stuffy and evil-reeking cabin, and the recollection of its brutal past to drop with a deck-load of iniquity behind him to the bottom of the Clyde. It is to be feared that in his unofficial moments he was inclined to be sentimental, and it seemed to him that the good ship Skyscraper henceforward carried an innocent freight not mentioned in her manifest, and that a gentle, ever-smiling figure, not entered on her books, had invisibly taken a place at her wheel.

But he was recalled to himself by a slight altercation on deck. The young girl and the passenger had just returned from the cabin. The consul, after a discreetly careless pause, had lifted his eyes to the young girl's face, and saw that it was singularly pretty in color and outline, but perfectly self-composed and serenely unconscious. And he was a little troubled to observe that the passenger was a middle-aged man, whose hard features were already considerably worn with trial and experience.

Both he and the girl were listening with sympathizing but cautious interest to her father's contention with the boatman who had brought them from shore, and who was now inclined to demand an extra fee for returning with them. The boatman alleged that he had been detained beyond "kirk time," and that this imperiling of his salvation could only be compensated by another shilling. To the consul's surprise, this extraordinary argument was recognized by the father, who, however, contented himself by simply contending that it had not been stipulated in the bargain. The issue was, therefore, limited, and the discussion progressed slowly and deliberately, with a certain calm dignity and argumentative satisfaction on both sides that exalted the subject, though it irritated the captain.

"If ye accept the premises that I 've just laid down, that it 's a contract" — began the boatman.

"Dry up! and haul off," said the captain.

"One moment," interposed the consul, with a rapid glance at the slight trouble in the young girl's face. Turning to the father, he went on: "Will you allow me to offer you and your daughter a seat in my boat?"

It was an unlooked-for and tempting proposal. The boatman was lazily lying on his oars, secure in self-righteousness and the conscious possession of the only available boat to shore; on the other hand, the smart gig of the consul, with its four oars, was not only a providential escape from a difficulty, but even to some extent a quasi-official indorsement of his contention. Yet he hesitated.

"It 'll be costin' ye no more?" he said interrogatively, glancing at the consul's boat crew, "or ye 'll be askin' me a fair proportion."

"It will be the gentleman's own boat," said the girl, with a certain shy assurance, "and he 'll be paying his boatmen by the day."

The consul hastened to explain that their passage would involve no additional expense to anybody, and added, tactfully, that he was glad to enable them to oppose extortion.

"Ay, but it 's a preencipel," said the father proudly, "and I 'm pleased, sir, to see ye recognize it."

He proceeded to help his daughter into the boat without any further leave-taking of the passenger, to the consul's great surprise, and with only a parting nod from the young girl. It was as if this momentous incident were a sufficient reason for the absence of any further trivial sentiment.

Unfortunately the father chose to add an exordium for

the benefit of the astonished boatman still lying on his oars.

"Let this be a lesson to ye, ma frien', when ye 're ower sure! Ye 'll ne'er say a herrin' is dry until it be reestit an' reekit."

"Ay," said the boatman, with a lazy, significant glance at the consul, "it wull be a lesson to me not to trust to a lassie's *gangin'* jo, when thair 's anither yin comin'."

"Give way," said the consul sharply.

Yet his was the only irritated face in the boat as the men bent over their oars. The young girl and her father looked placidly at the receding ship, and waved their hands to the grave, resigned face over the taffrail. The consul examined them more attentively. The father's face showed intelligence and a certain probity in its otherwise commonplace features. The young girl had more distinction, with, perhaps, more delicacy of outline than of texture. Her hair was dark, with a burnished copper tint at its roots, and eyes that had the same burnished metallic lustre in their brown pupils. Both sat respectfully erect, as if anxious to record the fact that the boat was not their own to take their ease in; and both were silently reserved, answering briefly to the consul's remarks as if to indicate the formality of their presence there. But a distant railway whistle startled them into emotion.

"We 've lost the train, father!" said the young girl.

The consul followed the direction of her anxious eyes; the train was just quitting the station at Bannock.

"If ye had not lingered below with Jamie, we 'd have been away in time, ay, and in our own boat," said the father, with marked severity.

The consul glanced quickly at the girl. But her face betrayed no consciousness, except of their present disappointment.

"There 's an excursion boat coming round the Point,"

he said, pointing to the black smoke trail of a steamer at the entrance of a loch, "and it will be returning to St. Kontigern shortly. If you like, we 'll pull over and put you aboard."

"Eh! but it 's the Sabbath-breaker!" said the old man harshly.

The consul suddenly remembered that that was the name which the righteous St. Kentigerners had given to the solitary bold, bad pleasure-boat that defied their Sabbatical observances.

"Perhaps you won't find very pleasant company on board," said the consul smiling; "but, then, you 're not seeking *that.* And as you would be only using the boat to get back to your home, and not for Sunday recreation, I don't think your conscience should trouble you."

"Ay, that 's a fine argument, Mr. Consul, but I 'm thinkin' it 's none the less sopheestry for a' that," said the father grimly. "No; if ye 'll just land us yonder at Bannock pier, we 'll be ay thankin' ye the same."

"But what will you do there? There 's no other train to-day."

"Ay, we 'll walk on a bit."

The consul was silent. After a pause the young girl lifted her clear eyes, and with a half pathetic, half childish politeness, said: "We 'll be doing very well — my father and me. You 're far too kind."

Nothing further was said as they began to thread their way between a few large ships and an ocean steamer at anchor, from whose decks a few Sunday-clothed mariners gazed down admiringly on the smart gig and the pretty girl in a tam o' shanter in its stern-sheets. But here a new idea struck the consul. A cable's length ahead lay a yacht, owned by an American friend, and at her stern a steam launch swung to its painter. Without intimating his intention to his passengers he steered for it. "Bow!

— way enough," he called out as the boat glided under the yacht's counter, and, grasping the companion-ladder ropes, he leaped aboard. In a few hurried words he explained the situation to Mr. Robert Gray, her owner, and suggested that he should send the belated passengers to St. Kentigern by the launch. Gray assented with the easy good-nature of youth, wealth, and indolence, and lounged from his cabin to the side. The consul followed. Looking down upon the boat he could not help observing that his fair young passenger, sitting in her demure stillness at her father's side, made a very pretty picture. It was possible that "Bob Gray" had made the same observation, for he presently swung himself over the gangway into the gig, hat in hand. The launch could easily take them; in fact, he added unblushingly, it was even then getting up steam to go to St. Kentigern. Would they kindly come on board until it was ready? At an added word or two of explanation from the consul, the father accepted, preserving the same formal pride and stiffness, and the transfer was made. The consul, looking back as his gig swept round again towards Bannock pier, received their parting salutations, and the first smile he had seen on the face of his grave little passenger. He thought it very sweet and sad.

He did not return to the consulate at St. Kentigern until the next day. But he was somewhat surprised to find Mr. Robert Gray awaiting him, and upon some business which the young millionaire could have easily deputed to his captain or steward. As he still lingered, the consul pleasantly referred to his generosity on the previous day, and hoped the passengers had given him no trouble.

"No," said Gray with a slight simulation of carelessness. "In fact I came up with them myself. I had nothing to do; it was Sunday, you know."

The consul lifted his eyebrows slightly.

"Yes, I saw them home," continued Gray lightly. "In one of those bystreets not far from here; neat-looking house outside; inside, corkscrew stone staircase like a lighthouse; fourth floor, no lift, but *she* circled up like a swallow! Flat — sitting-room, two bedrooms, and a kitchen — mighty snug and shipshape and pretty as a pink. They *own* it too — fancy *owning* part of a house! Seems to be a way they have here in St. Kentigern." He paused and then added: "Stayed there to a kind of high tea!"

"Indeed," said the consul.

"Why not? The old man wanted to return my 'hospitality' and square the account! He was n't going to lie under any obligation to a stranger, and, by Jove! he made it a special point of honor! A Spanish grandee could n't have been more punctilious. And with an accent, Jerusalem! like a northeaster off the Banks! But the feed was in good taste, and he only a mathematical-instrument maker, on about twelve hundred dollars a year!"

"You seem to know all about him," said the consul smilingly.

"Not so much as he does about me," returned Gray, with a half perplexed face; "for he saw enough to admonish me about my extravagance, and even to intimate that that rascal Saunderson, my steward, was imposing on me. *She* took me to task, too, for not laying the yacht up on Sunday that the men could go 'to kirk,' and for swearing at a bargeman who ran across our bows. It 's their perfect simplicity and sincerity in all this that gets me! You 'd have thought that the old man was my guardian, and the daughter my aunt." After a pause he uttered a reminiscent laugh. "She thought we ate and drank too much on the yacht, and wondered what we could find to do all day. All this, you know, in the gentlest, caressing sort of voice, as if she was really concerned, like one's own sister.

Well, not exactly like mine"—he interrupted himself grimly—"but, hang it all, you know what I mean. You know that our girls over there have n't got *that* trick of voice. Too much self-assertion, I reckon; things made too easy for them by us men. Habit of race, I dare say." He laughed a little. "Why, I mislaid my glove when I was coming away, and it was as good as a play to hear her commiserating and sympathizing, and hunting for it as if it were a lost baby."

"But you 've seen Scotch girls before this," said the consul. "There were Lady Glairn's daughters, whom you took on a cruise."

"Yes, but the swell Scotch all imitate the English, as everybody else does, for the matter of that, our girls included; and they 're all alike. Society makes 'em fit in together like tongued and grooved planks that will take any amount of holystoning and polish. It 's like dropping into a dead calm, with every rope and spar that you know already reflected back from the smooth water upon you. It 's mighty pretty, but it is n't getting on, you know." After a pause he added: "I asked them to take a little holiday cruise with me."

"And they declined," interrupted the consul.

Gray glanced at him quickly.

"Well, yes; that 's all right enough. They don't know me, you see, but they do know you; and the fact is, I was thinking that as you 're our consul here, don't you see, and sort of responsible for me, you might say that it was all right, you know. Quite the customary thing with us over there. And you might say, generally, who I am."

"I see," said the consul deliberately. "Tell them you 're Bob Gray, with more money and time than you know what to do with; that you have a fine taste for yachting and shooting and racing, and amusing yourself generally; that you find that *they* amuse you, and you would like your luxury and your dollars to stand as an equivalent to their independence and originality; that, being a good republican yourself, and recognizing no distinction of class, you don't care what this may mean to them, who are brought up differently; that after their cruise with you you don't care what life, what friends, or what jealousies they return to; that you know no ties, no responsibilities beyond the present, and that you are not a marrying man."

"Look here, I say, are n't you making a little too much of this?" said Gray stiffly.

The consul laughed. "I should be glad to know that I am."

Gray rose. "We 'll be dropping down the river to-morrow," he said, with a return of his usual lightness, "and I reckon I 'll be toddling down to the wharf. Good-by, if I don't see you again."

He passed out. As the consul glanced from the window he observed, however, that Mr. Gray was "toddling" in quite another direction than the wharf. For an instant he half regretted that he had not suggested, in some discreet way, the conclusion he had arrived at after witnessing the girl's parting with the middle-aged passenger the day before. But he reflected that this was something he had only accidentally overseen, and was the girl's own secret.

II

When the summer had so waxed in its fullness that the smoke of factory chimneys drifted high, permitting glimpses of fairly blue sky; when the grass in St. Kentigern's proudest park took on a less sober green in the comfortable sun, and even in the thickest shade there was no chilliness, the good St. Kentigerners recognized that the season had arrived to go "down the river," and that it was time for them to betake themselves, with rugs, mackintoshes, and umbrellas, to the breezy lochs and misty hillsides for which the neighborhood of St. Kentigern is justly famous. So when it came to pass that the blinds were down in the highest places, and the most exclusive pavements of St. Kentigern were echoless and desolate, the consul heroically tore himself from the weak delight of basking in the sunshine, and followed the others.

He soon found himself settled at the furthest end of a long narrow loch, made longer and narrower by the steep hillside of rock and heather which flanked its chilly surface on either side, and whose inequalities were lost in the firs and larches that filled ravine and chasm. The fragrant road which ran sinuously through their shadowy depths was invisible from the loch; no protuberance broke the seemingly sheer declivity; the even sky-line was indented in two places, — one where it was cracked into a fanciful resemblance to a human profile, the other where it was curved like a bowl. Need it be said that one was distinctly recognized as the silhouette of a prehistoric giant, and that the other was his drinking-cup? Need it be added that neither lent the slightest human suggestion to the solitude? A toy-like pier extending into the loch, midway from the barren shore, only heightened the desolation. And when the little steamboat that occasionally entered the loch took away a solitary passenger from the pier-head, the simplest parting was invested with a dreary loneliness that might have brought tears to the most hardened eye.

Still, when the shadow of either hillside was not reaching across the loch, the meridian sun, chancing upon this coy mirror, made the most of it. Then it was that, seen from above, it flashed like a falchion lying between the hills; then its reflected glory, striking up, transfigured the two acclivities, tipped the cold heather with fire, gladdened the funereal pines, and warmed the ascetic rocks. And it was in one of those rare, passionate intervals that the consul, riding along the wooded track and turning his eyes from their splendors, came upon a little house.

It had once been a sturdy cottage, with a grim endurance and inflexibility which even some later and lighter additions had softened rather than changed. On either side of the door, against the bleak whitewashed wall, two tall fuchsias relieved the rigid blankness with a show of color. The windows were prettily draped with curtains caught up with gay ribbons. In a stony pound-like inclosure there was some attempt at floral cultivation, but all quite recent. So, too, were a wicker garden seat, a bright Japanese umbrella, and a tropical hammock suspended between two arctic-looking bushes, which the rude and rigid forefathers of the hamlet would have probably resented.

He had just passed the house when a charming figure slipped across the road before him. To his surprise it was the young girl he had met a few months before on the Skyscraper. But the tam o' shanter was replaced by a little straw hat; and a light dress, summery in color and texture, but more in keeping with her rustic surroundings, seemed as grateful and rare as the sunshine. Without knowing why, he had an impression that it was of her own making, — a gentle plagiarism of the style of her more fortunate sisters, but with a demure restraint all her own. As she recognized him a faint color came to her cheek, partly from surprise, partly from some association. To his delighted greeting she responded by informing him that her father had taken the cottage he had just passed, where they were spending a three weeks' vacation from his business. It was not so far from St. Kentigern but that he could run up for a day to look after the shop. Did the consul not think it was wise?

Quite ready to assent to any sagacity in those clear brown eyes, the consul thought it was. But was it not, like wisdom, sometimes lonely?

Ah, no. There was the loch, and the hills and the heather; there were her flowers; did he not think they were growing well? and at the head of the loch there was the old tomb of the McHulishes, and some of the coffins were still to be seen.

Perhaps emboldened by the consul's smile, she added, with a more serious precision which was, however, lost in the sympathizing caress of her voice, "And would you not be getting off and coming in and resting a wee bit before you go further? It would be so good of you, and father would think it so kind. And he will be there now, if you 're looking."

The consul looked. The old man was standing in the doorway of the cottage, as respectably uncompromising as ever, with the slight concession to his rural surroundings of wearing a tam o' shanter and easy slippers. The consul dismounted and entered. The interior was simply but tastefully furnished. It struck him that the Scotch prudence and economy, which practically excluded display and meretricious glitter, had reached the simplicity of the truest art and the most refined wealth. He felt he could understand Gray's enthusiasm, and by an odd association of ideas he found himself thinking of the resigned face of the lonely passenger on the Skyscraper.

"Have you heard any news of your friend who went to Rio?" he asked pleasantly, but without addressing himself particularly to either.

There was a perceptible pause, doubtless of deference to her father on the part of the young girl, and of the usual native conscientious caution on the part of the father, but neither betrayed any embarrassment or emotion. "No; he would not be writing yet," she at length said simply; "he would be waiting until he was settled to his business. Jamie would be waiting until he could say how he was doing, father?" she appealed interrogatively to the old man.

"Ay, James Gow would not fash himself to write compliments and gossip till he knew his position and work," corroborated the old man. "He 'll not be going two thousand miles to send us what we can read in the 'St. Kentigern Herald.' But," he added, suddenly, with a recall of cautiousness, "perhaps *you* will be hearing of the ship?"

"The consul will not be remembering what he hears of all the ships," interposed the young girl, with the same gentle affectation of superior worldly knowledge which had before amused him. "We 'll be wearying him, father;" and the subject dropped.

The consul, glancing around the room again, but always returning to the sweet and patient seriousness of the young girl's face and the grave decorum of her father, would have liked to ask another question, but it was presently anticipated; for when he had exhausted the current topics, in which both father and daughter displayed a quiet sagacity, and he had gathered a sufficient knowledge of their character to seem to justify Gray's enthusiasm, and was rising to take his leave, the young girl said timidly: —

"Would ye not let Bessie take your horse to the grass field over yonder, and yourself stay with us to dinner? It would be most kind, and you would meet a great friend of yours who will be here."

"Mr. Gray?" suggested the consul audaciously. Yet he was greatly surprised when the young girl said quietly, "Ay."

"He 'll be coming in the loch with his yacht," said the old man. "It 's not so expensive lying here as at Bannock, I 'm thinking; and the men cannot gang ashore for drink. Eh, but it 's an awful waste o' pounds, shillings, and pence, keeping these gowks in idleness with no feeshin' nor carrying of passengers."

"Ay, but it 's better Mr. Gray should pay them for

being decent and well-behaved on board his ship, than that they should be out of work and rioting in taverns and lodging-houses. And you yourself, father, remember the herrin' fishers that come ashore at Ardie, and the deck hands of the excursion boat, and the language they 'll be using."

"Have you had a cruise in the yacht?" asked the consul quickly.

"Ay," said the father, "we have been up and down the loch, and around the far point, but not for boardin' or lodgin' the night, nor otherwise conteenuing or parteecipating. I have explained to Mr. Gray that we must return to our own home and our own porridge at evening, and he has agreed, and even come with us. He 's a decent enough lad, and not above instructin', but extraordinar' extravagant."

"Ye know, father," interposed the young girl, "he talks of fitting up the yacht for the fishing, and taking some of his most decent men on shares. He says he was very fond of fishing off the Massachusetts coast, in America. It will be, I 'm thinking," she said, suddenly turning to the consul with an almost pathetic appeal in her voice, "a great occupation for the rich young men over there."

The consul, desperately struggling with a fanciful picture of Mr. Robert Gray as a herring fisher, thought gravely that it "might be." But he thought still more gravely, though silently, of this singular companionship, and was somewhat anxious to confront his friend with his new acquaintances. He had not long to wait. The sun was just dipping behind the hill when the yacht glided into the lonely loch. A boat was put off, and in a few moments Robert Gray was climbing the little path from the loch.

Had the consul expected any embarrassment or lover-like consciousness on the face of Mr. Gray at their unexpected meeting, he would have been disappointed. Nor was the young man's greeting of father and daughter, whom he addressed as Mr. and Miss Callender, marked by any tenderness or hesitation. On the contrary, a certain seriousness and quiet reticence, unlike Gray, which might have been borrowed from his new friends, characterized his speech and demeanor. Beyond this freemasonry of sad repression there was no significance of look or word passed between these two young people. The girl's voice retained its even pathos. Gray's grave politeness was equally divided between her and her father. He corroborated what Callender had said of his previous visits without affectation or demonstration; he spoke of the possibilities of his fitting up the yacht for the fishing season with a practical detail and economy that left the consul's raillery ineffective. Even when, after dinner, the consul purposely walked out in the garden with the father, Gray and Ailsa presently followed them without lingering or undue precipitation, and with no change of voice or manner. The consul was perplexed. Had the girl already told Gray of her lover across the sea, and was this singular restraint their joint acceptance of their fate; or was he mistaken in supposing that their relations were anything more than the simple friendship of patron and protégée? Gray was rich enough to indulge in such a fancy, and the father and daughter were too proud to ever allow it to influence their own independence. In any event the consul's right to divulge the secret he was accidentally possessed of seemed more questionable than ever. Nor did there appear to be any opportunity for a confidential talk with Gray, since it was proposed that the whole party should return to the yacht for supper, after which the consul should be dropped at the pier-head, distant only a few minutes from his hotel, and his horse sent to him the next day.

A faint moon was shimmering along the surface of Loch Dour in icy little ripples when they pulled out from the shadows of the hillside. By the accident of position, Gray, who was steering, sat beside Ailsa in the stern, while the consul and Mr. Callender were further forward, although within hearing. The faces of the young people were turned towards each other, yet in the cold moonlight the consul fancied they looked as impassive and unemotional as statues. The few distant, far-spaced lights that trembled on the fading shore, the lonely glitter of the water, the blackness of the pine-clad ravines seemed to be a part of this repression, until the vast melancholy of the lake appeared to meet and overflow them like an advancing tide. Added to this, there came from time to time the faint sound and smell of the distant, desolate sea.

The consul, struggling manfully to keep up a spasmodic discussion on Scotch diminutives in names, found himself mechanically saying: —

"And James you call Jamie?"

"Ay; but ye would say, to be pure Scotch, 'Hamish,'" said Mr. Callender precisely. The girl, however, had not spoken; but Gray turned to her with something of his old gayety.

"And I suppose you would call me 'Robbie'?"

"Ah, no!"

"What then?"

"Robin."

Her voice was low yet distinct, but she had thrown into the two syllables such infinite tenderness, that the consul was for an instant struck with an embarrassment akin to that he had felt in the cabin of the Skyscraper, and half expected the father to utter a shocked protest. And to save what he thought would be an appalling silence, he said with a quiet laugh: —

"That 's the fellow who 'made the assembly shine' in the song, is n't it?"

I suppose you would call me Robbie

"That was Robin Adair," said Gray quietly; "unfortunately I would only be 'Robin Gray,' and that 's quite another song."

"*Auld* Robin Gray, sir, deestinctly 'auld' in the song," interrupted Mr. Callender with stern precision; "and I 'm thinking he was not so very unfortunate either."

The discussion of Scotch diminutives halting here, the boat sped on silently to the yacht. But although Robert Gray, as host, recovered some of his usual lightheartedness, the consul failed to discover anything in his manner to indicate the lover, nor did Miss Ailsa after her single lapse of tender accent exhibit the least consciousness. It was true that their occasional frank allusions to previous conversations seemed to show that their opportunities had not been restricted, but nothing more. He began again to think he was mistaken.

As he wished to return early, and yet not hasten the Callenders, he prevailed upon Gray to send him to the pier-head first, and not disturb the party. As he stepped into the boat, something in the appearance of the coxswain awoke an old association in his mind. The man at first seemed to avoid his scrutiny, but when they were well away from the yacht he said hesitatingly: —

"I see you remember me, sir. But if it 's all the same to you, I 've got a good berth here and would like to keep it."

The consul had a flash of memory. It was the boatswain of the Skyscraper, one of the least objectionable of the crew. "But what are you doing here? you shipped for the voyage," he said sharply.

"Yes, but I got away at Key West, when I knew what was coming. I was n't on her when she was abandoned."

"Abandoned!" repeated the consul. "What the d—l! Do you mean to say she was wrecked?"

"Well, yes — you know what I mean, sir. It was an

understood thing. She was over-insured, and scuttled in the Bahamas. It was a put-up job, and I reckoned I was well out of it."

"But there was a passenger! What of him?" demanded the consul anxiously.

"Dunno! But I reckon he got away. There was n't any of the crew lost that I know of. Let 's see, he was an engineer, was n't he? I reckon he had to take a hand at the pumps, and his chances with the rest."

"Does Mr. Gray know of this?" asked the consul after a pause.

The man stared.

"Not from me, sir. You see it was nothin' to him, and I did n't care talking much about the Skyscraper. It was hushed up in the papers. You won't go back on me, sir?"

"You don't know what became of the passenger?"

"No! But he was a Scotchman, and they 're bound to fall on their feet somehow!"

III

The December fog that overhung St. Kentigern had thinned sufficiently to permit the passage of a few large snowflakes, soiled in their descent, until in color and consistency they spotted the steps of the consulate and the umbrellas of the passers-by like sprinklings of gray mortar. Nevertheless the consul thought the streets preferable to the persistent gloom of his office, and sallied out. Youthful mercantile St. Kentigern strode sturdily past him in the lightest covert coats; collegiate St. Kentigern fluttered by in the scantiest of red gowns, shaming the furs that defended his more exotic blood; and the bare red feet of a few factory girls, albeit their heads and shoulders were draped and hooded in thick shawls, filled him with a keen sense of his effeminacy. Everything of earth, air, and sky, and even the faces of those he looked upon, seemed to be set in the hard, patient endurance of the race. Everywhere on that dismal day he fancied he could see this energy without restlessness, this earnestness without geniality, all grimly set against the hard environment of circumstance and weather.

The consul turned into one of the main arteries of St. Kentigern, a wide street that, however, began and ended inconsequently, and with half a dozen social phases in as many blocks. Here the snow ceased, the fog thickened suddenly with the waning day, and the consul found himself isolated and cut off on a block which he did not remember, with the clatter of an invisible tramway in his ears. It was a block of small houses with smaller shop-fronts. The one immediately before him seemed to be an optician's, but the dimly lighted windows also displayed the pathetic reinforcement of a few watches, cheap jewelry on cards, and several cairngorm brooches and pins set in silver. It occurred to him that he wanted a new watch crystal, and that he would procure it here and inquire his way. Opening the door he perceived that there was no one in the shop, but from behind the counter another open door disclosed a neat sitting-room, so close to the street that it gave the casual customer the sensation of having intruded upon domestic privacy. The consul's entrance tinkled a small bell which brought a figure to the door. It was Ailsa Callender.

The consul was startled. He had not seen her since he had brought to their cottage the news of the shipwreck with a precaution and delicacy that their calm self-control and patient resignation, however, seemed to make almost an impertinence. But this was no longer the handsome shop in the chief thoroughfare with its two shopmen, which he previously knew as "Callender's." And Ailsa here! What misfortune had befallen them?

Whatever it was, there was no shadow of it in her clear eyes and frank yet timid recognition of him. Falling in with her stoical and reticent acceptance of it, he nevertheless gathered that the Callenders had lost money in some invention which James Gow had taken with him to Rio, but which was sunk in the ship. With this revelation of a business interest in what he had believed was only a sentimental relation, the consul ventured to continue his inquiries. Mr. Gow had escaped with his life and had reached Honduras, where he expected to try his fortunes anew. It might be a year or two longer before there were any results. Did the consul know anything of Honduras? There was coffee there, — so she and her father understood. All this with little hopefulness, no irritation, but a divine patience in her eyes. The consul, who found that his watch required extensive repairing, and had suddenly developed an inordinate passion for cairngorms, watched her as she opened the showcase with no affectation of unfamiliarity with her occupation, but with all her old serious concern. Surely she would have made as thorough a shop-girl as she would — His half-formulated thought took the shape of a question.

"Have you seen Mr. Gray since his return from the Mediterranean?"

Ah! one of the brooches had slipped from her fingers to the bottom of the case. There was an interval or two of pathetic murmuring, with her fair head under the glass, before she could find it; then she lifted her eyes to the consul. They were still slightly suffused with her sympathetic concern. The stone, which was set in a thistle — the national emblem — did he not know it? — had dropped out. But she could put it in. It was pretty and not expensive. It was marked twelve shillings on the card, but he could have it for ten shillings. No, she had not seen Mr. Gray since they had lost their fortune. (It struck the consul as none the less pathetic that she seemed really to believe in their former opulence.) They could not be seeing him there in a small shop, and they could not see him elsewhere. It was far better as it was. Yet she paused a moment when she had wrapped up the brooch. "You 'd be seeing him yourself some time?" she added gently.

"Perhaps."

"Then you 'll not mind saying how my father and myself are sometimes thinking of his goodness and kindness," she went on, in a voice whose tenderness seemed to increase with the formal precision of her speech.

"Certainly."

"And you 'll say we 're not forgetting him."

"I promise."

As she handed him the parcel her lips softly parted in what might have been equally a smile or a sigh.

He was able to keep his promise sooner than he had imagined. It was only a few weeks later that, arriving in London, he found Gray's hatbox and bag in the vestibule of his club, and that gentleman himself in the smoking-room. He looked tanned and older.

"I only came from Southampton an hour ago, where I left the yacht. And," shaking the consul's hand cordially, "how 's everything and everybody up at old St. Kentigern?"

The consul thought fit to include his news of the Callenders in reference to that query, and with his eyes fixed on Gray dwelt at some length on their change of fortune. Gray took his cigar from his mouth, but did not lift his eyes from the fire. Presently he said, "I suppose that 's why Callender declined to take the shares I offered him in the fishing scheme. You know I meant it, and would have done it."

"Perhaps he had other reasons."

"What do you mean?" said Gray, facing the consul suddenly.

"Look here, Gray," said the consul, "did Miss Callender or her father ever tell you she was engaged?"

"Yes; but what 's that to do with it?"

"A good deal. Engagements, you know, are sometimes forced, unsuitable, or unequal, and are broken by circumstances. Callender is proud."

Gray turned upon the consul the same look of gravity that he had worn on the yacht, — the same look that the consul even fancied he had seen in Ailsa's eyes. "That 's exactly where you 're mistaken in her," he said slowly. "A girl like that gives her word and keeps it. She waits, hopes, accepts what may come, — breaks her heart, if you will, but not her word. Come, let 's talk of something else. How did he — that man Gow — lose Callender's money?"

The consul did not see the Callenders again on his return, and perhaps did not think it necessary to report the meeting. But one morning he was delighted to find an official document from New York upon his desk, asking him to communicate with David Callender of St. Kentigern, and, on proof of his identity, giving him authority to draw the sum of five thousand dollars damages awarded for the loss of certain property on the Skyscraper, at the request of James Gow. Yet it was with mixed sensations that the consul sought the little shop of the optician with this convincing proof of Gow's faithfulness and the indissolubility of Ailsa's engagement. That there was some sad understanding between the girl and Gray he did not doubt, and perhaps it was not strange that he felt a slight partisanship for his friend, whose nature had so strangely changed. Miss Ailsa was not there. Her father explained that her health had required a change, and she was visiting some friends on the river.

"I 'm thinkin' that the atmosphere is not so pure here. It is deficient in ozone. I noticed it myself in the early morning. No! it was not the confinement of the shop, for she never cared to go out."

He received the announcement of his good fortune with unshaken calm and great practical consideration of detail. He would guarantee his identity to the consul. As for James Gow, it was no more than fair, and what he had expected of him. As to its being an equivalent of his loss, he could not tell until the facts were before him.

"Miss Ailsa," suggested the consul venturously, "will be pleased to hear again from her old friend, and know that he is succeeding."

"I 'm not so sure that ye could call it 'succeeding,'" returned the old man, carefully wiping the glasses of a pair of spectacles that he held critically to the light, "when ye consider that, saying nothing of the waste of valuable time, it only puts James Gow back where he was when he went away."

"But any man who has had the pleasure of knowing Mr. and Miss Callender would be glad to be on that footing," said the consul, with polite significance.

"I 'm not agreeing with you there," said Mr. Callender quietly; "and I 'm observing in ye of late a tendency to combine business wi' compleement. But it was kind of ye to call; and I 'll be sending ye the authorization."

Which he did. But the consul, passing through the locality a few weeks later, was somewhat concerned to find the shop closed, with others on the same block, behind a hoarding that indicated rebuilding and improvement. Further inquiry elicited the fact that the small leases had been bought up by some capitalist, and that Mr. Callender, with the others, had benefited thereby. But there was no trace nor clue to his present locality. He and his daughter seemed to have again vanished with this second change in their fortunes.

It was a late March morning, when the streets were dumb with snow, and the air was filled with flying granulations that tinkled against the windows of the consulate like fairy sleigh-bells, when there was the stamping of snow-clogged feet in the outer hall, and the door was opened to Mr. and Miss Callender. For an instant the consul was startled. The old man appeared as usual, — erect, and as frigidly respectable as one of the icicles that fringed the window; but Miss Ailsa was, to his astonishment, brilliant with a new-found color, and sparkling with health and only half repressed animation. The snowflakes, scarcely melting on the brown head of this true daughter of the North, still crowned her hood; and as she threw back her brown cloak and disclosed a plump little scarlet jacket and brown skirt, the consul could not resist her suggested likeness to some bright-eyed robin redbreast, to whom the inclement weather had given a charming audacity. And shy and demure as she still was, it was evident that some change had been wrought in her other than that evoked by the stimulus of her native sky and air.

To his eager questioning, the old man replied briefly that he had bought the old cottage at Loch Dour, where they were living, and where he had erected a small manufactory and laboratory for the making of his inventions, which had become profitable. The consul reiterated his delight at meeting them again.

"I 'm not so sure of that, sir, when you know the business on which I come," said Mr. Callender, dropping rigidly into a chair, and clasping his hands over the crutch of a shepherd-like staff. "Ye mind, perhaps, that ye conveyed to me, osteensibly at the request of James Gow, a certain sum of money, for which I gave ye a good and sufficient guarantee. I thought at the time that it was a most feckless and unbusiness-like proceeding on the part of

James, as it was without corroboration or advice by letter; but I took the money."

"Do you mean to say that he made no allusion to it in his other letters?" interrupted the consul, glancing at Ailsa.

"There were no other letters at the time," said Callender dryly. "But about a month afterwards we *did* receive a letter from him inclosing a draft and a full return of the profits of the invention, which *he had sold in Honduras.* Ye 'll observe the deescrepancy! I then wrote to the bank on which I had drawn as you authorized me, and I found that they knew nothing of any damages awarded, but that the sum I had drawn had been placed to my credit by Mr. Robert Gray."

In a flash the consul recalled the one or two questions that Gray had asked him, and saw it all. For an instant he felt the whole bitterness of Gray's misplaced generosity — its exposure and defeat. He glanced again hopelessly at Ailsa. In the eye of that fresh, glowing, yet demure young goddess, unhallowed as the thought might be, there was certainly a distinctly tremulous wink.

The consul took heart. "I believe I need not say, Mr. Callender," he began with some stiffness, "that this is as great a surprise to me as to you. I had no reason to believe the transaction other than bona fide, and acted accordingly. If my friend, deeply sympathizing with your previous misfortune, has hit upon a delicate, but unbusinesslike way of assisting you temporarily — I say *temporarily*, because it must have been as patent to him as to you that you would eventually find out his generous deceit — you surely can forgive him for the sake of his kind intention. Nay, more; may I point out to you that you have no right to assume that this benefaction was intended exclusively for you; if Mr. Gray, in his broader sympathy with you and your daughter, has in this way chosen to assist and strengthen the position of a gentleman so closely connected with you, but still struggling with hard fortune" —

"I 'd have ye know, sir," interrupted the old man, rising to his feet, "that ma frien' Mr. James Gow is as independent of yours as he is of me and mine. He has married, sir, a Mrs. Hernandez, the rich widow of a coffee-planter, and now is the owner of the whole estate, minus the encumbrance of three children. And now, sir, you 'll take this," — he drew from his pocket an envelope. "It 's a draft for five thousand dollars, with the ruling rate of interest computed from the day I received it till this day, and ye 'll give it to your frien' when ye see him. And ye 'll just say to him from me" —

But Miss Ailsa, with a spirit and independence that challenged her father's, here suddenly fluttered between them with sparkling eyes and outstretched hands.

"And ye 'll say to him from *me* that a more honorable, noble, and generous man, and a kinder, truer, and better friend than he, cannot be found anywhere! And that the foolishest and most extravagant thing he ever did is better than the wisest and most prudent thing that anybody else ever did, could, or would do! And if he was a bit over-proud — it was only because those about him were over-proud and foolish. And you 'll tell him that we 're wearying for him! And when you give him that daft letter from father you 'll give him this bit line from me," she went on rapidly as she laid a tiny note in his hand. "And," with wicked dancing eyes that seemed to snap the last bond of repression, "ye 'll give him *that* too, and say I sent it!"

There was a stir in the official apartment! The portraits of Lincoln and Washington rattled uneasily in their frames; but it was no doubt only a discreet blast of the north wind that drowned the echo of a kiss.

"Ailsa!" gasped the shocked Mr. Callender.

"Ah! but, father, if it had not been for *him* we would not have known Robin."

. . . .

It was the last that the consul saw of Ailsa Callender; for the next summer when he called at Loch Dour she was Mrs. Gray.

A LEGEND OF SAMMTSTADT

It was the sacred hour of noon at Sammtstadt. Everybody was at dinner; and the serious Kellner of "Der Wildemann" glanced in mild reproach at Mr. James Clinch, who, disregarding that fact and the invitatory table d'hôte, stepped into the street. For Mr. Clinch had eaten a late breakfast at Gladbach, was dyspeptic and American, and, moreover, preoccupied with business. He was consequently indignant, on entering the garden-like court and cloister-like counting-house of "Von Becheret, Sons, Uncles, and Cousins," to find the comptoir deserted even by the porter, and was furious at the maid-servant, who offered the sacred shibboleth "Mittagsessen" as a reasonable explanation of the solitude. "A country," said Mr. Clinch to himself, "that stops business at midday to go to dinner, and employs women-servants to talk to business-men, is played out."

He stepped from the silent building into the equally silent Kronprinzen Strasse. Not a soul to be seen anywhere. Rows on rows of two-storied, gray-stuccoed buildings that might be dwellings, or might be offices, all showing some traces of feminine taste and supervision in a flower or a curtain that belied the legended "Comptoir," or "Direction," over their portals. Mr. Clinch thought of Boston and State Street, of New York and Wall Street, and became coldly contemptuous.

Yet there was clearly nothing to do but to walk down the formal rows of chestnuts that lined the broad Strasse, and then walk back again. At the corner of the first cross-street he was struck with the fact that two men who were standing in front of a dwelling-house appeared to be as inconsistent, and out of proportion to the silent houses, as were the actors on a stage to the painted canvas thoroughfares before which they strutted. Mr. Clinch usually had no fancies, had no eye for quaintness; besides, this was not a quaint nor romantic district, only an entrepôt for silks and velvets, and Mr. Clinch was here, not as a tourist, but as a purchaser. The guide-books had ignored Sammtstadt, and he was too good an American to waste time in looking up uncatalogued curiosities. Besides, he had been here once before, — an entire day!

One o'clock. Still a full hour and a half before his friend would return to business. What should he do? The Verein where he had once been entertained was deserted even by its waiters; the garden, with its ostentatious out-of-door tables, looked bleak and bare. Mr. Clinch was not artistic in his tastes; but even he was quick to detect the affront put upon Nature by this continental theatrical gardening, and turned disgustedly away. Born near a "lake" larger than the German Ocean, he resented a pool of water twenty-five feet in diameter under that alluring title; and, a frequenter of the Adirondacks, he could scarce contain himself over a bit of rock-work twelve feet high. "A country," said Mr. Clinch, "that" — but here he remembered that he had once seen in a park in his native city an imitation of the Drachenfels in plaster, on a scale of two inches to the foot, and checked his speech.

He turned into the principal allée of the town. There was a long white building at one end, — the Bahnhof; at the other end he remembered a dyehouse. He had, a year ago, met its hospitable proprietor; he would call upon him now.

But the same solitude confronted him as he passed the porter's lodge beside the gateway. The counting-house.

half villa, half factory, must have convoked its humanity in some out-of-the-way refectory, for the halls and passages were tenantless. For the first time he began to be impressed with a certain foreign quaintness in the surroundings; he found himself also recalling something he had read when a boy, about an enchanted palace whose inhabitants awoke on the arrival of a long-predestined Prince. To assure himself of the absolute ridiculousness of this fancy, he took from his pocket the business-card of its proprietor, a sample of dye, and recalled his own personality in a letter of credit. Having dismissed this idea from his mind, he lounged on again through a rustic lane that might have led to a farmhouse, yet was still, absurdly enough, a part of the factory gardens. Crossing a ditch by a causeway, he presently came to another ditch and another causeway, and then found himself idly contemplating a massive, ivy-clad, venerable brick wall. As a mere wall it might not have attracted his attention; but it seemed to enter and bury itself at right angles in the side-wall of a quite modern-looking dwelling. After satisfying himself of this fact, he passed on before the dwelling, but was amazed to see the wall reappear on the other side exactly the same, — old, ivy-grown, sturdy, uncompromising, and ridiculous. Could it actually be a part of the house? He turned back, and repassed the front of the building. The entrance-door was hospitably open. There was a hall and a staircase, but — by all that was preposterous! — they were built *over* and *around* the central brick intrusion. The wall actually ran through the house! "A country," said Mr. Clinch to himself, "where they build their houses over ruins to accommodate them, or save the trouble of removal is," — but a very pleasant voice addressing him here stopped his usual hasty conclusion.

"Guten Morgen!"

Mr. Clinch looked hastily up. Leaning on the parapet

of what appeared to be a garden on the roof of the house was a young girl, red-cheeked, bright-eyed, blond-haired. The voice was soft, subdued, and mellow; it was part of the new impression he was receiving that it seemed to be in some sort connected with the ivy-clad wall before him. His hat was in his hand as he answered, —

"Guten Morgen!"

Was the Herr seeking anything?

The Herr was only waiting a long-time-coming friend, and had strayed here to speak with the before-known proprietor.

So? But, the before-known proprietor sleeping well at present after dinner, would the Herr on the terrace still a while linger?

The Herr would, but looked around in vain for the means to do it. He was thinking of a scaling-ladder, when the young woman reappeared at the open door, and bade him enter.

Following his youthful hostess, Mr. Clinch mounted the staircase, but, passing the mysterious wall, could not forbear an allusion to it.

"It is old, very old," said the girl; "it was here when I came."

"That was not very long ago," said Mr. Clinch gallantly.

"No; but my grandfather found it here too."

"And built over it?"

"Why not? It is very, very hard, and *so* thick."

Mr. Clinch here explained, with masculine superiority, the existence of such modern agents as nitro-glycerine, and dynamite, persuasive in their effects upon time-honored obstructions and encumbrances.

"But there was not then what you call — this — ni — nitro-glycerine."

"But since then?"

The young girl gazed at him in troubled surprise.

"My great-grandfather did not take it away when he built the house; why should we?"

"Oh!"

They had passed through a hall and dining-room, and suddenly stepped out of a window upon a graveled terrace. From this a few stone steps descended to another terrace, on which trees and shrubs were growing; and yet, looking over the parapet, Mr. Clinch could see the road some twenty feet below. It was nearly on a level with, and part of, the second story of the house. Had an earthquake lifted the adjacent ground, or had the house burrowed into a hill? Mr. Clinch turned to his companion, who was standing close beside him, breathing quite audibly, and leaving an impression on his senses as of a gentle and fragrant heifer.

"How was all this done?"

The maiden did not know. "It was always here."

Mr. Clinch reascended the steps. He had quite forgotten his impatience. Possibly it was the gentle, equable calm of the girl, who but for her ready color did not seem to be moved by anything; perhaps it was the peaceful repose of this mausoleum of the dead and forgotten wall that subdued him, but he was quite willing to take the old-fashioned chair on the terrace which she offered him, and follow her motions with not altogether mechanical eyes as she drew out certain bottles and glasses from a mysterious closet in the wall. Mr. Clinch had the weakness of a majority of his sex in believing that he was a good judge of wine and women. The latter, as shown in the specimen before him, he would have invoiced as a fair sample of the middle-class German woman, — healthy, comfort-loving, home-abiding, the very genius of domesticity. Even in her virgin outlines the future wholesome matron was already forecast, from the curves of her broad hips, to the flat lines of her back and shoulders. Of the wine he was to judge later. *That* required an even more subtle and unimpassioned intellect.

She placed two bottles before him on the table, — one, the traditional long-necked, amber-colored Rheinflasche; the other, an old, quaint, discolored, amphora-patterned glass jug. The first she opened.

"This," she said, pointing to the other, "cannot be opened."

Mr. Clinch paid his respects first to the opened bottle, a good quality of Niersteiner. With his intellect thus clarified, he glanced at the other.

"It is from my great-grandfather. It is old as the wall."

Mr. Clinch examined the bottle attentively. It seemed to have no cork. Formed of some obsolete, opaque glass, its twisted neck was apparently hermetically sealed by the same material. The maiden smiled, as she said, —

"It cannot be opened now without breaking the bottle. It is not good luck to do so. My grandfather and my father would not."

But Mr. Clinch was still examining the bottle. Its neck was flattened towards the mouth; but a close inspection showed it was closed by some equally hard cement, but not glass.

"If *I* can open it without breaking the bottle, have I your permission?"

A mischievous glance rested on Mr. Clinch, as the maiden answered, —

"*I* shall not object; but for what will you do it?"

"To taste it, to try it."

"You are not afraid?"

There was just enough obvious admiration of Mr. Clinch's audacity in the maiden's manner to impel him to any risk. His only answer was to take from his pocket a small steel instrument. Holding the neck of the bottle firmly in one hand, he passed his thumb and the steel twice or thrice around it. A faint rasping, scratching sound was all the wondering girl heard. Then, with a sudden, dexterous twist of his thumb and finger, to her utter astonishment he laid the top of the neck, neatly cut off, in her hand.

"There 's a better and more modern bottle than you had before," he said, pointing to the cleanly-divided neck, "and any cork will fit it now."

But the girl regarded him with anxiety. "And you still wish to taste the wine?"

"With your permission, yes!"

He looked up in her eyes. There was permission; there was something more, that was flattering to his vanity. He took the wine-glass, and, slowly and in silence, filled it from the mysterious flask.

The wine fell into the glass clearly, transparently, heavily, but still and cold as death. There was no sparkle, no cheap ebullition, no evanescent bubble. Yet it was so clear, that, but for a faint amber-tinting, the glass seemed empty. There was no aroma, no ethereal diffusion from its equable surface. Perhaps it was fancy, perhaps it was from nervous excitement; but a slight chill seemed to radiate from the still goblet, and bring down the temperature of the terrace. Mr. Clinch and his companion both insensibly shivered.

But only for a moment. Mr. Clinch raised the glass to his lips. As he did so, he remembered seeing distinctly, as in a picture before him, the sunlit terrace, the pretty girl in the foreground, — an amused spectator of his sacrilegious act, — the outlying ivy-crowned wall, the grass-grown ditch, the tall factory chimneys rising above the chestnuts, and the distant poplars that marked the Rhine.

The wine was delicious; perhaps a *trifle*, only a trifle,

heady. He was conscious of a slight exaltation. There was also a smile upon the girl's lip and a roguish twinkle in her eye as she looked at him.

"Do you find the wine to your taste?" she asked.

"Fair enough, I warrant," said Mr. Clinch with ponderous gallantry; "but methinks 't is nothing compared with the nectar that grows on those ruby lips. Nay, by St. Ursula, I swear it!"

No sooner had this solemnly ridiculous speech passed the lips of the unfortunate man than he would have given worlds to have recalled it. He knew that he must be intoxicated; that the sentiment and language were utterly unlike him, he was miserably aware; that he did not even know exactly what it meant, he was also hopelessly conscious. Yet feeling all this, — feeling, too, the shame of appearing before her as a man who had lost his senses through a single glass of wine, — nevertheless he rose awkwardly, seized her hand, and by sheer force drew her towards him, and kissed her. With an exclamation that was half a cry and half a laugh, she fled from him, leaving him alone and bewildered on the terrace.

For a moment Mr. Clinch supported himself against the open window, leaning his throbbing head on the cold glass. Shame, mortification, an hysterical half-consciousness of his utter ridiculousness, and yet an odd, undefined terror of something, by turns possessed him. Was he ever before guilty of such perfect folly? Had he ever before made such a spectacle of himself? Was it possible that he, Mr. James Clinch, the coolest head at a late supper, — he, the American, who had repeatedly drunk Frenchmen and Englishmen under the table — could be transformed into a sentimental, stagey idiot by a single glass of wine? He was conscious, too, of asking himself these very questions in a stilted sort of rhetoric, and with a rising brutality of anger that was new to him. And then everything swam before him, and he seemed to lose all consciousness.

But only for an instant. With a strong effort of his will he again recalled himself, his situation, his surroundings, and, above all, his appointment. He rose to his feet, hurriedly descended the terrace-steps, and, before he well knew how, found himself again on the road. Once there, his faculties returned in full vigor; he was again himself. He strode briskly forward toward the ditch he had crossed only a few moments before, but was suddenly stopped. It was filled with water! He looked up and down. It was clearly the same ditch; but a flowing stream thirty feet wide now separated him from the other bank.

The appearance of this unlooked-for obstacle made Mr. Clinch doubt the full restoration of his faculties. He stepped to the brink of the flood to bathe his head in the stream, and wash away the last vestiges of his potations. But as he approached the placid depths, and knelt down, he again started back, and this time with a full conviction of his own madness; for reflected from its mirror-like surface was a figure he could scarcely call his own, although here and there some trace of his former self remained.

His close-cropped hair, trimmed à la mode, had given way to long, curling locks that dropped upon his shoulders. His neat mustache was frightfully prolonged, and curled up at the ends stiffly. His Piccadilly collar had changed shape and texture, and reached — a mass of lace — to a point midway of his breast. His boots, — why had he not noticed his boots before? — these triumphs of his Parisian boot-maker, were lost in hideous leathern cases that reached half way up his thighs. In place of his former high silk hat, there lay upon the ground beside him the awful thing he had just taken off, — a mass of thickened felt, flap, feather, and buckle that weighed at least a stone.

A single terrible idea now took possession of him. He

had been "sold," "taken in," "done for." He saw it all. In a state of intoxication he had lost his way, had been dragged into some vile den, stripped of his clothes and valuables, and turned adrift upon the quiet town in this shameless masquerade. How should he keep his appointment? how inform the police of this outrage upon a stranger and an American citizen? how establish his identity? Had they spared his papers? He felt feverishly in his breast. Ah! — his watch? Yes, a watch — heavy, jeweled, enameled — and, by all that was ridiculous, *five others!* He ran his hands into his capacious trunk hose. What was this? Brooches, chains, finger-rings, — one large episcopal one, — ear-rings, and a handful of battered gold and silver coins. His papers, his memorandums, his passport — all proofs of his identity — were gone! In their place was the unmistakable *omnium gatherum* of an accomplished knight of the road. Not only was his personality, but his character, gone forever.

It was a part of Mr. Clinch's singular experience that this last stroke of ill fortune seemed to revive in him something of the brutal instinct he had felt a moment before. He turned eagerly about with the intention of calling some one — the first person he met — to account. But the house that he had just quitted was gone! The wall! Ah, there it was, no longer purposeless, intrusive, and ivy-clad, but part of the buttress of another massive wall that rose into battlements above him. Mr. Clinch turned again hopelessly toward Sammtstadt. There was the fringe of poplars on the Rhine, there were the outlying fields lit by the same meridian sun; but the characteristic chimneys of Sammtstadt were gone. Mr. Clinch was hopelessly lost.

The sound of a horn breaking the stillness recalled his senses. He now for the first time perceived that a little distance below him, partly hidden in the trees, was a queer, tower-shaped structure with chains and pulleys, that in some strange way recalled his boyish reading. A drawbridge and portcullis! And on the battlement a figure in a masquerading dress as absurd as his own, flourishing a banner and trumpet, and trying to attract his attention.

"Was wollen Sie?"

"I want to see the proprietor," said Mr. Clinch, choking back his rage.

There was a pause, and the figure turned apparently to consult with some one behind the battlements. After a moment he reappeared, and in a perfunctory monotone, with an occasional breathing spell on the trumpet, began, —

"You do give warranty as a good knight and true, as well as by the bones of the blessed St. Ursula, that you bear no ill will, secret enmity, wicked misprise or conspiracy, against the body of our noble lord and master Von Kölnsche? And you bring with you no ambush, siege, or surprise of retainers, neither secret warrant nor lettres de cachet, nor carry on your knightly person poisoned dagger, magic ring, witch-powder, nor enchanted bullet, and that you have entered into no unhallowed alliance with the Prince of Darkness, gnomes, hexies, dragons, Undines, Loreleis, nor the like?"

"Come down out of that, you d—d old fool!" roared Mr. Clinch, now perfectly beside himself with rage, — "come down, and let me in!"

As Mr. Clinch shouted out the last words, confused cries of recognition and welcome, not unmixed with some consternation, rose from the battlements: "Ach Gott!" "Mutter Gottes — it is he! It is Jann, Der Wanderer. It is himself." The chains rattled, the ponderous drawbridge creaked and dropped; and across it a medley of motley figures rushed pell-mell. But, foremost among them, the very maiden whom he had left not ten minutes before flew into his arms, and with a cry of joyful greeting sank upon his breast. Mr. Clinch looked down upon the fair head and long braids. It certainly was the same maiden, his cruel enchantress; but where did she get those absurd garments?

"Willkommen," said a stout figure, advancing with some authority, and seizing his disengaged hand; "where hast thou been so long?"

Mr. Clinch, by no means placated, coldly dropped the extended hand. It was *not* the proprietor he had known. But there was a singular resemblance in his face to some one of Mr. Clinch's own kin; but who, he could not remember. "May I take the liberty of asking your name?" he asked coldly.

The figure grinned. "Surely; but, if thou standest upon punctilio, it is for *me* to ask thine, most noble Freiherr," said he, winking upon his retainers. "Whom have *I* the honor of entertaining?"

"My name is Clinch, — James Clinch of Chicago, Ill."

A shout of laughter followed. In the midst of his rage and mortification Mr. Clinch fancied he saw a shade of pain and annoyance flit across the face of the maiden. He was puzzled, but pressed her hand, in spite of his late experiences, reassuringly. She made a gesture of silence to him, and then slipped away in the crowd.

"Schames K'l'n'sche von Schekargo," mimicked the figure, to the unspeakable delight of his retainers. "So! *That* is the latest French style. Holy St. Ursula! Hark ye, nephew! *I* am not a traveled man. Since the Crusades we simple Rhine gentlemen have stayed at home. But I call myself Kölnsche of Köln, at your service."

"Very likely you are right," said Mr. Clinch hotly, disregarding the caution of his fair companion; "but, whoever *you* are, *I* am a stranger entitled to protection. I have been robbed."

If Mr. Clinch had uttered an exquisite joke instead of

a very angry statement, it could not have been more hilariously received. He paused, grew confused, and then went on hesitatingly, —

"In place of my papers and credentials I find only these." And he produced the jewelry from his pockets.

Another shout of laughter and clapping of hands followed this second speech; and the baron, with a wink at his retainers, prolonged the general mirth by saying, "By the way, nephew, there is little doubt but there has been robbery — somewhere."

"It was done," continued Mr. Clinch, hurrying to make an end of his explanation, "while I was inadvertently overcome with liquor, — drugged liquor."

The laughter here was so uproarious that the baron, albeit with tears of laughter in his own eyes, made a peremptory gesture of silence. The gesture was peculiar to the baron, efficacious and simple. It consisted merely in knocking down the nearest laugher. Having thus restored tranquillity, he strode forward, and took Mr. Clinch by the hand. "By St. Adolph, I did doubt thee a moment ago, nephew; but this last frank confession of thine shows me I did thee wrong. Willkommen zu Hause, Jann, drunk or sober, willkommen zu Cracowen."

More and more mystified, but convinced of the folly of any further explanation, Mr. Clinch took the extended hand of his alleged uncle, and permitted himself to be led into the castle. They passed into a large banqueting-hall adorned with armor and implements of the chase. Mr. Clinch could not help noticing that, although the appointments were liberal and picturesque, the ventilation was bad, and the smoke from the huge chimney made the air murky. The oaken tables, massive in carving and rich in color, were unmistakably greasy; and Mr. Clinch slipped on a piece of meat that one of the dozen half-wild dogs who were occupying the room was tearing on the floor.

The dog, yelping, ran between the legs of a retainer, precipitating him upon the baron, who instantly, with the "equal foot" of fate, kicked him and the dog into a corner.

"And whence came you last?" asked the baron, disregarding the little contretemps, and throwing himself heavily on an oaken settle, while he pushed a queer, uncomfortable-looking stool, with legs like a Siamese-twin-connected double X, towards his companion.

Mr. Clinch, who had quite given himself up to fate, answered mechanically, —

"Paris."

The baron winked his eye with unutterable, elderly wickedness. "Ach Gott! it is nothing to what it was when I was your age. Ah! there was Manon, — Sieur Manon we used to call her. I suppose she 's getting old now. How goes on the feud between the students and the citizens? Eh? Did you go to the bal in la Cité?"

Mr. Clinch stopped the flow of those Justice-Shallow-like reminiscences by an uneasy exclamation. He was thinking of the maiden who had disappeared so suddenly. The baron misinterpreted his nervousness. "What, ho, within there! — Max, Wolfgang, — lazy rascals! Bring some wine."

At the baleful word Mr. Clinch started to his feet. "Not for me! Bring me none of your body-and-soul-destroying poison! I 've enough of it!"

The baron stared. The servitors stared also.

"I beg your pardon," said Mr. Clinch, recalling himself slowly; "but I fear that Rhine wine does not agree with me."

The baron grinned. Perceiving, however, that the three servitors grinned also, he kicked two of them into obscurity, and felled the third to the floor with his fist. "Hark ye, nephew," he said, turning to the astonished

Clinch, "give over this nonsense! By the mitre of Bishop Hatto, thou art as big a fool as he!"

"Hatto," repeated Clinch mechanically. "What! he of the Mouse Tower?"

"Ay, of the Mouse Tower!" sneered the baron. "I see you know the story."

"Why am I like him?" asked Mr. Clinch in amazement.

The baron grinned. "*He* punished the Rheinish wine as thou dost, without judgment. He had" —

"The jim-jams," said Mr. Clinch mechanically again.

The baron frowned. "I know not what gibberish thou sayest by 'jim-jams;' but he had, like thee, the wildest fantasies and imaginings; saw snakes, toads, rats, in his boots, but principally *rats;* said they pursued him, came to his room, his bed — ach Gott!"

"Oh!" said Mr. Clinch, with a sudden return to his firmer self and his native inquiring habits; "then *that* is the fact about Bishop Hatto of the story?"

"His enemies made it the subject of a vile slander of an old friend of mine," said the baron; "and those cursed poets, who believe everything, and then persuade others to do so, — may the Devil fly away with them! — kept it up."

Here were facts quite to Mr. Clinch's skeptical mind. He forgot himself and his surroundings.

"And that story of the Drachenfels?" he asked insinuatingly, — "the dragon, you know. Was he too" —

The baron grinned. "A boar transformed by the drunken brains of the Bauers of the Siebengebirge. Ach Gott! Ottefried had many a hearty laugh over it; and it did him, as thou knowest, good service with the nervous mother of the silly maiden."

"And the seven sisters of Schönberg?" asked Mr. Clinch persuasively.

"Schönberg! Seven sisters! What of them?" demanded the baron sharply.

"Why, you know, — the maidens who were so coy to their suitors, and — don't you remember? — jumped into the Rhine to avoid them."

"Coy? Jumped into the Rhine to avoid suitors?" roared the baron, purple with rage. "Hark ye, nephew! I like not this jesting. Thou knowest I married one of the Schönberg girls, as did thy father. How 'coy' they were is neither here nor there; but mayhap *we* might tell another story. Thy father, as weak a fellow as thou art where a petticoat is concerned, could not as a gentleman do other than he did. And *this* is his reward? Ach Gott! Coy! And *this*, I warrant, is the way the story is delivered in Paris."

Mr. Clinch would have answered that this was the way he read it in a guide-book, but checked himself at the hopelessness of the explanation. Besides, he was on the eve of historic information; he was, as it were, interviewing the past; and, whether he would ever be able to profit by the opportunity or not, he could not bear to lose it. "And how about the Lorelei — is she, too, a fiction? he asked glibly.

"It was said," observed the baron sardonically, "that when thou disappeared with the gamekeeper's daughter at Obercassel — Heaven knows where! — thou wast swallowed up in a whirlpool with some creature. Ach Gott! I believe it! But a truce to this balderdash. And so thou wantest to know of the 'coy' sisters of Schönberg? Hark ye, Jann, that cousin of thine is a Schönberg. Call you her 'coy'? Did I not see thy greeting? Eh? By St. Adolph, knowing thee as she does to be robber and thief, call you her greeting 'coy'?"

Furious as Mr. Clinch inwardly became under these epithets, he felt that his explanation would hardly relieve the maiden from deceit, or himself from weakness. But out of his very perplexity and turmoil a bright idea was born. He turned to the baron, —

"Then you have no faith in the Rhine legends?"

The baron only replied with a contemptuous shrug of his shoulders.

"But what if I told you a new one?"

"You?"

"Yes; a part of my experience?"

The baron was curious. It was early in the afternoon, just after dinner. He might be worse bored.

"I 've only one condition," added Mr. Clinch; "the young lady — I mean, of course, my cousin — must hear it too."

"Oh, ay! I see. Of course — the old trick! Well, call the jade. But mark ye, Sir Nephew, no enchanted maidens and knights. Keep to thyself. Be as thou art, vagabond Jann Kölnsche, knight of the road. What ho there, scoundrels! Call the Lady Wilhelmina."

It was the first time Mr. Clinch had heard his fair friend's name; but it was not, evidently, the first time she had seen him, as the very decided wink the gentle maiden dropped him testified. Nevertheless, with hands lightly clasped together, and downcast eyes, she stood before them.

Mr. Clinch began. Without heeding the baron's scornful grin, he graphically described his meeting, two years before, with a Lorelei, her usual pressing invitation, and his subsequent plunge into the Rhine.

"I am free to confess," added Mr. Clinch, with an affecting glance to Wilhelmina, "that I was not enamored of the graces of the lady, but was actuated by my desire to travel, and explore hitherto unknown regions. I wished to travel, to visit" —

"Paris," interrupted the baron sarcastically.

"America," continued Mr. Clinch.

"What?"

"America."

"'T is a gnome-like sounding name, this Meriker. Go on, nephew: tell us of Meriker."

With the characteristic fluency of his nation, Mr. Clinch described his landing on those enchanted shores, viz., the Rhine Whirlpool and Hell Gate, East River, New York. He described the railways, tramways, telegraphs, hotels, phonograph, and telephone. An occasional oath broke from the baron, but he listened attentively; and in a few moments Mr. Clinch had the raconteur's satisfaction of seeing the vast hall slowly filling with open-eyed and open-mouthed retainers hanging upon his words. Mr. Clinch went on to describe his astonishment at meeting on these very shores some of his own blood and kin. "In fact," said Mr. Clinch, "here were a race calling themselves 'Clinch,' but all claiming to have descended from Kölnsche."

"And how?" sneered the baron.

"Through James Kölnsche and Wilhelmina his wife," returned Mr. Clinch boldly. "They emigrated from Köln and Crefeld to Philadelphia, where there is a quarter named Crefeld." Mr. Clinch felt himself shaky as to his chronology, but wisely remembered that it was a chronology of the future to his hearers, and they could not detect an anachronism. With his eyes fixed upon those of the gentle Wilhelmina, Mr. Clinch now proceeded to describe his return to his fatherland, but his astonishment at finding the very face of the country changed, and a city standing on those fields he had played in as a boy; and how he had wandered hopelessly on, until he at last sat wearily down in a humble cottage built upon the ruins of a lordly castle. "So utterly travel-worn and weak had I become," said Mr. Clinch, with adroitly simulated pathos, "that a single glass of wine offered me by the simple cottage maiden affected me like a prolonged debauch."

A long-drawn snore was all that followed this affecting climax. The baron was asleep; the retainers were also asleep. Only one pair of eyes remained open, — arch, luminous, blue, — Wilhelmina's.

"There is a subterranean passage below us to Linn. Let us fly!" she whispered.

"But why?"

"They always do it in the legends," she murmured modestly.

"But your father?"

"He sleeps. Do you not hear him?"

Certainly somebody was snoring. But, oddly enough, it seemed to be Wilhelmina. Mr. Clinch suggested this to her.

"Fool, it is yourself!"

Mr. Clinch, struck with the idea, stopped to consider. She was right. It certainly *was* himself.

With a struggle he awoke. The sun was shining. The maiden was looking at him. But the castle — the castle was gone!

"You have slept well," said the maiden archly. "Everybody does after dinner at Sammtstadt. Father has just awakened, and is coming."

Mr. Clinch stared at the maiden, at the terrace, at the sky, at the distant chimneys of Sammtstadt, at the more distant Rhine, at the table before him, and finally at the empty glass. The maiden smiled. "Tell me," said Mr. Clinch, looking in her eyes, "is there a secret passage underground between this place and the Castle of Linn?"

"An underground passage?"

"Ay — whence the daughter of the house fled with a stranger knight."

"They say there is," said the maiden, with a gentle blush.

"Can you show it to me?"

She hesitated. "Papa is coming; I'll ask him."

I presume she did. At least the Herr Consul at Sammtstadt informs me of a marriage-certificate issued to one Clinch of Chicago, and Kölnsche of Köln; and there is an amusing story extant in the Verein at Sammtstadt, of an American connoisseur of Rhine wines, who mistook a flask of Cognac and rock-candy, used for "craftily qualifying" lower grades of wine to the American standard, for the rarest Rüdesheimerberg.

VIEWS FROM A GERMAN SPION

OUTSIDE of my window, two narrow perpendicular mirrors, parallel with the casement, project into the street, yet with a certain unobtrusiveness of angle that enables them to reflect the people who pass, without any reciprocal disclosure of their own. The men and women hurrying by not only do not know they are observed, but, what is worse, do not even see their own reflection in this hypocritical plane, and are consequently unable, through its aid, to correct any carelessness of garb, gait, or demeanor. At first this seems to be taking an unfair advantage of the human animal, who invariably assumes an attitude when he is conscious of being under human focus. But I observe that my neighbors' windows, right and left, have a similar apparatus, that this custom is evidently a local one, and the locality is German. Being an American stranger, I am quite willing to leave the morality of the transaction with the locality, and adapt myself to the custom; indeed, I had thought of offering it, figuratively, as an excuse for any unfairness of observation I might make in these pages. But my German mirrors reflect without prejudice, selection, or comment; and the American eye, I fear, is but mortal, and like all mortal eyes, figuratively as well as in that literal fact noted by an eminent scientific authority, infinitely inferior to the work of the best German opticians.

And this leads me to my first observation, namely, that a majority of those who pass my mirror have weak eyes, and have already invoked the aid of the optician. Why are these people, physically in all else so much stronger than my countrymen, deficient in eyesight? Or, to omit the passing testimony of my Spion, and take my own personal experience, why does my young friend Max, brightest of all schoolboys, who already wears the cap that denotes the highest class, — why does he shock me by suddenly drawing forth a pair of spectacles, that upon his fresh, rosy face would be an obvious mocking imitation of the Herr Papa — if German children could ever, by any possibility, be irreverent? Or why does the Fräulein Marie, his sister, pink as Aurora, round as Hebe, suddenly veil her blue eyes with a golden lorgnette in the midst of our polyglot conversation? Is it to evade the direct, admiring glance of the impulsive American? Dare I say *No?* Dare I say that that frank, clear, honest, earnest return of the eye, which has on the Continent most unfairly brought my fair countrywomen under criticism, is quite as common to her more carefully-guarded, tradition-hedged German sisters? No, it is not that. Is it anything in these emerald and opal tinted skies, which seem so unreal to the American eye, and for the first time explain what seemed the unreality of German art? in these mysterious yet restful Rhine fogs, which prolong the twilight, and hang the curtain of romance even over midday? Surely not. Is it not rather, O Herr Professor profound in analogy and philosophy! — is it not rather this abominable black-letter, this elsewhere-discarded, uncouth, slowly-decaying text known as the German Alphabet, that plucks out the bright eyes of youth, and bristles the gateways of your language with a cheval de frise of splintered rubbish? Why must I hesitate whether it is an accident of the printer's press, or the poor quality of the paper, that makes this letter a "*k*" or a "*t*"? Why must I halt in an emotion or a thought because "*s*" and "*f*" are so nearly alike? Is it not enough that I, an impulsive American, accustomed to do a thing first, and reflect upon it afterwards, must grope my way through a blind alley of substantives and adjectives, only to find the verb of action in an obscure corner, without ruining my eyesight in the groping?

But I dismiss these abstract reflections for a fresh and active resentment. This is the fifth or sixth dog that has passed my Spion, harnessed to a small barrow-like cart, and tugging painfully at a burden so ludicrously disproportionate to his size that it would seem a burlesque, but for the poor dog's sad sincerity. Perhaps it is because I have the barbarian's fondness for dogs, and for their lawless, gentle, loving uselessness, that I rebel against this unnatural servitude. It seems as monstrous as if a child were put between the shafts, and made to carry burdens; and I have come to regard those men and women, who in the weakest perfunctory way affect to aid the poor brute by laying idle hands on the barrow behind, as I would unnatural parents. Pegasus harnessed to the Thracian herdsman's plough was no more of a desecration. I fancy the poor dog seems to feel the monstrosity of the performance, and, in sheer shame for his master, forgivingly tries to assume it is *play;* and I have seen a little collie running along, barking, and endeavoring to leap and gambol in the shafts, before a load that any one out of this locality would have thought the direst cruelty. Nor do the older or more powerful dogs seem to become accustomed to it. When his cruel taskmaster halts with his wares, instantly the dog, either by sitting down in his harness, or crawling over the shafts, or by some unmistakable dog-like trick, utterly scatters any such delusion of even the habit of servitude. The few of his race who do not work in this ducal city seem to have lost their democratic canine sympathies, and look upon him with something of that indifferent calm with which yonder officer eyes the road-mender in the ditch below him. He loses even the characteristics of species. The common cur and mastiff look alike in harness. The burden levels all distinctions. I have said that he was generally sincere in his efforts. I recall but one instance to the contrary. I remember a young collie who first attracted my attention by his persistent barking. Whether he did this, as the plough-boy whistled, "for want of thought," or whether it was a running protest against his occupation, I could not determine, until one day I noticed that, in barking, he slightly threw up his neck and shoulders, and that the two-wheeled barrow-like vehicle behind him, having its weight evenly poised on the wheels by the trucks in the hands of its driver, enabled him by this movement to cunningly throw the centre of gravity and the greater weight on the man, — a fact which that less sagacious brute never discerned. Perhaps I am using a strong expression regarding his driver. It may be that the purely animal wants of the dog, in the way of food, care, and shelter, are more bountifully supplied in servitude than in freedom; becoming a valuable and useful property, he may be cared for and protected as such (an odd recollection that this argument had been used forcibly in regard to human slavery in my own country strikes me here); but his picturesqueness and poetry are gone, and I cannot help thinking that the people who have lost this gentle, sympathetic, characteristic figure from their domestic life and surroundings have not acquired an equal gain through his harsh labors.

To the American eye there is, throughout the length and breadth of this foreign city, no more notable and striking object than the average German house-servant. It is not that she has passed my Spion a dozen times within the last hour, — for here she is messenger, porter, and commissionnaire, as well as housemaid and cook, — but that she is always a phenomenon to the American stranger, accustomed to be abused in his own country by his foreign Irish handmaiden. Her presence is as refreshing and grateful as the morning light, and as inevitable and regular. When I add that with the novelty of being well served is combined the satisfaction of knowing that you have in your household an intelligent being who reads and writes with fluency, and yet does not abstract your books, nor criticise your literary composition; who is cleanly clad, and neat in her person, without the suspicion of having borrowed her mistress's dresses; who may be good-looking without the least imputation of coquetry or addition to her followers; who is obedient without servility, polite without flattery, willing and replete with supererogatory performance, without the expectation of immediate pecuniary return, what wonder that the American householder translated into German life feels himself in a new Eden of domestic possibilities unrealized in any other country, and begins to believe in a present and future of domestic happiness! What wonder that the American bachelor living in German lodgings feels half the terrors of the conjugal future removed, and rushes madly into love — and housekeeping! What wonder that I, a long-suffering and patient master, who have been served by the reticent but too imitative Chinaman; who have been "Massa" to the childlike but untruthful negro; who have been the recipient of the brotherly but uncertain ministrations of the South-Sea Islander, and have been proudly disregarded by the American aborigine, only in due time to meet the fate of my countrymen at the hands of Bridget the Celt, — what wonder that I gladly seize this opportunity to sing the praises of my German handmaid! Honor to thee, Lenchen, wherever thou goest! Heaven bless thee in thy walks abroad! whether with that tightly-booted cavalryman in thy Sunday gown and best, or in blue polka-dotted apron and bare head as thou trottest nimbly on mine errands, —

errands which Bridget O'Flaherty would scorn to undertake, or, undertaking, would hopelessly blunder in. Heaven bless thee, child, in thy early risings and in thy later sittings, at thy festive board overflowing with Essig and Fett, in the mysteries of thy Kuchen, in the fullness of thy Bier, and in thy nightly suffocations beneath mountainous and multitudinous feathers! Good, honest, simple-minded, cheerful, duty-loving Lenchen! Have not thy brothers, strong and dutiful as thou, lent their gravity and earnestness to sweeten and strengthen the fierce youth of the republic beyond the seas? And shall not thy children inherit the broad prairies that still wait for them, and discover the fatness thereof, and send a portion transmuted in glittering shekels back to thee?

Almost as notable are the children whose round faces have as frequently been reflected in my Spion. Whether it is only a fancy of mine that the average German retains longer than any other race his childish simplicity and unconsciousness, or whether it is because I am more accustomed to the extreme self-assertion and early maturity of American children, I know not; but I am inclined to believe that among no other people is childhood so perennial, and to be studied in such characteristic and quaint and simple phases, as here. The picturesqueness of Spanish and Italian childhood has a faint suspicion of the pantomime and the conscious attitudinizing of the Latin races. German children are not exuberant or volatile: they are serious, — a seriousness, however, not to be confounded with the grave reflectiveness of age, but only the abstract wonderment of childhood; for all those who have made a loving study of the young human animal will, I think, admit that its dominant expression is *gravity*, and not playfulness, and will be satisfied that he erred pitifully who first ascribed "light-heartedness" and "thoughtlessness" as part of its phenomena. These little creatures I meet upon the street — whether in quaint wooden shoes and short woolen petticoats, or neatly booted and furred, with school knapsacks jauntily borne upon little square shoulders — all carry likewise in their round chubby faces their profound wonderment and astonishment at the big busy world into which they have so lately strayed. If I stop to speak with this little maid who scarcely reaches to the top-boots of yonder cavalry officer, there is less of bashful self-consciousness in her sweet little face than of grave wonder at the foreign accent and strange ways of this new figure obtruded upon her limited horizon. She answers honestly, frankly, prettily, but gravely. There is a remote possibility that I might bite; and, with this suspicion plainly indicated in her round blue eyes, she quietly slips her little red hand from mine, and moves solemnly away. I remember once to have stopped in the street with a fair countrywoman of mine to interrogate a little figure in sabots, — the one quaint object in the long, formal perspective of narrow, gray bastard-Italian façaded houses of a Rhenish German Strasse. The sweet little figure wore a dark blue woolen petticoat that came to its knees; gray woolen stockings covered the shapely little limbs below; and its very blond hair, the color of a bright dandelion, was tied in a pathetic little knot at the back of its round head, and garnished with an absurd green ribbon. Now, although this gentlewoman's sympathies were catholic and universal, unfortunately their expression was limited to her own mother-tongue. She could not help pouring out upon the child the maternal love that was in her own womanly breast, nor could she withhold the "baby-talk" through which it was expressed. But, alas! it was in English. Hence ensued a colloquy, tender and extravagant on the part of the elder, grave and wondering on the part of the child. But the lady had a natural feminine desire for reciprocity, particularly in the presence of our emotion-scorning sex, and as a last resource she emptied the small silver of her purse into the lap of the coy maiden. It was a declaration of love, susceptible of translation at the nearest cake-shop. But the little maid, whose dress and manner certainly did not betray an habitual disregard of gifts of this kind, looked at the coin thoughtfully, but not regretfully. Some innate sense of duty, equally strong with that of being polite to strangers, filled her consciousness. With the utterly unexpected remark that her father *did not allow her to take money*, the queer little figure moved away, leaving the two Americans covered with mortification. The rare American child who could have done this would have done it with an attitude. This little German bourgeoise did it naturally. I do not intend to rush to the deduction that German children of the lower classes habitually refuse pecuniary gratuities; indeed, I remember to have wickedly suggested to my companion that, to avoid impoverishment in a foreign land, she should not repeat the story nor the experiment. But I simply offer it as a fact, and to an American, at home or abroad, a novel one.

I owe to these little figures another experience quite as strange. It was at the close of a dull winter's day, — a day from which all out-of-door festivity seemed to be naturally excluded; there was a baleful promise of snow in the air and a dismal reminiscence of it under foot, when suddenly, in striking contrast with the dreadful bleakness of the street, a half-dozen children, masked and bedizened with cheap ribbons, spangles, and embroidery, flashed across my Spion. I was quick to understand the phenomenon. It was the Carnival season. Only the night before I had been to the great opening masquerade, — a famous affair, for which this art-loving city is noted, and to which strangers are drawn from all parts of the Continent. I remember to have wondered if the pleasure-loving German in America had not broken some of his conventional shackles in emigration; for certainly I had found the Carnival balls of the "Lieder Kranz Society" in New York, although decorous and fashionable to the American taste, to be wild dissipations compared with the practical seriousness of this native performance, and I hailed the presence of these children in the open street as a promise of some extravagance, real, untrammeled, and characteristic. I seized my hat and — *overcoat*, — a dreadful incongruity to the spangles that had whisked by, — and followed the vanishing figures round the corner. Here they were reenforced by a dozen men and women, fantastically, but not expensively arrayed, looking not unlike the supernumeraries of some provincial opera troupe. Following the crowd, which already began to pour in from the side-streets, in a few moments I was in the broad, grove-like allée, and in the midst of the masqueraders.

I remember to have been told that this was a characteristic annual celebration of the lower classes, anticipated with eagerness, and achieved with difficulty, indeed, often only through the alternative of pawning clothing and furniture to provide the means for this ephemeral transformation. I remember being warned, also, that the buffoonery was coarse, and some of the slang hardly fit for "ears polite." But I am afraid that I was not shocked at the prodigality of these poor people, who purchased a holiday on such hard conditions; and, as to the coarseness of the performance, *I* felt that I certainly might go where these children could.

At first the masquerading figures appeared to be mainly composed of young girls of ages varying from nine to eighteen. Their costumes — if what was often only the addition of a broad, bright-colored stripe to the hem of a short dress could be called a costume — were plain, and seemed to indicate no particular historical epoch or character. A general suggestion of the peasant's holiday attire was dominant in all the costumes. Everybody was closely masked. All carried a short, gayly-striped bâton of split wood, called a Pritsche, which, when struck sharply on the back or shoulders of some spectator or sister-masker, emitted a clattering rasping sound. To wander hand in hand down this broad allée, to strike almost mechanically, and often monotonously, at each other with their bâtons, seemed to be the extent of that wild dissipation. The crowd thickened. Young men with false noses, hideous masks, cheap black or red cotton dominoes, soldiers in uniform, crowded past each other up and down the promenade, all carrying a Pritsche, and exchanging blows with each other, but always with the same slow seriousness of demeanor, which, with their silence, gave the performance the effect of a religious rite. Occasionally some one shouted; perhaps a dozen young fellows broke out in song; but the shout was provocative of nothing, the song faltered as if the singers were frightened at their own voices. One blithe fellow, with a bear's head on his fur-capped shoulders, began to dance; but, on the crowd stopping to observe him seriously, he apparently thought better of it, and slipped away. Nevertheless, the solemn beating of Pritsche over each other's backs went on. I remember that I was followed the whole length of the allée by a little girl scarcely twelve years old, in a bright striped skirt and black mask, who from time to time struck me over the shoulders with a regularity and sad persistency that was peculiarly irresistible to me; the more so as I could not help thinking that it was not half as amusing to herself. Once only did the ordinary brusque gallantry of the Carnival spirit show itself. A man with an enormous pair of horns, like a half-civilized satyr, suddenly seized a young girl, and endeavored to kiss her. A slight struggle ensued, in which I fancied I detected in the girl's face and manner the confusion and embarrassment of one who was obliged to overlook, or seem to accept, a familiarity that was distasteful, rather than be laughed at for prudishness or ignorance. But the incident was exceptional. Indeed, it was particularly notable to my American eyes to find such decorum where there might easily have been the greatest license. I am afraid that an American mob of this class would have scarcely been as orderly and civil under the circumstances. They might have shown more humor, but there would have probably been more effrontery; they might have been more exuberant; they would certainly have been drunker. I did not notice a single masquerader unduly excited by liquor; there was not a word or motion from the lighter sex that could have been construed into an impropriety. There was something almost pathetic to me in this attempt to wrest gayety and excitement out of these dull materials; to fight against the blackness of that wintry sky, and the stubborn hardness of the frozen soil, with these painted sticks of wood; to mock the dreariness of their poverty with these flaunting raiments. It did not seem like them, or rather, consistent with my idea of them. There was incongruity deeper than their bizarre externals; a half-melancholy, half-crazy absurdity in their action, the substitution of a grim spasmodic frenzy for levity, that rightly or wrongly impressed me. When the increasing gloom of the evening made their figures undistinguishable, I turned into the first cross-street. As I lifted my hat to my persistent young friend with the Pritsche, I fancied she looked as relieved as myself. If, however, I was mistaken; if that child's pathway through life be strewn with rosy recollections of the unresisting back of the stranger American; if any burden, O Gretchen, laid upon thy young shoulders, be lighter for the trifling one thou didst lay upon mine, — know, then, that I, too, am content.

And so, day by day, has my Spion reflected the various changing forms of life before it. It has seen the first flush of spring in the broad allée, when the shadows of tiny leaflets overhead were beginning to checker the cool, square flagstones. It has seen the glare and fullness of summer sunshine and shadow, the flying of November gold through the air, the gaunt limbs, and stark, rigid, death-like whiteness of winter. It has seen children in their queer wicker baby-carriages, old men and women, and occasionally that grim usher of death, in sable cloak and cocked hat, — a baleful figure for the wandering invalid tourist to meet, — who acts as undertaker for this ducal city, and marshals the last melancholy procession. I well remember my first meeting with this ominous functionary. It was an early autumnal morning; so early, that the long formal perspective of the allée, and the decorous, smooth vanishing-lines of cream-and-gray fronted houses, were unrelieved by a single human figure. Suddenly a tall black spectre, as theatrical and as unreal as the painted scenic distance, turned the corner from a cross-street, and moved slowly towards me. A long black cloak, falling from its shoulders to its feet, floated out on either side like sable wings; a cocked hat trimmed with crape, and surmounted by a hearse-like feather, covered a passionless face; and its eyes, looking neither left nor right, were fixed fatefully upon some distant goal. Stranger as I was to this Continental ceremonial figure, there was no mistaking his functions as the grim messenger, knocking "with equal foot" on every door; and, indeed, so perfectly did he act and look his rôle, that there was nothing ludicrous in the extraordinary spectacle. Facial expression and dignity of bearing were perfect; the whole man seemed saturated with the accepted sentiment of his office. Recalling the half-confused and half-conscious ostentatious hypocrisy of the American sexton, the shameless absurdities of the

English mutes and mourners, I could not help feeling that, if it were demanded that Grief and Fate should be personified, it were better that it should be well done. And it is one observation of my Spion, that this sincerity and belief is the characteristic of all Continental functionaries.

It is possible that my Spion has shown me little that is really characteristic of the people, and the few observations I have made I offer only as an illustration of the impressions made upon two thirds of American strangers in the larger towns of Germany. Assimilation goes on more rapidly than we are led to imagine. As I have seen my friend Karl, fresh and awkward in his first uniform, lounging later down the allée with the blasé listlessness of a full-blown militaire, so I have seen American and English residents gradually lose their peculiarities, and melt and merge into the general mass. Returning to my Spion after a flying trip through Belgium and France, as I look down the long perspective of the Strasse, I am conscious of recalling the same style of architecture and humanity at Aachen, Brussels, Lille, and Paris, and am inclined to believe that, even as I would have met, in a journey of the same distance through a parallel of the same latitude in America, a greater diversity of type and character, and a more distinct flavor of locality, even so would I have met a more heterogeneous and picturesque display from a club window on Fifth Avenue, New York, or Montgomery Street, San Francisco.

THE INDISCRETION OF ELSBETH

THE American paused. He had evidently lost his way. For the last half-hour he had been wandering in a mediæval town, in a profound mediæval dream. Only a few days had elapsed since he had left the steamship that carried him hither; and the accents of his own tongue, the idioms of his own people, and the sympathetic community of New World tastes and expressions still filled his mind until he woke up, or rather, as it seemed to him, was falling asleep in the past of this Old World town which had once held his ancestors. Although a republican, he had liked to think of them in quaint distinctive garb, representing state and importance, — perhaps even aristocratic preëminence, — content to let the responsibility of such "bad eminence" rest with them entirely; but a habit of conscientiousness and love for historic truth eventually led him also to regard an honest bauer standing beside his cattle in the quaint market-place, or a kindly-faced black-eyed dienstmädchen in a doorway, with a timid, respectful interest, as a possible type of his progenitors. For, unlike some of his traveling countrymen in Europe, he was not a snob, and it struck him — as an American — that it was, perhaps, better to think of his race as having improved than as having degenerated. In these ingenuous meditations he had passed the long rows of quaint, high houses, whose sagging roofs and unpatched dilapidations were yet far removed from squalor, until he had reached the road bordered by poplars, all so unlike his own country's waysides — and knew that he had wandered far from his hotel.

He did not care, however, to retrace his steps and return by the way he had come. There was, he reasoned, some other street or turning that would eventually bring him to the market-place and his hotel, and yet extend his experience of the town. He turned at right angles into a narrow grass lane, which was, however, as neatly kept and apparently as public as the highway. A few moments' walking convinced him that it was not a thoroughfare and that it led to the open gates of a park. This had something of a public look, which suggested that his intrusion might be, at least, a pardonable trespass, and he relied, like most strangers, on the exonerating quality of a stranger's ignorance. The park lay in the direction he wished to go, and yet it struck him as singular that a park of such extent should be allowed to still occupy such valuable urban space. Indeed, its length seemed to be illimitable as he wandered on, until he became conscious that he must have again lost his way, and he diverged toward the only boundary, a high, thick-set hedge to the right, whose line he had been following.

As he neared it he heard the sound of voices on the other side, speaking in German, with which he was unfamiliar. Having, as yet, met no one, and being now impressed with the fact that for a public place the park was singularly deserted, he was conscious that his position was getting serious, and he determined to take this only chance of inquiring his way. The hedge was thinner in some places than in others, and at times he could see not only the light through it but even the moving figures of the speakers, and the occasional white flash of a summer gown. At last he determined to penetrate it, and with little difficulty emerged on the other side. But here he paused motionless. He found himself behind a somewhat formal and symmetrical group of figures with their backs toward him, but all stiffened into attitudes as motionless as his own, and all gazing with a monotonous intensity in the direction of a handsome building, which had been invisible above the hedge, but which now seemed to arise suddenly before him. Some of the figures were in uniform. Immediately before him, but so slightly separated from the others that he was enabled to see the house between her and her companions, he was confronted by the pretty back, shoulders and blond braids of a young girl of twenty. Convinced that he had unwittingly intruded upon some august ceremonial, he instantly slipped back into the hedge, but so silently that his momentary presence was evidently undetected. When he regained the park side he glanced back through the interstices; there was no movement of the figures nor break in the silence to indicate that his intrusion had been observed. With a long breath of relief he hurried from the park.

It was late when he finally got back to his hotel. But his little modern adventure had, I fear, quite outrun his previous mediæval reflections, and almost his first inquiry of the silver-chained porter in the courtyard was in regard to the park. There was no public park in Alstadt! The Herr possibly alluded to the Hof Gardens — the Schloss, which was in the direction he indicated. The Schloss was the residency of the hereditary Grand Duke. Ja wohl! He was stopping there with several Hoheiten. There was naturally a party there, — a family reunion. But it was a private inclosure. At times, when the Grand Duke was not "in residence," it was open to the public. In point of fact, at such times tickets of admission were to be had at the hotel for fifty pfennige each. There was not, of truth, much to see except a model farm and dairy, — the pretty toy of a previous Grand Duchess.

But he seemed destined to come into closer collision with the modern life of Alstadt. On entering the hotel, wearied by his long walk, he passed the landlord and a man in half-military uniform on the landing near his room. As he entered his apartment he had a vague impression, without exactly knowing why, that the landlord and the military stranger had just left it. This feeling was deepened by the evident disarrangement of certain articles in his unlocked portmanteau and the disorganization of his writing-case. A wave of indignation passed over him. It was followed by a knock at the door, and the landlord blandly appeared with the stranger.

"A thousand pardons," said the former smilingly, "but Herr Sanderman, the Ober-Inspector of Police, wishes to speak with you. I hope we are not intruding?"

"Not *now*," said the American, dryly.

The two exchanged a vacant and deprecating smile.

"I have to ask only a few formal questions," said the Ober-Inspector in excellent but somewhat precise English, "to supplement the report which, as a stranger, you may not know is required by the police from the landlord in regard to the names and quality of his guests who are foreign to the town. You have a passport?"

"I have," said the American still more dryly. "But I do not keep it in an unlocked portmanteau or an open writing-case."

"An admirable precaution," said Sanderman, with unmoved politeness. "May I see it? Thanks," he added, glancing over the document which the American produced from his pocket. "I see that you are a born American citizen — and an earlier knowledge of that fact would have prevented this little contretemps. You are aware, Mr. Hoffman, that your name is German?"

"It was borne by my ancestors, who came from this country two centuries ago," said Hoffman curtly.

"We are indeed honored by your return to it," returned Sanderman suavely, "but it was the circumstance of your name being a local one, and the possibility of your still being a German citizen liable to unperformed military duty, which has caused the trouble." His manner was clearly civil and courteous, but Hoffman felt that all the time his own face and features were undergoing a profound scrutiny from the speaker.

"And you are making sure that you will know me again?" said Hoffman, with a smile.

"I trust, indeed, both," returned Sanderman, with a bow, "although you will permit me to say that your description here," pointing to the passport, "scarcely does you justice. Ach Gott! it is the same in all countries; the official eye is not that of the young Damen."

Hoffman, though not conceited, had not lived twenty years without knowing that he was very good-looking, yet there was something in the remark that caused him to color with a new uneasiness. The Ober-Inspector rose with another bow, and moved toward the door. "I hope you will let me make amends for this intrusion by doing anything I can to render your visit here a pleasant one. Perhaps," he added, "it is not for long."

But Hoffman evaded the evident question as he resented what he imagined was a possible sneer.

"I have not yet determined my movements," he said.

The Ober-Inspector brought his heels together in a somewhat stiffer military salute and departed.

Nothing, however, could have exceeded the later almost servile urbanity of the landlord, who seemed to have been proud of the official visit to his guest. He was profuse in his attentions, and even introduced him to a singularly artistic-looking man of middle age, wearing an order in his buttonhole, whom he met casually in the hall.

"Our Court photographer," explained the landlord with some fervor, "at whose studio, only a few houses distant, most of the Hoheiten and Prinzessinnen of Germany have sat for their likenesses."

"I should feel honored if the distinguished American Herr would give me a visit," said the stranger gravely, as he gazed at Hoffman with an intensity which recalled the previous scrutiny of the Police-Inspector, "and I would be charmed if he would avail himself of my poor skill to transmit his picturesque features to my unique collection."

Hoffman returned a polite evasion to this invitation, although he was conscious of being struck with this second examination of his face, and the allusion to his personality.

The next morning the porter met him with a mysterious air. The Herr would still like to see the Schloss? Hoffman, who had quite forgotten his adventure in the park, looked vacant. Ja wohl — the Hof authorities had no doubt heard of his visit and had intimated to the hotel proprietor that he might have permission to visit the model farm and dairy. As the American still looked indifferent the porter pointed out with some importance that it was a Ducal courtesy not to be lightly treated; that few, indeed, of the burghers themselves had ever been admitted to this eccentric whim of the late Grand Duchess. He would, of course, be silent about it; the Court would not like it known that they had made an exception to their rules in favor of a foreigner; he would enter quickly and boldly alone. There would be a housekeeper or a dairymaid to show him over the place.

More amused at this important mystery over what he, as an American, was inclined to classify as a "free pass" to a somewhat heavy "side show," he gravely accepted the permission, and the next morning after breakfast set out to visit the model farm and dairy. Dismissing his driver, as he had been instructed, Hoffman entered the gateway with a mingling of expectancy and a certain amusement over the "boldness" which the porter had suggested should characterize his entrance. Before him was a beautifully-kept lane bordered by arbored and trellised roses, which seemed to sink into the distance. He was instinctively following it when he became aware that he was mysteriously accompanied by a man in the livery of a chasseur, who was walking among the trees almost abreast of him, keeping pace with his step, and after the first introductory military salute preserving a ceremonious silence. There was something so ludicrous in this solemn procession toward a peaceful, rural industry that by the time they had reached the bottom of the lane the American had quite recovered his good humor. But here a new astonishment awaited him. Nestling before him in a green amphitheatre lay a little wooden farmyard and outbuildings, which irresistibly suggested that it had been recently unpacked and set up from a box of Nuremberg toys. The symmetrical trees, the galleried houses with preternaturally glazed windows, even the spotty, disproportionately sized cows in the white-fenced barnyards were all unreal, wooden, and toylike.

Crossing a miniature bridge over a little stream, from which he was quite prepared to hook metallic fish with a magnet their own size, he looked about him for some real being to dispel the illusion. The mysterious chasseur had disappeared. But under the arch of an arbor, which seemed to be composed of silk ribbons, green glass, and pink tissue paper, stood a quaint but delightful figure.

At first it seemed as if he had only dispelled one illusion for another. For the figure before him might have been made of Dresden china — so daintily delicate and unique it was in color and arrangement. It was that of a young girl dressed in some forgotten mediæval peasant garb of velvet braids, silver stay-laced corsage, lace sleeves, and helmeted metallic comb. But, after the Dresden method, the pale yellow of her hair was repeated in her bodice, the pink of her cheeks was in the roses of her chintz overskirt. The blue of her eyes was the blue of her petticoat; the dazzling whiteness of her neck shone again in the sleeves and stockings. Nevertheless she was real and human, for the pink deepened in her cheeks as Hoffman's hat flew from his head, and she recognized the civility with a grave little courtesy.

"You have come to see the dairy," she said in quaintly accurate English; "I will show you the way."

"If you please," said Hoffman gayly, "but" —

"But what?" she said, facing him suddenly with absolutely astonished eyes.

Hoffman looked into them so long that their frank wonder presently contracted into an ominous mingling of restraint and resentment. Nothing daunted, however, he went on: —

"Could n't we shake all that?"

The look of wonder returned. "Shake all that?" she repeated. "I do not understand."

"Well! I 'm not positively aching to see cows, and you must be sick of showing them. I think, too, I 've about sized the whole show. Would n't it be better if we sat down in that arbor — supposing it won't fall down — and you told me all about the lot? It would save you a heap of trouble and keep your pretty frock cleaner than traipsing round. Of course," he said, with a quick transition to the gentlest courtesy, "if you 're conscientious about this thing we 'll go on and not spare a cow. Consider me in it with you for the whole morning."

She looked at him again, and then suddenly broke into a charming laugh. It revealed a set of strong white teeth, as well as a certain barbaric trace in its cadence which civilized restraint had not entirely overlaid.

"I suppose she really is a peasant, in spite of that pretty frock," he said to himself as he laughed too.

But her face presently took a shade of reserve, and with a gentle but singular significance she said: —

"I think you must see the dairy."

Hoffman's hat was in his hand with a vivacity that tumbled the brown curls on his forehead. "By all means," he said instantly, and began walking by her side in modest but easy silence. Now that he thought her a conscientious peasant he was quiet and respectful.

Presently she lifted her eyes, which, despite her gravity, had not entirely lost their previous mirthfulness, and said: —

"But you Americans — in your rich and prosperous country, with your large lands and your great harvests — you must know all about farming."

"Never was in a dairy in my life," said Hoffman gravely. "I 'm from the city of New York, where the cows give swill milk, and are kept in cellars."

Her eyebrows contracted prettily in an effort to understand. Then she apparently gave it up, and said with a slanting glint of mischief in her eyes: —

"Then you come here like the other Americans in hope to see the Grand Duke and Duchess and the Princesses?"

"No. The fact is I almost tumbled into a lot of 'em — standing like wax figures, — the other side of the park lodge, the other day — and got away as soon as I could. I think I prefer the cows."

Her head was slightly turned away. He had to content himself with looking down upon the strong feet in their serviceable but smartly-buckled shoes that uplifted her upright figure as she moved beside him.

"Of course," he added with boyish but unmistakable courtesy, "if it 's part of your show to trot out the family, why I 'm in that, too. I dare say you could make them interesting."

"But why," she said with her head still slightly turned away toward a figure, — a sturdy-looking woman, which, for the first time, Hoffman perceived was walking in a line with them as the chasseur had done, — "why did you come here at all?"

"The first time was a fool accident," he returned frankly. "I was making a short cut through what I thought was a public park. The second time was because I had been rude to a Police-Inspector whom I found going through my things, but who apologized — as I suppose — by getting me an invitation from the Grand Duke to come here, and I thought it only the square thing to both of 'em to accept it. But I 'm mighty glad I came; I would n't have missed *you* for a thousand dollars. You see I have n't struck any one I cared to talk to since." Here he suddenly remarked that she had n't looked at him, and that the delicate whiteness of her neck was quite suffused with pink, and stopped instantly. Presently he said quite easily: —

"Who 's the chorus?

"The lady?"

"Yes. She 's watching us as if she did n't quite approve, you know, — just as if she did n't catch on."

"She 's the head housekeeper of the farm. Perhaps you would prefer to have her show you the dairy; shall I call her?"

The figure in question was very short and stout, with voluminous petticoats.

"Please don't; I 'll stay without your setting that paperweight on me. But here 's the dairy. Don't let her come inside among those pans of fresh milk with that smile, or there 'll be trouble."

The young girl paused too, made a slight gesture with her hand, and the figure passed on as they entered the dairy. It was beautifully clean and fresh. With a persistence that he quickly recognized as mischievous and ironical, and with his characteristic adaptability accepted with even greater gravity and assumption of interest, she showed him all the details. From thence they passed to the farmyard, where he hung with breathless attention over the names of the cows and made her repeat them. Although she was evidently familiar with the subject he could see that her zeal was fitful and impatient.

"Suppose we sit down," he said, pointing to an ostentatious rustic seat in the centre of the green.

"Sit down?" she repeated wonderingly. "What for?"

"To talk. We'll knock off and call it half a day."

"But if you are not looking at the farm you are, of course, going," she said quickly.

"Am I? I don't think these particulars were in my invitation."

She again broke into a fit of laughter, and, at the same time, cast a bright eye around the field.

"Come," he said gently, "there are no other sightseers waiting, and your conscience is clear," and he moved toward the rustic seat.

"Certainly not — there," she added in a low voice.

They moved on slowly together to a copse of willows which overhung the miniature stream.

"You are not staying long in Alstadt?" she said.

"No; I only came to see the old town that my ancestors came from."

They were walking so close together that her skirt brushed his trousers, but she suddenly drew away from him, and looking him fixedly in the eye said: —

"Ah, you have relations here?"

"Yes, but they are dead two hundred years."

She laughed again with a slight expression of relief. They had entered the copse and were walking in dense shadow when she suddenly stopped and sat down upon a rustic bench. To his surprise he found that they were quite alone.

"Tell me about these relatives," she said, slightly drawing aside her skirt to make room for him on the seat.

He did not require a second invitation. He not only told her all about his ancestral progenitors, but, I fear, even about those more recent and more nearly related to him; about his own life, his vocation, — he was a clever newspaper correspondent with a roving commission, — his ambitions, his beliefs, and his romance.

"And then, perhaps, of this visit — you will also make 'copy'?"

He smiled at her quick adaptation of his professional slang, but shook his head.

"No," he said gravely. "No — this is *you*. The 'Chicago Interviewer' is big pay and is rich, but it has n't capital enough to buy you from me."

He gently slid his hand toward hers and slipped his fingers softly around it. She made a slight movement of withdrawal, but even then — as if in forgetfulness or indifference — permitted her hand to rest unresponsively in his. It was scarcely an encouragement to gallantry, neither was it a rejection of an unconscious familiarity.

"But you have n't told me about yourself," he said.

"Oh, I" — she returned, with her first approach to coquetry in a laugh and a sidelong glance, "of what importance is that to you? It is the Grand Duchess and Her Highness the Princess that you Americans seek to know. I am — what I am — as you see."

"You bet," said Hoffman with charming decision.

"I *what?*"

"You *are*, you know, and that 's good enough for me but I don't even know your name."

She laughed again, and after a pause, said: "Elsbeth."

"But I could n't call you by your first name on our first meeting, you know."

"Then you Americans are really so very formal — eh?" she said slyly, looking at her imprisoned hand.

"Well, yes," returned Hoffman, disengaging it. "I

suppose we are respectful, or mean to be. But whom am I to inquire for? To write to?"

"You are neither to write nor inquire."

"What?" She had moved in her seat so as to half face him with eyes in which curiosity, mischief, and a certain seriousness alternated, but for the first time seemed conscious of his hand, and accented her words with a slight pressure.

"You are to return to your hotel presently, and say to your landlord: 'Pack up my luggage. I have finished with this old town and my ancestors, and the Grand Duke whom I do not care to see, and I shall leave Alstadt to-morrow!'"

"Thank you! I don't catch on."

"Of what necessity should you? I have said it. That should be enough for a chivalrous American like you." She again significantly looked down at her hand.

"If you mean that you know the extent of the favor you ask of me, I can say no more," he said seriously; "but give me some reason for it."

"Ah, so!" she said, with a slight shrug of her shoulders. "Then I must tell you. You say you do not know the Grand Duke and Duchess. Well! *they know you.* The day before yesterday you were wandering in the park, as you admit. You say, also, you got through the hedge and interrupted some ceremony. That ceremony was not a Court function, Mr. Hoffman, but something equally sacred, — the photographing of the Ducal family before the Schloss. You say that you instantly withdrew. But after the photograph was taken the plate revealed a stranger standing actually by the side of the Princess Alexandrine, and even taking the pas of the Grand Duke himself. That stranger was you!"

"And the picture was spoiled," said the American, with a quiet laugh.

"I should not say that," returned the lady, with a demure glance at her companion's handsome face, "and I do not believe that the Princess — who first saw the photograph — thought so either. But she is very young and willful, and has the reputation of being very indiscreet, and unfortunately she begged the photographer not to destroy the plate, but to give it to her, and to say nothing about it, except that the plate was defective, and to take another. Still it would have ended there if her curiosity had not led her to confide a description of the stranger to the Police Inspector, with the result you know."

"Then I am expected to leave town because I accidentally stumbled into a family group that was being photographed?"

"Because a certain Princess was indiscreet enough to show her curiosity about you," corrected the fair stranger.

"But look here! I'll apologize to the Princess, and offer to pay for the plate."

"Then you do want to see the Princess?" said the young girl smiling; "you are like the others."

"Bother the Princess! I want to see *you*. And I don't see how they can prevent it if I choose to remain."

"Very easily. You will find that there is something wrong with your passport, and you will be sent on to Pumpernickel for examination. You will unwittingly transgress some of the laws of the town and be ordered to leave it. You will be shadowed by the police until you quarrel with them — like a free American — and you are conducted to the frontier. Perhaps you will strike an officer who has insulted you, and then you are finished on the spot."

The American's crest rose palpably until it cocked his straw hat over his curls.

"Suppose I am content to risk it — having first laid the whole matter and its trivial cause before the American

Minister, so that he could make it hot for this whole caboodle of a country if they happened to 'down me.' By Jove! I should n't mind being the martyr of an international episode if they 'd spare me long enough to let me get the first 'copy' over to the other side." His eyes sparkled.

"You could expose them, but they would then deny the whole story, and you have no evidence. They would demand to know your informant, and I should be disgraced, and the Princess, who is already talked about, made a subject of scandal. But no matter! It is right that an American's independence shall not be interfered with."

She raised the hem of her handkerchief to her blue eyes and slightly turned her head aside. Hoffman gently drew the handkerchief away, and in so doing possessed himself of her other hand.

"Look here, Miss — Miss — Elsbeth. You know I would n't give you away, whatever happened. But could n't I get hold of that photographer — I saw him, he wanted me to sit to him — and make him tell me?"

"He wanted you to sit to him," she said hurriedly, "and did you?"

"No," he replied. "He was a little too fresh and previous, though I thought he fancied some resemblance in me to somebody else."

"Ah!" She said something to herself in German which he did not understand, and then added aloud: —

"You did well; he is a bad man, this photographer. Promise me you shall not sit for him."

"How can I if I 'm fired out of the place like this?" He added ruefully, "But I 'd like to make him give himself away to me somehow."

"He will not, and if he did he would deny it afterward. Do not go near him nor see him. Be careful that he does not photograph you with his instantaneous instrument when you are passing. Now you must go. I must see the Princess."

"Let me go, too. I will explain it to her," said Hoffman.

She stopped, looked at him keenly, and attempted to withdraw her hands. "Ah, then it *is* so. It is the Princess you wish to see. You are curious — you, too; you wish to see this lady who is interested in you. I ought to have known it. You are all alike."

He met her gaze with laughing frankness, accepting her outburst as a charming feminine weakness, half jealousy, half coquetry, — but retained her hands.

"Nonsense," he said. "I wish to see her that I may have the right to see you — that you shall not lose your place here through me; that I may come again."

"You must never come here again."

"Then you must come where I am. We will meet somewhere when you have an afternoon off. You shall show me the town — the houses of my ancestors — their tombs; possibly — if the Grand Duke rampages — the probable site of my own."

She looked into his laughing eyes with her clear, steadfast, gravely-questioning blue ones. "Do not you Americans know that it is not the fashion here, in Germany, for the young men and the young women to walk together — unless they are verlobt?"

"Ver — which?"

"Engaged." She nodded her head thrice; viciously, decidedly, mischievously.

"So much the better."

"Ach Gott!" She made a gesture of hopelessness at his incorrigibility, and again attempted to withdraw her hands.

"I must go now."

"Well then, good-by."

It was easy to draw her closer by simply lowering her still captive hands. Then he suddenly kissed her coldly-startled lips, and instantly released her. She as instantly vanished.

"Elsbeth," he called quickly. "Elsbeth!"

Her now really frightened face reappeared with a heightened color from the dense foliage — quite to his astonishment.

"Hush," she said, with her finger on her lips. "Are you mad?"

"I only wanted to remind you to square me with the Princess," he laughed, as her head disappeared.

He strolled back toward the gate. Scarcely had he quitted the shrubbery before the same chasseur made his appearance with precisely the same salute; and, keeping exactly the same distance, accompanied him to the gate. At the corner of the street he hailed a drosky and was driven to his hotel.

The landlord came up smiling. He trusted that the Herr had greatly enjoyed himself at the Schloss. It was a distinguished honor, — in fact, quite unprecedented. Hoffman, while he determined not to commit himself nor his late fair companion, was, nevertheless, anxious to learn something more of her relations to the Schloss. So pretty, so characteristic and marked a figure must be well known to sightseers. Indeed, once or twice the idea had crossed his mind with a slightly jealous twinge that left him more conscious of the impression she had made on him than he had deemed possible. He asked if the model farm and dairy were always shown by the same attendants.

"Ach Gott! no doubt, yes; His Royal Highness had quite a retinue when he was in residence."

"And were these attendants in costume?"

"There was undoubtedly a livery for the servants."

Hoffman felt a slight republican irritation at the epithet, — he knew not why. But this costume was rather an historical one; surely it was not intrusted to every-day menials, — and he briefly described it.

His host's blank curiosity suddenly changed to a look of mysterious and arch intelligence.

"Ach Gott! yes!" He remembered now (with his finger on his nose) that when there was a feast at the Schloss the farm and dairy were filled with shepherdesses in quaint costume worn by the ladies of the Grand Duke's own theatrical company, who assumed the characters with great vivacity. Surely it was the same, and the Grand Duke had treated the Herr to this special courtesy. Yes — there was one pretty, blonde young lady — the Fräulein Wimpfenbuttel, a most popular soubrette, who would play it to the life! And the description fitted her to a hair! Ah, there was no doubt of it; many persons, indeed, had been so deceived.

But happily, now that he had given him the wink, the Herr could corroborate it himself by going to the theatre to-night. Ah, it would be a great joke — quite colossal! if he took a front seat where she could see him. And the good man rubbed his hands in gleeful anticipation.

Hoffman had listened to him with a slow repugnance that was only equal to his gradual conviction that the explanation was a true one, and that he himself had been ridiculously deceived. The mystery of his fair companion's costume, which he had accepted as part of the "show"; the inconsistency of her manner and her evident occupation; her undeniable wish to terminate the whole episode with that single interview; her mingling of worldly aplomb and rustic innocence; her perfect self-control and experienced acceptance of his gallantry under the simulated attitude of simplicity, — all now struck him as perfectly comprehensible. He recalled the actress's inimitable touch in certain picturesque realistic details in the dairy — which she had not spared him; he recognized it now even in their bowered confidences (how like a pretty ballet scene their whole interview on the rustic bench was!), and it breathed through their entire conversation — to their theatrical parting at the close! And the whole story of the photograph was, no doubt, as pure a dramatic invention as the rest! The Princess's romantic interest in him — that Princess who had never appeared (why had he not detected the old, well-worn, sentimental situation here?) — was all a part of it. The dark, mysterious hint of his persecution by the police was a necessary culmination to the little farce. Thank Heaven! he had not "risen" at the Princess, even if he had given himself away to the clever actress in her own humble rôle. Then the humor of the whole situation predominated and he laughed until the tears came to his eyes, and his forgotten ancestors might have turned over in their graves without his heeding them. And with this humanizing influence upon him he went to the theatre.

It was capacious even for the town, and although the performance was a special one he had no difficulty in getting a whole box to himself. He tried to avoid this public isolation by sitting close to the next box, where there was a solitary occupant — an officer — apparently as lonely as himself. He had made up his mind that when his fair deceiver appeared he would let her see by his significant applause that he recognized her, but bore no malice for the trick she had played on him. After all, he had kissed her, — he had no right to complain. If she should recognize him, and this recognition led to a withdrawal of her prohibition, and their better acquaintance, he would be a fool to cavil at her pleasant artifice. Her vocation was certainly a more independent and original one than that he had supposed; for its social quality and inequality he cared nothing. He found himself longing for the glance of her calm blue eyes, for the pleasant smile that broke the seriousness of her sweetly-restrained lips. There was no doubt that he should know her even as the heroine of "Der Czar und der Zimmermann" on the bill before him. He was becoming impatient. And the performance evidently was waiting. A stir in the outer gallery, the clatter of sabres, the filing of uniforms into the royal box, and a triumphant burst from the orchestra showed the cause. As a few ladies and gentlemen in full evening dress emerged from the background of uniforms and took their places in the front of the box, Hoffman looked with some interest for the romantic Princess. Suddenly he saw a face and shoulders in a glitter of diamonds that startled him, and then a glance that transfixed him.

He leaned over to his neighbor. "Who is the young lady in the box?"

"The Princess Alexandrine."

"I mean the young lady in blue with blond hair and blue eyes."

"It is the Princess Alexandrine Elsbeth Marie Stephanie, the daughter of the Grand Duke — there is none other there."

"Thank you."

He sat silently looking at the rising curtain and the stage. Then he rose quietly, gathered his hat and coat, and left the box. When he reached the gallery he turned instinctively and looked back at the royal box. Her eyes had followed him, and as he remained a moment motionless in the doorway her lips parted in a grateful smile, and she waved her fan with a faint but unmistakable gesture of farewell.

The next morning he left Alstadt. There was some little delay at the Zoll on the frontier, and when Hoffman received back his trunk it was accompanied by a little sealed packet which was handed to him by the Custom-house Inspector. Hoffman did not open it until he was alone.

. . . .

There hangs upon the wall of his modest apartment in New York a narrow, irregular photograph ingeniously framed, of himself standing side by side with a young German girl, who, in the estimation of his compatriots, is by no means stylish and only passably good-looking. When he is joked by his friends about the post of honor given to this production, and questioned as to the lady, he remains silent. The Princess Alexandrine Elsbeth Marie Stephanie von Westphalen-Alstadt, among her other royal qualities, knew whom to trust.